To Glen -
Hope you enjoy
FAT PROFITS.

Brian
Bradley

FAT

PROFIT$

FAT
PROFIT$

BRUCE BRADLEY

HowlingHound
PRESS

HowlingHound
PRESS

Published by Howling Hound Press
P.O. Box 46012
Minneapolis, MN 55446

or contact via e-mail at:
info@howlinghoundpress.com

First Edition: August 2012

Publisher's Cataloging-In-Publication Data

Bradley, Bruce.
Fat profits / Bruce Bradley. -- 1st ed.

p. ; cm.

ISBN: 978-1-938053-07-8

1. Food industry and trade--Corrupt practices--United States--Fiction.
2. Divorced fathers--United States--Fiction. 3. Conspiracies--United States--Fiction.
4. Lobbyists--United States--Fiction. 5. Minneapolis (Minn.)--Fiction.
6. Washington (D.C.)--Fiction. 7. Suspense fiction. I. Title. II. Title: Fat profits

PS3602.R23 F28 2012
813/.6   2012938674

PRINTED IN THE UNITED STATES OF AMERICA

This is a work of fiction. Characters, corporations, institutions, and organizations in this novel are the product of the author's imagination, or, if real, are
used fictitiously without any intent to describe their actual conduct.

Dedicated to my son, Ben...
May you learn from my journey that
reaching your dreams is always possible,
but rarely easy.
Discover *your* dreams,
work hard, and make them come true.
Love always...
Dad

Acknowledgements

You never know exactly where life is going to take you. I certainly never imagined in a million years I'd be living the life I am today. Some of the differences are amazing, while others, not as ideal. Regardless, it's that special mixture of ups and downs that has made me who I am today, and it has helped make my dream of writing my first novel possible.

Along my journey, there are some special people I'd like to acknowledge and thank. The first is my family, and on the top of that list is my son. Ben, you are the greatest gift I've ever received. I feel so lucky and thankful to be your dad. To watch you grow up is both the hardest and most wonderful thing. Hard because I cherish that little boy I am losing. Wonderful because I am thrilled at the man you are becoming. Thank you for being you, and for your encouragement on my quest.

To Ben's mom, thanks for loving Ben as only a mother can. Thank you for bringing your gifts as a parent to him. Although divorce is never easy, I am very thankful we have found peace, and I am grateful that Ben is a thriving young man.

To my parents, I know you both sacrificed so much for me, and I can never say thank you enough. Mom, your drive and spunk have taught me to never give up. That grit that makes you push through harder even when you think all is lost has helped me just dig deeper when I've struggled to write, doubted myself, or just felt lazy. Dad, when you were getting so sick, and I told you about my dream of writing a novel, I remember your words of encouragement and support. That meant the world to me, and since your death, I have felt your help, by my side. Thank you.

To my brothers Kirk and John, what can I say? We joke and play around with each other constantly, sometimes ruthlessly. But when the chips are down, we are always there for each other. Both of you have proved that to me time and again. Thanks for always being in my corner. I will always have your backs.

To my sister-in-law, Casey, thanks for being such a wonderful addition to our family, and an avid reader to boot! You were my first reader, and although you may not realize it, that shows how much I respect and trust you. Thank you for your encouragement and honesty.

To my friends, so many of you have offered your kind words of support. At the top of my list are three special callouts. Betsie, you believed in me more than I believed in myself. You helped nurture my dream, and you have always been there for me. You are a true friend, tested by time and tribulation. Your gift of friendship is priceless to me. Thank you for being such a wonderful friend and person. Ellen, as I was making so many changes in my life, you spurred me on to go for it. Thanks for believing in me. To Kirsten A., thank you for all your support. Writing can be a lonely sport. Our writer's group gave me a place to share and wonder, support and be supported. I know you have given me more than I have given you. Thank you, my writing friend. Here's to the success of your book when you're ready!

To Dr. Kirsten Lysne, you were my lighthouse through my divorce. Your coaching helped me navigate those troubled waters and become a better parent and person. Then, years later, when I came to you, struggling with my dream of writing a novel, you helped me come up with my plan and regain my confidence. I will always treasure your kind words, thoughtful support, and fun spirit. Thank you.

To Alan Rinzler, thank you for providing the sage advice of a seasoned editor. To Gabe Robinson, Esther Porter, and Diana

Cox, your help getting my manuscript cleaned up and ready for publication was just what I needed.

To Jeannemarie, Marina, Gerald, Curt, Terry, and Steve, thank you for helping me get the facts and details right. For any remaining errors, I have only myself to blame. And to my early readers, thanks for pushing through an unedited manuscript. Your encouragement and feedback helped make it all possible.

Finally, to Katie, our goldendoodle. No one does unconditional love better than you. No matter what the day brings, a blank page or a bounty of words, you can always make me smile and act like a kid. Thanks for being a big part of our small family.

FAT

PROFIT$

ONE

THE REAL RULES of business are unwritten. Navigating corporate America's cutthroat game of politics and power-mongering requires keen instincts, and though only thirty-one years old, Becky Clausen was a savvy player. Or at least she thought so.

Today's game was an urgent, hush-hush trip to Washington, DC. Becky and four of her coworkers had been summoned for a crucial job. Some old research had just resurfaced that could derail the FDA approval of Redu, a key ingredient in International Food & Milling's biggest new product launch in years. But no matter what happened, Becky knew she would come out on top. Three months prior she had been promoted to Director of Health and Nutrition for IFM's domestic Food and Beverage

1

divisions as a reward for her outstanding performance. She was in the fast lane, and her first trip on the corporate jet proved she was making it.

Becky arrived at the Minneapolis/St. Paul International Airport at 5:15 a.m., but struggled to find IFM's corporate hangar and executive lounge. Dawn had broken, but with only a glimmer of daylight in the sky, it took several drive-bys along a deserted stretch of road to finally see the discrete, unlit International Food & Milling sign hanging on the chain-link fence securing the building. Upon entering the driveway, she buzzed the office to announce her arrival, then a large, metal gate lumbered open, rolling sideways.

After parking her car, Becky grabbed her bags and walked into the hangar's lounge, only to be disappointed by the absence of any executives she could chat up. Determined to build her network, Becky quickly toured around the building and managed to meet the pilots for her flight. She wanted to know them. Becky had plans to be a frequent flier, and it always made sense to grease the skids.

In a matter of minutes, Becky learned all about Jim Donns and Mark Jonicus. Combined they had been flying for the company for over forty-four years. When Jim started, IFM only had two corporate jets. After eight acquisitions and impressive growth, IFM's fleet now numbered twelve jets, more than their archrival, Nutrisense, the largest food company in the world. These and many of IFM's other corporate toys were thanks to Aidan Toole, its CEO. He had the biggest ego on the block, and materialistic symbols like planes and a lavish headquarters helped him compensate for still being number two to Nutrisense and for the unsophisticated reputation of IFM's hometown, Minneapolis.

"So give me the scoop, guys. What are the rules on board this jet?" Becky asked. "This is my first flight, and I don't want to screw it up."

"Rules? No rules. Just relax and enjoy the flight."

"Come on, how does it work? Who sits where? Is there food on board? Who serves it?"

"Calm down," Jim laughed. "There are no assigned seats, but the most senior people usually sit toward the back. And don't worry, there's always some food. You don't think IFM would let anyone starve, do you? Morning flights usually have catered plates with fresh fruit, a bagel, and yogurt. And of course there are always IFM snacks, cereals, candies, juices, and soft drinks."

"Is there a flight attendant?"

"Not unless Mr. Toole is on board one of our larger jets for a longer flight. It's all self-serve. Usually someone junior ends up seated toward the front and passes back the food and drinks."

Becky had no intention of doing anything menial, so like any meeting, getting the power seat was crucial.

"How about cell phones? Can we use them?"

"Well, the FCC and FAA say no, but we sure won't be policing that. We're up in the cockpit. But watch out for the reception. As soon as we get up around twelve thousand feet, you'll start losing your signal."

Within thirty minutes, all of the passengers had arrived. Craig Bonesteel, Derrick Bates, and Ginny Lawrence were Becky's counterparts. As Directors of Health & Nutrition at IFM, they each managed a portion of the company's vast $98 billion food empire. Although they weren't lawyers, they ensured all IFM businesses complied with food handling, packaging, and marketing regulations. The fifth and final passenger was Vicki Trease. She was the lawyer of the group and headed up IFM's Legal and Regulatory team.

As they crossed the hangar, Becky quickened her step so she could board first. According to the pilots, the plane was a Citation III. It was IFM's oldest and smallest jet, but to Becky it was a whole new class of living. Adorned with cappuccino leather seats, plush satin tan carpeting, mahogany cabinetry, and six personal flight entertainment systems, the jet smelled of luxury and excess. Becky jockeyed herself into the rear of the plane, settled in, and then immediately got to work on her cell phone. After all, there was no better way to show off her newfound importance than to make a few phone calls from the corporate jet.

She decided to call Andrew Hastings, the Marketing Manager for Uncle Chuck's new, healthy line of B-Lean salty snacks. It was too early for him to be at his desk, so a voice mail would have to suffice.

"Hey, Andrew, this is Becky. I'm heading out of town for an urgent meeting. Keep this to yourself, but we've hit a real snag. Some old research just surfaced that may cause a big delay for Redu and your B-Lean Snacks lineup. I'm taking the corporate jet to DC for a strategy meeting with our legal team. I'll let you know more when I can. Please, keep this quiet."

Craig Bonesteel couldn't help overhearing Becky.

"What are you doing, Becky?"

"Oh, just updating the team a bit. We have some crucial deadlines in front of us, and I don't want us to be caught holding the bag."

"You're crazy! Chloe just reminded us again yesterday not to leak a word to anyone about the trouble with Redu until we've come up with a plan to handle this mess."

"I know, I know," Becky said in a dismissive tone. "Let me worry about how I handle it."

The jet engines had started and the plane quickly taxied into position. Everything seemed to happen so much faster on the corporate jet. No security checkpoints, no lines to board, and before Becky knew it, the plane was streaking down the runway, its nose quickly lifting into the air.

As the plane gained altitude, Becky saw Lake Nokomis below and then moments later Lake Harriet. Then, when the plane banked to the south, she spotted her neighborhood and remembered she needed to call her husband. It was a few minutes after six and Bill was undoubtedly up with the girls by now. A faithful and dedicated househusband of two years, he managed the home since Becky was working ten-hour days and weekends as she rose up the corporate ranks of IFM.

"Hey, hon, how's it going?"

"Ah, good here," Bill replied. "Lizzie and Maureen are up, and

I'm just getting breakfast ready. So where are you now? It sounds awfully noisy."

"I'm flying high. Right over our house in fact! Honey, you wouldn't believe this. It's so cool. You can bet not just anyone gets to take a ride on the corporate jet."

"That's great, Becky," Bill said smiling, genuinely proud of his wife. "You've worked so hard for this. You deserve it and a lot more. Want to say a quick hello to the girls?"

"Sure, put them on. Oh, one sec though. I realized on the way to the airport that I left some papers I need on the nightstand. Could you scan and send them to my gmail address? I need them for my meetings, and Chloe would kill me if she knew I left them at home."

"Tell that boss of yours to just relax. She has you so scared. You've barely said two words to me about this crazy project."

"I know, I know. But I've told you, this is IFM's biggest new product initiative ever."

"Blah, blah, blah. I'll get your stuff to you. Don't worry. Love you. Here are the girls."

"Cool, put them on speakerphone." The phone made a click, and Becky's voice jumped up an octave. "Hi, sweeties. Mommy is in a cool plane flying on a trip for work."

The noise and commotion of the kitchen buzzed in the background and nearly droned out the faint sound of the girls.

"Hi, Mommy. Can you see any birds?"

Becky strained to hear her daughter Maureen's voice. Just a month shy of five years old, Maureen was a typical first-born child—reliable, conscientious, and she didn't like surprises. Lizzie, on the other hand, was her mischievous, rule-breaking three-year-old. Bill and Becky kept hoping Lizzie would calm down as she got older, but she showed no signs of easing up any time soon.

"No, no birds, but I could see the lake a minute ago. I was right over our house."

"Wow. Can you see me, Mommy? I'm waving…"

"Yes, yes, honey…I can see you. But where's Lizzie?"

Becky waited for a response but could only hear the buzzing of the speakerphone and some crackling noise as the signal began to fade.

"Can you hear me? Kisses to both of you. Mommy loves you up to the sky." She waited again but could only hear static. "Losing the signal here, Bill." More static. "Okay, bye."

After hanging up, Becky took a brief moment to look out the windows. The plane had completed its turn southeast, and acres of corn streamed below as far as the eye could see. It was tough leaving Lizzie and Maureen overnight, and she knew it would get worse when they got older and needed more quality time with their mother. But Becky didn't want her mind to go there now. Instead she settled in for the flight and turned on her laptop.

As she started to dig into her e-mails, the plane groaned and listed to the left as an ever-so-slight aroma of something burning wafted through the cabin. At first Becky cast it off, unwilling to appear as an unseasoned traveler. She glanced over to the in-flight monitor that was tracking their progress to DC. Everything seemed fine. But just as Becky started to refocus on her work, the plane groaned again and shook, and her nerves got the better of her.

"What's happening?" Becky exclaimed, reaching her arms into the air looking for a call button.

The other passengers shared Becky's concern. They were just doing a better job of staying calm.

"I'm sure it's nothing," Craig replied. Becky stared at him briefly, not knowing whether to trust his opinion.

The plane rocked again, this time much more severely than before, and now the screen for her in-flight monitor went dark. Becky looked around in a panic. It wasn't just her monitor. The whole cabin had lost power.

Just as she was going to announce her latest discovery, alarms sounded and flashed in the cockpit.

"What the hell is happening?" she cried, looking out the window for clues.

Suddenly, the plane dropped rapidly with a violent plunge from the sky, and Becky's laptop flew through the air and slammed into her forehead, knocking her out. The chaos continued briefly as blood started to drip into her eyes. Then, the plane exploded and the sky glowed with a blazing, intense red light.

Chunks of metal and bodies blasted out concentrically toward the horizon, then fell to the earth far below.

Yes, everything happened faster on this corporate jet.

TWO

IFM Headquarters
Wayzata, Minnesota
Wednesday, June 2
7:00 A.M.

A COOL SUMMER MIST hung over Lake Minnetonka as birds skimmed near the surface looking for their morning meal. The water was calm. It was early and most boats were still docked alongside their multimillion-dollar estates or at one of the many marinas that dappled the bays and coves of the lake.

IFM's headquarters was just coming to life. A shimmering gem placed right next to Lake Minnetonka, it was composed of three glass, steel, and slate buildings that hugged the shore, while another six buildings and two parking decks sprawled across the rest of the property. All the buildings were interconnected with skyways or underground tunnels to allow their inhabitants to move freely year-round. After all, in the dead of winter, weeks of subzero temperatures were the norm, and the powers that be wanted to keep their people attending meetings, working hard, and selling their products.

The sixty-acre campus was meticulously maintained. The landscaping was a beautiful, natural outcropping of the lake. Gardens and statuary adorned the grounds and created the appearance of an idyllic corporate paradise. Although many locals didn't approve of large, five-story commercial buildings situated right on the lake, in this town, what IFM wanted, IFM got. Even if it took a while, careful planning and the right donations always succeeded in getting the public to line up with IFM's interests.

Andrew Hastings walked up to the employee entrance at seven o'clock. Many office lights were already on in the Sales and Operations floors of headquarters. They were the early birds at IFM. Marketers like Andrew were notorious for rolling in well after eight, but their hours were grueling and they often worked late into the night. At food companies like IFM, Marketing ran the company. Well-educated MBAs from the best schools in the world, these marketers were not only responsible for driving great advertising and promotions, but they were also the so-called hub of the wheel, leading cross-functional teams to build and grow IFM's brands. Yes, they would collaborate with Sales, Operations, and R&D, but ultimately Marketing made the decisions.

"Good morning, Andrew," greeted Barney Fisher. Barney had been with IFM for over twenty years. Although he was officially part of IFM's campus security, he was much more than a guard. He was affable, well-dressed, and knew everyone by name. Employees like Barney were the heart and soul of IFM—hardworking, caring, and determined to do their jobs better than anyone else.

"Good morning, Barney. How's it going?" Andrew asked.

"Great here. How's Ethan? He must be with your ex today? You aren't usually in so early on Wednesdays."

"Ethan is great. Thanks for asking. Yep, just me today. I traded some time with his mom, so I am getting in early to work, work, work. Have a great day, Barney."

Andrew walked down the main corridor of the employee entrance. Bright and filled with glass and chrome, it led to a multimedia extravaganza with product displays, community outreach efforts, company club kiosks, and flat-screen televisions showing reels of IFM's most recent and classic commercials. Then the hallway opened up into a grand space called the Commons. Here all the basic needs of any IFM employee were met with a credit union, coffee house, dry cleaners, convenience store, company store, cafeteria, clothing store, doctor's office, dentist's office, three of IFM's largest fast food chains, and a concierge service center to cover anything else that wasn't available. IFM had been written up in *Moms at Work*, *Corporate Weekly*, and *Riches* magazine as one of the top companies in the world to work for, and the impressive headquarters and special perks made it easy to see why.

Five minutes later, Andrew had made his way up to his office. The massive main building, almost twice as big as the two wings that flanked it, housed all the domestic operating grocery divisions, except for Beverages, which shared a separate building with the Restaurant, Foodservice, and International Divisions. The executive wing, legal, and other corporate level functions were on the fifth floor of this main building.

Andrew got off the elevator on the fourth floor, home of Uncle Chuck's, IFM's Snacks Division. Snack foods were at the core of the company and its heritage. In 1932, IFM introduced the first nationally distributed snack, Corn Crunchers, and after years of new products and line extensions, IFM was the category leader with over 40 percent market share. But over the last twelve years, Nutrisense had made inroads and IFM was now on the defensive. As the Marketing Manager for Uncle Chuck's transformational new products, Andrew intended to reverse that trend with his new, healthy, salty-snacks initiative. Part of a broader B-Lean brand launch that spanned IFM's snacks, cereals, desserts, foodservice, and fast food businesses, Andrew's project was likened to what Diet X-cite cola did for IFM's Beverage Division back in the 1980s. This was Andrew's shot to make director, and he knew it. Failure was not an option.

Andrew settled in to prep for his nine o'clock meeting with Sales. He knew the drill. Sales didn't like to rock the boat or make their accounts nervous. They only wanted to sell sure bets. A tasty product that scored well with consumers with some great advertising wasn't enough. If a new item was going to be successful, great product scores had to be accompanied by lots of trade dollars to buy shelf space and fund jaw-dropping sale prices and displays.

Sure, being innovative and on-trend was important, just as long as you weren't ahead of the times. Yes, perfect timing was also imperative. But almost more important than anything else was guaranteed product availability. Grocers planned their shelves and sale circulars months in advance. Selling them a product that you couldn't deliver on time or supply enough of was a salesman's nightmare, even worse than an item that didn't sell. Today's meeting objective was to reassure Sales that the B-Lean Snacks launch would have plenty of supply, because if Sales got spooked, they wouldn't sell aggressively.

As Andrew fired up his laptop, he noticed his voice mail light glowing. Hoping it was a message from Dan Murdock with some feedback on the draft for today's presentation, he picked up the phone, only to shake his head in disbelief as he started to listen. It was Becky Clausen, the team's top regulatory contact, and she was giving Andrew a heads-up on more problems. Just what he needed. The sky had been falling so many times on this project he could hardly count them. But rather than get rattled, Andrew got back to work and decided to deal with Becky later.

Within thirty minutes, he put the finishing touches on a five-page PowerPoint presentation full of pictures, graphs, and a great product availability story to pitch to Sales. Heading over to the printer to pick up copies for his meeting, he saw Stephanie Kingston, his administrative assistant, running toward him.

"Good morning, Steph. Why the rush?" Andrew asked.

"Go to the lobby. There was a plane crash. It was one of our jets. It's all over the news."

Steph dropped her stuff at her desk, and Andrew ran with her toward the main reception area on the fourth floor. Despite the early hour, a crowd of more than thirty people gathered around the flat-screen television, watching the live news report.

The images were bleak and horrifying. The smoking wreckage of a plane was strewn across a cornfield. As the camera panned, Andrew saw jagged chunks of smoldering debris scattered in a vast radius among verdant green seedlings. The on-the-scene reporter, Heidi Pearson, stammered then paused briefly to get control of her emotions.

Andrew stared into the reporter's compassionate eyes then finally asked, "Do we know who was on the plane?"

"No. No details yet," replied Steph.

As they watched in horror, Andrew whispered to her, "I just got a message from Becky this morning. She was on her way to DC on the corporate jet. This could be her plane."

"Oh my goodness, no. Doesn't she have two little girls at home?"

"Yes," Andrew replied, biting his lip and shaking his head. *No, this can't be her plane. IFM has lots of jets*, he thought, trying to convince himself that Becky was all right. *Maybe I should call Bill and see if he knows anything.* But he decided that would only make the poor guy worry, so he did nothing, at least for the moment.

The television broadcast shifted back to the newsroom where the anchor went on and on, reporting the same few facts again and again—an IFM corporate jet crashed southeast of the airport—early that morning an IFM corporate jet crashed shortly after taking off from Minneapolis—breaking news, an IFM corporate jet crashed in a field northeast of Zumbrota—all interspersed with footage of the sparse, hideous remains of a plane. Human tragedy had once more been transformed into the latest ratings game.

THE PLANE CRASH dominated the chatter throughout IFM. From break rooms to the cafeteria, the talk was constant. But work had to go on. Meetings had to happen. Deadlines couldn't be moved. Andrew knew the possible loss of a friend and coworker wasn't enough to call off his meeting. Regional sales directors were in town. If canceled, rescheduling it could take weeks. This was a command performance.

As the fourth floor conference room filled up with over twenty attendees, Andrew passed around copies of the presentation. The morning light reflected off the lake so brightly that it blinded half of the room. As he greeted a few stragglers, Andrew walked over to the command console and lowered the blinds to help ensure a comfortable, attentive audience.

Despite it already being five past nine, Andrew decided to wait a few minutes longer. Art Jacobson, President of US Retail Sales, and Dan Murdock, Andrew's temporary boss and Chief Operating Officer of US Retail, had not arrived yet. His real boss, Angie Green, who would normally lead this meeting, was out on maternity leave. A hard worker and dedicated businesswoman, Angie had agreed to an abbreviated, six-week maternity leave in exchange for a guarantee from IFM to hold her prized position as Transformative New Products Director.

Although there was much speculation over this unusual plan, Andrew was glad to pinch-hit. Angie was a single mom and needed all the help she could get. Andrew also knew that her maternity leave was his big chance to step up. Most managers would kill to report to Dan Murdock since he was arguably on a very short list to succeed Aidan Toole as CEO of IFM. But working for Dan was very challenging, since he was extremely busy, rarely available for input, and always hypercritical—a deadly combination for any boss. Today's meeting was no exception. Andrew had sent Dan an e-mail outlining the key objectives of the meeting and attached a well-crafted draft of the presentation. After waiting for Dan's input for over a week, he finally gave up. It was all Andrew's to win or lose.

Andrew looked around the room as he got ready to present. *Impressive,* he thought. You couldn't assemble a group of smarter, better dressed people if you tried. Although IFM had adopted a business casual policy years earlier, the upwardly mobile sales managers and directors in this room didn't use that as an excuse to look shoddy. The men looked like they had walked out of a Brooks Brothers catalog with their gabardine dress slacks, neatly pressed long-sleeve, cotton shirts, and an occasional sport coat.

The women flaunted more color and variety, but they were equally professional. But what stood out more than anything else was that there wasn't an average-looking face in the crowd. IFM had an affinity for recruiting not only the brightest, but also the best-looking candidates.

In many ways, Andrew fit IFM's bill. At six foot two, his blond-haired, blue-eyed good looks were classic. Andrew ran, biked, worked out, and loved to hike and camp. Graduating from the top of his class at Carleton College, then getting his MBA from Stanford, his credentials were impeccable. The only stain on his career had been a messy divorce.

Four years into his career, Andrew's wife, Lydia, had left him. They had drifted apart—their relationship compromised by their stressful jobs. But what proved more damaging was Lydia's growing frustration with Andrew's slow climb up the corporate ladder. Lydia had high aspirations, and when Great Sioux National Bank promoted her to City Executive, she realized Andrew was holding her back. Finally, after deciding Andrew would never have the drive to be an executive, Lydia just wanted out.

Her demands were simple—full custody of their son and all of their assets. Two years and many legal battles later, Andrew emerged poorer financially, but much richer as a man and father. With the support of friends and a great boss, Andrew restarted his life with joint custody of his son, a used car, and $10,000. But no matter how much things returned to normal on the surface, Andrew found it hard to trust anyone again, especially Lydia. While he could accept his failure as a husband, he could never understand why she tried to take his son away from him.

The divorce had certainly set Andrew back on the promotion track. Six members of his hiring class had already made it to director. While that bothered him on some level, Andrew realized his priorities were different. IFM had been good to him, but it wasn't his life. He knew there were more important things than work. But today, right now, he had to knock it out of the park.

Finally, at eight minutes after nine, Dan and Art wandered

in chatting together. As they found their seats, the room quieted and Andrew quickly took control of the meeting.

"Good morning. I know we all have a lot of things distracting us right now with the horrible news of the plane crash, but we need to press forward and discuss our exciting new snack launch."

No one was smiling, but at least he had their attention. He went on.

"As most of you know, we're ready to transform the way Americans eat with our new B-Lean Snacks. These snacks contain IFM's proprietary Ultra-Hi Resistant Starch blend called Redu. IFM will be introducing B-Lean items across its vast food holdings, and in so doing will truly revolutionize how we eat and lose weight. The Snacks, Cereals, Desserts, Bakery, Foodservice, and Fast Food Divisions will all be flooding the media with B-Lean advertising in January. In order to be on shelf by then, we're targeting a November 1 start ship. We expect to receive final FDA approval by June 15. Sales materials and sales samples are set to ship shortly after, on June 21."

Before Andrew could move on to his next page, Scott Tishman, head of the Central Region, jumped in and asked, "Yeah, excuse me, Andrew. But how in the world are we supposed to get retailers on board with resetting shelves during the busy holiday season?"

Caught a bit off guard, Andrew hesitated. "Well, we agreed to that date months ago. Our timelines are very aggressive." Realizing that a defensive stance never worked with Sales, Andrew leaned forward, and started selling. "Scott, I don't underestimate the challenge of the job. We know it is very difficult. But I also know we have the best sales force out there. With a great product, and your team's salesmanship, I know you can get retailers to do just about anything we ask them." Andrew was no fool. He knew some pandering thrown in there to feed the egos of his audience wouldn't hurt. "You know our job is to sell this as a once-in-a-lifetime launch. And we all know weight-loss season kicks off every January with New Year's resolutions."

Art piped in. "Scotty, Andrew's right. This is a make or break deal for IFM. Our leaders have invested millions in developing and bringing this technology to market. We've leapfrogged the competition. We have patents. We're ready."

"Yes, I get that, but I'm still concerned." Scott's tone changed. It was easy to slice up a marketing guy, but Scott wanted Art's job someday, and to get there he needed to show Art respect, courage, and some modicum of intelligence. "The FDA hasn't approved Redu as a food ingredient, yet here we are supposedly selling these various product lines in less than two weeks. First, are we sure it's really going to get the green light? And second, are we prepared to launch it when it does? Do we have the appropriate inventory on hand to supply such a big launch?"

Andrew jumped in, desperately trying to make sure the meeting didn't spin out of control. "Scott, we're confident that we're on the path to FDA approval. The FDA-appointed Food Advisory Committee recommended approval back in April. The Regulatory Decision Team, or RDT as the press likes to call it, should make its recommendation to the Commissioner anytime now, with a final decision promised by June 15. All indicators are positive. As for being prepared, I can assure you we're ready."

"Assure?" asked Scott. "What's that supposed to mean? We need solid facts to answer retailer questions. Our first top-to-top is with Klout here at headquarters on June 21. They're the second biggest retailer. There's no screwing around with them. I mean—"

Andrew interrupted. "I understand, Scott. I promise to answer all your questions. Please, give me a chance first. Let's move on to page two." The papers around the desk shuffled, and Andrew moved on quickly to his other points.

"As you can see here, IFM has been producing supplies of Redu since last crop year. Already over two hundred million pounds of corn, wheat, rice, and barley have been processed into Redu. Sales sample quantities of all B-Lean Snacks are ready to ship June 16. After the FDA's approval, manufacturing of retail sale products will begin in late June. If you turn to the next page, you will see that by early October, four months' supply of each variety of B-Lean Snacks will be on hand. By start ship, over six months will be on hand. If we oversell our expectations, which I believe we will, we have the capacity to produce over 50 percent more and maintain 100 percent service levels."

These numbers were staggering to Scott and the rest of the team. Typically IFM started shipping new items with two to three months of supply. If the items were a hit, logistics would start cutting orders. Service levels of 50 percent or below were not unheard of on blockbuster new items. The problem was, customers like Klout hated when orders got cut. Their precious shelf space would be empty, selling nothing. Or even worse, they might advertise a hot price point and plan for end-cap displays, only to curse IFM for not having enough inventory to keep up with consumer demand.

"How can we afford all this? We're always told it's too expensive to do things this way," commented Joe Spenz, who held Scott's position in the Eastern Region.

"Well, Aidan Toole and his leadership team have pulled out all the stops on this launch. It's expected to be the biggest new product introduction in IFM's history. No expense has been spared. The grain alone processed in advance of this year's production cost an estimated $20 million."

Undeterred, Scott jumped back in, "This all sounds great, but again, how can we be so confident the FDA will approve Redu? Aren't we betting the bank on this?"

Just as Andrew hesitated for a breath, Dan Murdock jumped in.

"Hold on, guys—no offense to you ladies," Dan said, flashing his sparkling smile to the ten or so women sitting around the table. "We've tested Redu. It's passed all the tests. Without a doubt, it's safe. The FDA's approval is on its way. We're just working through some final red tape."

"But what about all the objections I read in the news? The Ethical Food Coalition and other watchdog groups say they won't let this stuff get onto America's plates. I mean, these EFC guys are hard core."

"They're a bunch of radicals," Dan snapped back, "and the FDA sees them for what they are. I can't put it any other way, Scotty. I know I've done my job. You have a healthy, delicious, weight-loss product to sell. We're light years ahead of the competition. Now just get off your ass and sell."

Silence filled the room as the sales team glanced over at Scott to see if he was up for another round with Dan. But Scott settled back in his chair, eyes looking to the floor like a scolded dog.

"Thanks, Dan. We get it," proclaimed Art. "You can count on us to get it done."

Not knowing exactly what to do next, Andrew stepped in, walked the group through the last couple pages, and asked for any other questions. By this time, the deal was done. Sales was on board, in part because of his work, but mostly because Dan told them to just do it.

Soon the meeting was over, and the room started to empty. Andrew chatted briefly and personally thanked some of the attendees. As he walked with Joe Spenz to the door, he saw Steph waiting outside the conference room. With a mere glance, he could see she'd been crying, so with a final shake of hands, he said good-bye to Joe, picked up his things, and hurried out of the room.

"What's wrong, Steph?"

"You were right, Andrew. It was Becky's plane that went down. They just announced that she and six other employees were on the plane."

Speechless, Andrew's thoughts quickly shifted to Becky's family.

"Steph, I'm sorry, but please excuse me. I need to call Becky's husband. He must be devastated."

Ducking into a small, empty conference room, Andrew grabbed his cell phone and found Bill's home number. Andrew was sure he would get the Clausen's voice mail, but he had to at least try to reach Bill.

"Hello?" a dry, raspy voice answered.

"Bill? This is Andrew. I just heard about the crash. I'm so sorry."

Bill cleared his throat unsuccessfully a couple times, trying to find his voice. "Andrew, I just don't know what I'm going to do without her..."

Andrew could hear the muffled cries as his friend tried to be strong. "Bill, I'm going to come over right now. Can I bring over anything for you or the girls?"

"No, Andrew, please don't come right now. Becky's sister, Hope, is here already helping me with the girls. My in-laws and Becky's brothers will be here any minute," Bill paused and took a deep breath. "I'm going to be okay. I just need to be strong for the girls."

"Well, what can I do? Can I bring over dinner this evening?"

"One of our neighbors has already offered, but thank you."

"I'd still like to help. Let me organize meals for the next couple weeks. I'm sure plenty of Becky's coworkers and friends from church would love to help out."

"That would be great, Andrew."

Andrew could hear some commotion in the background.

"Andrew, I need to get going. Becky's mom and dad just walked in the door. Thank you so much for your call."

"Please, Bill, don't hesitate to call me for anything. You hear me?"

"I promise. I'll talk to you soon."

WMSP-TV Headquarters
St. Louis Park, Minnesota
Wednesday, June 2nd
10:00 A.M.

WMSP-TV'S HEADQUARTERS was located fifteen minutes west of downtown Minneapolis in the suburb of St. Louis Park. The building was classic 1960s architecture with flat lines and exposed concrete and metal. Tall antennae, satellite dishes, and weather radar littered the roof, giving it the look of a galactic junkyard.

Despite years of complaints from the neighborhood association, the time for improving this eyesore had passed. The recession had hurt the station's advertising revenues badly, and the news business was bleeding out as the digital age put the screws to their outdated business model. Five rounds of layoffs over five years made it a tough place to work. But for Heidi Pearson, Minneapolis was her home, and she was willing to gut it out to stay near her friends and family.

Heidi stared out of the conference room windows overlooking the newsroom, watching as Erika tried to gather the group. It was almost comical. Getting reporters into a room was like herding cats, but it could be done. It just required some leadership and charisma, two qualities Erika sorely lacked.

Erika Braker ran the early news shift. She was intelligent enough, but she was very green with less than three years of experience. The news world was littered with Erikas now—young, poorly paid journalism majors with no true understanding of running a newsroom or reporting ethics. The industry just didn't have the time or money for the luxury of better qualified personnel anymore.

Finally, after ten minutes, Heidi, out of sheer frustration, took over and corralled the renegades.

As the group got seated around the table, they looked to Heidi to get things started. She was a natural leader. Her enthusiasm and energy were contagious, and she could rally the team to do just about anything. With gorgeous blond hair, incredible blue eyes, and an unflappable personality, Heidi had been recruited to be a news anchor on several occasions. But she hated the idea of being tethered to a desk, so she always politely refused. Her independent streak often put her at odds with news directors and producers, but when she stood her ground, she usually had good cause. Today, she was just a reporter, and she wanted to get to work.

"So, Erika, where do you want to begin?" Heidi asked, hoping to get the group focused on the task at hand.

"Well, as you all know, one of IFM's corporate jets crashed just southeast of the airport early this morning. This will be our lead story for the evening news. I've shared our latest briefing with each of you. It includes the names of each of the victims, addresses, and any family details. I have assigned each of you a family to cover. You know the deal. Tearful, emotional tragedy or anger makes great news. Heidi, you will play point. I also need you to interview officials at IFM, the National Transportation Safety Board, and other local authorities."

Erika looked around the room to make sure everyone was following her, then she asked, "Does anyone know if any videos of the actual crash have surfaced?"

"We interviewed several witnesses while we were down in Zumbrota, but so far we haven't found anyone that videoed the crash," Heidi replied.

Just as Erika was about to ask another question, the glass door to the room flew open, causing her to jump in her seat. "Rusty, really? Do you really need to do that?" complained Erika.

"Yes ma'am," Rusty said, although his tone denoted anything but respect. "Well, I thought you'd be interested in this, Erika, but if not, I'll just leave."

Heidi interrupted. "Rusty, stop the games. We don't have time for it today. What do you have?"

"Whatever," Rusty said, looking at Heidi. "I just picked this up off the wire. Looks like the Ethical Food Coalition is claiming responsibility for the plane crash."

"What? Let me see that." Heidi spun around in her chair and grabbed the paper from Rusty's hands. As she read it, her brow furrowed with intensity.

"What are you thinking, Heidi?" Erika asked.

"I've reported on EFC in the past. They've clashed plenty with IFM over the years, but they've always adhered to a non-violent approach."

"Yeah, but they've been associated with blowing up plants and derailing trains," Rusty added.

"There's a violent, fringe element that claims to be part of EFC, but it really isn't. EFC has been forced to clarify this issue constantly. That said, even this fringe group doesn't believe in the loss of human life. Remember in that Nutrisense infant formula plant explosion, when a bomb threat was phoned in and the entire factory was evacuated? No one was injured in the blast. To kill seven people on this plane just doesn't add up."

"Could the crash have happened by mistake?" Erika asked. "Maybe they meant to blow the plane up in the hangar when nobody was on board."

"That's possible, but then why are they so anxious to take credit?" Rusty responded.

The briefing continued with more questions bantered back and forth. Finally, Heidi sent every reporter in the room out to cover some aspect of the crash location, survivors, the EFC, and both the criminal and safety investigations. Heidi stayed behind, setting up appointments over the phone. Calling and meeting with the victims' families was the hardest part. Most reporters exploited their fragile state to get the interview. Heidi refused to become a pushy, hearse-chasing journalist. Instead, her down-to-earth, honest style genuinely touched people, and helped them open up. People usually trusted her, and that always gave her an edge.

Within a few minutes, Heidi had scheduled interviews with Becky Clausen's husband, Bill, and her sister, Hope. Twenty minutes later, her day was set, and Heidi gathered her crew and headed out of the building. As she crossed the newsroom into the daylight of the employee entrance, Erika flagged her down.

"I just got word the network is looking to add your story. They're especially interested in the possible EFC involvement. Keep me posted and let's check-in before three."

"Will do," Heidi said, hoping the network brass wouldn't screw it up.

IFM Headquarters
Wednesday, June 2nd
11:30 A.M.

IFM POSTED a story about the plane crash on their company intranet site, and all televisions across headquarters were tuned into the local news for the latest details. Except for the names of the passengers and crew, not much was known.

After talking to Bill Clausen, Andrew had trouble getting back to work. He couldn't get Becky and her family off his mind. He talked with Steph for a while at her desk then decided to join two of his team members for lunch. Lourdes Perez was an Associate Marketing Manager who reported to him. She had been on his team for eight months now. She was sharp, hardworking, independent, and stunning with dark hair cut in a stylish, long bob and deep brown eyes that danced when she smiled or laughed. During her two years at IFM, she had earned a reputation for getting things done quickly, with her cross-functional team behind her the whole way. Lourdes was just the type of marketer that IFM wanted.

Rachel Sears, the team's Market Research Manager, was Lourdes's best friend. They ate lunch together most days and often socialized outside of work. A former college lacrosse player, Rachel was six foot one, lean, and wore her shocking red hair in a short pixie cut. Known as "the Belle" thanks to her North Carolina accent, Rachel was resourceful, funny, and outspoken. For the most part, Rachel's style was a nice change of pace, but occasionally her candor ruffled feathers and required extra work to pacify hurt feelings.

The cafeteria seemed busier than usual, and it took some hunting to find a place to sit. Perhaps everyone was lingering longer as they shared the latest news on the crash and played their own sick version of six degrees of Kevin Bacon, trying to make their most direct links to the victims. For Andrew's table, there was no game to play, no gossip, just sadness. Becky had been an original member of their cross-functional product launch team, and she continued to play a pivotal role even after her promotion. She was helpful and full of energy, and Andrew had always been able to count on Becky's can-do spirit to help rally the team to go the extra mile.

"It doesn't seem real. It's like some nightmare," said Lourdes.

"I know," Rachel replied. "Just last week Becky was laughing about her girls. She was telling me about how her husband had fallen asleep on the sofa watching television after dinner. Their younger daughter, Lizzie, took lipstick from Becky's bag and smeared it all over Bill's face. Becky couldn't stop laughing, and she had posted pictures of Bill on her Facebook page." Rachel started to tear up again as she laughed. Through her sniffling, she asked Andrew, "How close were you to Becky and Bill? It seems like you saw each other outside of work pretty often."

"We're good friends. We all go to the same church, so I see them most Sundays. For the past couple years I've chaired the annual family camp-out, and Bill has been great about getting involved and helping out. So I've gotten to know him well through that. He's a super nice guy, loves his girls, and adored Becky."

"Can you imagine being a single parent to those two little girls? A friend of mine who's divorced says being a single parent is impossible." Just as she said it, Rachel immediately wanted to take it back, and there was a long, awkward silence.

"It's okay, Rachel. Yes, I'm a single dad. A single, divorced dad. But Ethan still has both his parents. Even if his mom and I don't get along that well, we're both still there for him. Every kid deserves to have two parents, and now these poor little girls have had their mom taken away. It's just not right." As his lip trembled, he bit it and fought back a wave of tears. Whenever he talked of family, Andrew's emotions ran close to the surface. Family was sacred to him. He had lost so much during the past six years.

THREE

Plymouth, Minnesota
Wednesday, June 2
5:00 P.M.

A T FIVE O'CLOCK, a flood of people left IFM's head-quarters. The average employee had been there since eight o'clock and was ready to get out and enjoy a sunny Minnesota evening. Although most of Marketing would typically leave well after six, on Monday and Wednesday nights Andrew slipped out by five thirty to coach Ethan's soccer team. It was just a rec league, so it was a great way to spend time with Ethan and get to know his friends and their parents.

Andrew's drive home took less than fifteen minutes. His home was built in an older neighborhood in Plymouth. Andrew scrimped and saved for eighteen months after his divorce to afford the down payment. After living in a cramped, two-bedroom apartment for over three years, he was ready for a home, even if it came with a hefty mortgage.

Although Andrew's house was the smallest on the block, it

was still very comfortable with three bedrooms, two and a half baths, and a walkout basement. Most of his neighbors had three-car garages to store their jet-skis, boats, or snowmobiles, but a house with a two-car garage was all that would fit on this lot. The extra bay wasn't important to Andrew. He was more concerned about being near Ethan's friends and mom.

What finally sold him on the house was that it backed up to the Luce Line, an old railway that had since been converted to a path that led west past Lake Minnetonka and east toward downtown Minneapolis. Andrew loved to bike and run, so the added convenience of a great trail in his backyard sealed the deal.

Right now, there was no time for a bike ride or a run. His stop at home lasted less than ten minutes. After changing, he grabbed his soccer bag and drove to Parkers Lake fields where the boys practiced and played most of their games.

When he arrived a couple minutes after six, kids of all ages already covered the fields. Parents and siblings were busy setting up their chairs and blankets along the sidelines of each field. Trying not to be too late, Andrew started jogging to the field and spotted Ethan's tow-headed blond mop of hair in the sea of children. Of course Ethan's mom had him at practice on time. She made the high-powered working parent routine look so easy.

"Hey there, Ethan," Andrew shouted. "Can you give me a hand?"

Ethan turned his head, ran over, and gave his dad a big hug. Andrew dropped his bag and reached his arm around Ethan, giving him a squeeze.

"Hey, Dad."

"Can you take two of these balls over to center field?" Andrew asked as he unzipped his duffel bag. "I'll be there in a second. Get the guys arranged in two lines for a passing drill. Okay?"

"Sure."

Andrew dashed over to the sideline, greeting some parents along the way. Upon seeing his ex, Lydia, he gave her a friendly wave before setting down his bag, grabbing a drink of water, and running back onto the field.

Practice lasted an hour. During the first forty minutes the boys worked on several drills. Afterwards, they scrimmaged in a game of eight on eight. One side was short a player, so Andrew filled in as a fullback. Ethan and the rest of the boys loved nothing better than outmaneuvering their coach, and it was happening more often. The past couple years Andrew wondered if he should quit coaching since the kids' skills were quickly outpacing his, but somehow Ethan convinced him to do it again and again. And as long as there wasn't someone more qualified volunteering, Andrew was willing to keep doing his best.

"Okay, guys, let's head in," said Andrew.

Slowly the kids walked to the sidelines where one of the parents was breaking out some snacks. As soon as the kids saw the ice cream sandwiches being passed out, the field cleared quickly. Andrew picked up the soccer balls, zipped them up in his bag, and walked over to Ethan, who was goofing around with his best friend, Mack.

"You guys were awesome tonight, Mack," said Andrew.

"Thanks, Coach Hastings."

"Are you going to be here for our game next Monday?" asked Andrew.

"I think so."

"Well, good. We need you out there. Hey, I need to talk to Ethan for a second, but we'll see you next week. Maybe you can come for a sleepover one night when we get back from vacation?"

"Sounds great, Coach. See you, Ethan."

Andrew turned and put his arm on Ethan's shoulder. "How was your second to last day as a fifth grader?"

"Boring."

"Are you excited about graduation tomorrow?"

"Kinda," Ethan paused. "It should be fun."

"Well, you should be proud of yourself. You've done a great job in elementary school. I still can't believe I'm going to be the father of a middle-schooler. It just sounds like crazy talk.

"Oh, before I forget, do you understand our schedule for the next week? Remember, it's a little different. Your mom and I made a couple trades so we can go on our trip to Hawaii."

"Yes, Dad, I know," Ethan said impatiently. "I'm at Mom's

this weekend, so I won't be back to our place until next Monday night, right?"

"You got it. But I'll see you tomorrow afternoon at graduation. Okay, buddy?"

"Deal." The two hugged, and Andrew kissed Ethan on his sweaty head. As they turned around, Andrew was startled. Lydia was standing right behind them.

"Oh, you scared me. I didn't realize you were right there."

"How are you, Andrew?" Lydia managed a faint smile. "Let's go, Ethan—time for dinner."

"Ethan and I were just chatting about the schedule for the next week, and his graduation tomorrow. I'm sure I'll see you there."

"Yes, of course I will be there," she replied.

"Well, see you tomorrow, buddy."

As Lydia and Ethan walked to her car, Andrew watched her put her arm around her son. She really did love him. For the most part, he and Lydia did their best to work together. But as hard as they tried, there was always something missing—trust.

Andrew collected his things, picked up some trash left on the fields, and walked toward his car. Fumbling in the side pocket of his bag, he grabbed for his phone. It was only a little past seven, and he could use some real exercise. With a few taps of his finger, he called his friend Josh.

"Hey, hey, mister. You doing okay?" answered Josh.

"It's been a hard day to say the least. Any chance you're up for a run?"

"You bet. I'm still here at IFM's crystal cage." Josh's slang for headquarters. "You want to run out here, or in the city?"

"Let's go in town and run Lake Calhoun. If we have time we can add on Lake Harriet as well."

"Great. Maybe we can even get a bite to eat?"

"Let's say outside your place at eight."

"Perfect."

Madison, Wisconsin
Wednesday, June 2
7:00 P.M.

LIA MERRIMAN savored the last spoonfuls of a delicious, Ethiopian peanut stew at a divey, bohemian restaurant in the heart of Madison. She liked visiting university towns. Not only did they have plenty of alternative restaurants that catered to her vegan diet, but they also had a vibrant energy that renewed her sense of hope and optimism—something she desperately needed today.

After dinner, Lia strolled down by Lake Mendota to rest and enjoy the view. It had been another long and difficult day, and it wasn't over yet. In a few minutes she had to deliver more bad news to her boss, Ken Luger. Today's meeting with Wally Babin, a former researcher on the Redu trials at Iowa Agriculture & Technology, had been a huge disappointment.

Lia worked for a Washington, DC-based consumer watchdog group called the Ethical Food Coalition. During six years plus of employment, Lia had traveled all over the United States and the world trying to improve the safety and quality of the food supply. Most days she felt good about her work. Although progress was slow and sometimes the wins were too far apart, she knew she was making a difference. But her current assignment seemed to be nothing but dead ends, and she was feeling defeated. She agreed with her bosses that something was up, but finding evidence to substantiate their instincts seemed impossible. Although Ken tried to keep her motivated, Lia could feel the growing desperation. The pressure was on to prove Redu was not safe, and EFC was running out of time.

Lia felt her cell phone vibrating in her pocket, so she quickly pulled it out and glanced at the caller ID. "Hi, Ken," she answered. "How are you?"

"I'm fine. And you? Any good news to report?"

"I'm okay," Lia replied, "but no good news here. Wally Babin appears to be another dead end."

"Really? I thought you were on to something with him."

"So did I. The details surrounding his sudden move to Madison certainly caught my attention, but I pressed him as hard as I could, and he didn't give me a thing."

"Damn!"

"I've run out of ideas here, so I'm heading home to DC. When I'm back I'll start digging again at the FDA and around congressional offices. Hopefully I can uncover a lead somewhere."

"At this point I'll take anything. We're running out of options."

"Agreed," Lia replied.

"By the way, did you hear about the IFM plane crash?"

"Yes, and the news reports are saying we may be involved," Lia replied, shaking her head.

"Well, you know those reports are a lie."

"I know, Ken. I wouldn't work for EFC if I thought we did business that way."

"I'm curious where these reports are coming from. Can you ask around?"

"Sure. I've got some connections. I'll see what people are saying."

"Thanks, Lia. It'd be great to get to the bottom of this if at all possible."

"No problem."

"Well, you travel home safely, and please keep me posted."

"Will do, Ken. Good night."

Just as Lia was about to get up and walk back to her hotel, the phone vibrated again. *Must be Ken,* she thought. *Maybe he forgot to tell me something.* But when she checked her caller ID, it displayed Gus's Car Wash with a Maryland area code. Although it was likely some telemarketer, screening calls wasn't an option in her line of business.

"Hello, this is Lia Merriman."

Lia could hear sounds on the other end of the line, but no voice.

"Hello?" she repeated. "Can you hear me?"

"Ms. Merriman," a hushed voice replied.

"Yes. I can barely hear you over that noise. Can you speak up?"

"No, I can't. I'm calling from a public phone. I'm afraid."

"Who are you? How can I help?"

"My name is Danielle Haley. We met several months ago. I work for the FDA in Director Epps's office. You gave me your card."

"Oh yes, Danielle. I remember you," Lia played along, although she honestly couldn't place her face.

"I was cleaning up some files the other day and found something regarding Redu that seemed strange."

"Really, what?"

"I don't want to say any more over the phone. I'd rather meet in person."

"When?"

"Can you meet tonight?"

"I'm in Wisconsin right now. How about tomorrow?"

The voice on the other end was silent.

"Danielle, are you there?"

"Yes. I can't talk. Someone is coming. I'll e-mail you a time and place. I've got to go."

Minneapolis, Minnesota
Wednesday, June 2
8:00 P.M.

JOSH'S CONDO SAT on the corner of Lake Street and Knox. Although a bit too modern and flashy for Andrew's tastes, Josh's sixth floor, northwest corner unit was very spacious and had one of the best views of Lake Calhoun and downtown Minneapolis in the city. And even though Josh never bragged, Andrew figured it must have cost over a million dollars, especially given how it was furnished. But that was nothing to Josh. He was single, earned six figures as an IT Director at IFM, and had an ample trust fund.

Although he liked to downplay it, Josh was an heir of the Sargent family, one of the founding families of Minneapolis. In 1872, Josh's great-great-great-grandfather, Joshua Klout Sargent, established Klout, a local trading and mercantile business. Over the years, it grew into the second largest grocery chain in the country. When the family sold the business ten years ago, they netted over $50 billion, with Josh's portion a mere $6 billion. Fortunately for Josh, his father refused to let his children become trust fund kids. Instead, he required that Josh and his two sisters have summer jobs in high school and work their way through college. By the time they were out in the real world, they understood the value of hard work, and each of the three children had jobs and became successful in his or her own right.

Josh came down from his condo at precisely eight o'clock. He was the antithesis of any IT nerd stereotype. Wearing Nike shorts, a tank top, and his latest hi-tech running shoes, he looked like he had walked right out of the pages of some fitness magazine. Although quite average in height at five foot ten, his body was perfectly sculpted. His brown hair was short, neat, and receded slightly at the temples. Deep brown eyes flecked with gold, dimples, a cleft chin, and a scruffy beard set off his square jaw and angular face.

"Are you ready to sweat?" asked Josh.

"Let's do it," Andrew replied.

As they ran across the street and down to the runner's path, Josh asked about Becky. He knew she was on Andrew's team, and Josh could tell Andrew was upset. But after Andrew gave several one- or two-word answers, Josh realized Andrew really didn't want to talk about it, so he quickly moved on to a happier topic.

"Are you and Ethan getting excited about your trip?" Josh asked.

"Yep. I can't believe it. We leave a week from this Friday. By the way, don't forget I'm still waiting for your recommendations on things we should do while in Maui and Kaua`i."

"I haven't forgotten. I'll try to e-mail you some stuff by this weekend."

"Thanks," Andrew replied. "I know it's crazy to take a vacation right before this big B-Lean launch, but if we don't go now, we won't have another chance this summer with all of Ethan's sports camps and his vacation with Lydia."

"What about soccer? Who's going to coach?"

"Oh, another father has volunteered to help out. While we're gone, there will be three games and a practice. Practices are the only thing it takes any effort to plan."

"And how is Lydia dealing with the whole vacation thing?"

"No different than usual. We even brought in our mediator. I understand she doesn't want to be away from Ethan that long. I don't like it when he's gone either. At least we're handling it like adults and keeping Ethan from feeling like he's caught in the middle."

Halfway around Lake Calhoun, they decided to make it a seven-mile run and ran through Berry Park to Lake Harriet. By this point they were both dripping with sweat, so they stopped at a water fountain for a drink then pulled off their shirts and wiped down their faces and chests. Although Josh's single life certainly afforded more trips to the gym, Andrew was also quite fit and his muscular, neatly-trimmed chest and abs shimmered in the golden light of dusk.

In just over an hour, they had completed their circuit, picked up some takeout from Chang Mai Thai, and were back at Josh's condo eating and watching the last hour of the Celtics-Lakers NBA finals game. Not fans of either team, they still enjoyed the close finish with the Celtics ultimately winning.

Andrew got up and took their dishes into the kitchen. "I should get going. I need to get into work early since I'm leaving after lunch for Ethan's graduation."

Lying on the couch, Josh continued watching television and muttered "Uh, huh." By now the news was on, and just as he decided to get up the lead story caught his eye. "Andrew, get back in here. Heidi's covering the crash."

"What?" Andrew wandered back into the room. Immediately Heidi's voice caught his attention. Her story was moving and meticulous. It included video of the crash site, eyewitness accounts, statements from IFM, and initial information from local police and the NTSB. When Heidi interviewed Becky's sister, Hope, her genuine concern and empathy transformed what could have been exploitive into a thoughtful, genuine story of a family experiencing unbearable loss.

Then as Heidi's story came to a close, she spoke briefly with Bill Clausen. Reaching out, she squeezed his hand and said, "I know you're struggling to even comprehend your loss, but if you can, what would you like us to know about your wife?"

Bill struggled to maintain his composure and swallowed hard. "Where do I begin?" he replied, looking forlorn and washed out. Then a smile crossed his face, and his bloodshot eyes glimmered toward the camera. "Becky always amazed me at how she could be a successful business woman and a great mom and still make me feel so loved. Although she died doing a job she adored, Becky was never afraid to let everyone know that it was her family that lit up her world."

Andrew took a deep breath. It felt like he had been holding it during the entire story.

"Have you spoken to Bill yet?" Josh asked.

"I called him this morning. Becky's family was coming over to the house, so he couldn't talk very long."

"How do you keep going after such a loss?"

"I don't know," Andrew replied. "He and Becky were so in love. They were the perfect couple."

Josh nodded as he picked up his dishes and walked into the kitchen. Raising his voice slightly so Andrew could still hear him, "I mean, those last words that Bill shared about Becky. How does Heidi get people to open up like that?"

"Heidi's pretty amazing, you know that," Andrew replied, following Josh into the kitchen.

"Yes, we both do." Josh paused and then asked, "So how long has it been since you've seen her?"

"Oh, I don't know. Probably six months."

Heidi had been a classmate of theirs at Carleton College. They met at freshman orientation, and quickly became best friends.

But by the time they left for summer vacation, Andrew knew he wanted to be more than just friends. He tried calling her over break, but she was never around. It wasn't until they returned to campus that Andrew realized why. Heidi had a new boyfriend, Tyler.

For months Andrew was depressed. Although he was still good friends with Heidi, he couldn't shake the feelings he had for her. So to help boost his best friend's spirits, Josh invited Andrew to a party his sister was throwing across town at St. Olaf College. It was there that he met Lydia. She was quick-witted and petite with beautiful emerald green eyes and highlighted blond hair. There was an immediate chemistry between the two of them, and Andrew enjoyed Lydia's aggressive pursuit. It was nice to be chased. Then after three years of tumultuous romance, Lydia wanted a ring. Andrew hesitated but finally relented to Lydia's determination. By the end of Andrew's senior year, they were engaged, and then married a year later.

It didn't take long for Lydia to try to re-cast Andrew's life. Jealous of his friendships with Josh and Heidi, Lydia made it increasingly difficult for Andrew to see them, especially after Heidi finally broke things off with Tyler. Ethan's birth and the pressures of fatherhood, work, and marriage reduced their friendships further. Andrew and Josh still got together for lunch and the occasional run at IFM, but gone were the days of hanging out with Heidi. Then, more than six years later, Andrew bumped into Heidi outside the Hennepin County Family Justice Center. Heidi was there covering a story. Andrew was coming out of family court. He was a broken shell of a man, having just been ordered to move out of his home within ten days.

Heidi invited Andrew and Josh over for dinner that weekend. They laughed about old times, and Heidi and Josh consoled their dear friend. Step by step they helped Andrew rebuild his life. From finding and furnishing his new apartment, to supporting him through a bitter divorce that threatened to leave him a father in name only, Josh and Heidi were there for Andrew.

Three years later, Andrew had persevered and flourished. The divorce was behind him. Ethan was thriving, spending half of his time with his dad, and half with his mom. Andrew had bought a home, and he threw a holiday party to celebrate his good fortune and to thank his friends. As Heidi helped Andrew clean up after the party, she kissed him, and turned his life upside down. He was in love.

The next nine months were wonderful. They agreed to take it slow, and just enjoy being together. Andrew still felt the scars of a bad marriage, and Ethan's well-being was his primary concern. He knew Ethan would love Heidi as a step-mom, but what if things didn't work out? Andrew didn't trust his instincts anymore, and he couldn't bear to have Ethan suffer another breakup. So to Ethan and much of the world, they were just friends. But as time passed, Heidi began pressing him for a commitment. She grew tired of keeping their relationship a secret. She was ready to get married, and although she adored Ethan, she also wanted kids of her own. Andrew felt pressured, and his fear of commitment grew. Finally, after they had dated for a year, Heidi forced the issue, and when Andrew said he wasn't ready yet, she ran.

"You haven't seen her in six months?" Josh knew to tread lightly. The topic of Heidi had been off limits for Andrew since they broke up, but Josh had successfully maintained friendships with both of them, mainly by minding his own business and trying not to meddle.

"We met a couple times to return some personal items to each other. Heidi was angry, and I was hurt. It was awkward."

"You know she still loves you."

"Really? Did she say that?" Andrew asked.

"No, but I can tell. I think she feels badly about what happened. Patience isn't Heidi's strength. She knew you needed more time."

"Well, that's all history now."

"Why do you say that?"

"I don't know. It's hard for me to trust anyone again after what I've been through. If there's anything I've learned from marriage, it's that I want a woman who will be there, no matter what." Andrew paused and asked, "How is she doing?"

"Okay. She's much more of a loner these days."

"Why do you say that?"

"She just doesn't talk much about doing stuff with other people—even her family. It's like work and exercise are all there is. You should give her a call."

Andrew couldn't make up his mind if Josh was right or not, but it was late, and he had to get going. So after cleaning up the last of the dishes, Andrew said good night and drove home, lost in thought.

IFM Headquarters
Wednesday, June 2
10:00 P.M.

AIDAN TOOLE'S OFFICE was a showplace. Perched atop IFM's headquarters, the view it provided was unrivaled. It was originally planned to be only a fraction of its current size, but Aidan had halted construction after visiting a grad school buddy's office in Manhattan. Not to be outdone, he worked with designers to reconfigure plans for his executive suite. He made space for his expansion by moving the chief counsel's office and a conference room to the opposite end of the floor. He didn't want a lawyer as his neighbor anyway.

The office had been built before "green" and "sustainability" were buzzwords, so Aidan had gotten away with furnishing it with rare Brazilian Ipe hardwood floors and handmade mahogany furniture from Peru. It was also constantly upgraded with the latest gadgetry, including three large flat-screens gracing the walls and the latest computing and video-conferencing accessories. The bathroom alone was larger than most IFM conference rooms, and it made quite an impression with gold plated fixtures, Persa Blue granite walls and countertops, a cedar sauna, whirlpool tub, and steam shower enclosure.

Aidan deserved it. Or at least he thought so. After all, he had sold his soul for this company.

Aidan stood by his desk, looking out over Lake Minnetonka. Peggy, his wife, chattered on and on over the phone, and Aidan did his best to listen and throw in the occasional "yes, dear" so as not to get called on the carpet for being uninterested. Aidan adored his wife, but tonight he was distracted, and she demanded more attention than he could muster.

They had celebrated their silver anniversary the previous summer, more a tribute to Peggy than him. His minor contribution was keeping his pants zipped when it came to the ladies. He figured it was the least he could do. Truth be told, he didn't consider himself a ladies' man. Although he was handsome, his short five-foot-six stature and balding blond hair weren't every woman's dream. To compensate, Aidan ran or swam most days and lifted weights at least three times a week. The result was an exception-ally fit fifty-eight-year-old man. Impeccably dressed and sporting dark tortoise shell glasses that hid his steel blue eyes, there was an air of mystery and self-imposed isolation to Aidan. Perhaps that came with leading a Fortune 100 company for almost ten years. However, on some level, Aidan was painfully aware of his own deep-seated insecurity that festered within his very core.

As Chloe Stiles knocked and entered his office, Aidan quickly muffled "I love you" and "good night" to Peggy and greeted Chloe.

Without even the briefest hello, Chloe asked nervously, "Have you heard from her?"

"Calm down. Laura is a professional," Aidan replied. "Let's wait for Dan." Glancing at his watch he went on, "Where the hell is he anyway? It's ten o'clock. He should be here."

Chloe opened Aidan's wet bar fridge, helped herself to a Diet X-cite cola, and sat down on the leather sofa. "Well, I'm sure it's not easy to get out of the house this late with five kids and a wife."

"Hell, you've done it."

"Oh, Aidan, I have two teenage boys, and they're at my ex's. It just makes life easier if they stay there during the week."

Chloe crossed her legs and sat nervously on the couch with her right leg fidgeting as if she was suffering from a case of restless leg syndrome. Her skittish behavior was hardly the image one would expect from IFM's President of Innovation, Technology, and Quality. But this was not a typical week for Chloe.

A beauty pageant star as a child, Chloe was now forty-eight and hanging on to her youth for dear life. Although certainly still beautiful, the telltale signs of age were gaining ground. Yoga, Botox, and countless surgical "procedures" weren't working anymore. Her long, straight, raven hair, once sleek and supple, had grown more brittle as dyes and age took a horrible toll. To complicate matters, Chloe still hadn't come to the realization that maintaining her size-two figure made it even harder to cover her age. Her face was drawn, her skin sagged, and her hands and arms were bony with prominent veins bulging to the surface. Yes, she could still fit into ultra mini-skirts and revealing tops, but her age-inappropriate fashion choices frequently made Chloe the butt of jokes.

Her love life was just as amusing. Married and divorced three times, Chloe was a woman who needed a man by her side but grew tired of his company quickly. There were a few who knew that there had actually been a fourth marriage, but it had lasted less than two weeks, so she didn't count it. Husband number two fathered her two children. They separated when the boys were three and five. Chloe left for a ski trip one weekend and never came back. These days she was single and sported such a constant flow of younger men on her arm that she earned the "Twin Cities Cougar of the Year" award from the local gossip rag—a title Chloe was secretly quite proud of.

Aidan continued pacing along the wall of glass overlooking Lake Minnetonka. The sun had set, and only the occasional blinking lights of a boat could be seen crossing the main channel. Finally, Dan Murdock walked into Aidan's office.

"Hi, sorry I'm late. The regional retail sales directors are in town, and I took them to Manny's for some drinks and steaks. I wanted to make sure they understood what a big deal the B-Lean launch is."

"What are you hearing from them?"

"They're impressed but still a little skeptical."

"Really, why?"

"I think they're so used to us saying this is our biggest launch ever, they don't understand we really mean it this time. But when they hear how much we're investing behind it, their eyes open and they start to see big bonus payouts."

"Well, that's good. Just as long as we have them on the hook to deliver big volume."

"Oh, we do. Art's signed them up for a forty million case increase. That alone will help us reach double-digit retail sales growth."

"Fantastic. I've always said there was money to be made in getting the bastards we've fattened up to slim down."

"Yeah!" Dan replied. "Now we can make money on the yo-yo dieters as their scales go up and down!" They both laughed.

Chloe got up from the sofa as it became apparent Aidan and Dan weren't coming to sit down anytime soon. She was growing tired of Dan taking all the credit. "Aidan, it's fantastic to see what we've been working so hard for the past nine years come to life. We've created a revolution in food, and we stand to reap huge rewards."

"Well, as you both know, we aren't at the finish line yet," Aidan said. "And after this morning's events, I know we're all anxious."

Chloe's face tightened, and she started to tap her foot.

"Let's go sit down." Aidan motioned to his desk then sat down facing Dan and Chloe.

"So, have you talked to her, Aidan?"

"Yes, Chloe. Laura called me earlier this evening. It looks like a clean hit." Chloe's eyes darted to the floor when Aidan said the word "hit."

"I knew Laura could do it," added Dan. "She's tough and reliable."

Chloe shifted in her chair. Still on edge, her shoulders drooped slightly as she digested the update.

"The news is reporting that EFC has claimed responsibility. What's that about?" she asked.

"Oh, Laura came up with that twist. She thought it would be

helpful to throw a red herring in the mix to use as cover," Dan replied.

"Well, I still don't like how all this went down," Chloe muttered. "I told both of you I could contain the issue with my people. Then you go off killing them."

"Hey there," Dan was getting upset and Chloe could tell. "Wait just one second. We agreed yesterday that too much was riding on this. What if your people started talking? Could we really afford to take that risk? Just one wrong word could have led a reporter or some EFC operative to uncover that damn early research from Dr. McNaulty."

"But I've made a lot of improvements since those early trials."

"That's great, Chloe, but don't you get it? We don't need to give anyone an excuse to go nosing around. Hell, so far we've hidden research, falsified trials, bribed government officials, and black-mailed researchers. If news of any of that leaks out, you know where the three of us will be? Jail. That's right! And that's not all. What about our big payout? Gone! We each stand to lose $250 million or more from our stock options alone if Redu goes down the tubes. So don't go pointing your finger, Chloe. You were there when we decided to take care of these loose ends."

"These so-called loose ends were people, Dan. You guys ganged up on me last night long after you and Laura had hatched a plan. I didn't have a choice."

"Oh, give me a break—"

Tired of the arguing, Aidan interrupted.

"Chloe, you know as well as I do, Dan is right. If the slightest inkling of impropriety were to get out, the press and food cops would treat it like blood in the water. It wouldn't take long for our transgressions to catch up with us. I agree with Dan. I don't want to end up in jail, and my guess is, neither do you. So stop the bickering. What's done is done. It was unfortunate but necessary. We need to move on quickly to make sure these actions weren't in vain."

"Yes, Aidan. You're completely right," Dan agreed.

Chloe stared at the floor. Aidan was right, but she still couldn't believe they had actually done it.

"First let's make sure our trail is clean," Aidan said. "Laura's very concerned about this. After all, that's how we got in this mess in the first place. She wants her chief IT person to do a complete and thorough audit of our networks and databases. Anything questionable will be isolated. Once a document has been quarantined only one of us can release it."

"Do we trust Laura?" Chloe asked. "I mean, she's brilliant, but she's also ruthless. Do we want her touching all of our data?"

"I don't think we have a choice," Aidan replied. "Our only other option is to bring our IT team into the mix to resolve this."

Dan rolled his eyes. Rick Dunlop was IFM's Chief of Information Systems. He had risen through the ranks quickly, but more for his golf game than for being smart or skilled. "Yeah, Rick's a nice guy and everything, but he's an idiot. Not only do I think he could screw this up, but I don't trust him."

Chloe turned to Dan. "It's refreshing how quickly you throw your buddies under the bus."

"What do you think we should do, Chloe?" Dan asked.

After squirming in her chair, she threw up her hands in disgust and shook her head. "You're right. We don't have a choice. I'm just scared of Laura. I'm convinced she would eat her own young if she had to."

Dan chuckled. "Well, you're right about that. She's tough, but that's what we need to get this done. Do you want me to follow up with Laura on this, Aidan, or do you want to handle it?"

"No, you can, Dan. You and Chloe are closer to what document vulnerabilities may exist. I expect a complete review by the end of this week so we can feel secure. Understand?"

"Perfectly."

"Good. Oh, by the way, I've called an emergency leadership team meeting for tomorrow morning."

"Yes, I saw that come through on my phone," Chloe said approvingly.

"In that meeting I will announce to the leadership team our

go-forward plan in light of the crash. Given the crucial nature of the B-Lean launch, I'm going to appoint both of you as special project chairmen. You will have the complete authority to pull in any resources necessary for the launch. My expectation is that you will personally lead this project through completion. Chloe, this means you need to pick up the reins. The FDA approval must happen by June 15. Got it?"

"Yes, I'll be in DC next Tuesday to make sure it happens."

"And, Dan, you need to have Marketing and Sales ready to make this our biggest launch ever."

"We're on it, Aidan," Dan said reassuringly. "Don't worry."

FOUR

Washington, D.C.
Thursday, June 3
8:00 A.M.

THE MORNING TRAFFIC was light. Congress was on recess for the week of Memorial Day, and the throngs of summer tourists were still at home battling carpools, final exams, and graduations. So today was a good day for Laura Long. She hated any inconvenience, especially traffic.

Her penthouse condo atop The Ritz-Carlton in Georgetown was five to twenty minutes from her office, all depending on DC's infamous gridlocked roads. This morning, Luis, her driver, navigated the least clogged route while Laura worked from her mobile office, the backseat of her Cadillac STS Platinum. Although it was quite comfortable by most standards, Laura was tough to please and she continued to miss her old BMW 750iL. But after forming The Center for Union Data, a thinly veiled lobbyist group funded by the Big USA automakers and other anti-union corporations, in 2005 she reluctantly traded in her import for this made-in-USA Caddie.

Luis headed east on M Street NW and turned onto Pennsylvania Avenue, smiling the whole way as he cruised along with no resistance. Laura's office was located in a modern, concrete and glass building just a block from the White House. The lease was held in the name of Long & Company, and it housed over two dozen lobbying entities. Each was formed as a tax-exempt, 501(c)3 US non-profit organization. As such, Laura avoided the messy business of disclosing any of her clients. The end result was a quarter of a billion dollars flowing into her coffers annually from countless, anonymous corporations around the world all for one purpose—for Ms. Long to be the front-woman in their fight to gain access to, and influence over, the government.

Laura's first non-profit, Diner's Choice, was founded in 1994. Funded by tobacco companies, it battled social discrimination against smokers in restaurants and other public areas, and tried to fight for smokers' rights by outlawing no smoking policies. As the fight for tobacco lost steam, Laura breathed new life into Diner's Choice by bringing in big liquor companies and restaurant chains who were looking for ways to battle Mothers Against Drunk Drivers' efforts to lower the legal blood-alcohol level below 0.10. From there, Laura formed new entities like The Center for Union Data and The Workers Policies Institute to battle unions and fight minimum wage increases, and Humane Guardian to attack the Humane Society and PETA by promoting activities like animal testing, factory farming, canned hunts, and fur farming.

Of all of her organizations, though, her most lucrative was the Council for American Liberties and Freedom (CALF). Established in 1998, this organization's sights were set to protect everyone's freedom to eat. Food companies and restaurants found themselves increasingly under attack. Food cops, dietitians, school boards, militant activists, and health care reformers were all taking aim and blaming them for the obesity epidemic. Laura quickly mobilized the food industry's fear of regulation and formed CALF, a powerful public relations and lobbying organization that defended everyone's right to eat whatever they want.

Of CALF's founding clients, IFM was by far the most generous and had earned a special place in Laura's priorities. Aidan Toole had helped rally support for CALF when he was Chief Marketing Officer at IFM. The CEO at the time, Geoff Henricks, was not fond of the relationship. Geoff was a CEO of a different generation. He fondly remembered when Tang was marketed as "the favorite drink of the space program." But the food marketer's landscape was changing quickly, and Aidan knew it. Gone were the days when IFM's products could be marketed as technological wonders. As time passed, all aspects of their products were increasingly scrutinized by consumer advocate groups, and the rumblings of more regulation were getting louder and harder to ignore.

So when Aidan took the helm of IFM, he doubled his support of CALF, and this investment had continued to increase over the past nine years. In doing so, he wanted not only to protect IFM's right to profit from the world's burgeoning waistlines, but also to make sure Laura Long knew where her loyalties were. Yes, other food manufacturers and restaurant chains were involved in CALF, but with IFM's investment accounting for over 50 percent of CALF's financial support, he ensured Laura was loyal to IFM first. Over the years, that loyalty had been tested time and again, and from making things happen or not happen on Capitol Hill to making pesky problems go away, Laura had passed the test every time.

As Luis approached Long & Company's office, he pulled up to the curb. After putting on his hazard lights, Luis quickly jumped out to open the door for Ms. Long. She was from Vietnam but her lineage was Chinese, and she was five foot three, thin, with dark hair styled in a shoulder-length blunt cut with straight bangs. Professionally dressed in black pants and jacket, a blue silk blouse, and thick, black-rimmed, rectangular glasses, Laura exuded a severe, unapproachable quality. Although she possessed an innate beauty, she did her best to obscure any feminine curves and harden her image. With her Asian face, that meant pinched lips and minimal make-up that enhanced her angular cheekbones, pointy chin, and dark, narrow eyes.

A creature of habit, Laura headed straight to Caribou Coffee for a cup of her favorite French Roast blend, and then went up to her offices on the eleventh and twelfth floors. Overlooking the Old Executive Office Building and just minutes from the White House and the Capitol, Laura Long's penthouse office cast a powerful shadow over Washington. Despite her proximity, though, none of her business was done on government property. Phone conversations and private dining rooms at the finest restaurants were her preferred domains for conducting her most important work.

As she rode up in the elevator, her phone vibrated. The caller ID showed Dan Murdock was calling again. It was his third call of the morning, and Laura was determined to make him wait. For Aidan she would answer on the first call, but in her book Dan was a self-aggrandizing ass, and she wanted him to squirm a little longer. Anyway, Aidan had filled her in the previous night after his meeting with Dan, and she already had her people working on his urgent request.

As Laura entered the office, the receptionist greeted her. "Good morning, Ms. Long."

Laura continued walking, ignoring the salutation as she reviewed her appointments for the day on her smartphone. As she passed by her secretary's desk, Joy tried to greet her as well, but Laura talked over her mutterings.

"Get me Larry and Ann," demanded Laura. "I need them in my office in five minutes."

"Certainly, Ms. Long."

Laura continued on, and Joy said to her back, "Is there anything else I can get for you?" Laura ignored her, walked into her office, shut the door, and settled into her chair.

Within a minute, Laura's office line buzzed announcing Dan Murdock was on the line. After keeping Dan on hold for a couple minutes while she settled in, she picked up the line.

"Good morning, Dan. How are you?"

"I've been better, Laura. I've been calling you since six this morning. Where have you been?"

"Calm down, Dan."

"So where do we stand?"

"We're all ready on our side. All we need is access to your servers."

"How can I do that without it being suspicious?"

"Well, I'm assuming you have a pretty high security clearance at IFM. Just ask your IT man to set up a new ID for you with unlimited access within the system. Get us that information, and we'll do the rest."

"You make it sound so easy."

"Just get it done." Laura contemplated throwing in some derogatory comment but changed her mind. She didn't like Dan, but she had to watch herself. Dan could be sitting in Aidan's chair someday.

"Okay, I will have it to you within the hour. Any idea how long it will take to complete your scan?"

"I've got our experts working on it right now. Once we have access, we should be able to put together a more complete timetable."

"Great. Oh, what are you hearing about the crash? Any rumblings or concerns?"

"No, no issues. Everything looks clean. We're monitoring the news media and local and federal authorities. If there's any unusual activity, we'll know about it."

"Sounds good."

"Leave me a message when you have access set up." She hung up abruptly without saying another word.

Laura got up from her chair, holding her coffee in her hands, and opened her door. Looking around, she yelled, "Where are Larry and Ann?"

"I called them right when you asked," replied Joy. "They should be here any second."

"Call them again!"

IFM Headquarters
Thursday, June 3
7:30 A.M.

AFTER A RESTLESS night's sleep, Andrew's alarm went off at five. Ten minutes later he was down in the basement lifting weights. His workout room wasn't large, but it was equipped with a treadmill, free weights, a bench, and a mat for sit-ups—everything Andrew needed to keep in shape and burn off stress.

By six thirty, Andrew was sitting in his office at IFM. There was no need to slip into his cube unnoticed this morning. No one was around this early. Although Andrew yearned for a real office, his cube was nothing to complain about. He was fortunate to score a magnificent lake view, real estate typically reserved for conference rooms, directors, or higher-ups. Although not spacious, it was big enough to pull in a couple extra chairs and have an impromptu meeting with four or five people. Privacy was the only issue, and sometimes Andrew would kill for four real walls, a ceiling, and a door.

After catching up on e-mails, Andrew prepared for his meeting with Lourdes. Today's topic was B-Lean Snacks marketing plans. Andrew was presenting plans to Dan and the Uncle Chuck's leadership team next Thursday. With any new product, there was always scrutiny, and as the leader of the B-Lean Snacks cross-functional team, Andrew was expected to be the expert on all aspects of the launch, from production start-ups to packaging inventories to product testing results. So to prepare, each cross-functional team member would update the marketing manager so any questions could be answered. With Becky gone, Andrew's team had lost all its expertise on Redu's FDA approval, and Andrew was frantic to get up to speed.

At exactly 7:30 a.m., Lourdes knocked at his cube doorway. "Does this time still work?"

"Yes, of course. Come on in. I'm sorry to drag you in here so early."

Lourdes took to heart the rule of dressing for success. Today's ensemble featured an ecru, pencil skirt that came just above the knee and an ivory jewel-neck crepe de Chine blouse topped with a cream and camel brown tweed Chanel-style cardigan jacket. For Lourdes, the look went far deeper than just dressing well. It was about all aspects of her work being in perfect order, a fact reaffirmed once again when she sat down for her update and opened her meticulously tabbed notebook.

"So did you get my e-mail yesterday? Are you ready to talk marketing plans?" Andrew asked.

"Yes," she replied. "I brought a couple documents with me." Lourdes pulled out a folder with several carefully prepared handouts. "First is the original planning timetable we agreed on in January. I updated it last night with our latest to-dos. Items marked in green are complete, yellow in process, and red are overdue."

Andrew scanned the timetable. It was gleaming with green and occasionally some yellow. The only red that could be seen was on follow-ups from the ad agency. The advertising campaign development was now at least six weeks off plan thanks to several missed attempts by their New York agency, Bingham & Morris.

"This looks fantastic. I know we have the ad agency coming in on Monday, so hopefully we can make some serious progress on that front next week. How's the actual presentation looking?"

"I updated the template per your feedback last week. Right now I'd say it's about 70 percent complete. I imagine by this weekend we should be down to just a couple pages that we'll need to focus on. Would you like to review it now?"

"No, if you can post the latest version by this evening, that would be great. I have to leave around one o'clock for Ethan's graduation, but I'll be online later. Are there any areas that you would like me to pay special attention to?"

"Well, I'm concerned about appearing knowledgeable regarding the approval process."

"I know that's going to be tough…with Becky gone—" Andrew

stopped mid-sentence and glanced away, and then tried to clear his throat.

"Are you okay?" Lourdes asked.

"Sorry. It's still hard to believe she's not coming back."

"I know," Lourdes replied. "Do you want me to leave?"

"No, I'll be okay," Andrew said, clearing his throat again. "Have you checked out the Knowledge Portal? Becky posted some great summaries there and the complete history of the approval process."

"Right. I have to go over that again."

"I e-mailed Chloe Stiles this morning to see if she could meet with me early next week. I want to make sure we have all the latest info."

"Chloe? That's going straight to the top."

"We go way back. I got to know her when I worked in the Beverages Division. She'd taken a special interest in a project I was working on. We had to travel together a lot, so we'd go out for drinks and dinner." Andrew hesitated.

"Sounds like there's more to that story."

"Nope. Never anything between us but business."

Lourdes raised one eyebrow, but she wasn't going to dig further despite Chloe's reputation for mixing business, pleasure, and handsome men.

"Seriously. It was nothing," Andrew objected again.

Finally he realized he would have to share more. "You see, we were out this one time and some guy started to make some aggressive moves on Chloe. So I came to her rescue. It's as simple as that. See, it was nothing."

"Ahhh...Prince Charming rescuing a damsel in distress."

"Hardly," Andrew replied. "But Chloe and I have some life experiences in common that have given us stuff to talk about. We're both divorced parents, and she has two boys. Hers are almost in college, so she's big on telling me what will come next with Ethan."

"I didn't even know she had kids."

"She takes a pretty hands-off approach to raising them. I think these days they're over at their dad's house most of the time, except for the occasional weekend."

"Well, it's great that you guys have a friendship, and that you can go directly to her."

"Yeah, I figure Chloe will help fill any knowledge gaps on the approval process. Now, you're taking the team through a rough draft of the presentation tomorrow, right?"

"Yes, it's on your schedule."

"Good. I'll try to have my edits and additions finished tonight. Then we can work together to wrap up the remaining holes in the presentation. Hopefully we should be all set by Tuesday with a couple days to spare."

"Perfect. Oh, after you review the presentation, let me know if there are some new visuals or props you'd like for your meeting next week."

"Sounds great. Lourdes, I couldn't do this without you. What am I going to do when we get you promoted?"

"I don't know, but..." Lourdes paused. "I hope we can find out soon."

"Don't worry. Your hard work is recognized. I can't promise you exactly when it will happen, but I know it will be soon. Okay?"

"I trust you, Andrew. You're one of the few managers around here that I'd say that about. You actually care about your people. You want to see them succeed."

A bit flushed, Andrew cleared his throat and said, "Thanks, Lourdes. That really means a lot, especially coming from you."

Long & Company Headquarters
Washington, D.C.
Thursday, June 3
8:30 A.M.

LARRY RUEHL walked down the main corridor leading to

Laura's office with Ann Verbena at his side. Dressed in a dark charcoal gray, pinstriped suit, white shirt, and blue tie, Larry was Laura's right arm. His dark brown hair was cut neat, with a light douse of pomade to hold it in place. Thankfully for the others in the office, he was a bit more diplomatic and polite than Laura.

As they approached Laura's office, Larry straightened his tie and buttoned his jacket. "Now let me handle the talking."

"I'm telling you, I can take care of myself. I'm not afraid of her," replied Ann.

Ann Verbena was new to Laura's operation. A recent recruit from a high-tech software company in California, she had only met Laura once before. Ann was brilliant, but Larry feared she wasn't tough enough to survive around Laura. Ann just seemed too feminine and mild. Her hair was soft brown with blond highlights, and her pale, baby soft skin was set off with huge, doe-like eyes. Her voice was high and sounded more like a kindergarten teacher's than a world-leading authority on systems and data mining. Unfortunately, her fashion sense didn't help either. Looking at her white blouse and fitted chinos that showed some bulge around the thighs, Larry winced, worrying Laura would criticize her.

As they approached Laura's office, Larry winked at Joy, who mouthed back "good luck."

Larry knocked and tentatively walked into Laura's office, saying, "Sorry we kept you waiting."

Laura grabbed the iPad off the corner of her desk. Other than her iMac, it was the only thing on the glass top. Papers and pencils never littered her desk. It made for a very sleek, minimalist look, which for Laura was all about efficiency.

Without acknowledging their tardiness, Laura said, "I spoke with Dan Murdock this morning. They want to move forward with the data cleaning operation. Have you put together a list of search words and phrases to trigger quarantined files?"

"Yes, it's right here," chimed Ann, holding out a piece of paper.

Laura raised her head slightly and peered over her glasses. "E-mail me a copy. I don't accept paper. I'll review it and get Dan's input."

"How very green of you," replied Ann.

Ouch, Larry thought. *Not a good time for joking.* He tried to jump in but hesitated for one moment too long.

"Let me be clear, Ann," Laura took off her glasses and stared through her. "This isn't about being green. This is about you getting me what I want, when I want it, and how I want it."

Larry intervened. "Laura, I went ahead and forwarded you both the screening methodology and the key words just before we came in."

"Thank you, Larry. Now if you can only teach your people how to follow protocol." A few moments passed as Laura pulled up the document. "It all looks in order. I'll run it by Dan."

"Yes, Ann did an excellent job putting it together," Larry piped in.

"How about the timeline, Ann?" asked Laura, setting another trap.

"Well, if we implement by noon, I think we should be done by Saturday night."

"Oh, you think. I'm going to tell our biggest client, who is on the precipice of a financial and legal disaster, that you 'think' you will be done Saturday night."

"Well, I don't know how much data we need to cover, or how quickly we will have access."

"Excuses, excuses. I told Larry you'd have access by noon. Don't you two talk?" As Ann tried to reply, Laura talked over her. "I don't care to hear your excuses. This operation is beyond crucial for the next couple weeks. If you slip up, you could bury IFM and maybe even us. I want no mistakes. Supposedly you are one of the world's most highly regarded data experts. Really? Really? I'm not seeing it."

Ann's face reddened.

"Calm down, Laura. Everything is okay. I know Ann can get the job done. Just let us get to work," Larry said.

Laura turned her chair around and looked out toward the Old Executive Office Building.

"No excuses."

Before Ann could utter another word, Larry grabbed her shoulder and ushered her out of the office.

At least we survived, he thought.

IFM Headquarters
Thursday, June 3
8:00 A.M.

IFM'S BOARDROOM WAS on the north side of the main building's fifth floor, just up the hall from the executive suites. Despite the short notice, all but two of Aidan's team made the emergency meeting—Joe Spears, President of IFM International, and Sumit Dharuna, President of Strategic Planning, were stuck in China negotiating a joint venture deal with the country's leading noodle company. The topic of Aidan's meeting was no secret. He had left a voice mail for his team late the previous night. Rumors swirled around IFM, and paralysis on the cusp of B-Lean's FDA approval and launch was unacceptable. His team and the company were getting their marching orders, and they knew it.

As the leadership team assembled, catering brought up a full assortment of beverages, bagels, pastries, cereals, snack bars, and three hot stations with breakfast sandwiches, pancakes, and breakfast meats. No one would go hungry.

At precisely 8:00 a.m., Aidan walked in, and the room quieted as people found their seats. "Good morning. I appreciate each of you juggling your personal and work schedules to make this meeting on such short notice. I'll keep it brief, I promise.

"Yesterday, our IFM family suffered a devastating loss. Seven hardworking employees died in a catastrophic crash on board one of our jets. While I don't have any details from the crash investigation, I did want you to know, we're taking care of our own. Each family will receive an immediate, post-tax distribution of $100,000 to alleviate any urgent financial concerns. This, of course, is in addition to the very generous life and AD&D insurance policies that already cover our entire IFM family. Also, IFM will pay for all funeral expenses, and we have dispatched funeral coordinators from Washburn-McReavy to assist each family's planning. Finally, I am completing work on full college scholarships for all the children of our lost team members. Certainly we cannot fill the loss, but I'm determined to take care of these families."

Dan stood up. "Aidan, I'm so proud to work for you and a company like IFM. You are always first class."

"Well, thank you, Dan. I appreciate all of your support in this effort, and if you have other suggestions on how we can help these families, please let me know.

"Now, moving over to pressing business matters. Our loss has also left our largest single initiative, the B-Lean launch, in peril. To prevent any slippage on this critical priority, I'm prepared to announce two temporary moves. Dan Murdock and Chloe Stiles will be Emergency Project Chairmen. In these roles, they have my complete authority. Anything that I could approve, they now can approve. Chloe will handle the sprint to the finish line for Redu's FDA approval as well as all issues getting B-Lean into production at all of our manufacturing sites. Whatever human resources or other corporate resources she needs to that end are hers. Dan Murdock will be responsible for the sales and marketing launch of B-Lean. This move is immediate, and is made with the express intention of setting the B-Lean launch as our clear priority. There will be no resource fights. Chloe and Dan understand our business issues. They will trump other priorities only when they need to. Any questions?"

There were some rumblings around the table, but no questions were asked.

"Okay, I'll be sending this directive out immediately via e-mail and posting it on the intranet. Thank you for coming this morning."

Before Aidan could get out of the room, Rick Dunlop, IT Chief, was on his tail.

"Excuse me, Aidan, but I'm guessing Dan's request to me this morning is related to this?"

"What request was that?"

"Well, he made the odd request to set up a new ID within the system. He said to set it up with unlimited access. That's quite unusual, you know."

"Rick, I appreciate you coming to me. I know Dan's request may seem unusual, but he's doing this with my full authority. He and Chloe have my complete trust."

"Okay, thank you, Aidan. You can count on me. I'll make it happen."

Dan was standing nearby and could overhear the entire conversation. As Aidan walked away, he winked at him and came up behind Rick, placing his hand on his shoulders. "Any questions there, buddy?"

"Oh, I didn't see you were standing there, Dan. Nope, not at all. I have my orders. You'll have your access set up by noon."

"Thanks, Rick, I appreciate it. Hey, what do you say we hit the links this weekend? Maybe we can get a foursome together?"

"Sure, sounds like fun."

"Great. I'll get us a tee time at Interlachen and invite a couple guys out."

EFC Headquarters
Washington, D.C.
Thursday, June 3
9:15 A.M.

GINA SILLS, the Executive Director of the Ethical Food Coalition, sat at her conference table reading through a series of news reports, shaking her head. Despite her best efforts, negative events attracted ten times more media coverage than her work advocating for public health and better food. The latest claim that EFC was responsible for the crash of an IFM corporate jet was preposterous. But sensationalized stories were so much more interesting to the news media than how fast food and salty snacks would likely reduce life expectancies of future generations.

Over the years, however, Gina had grown accustomed to going against the flow. As a PhD, Harvard-educated microbiologist, she had dedicated her life to improving the quality of the food supply. Dismayed by the chemical toolbox of big-business agriculture, food manufacturers, and restaurants, Gina founded EFC in 1992 to fight for quality food. Her leadership nurtured EFC from an unknown consumer advocacy group into one of the world's most powerful watchdogs. Now with five offices across the globe, 120 employees, and over one million e-mail subscribers, she believed she was finally amassing the critical mass to make a lasting impact.

As her top aides Henry Usher and Ken Luger walked into her office for their weekly strategy meeting, Gina asked, "Who do you think is behind this?" waving the latest newspaper article.

"We aren't sure," replied Henry. "We've been polling our teams across the country to see if there were any fringe associates that could be linked to the event."

"And?" Gina jumped in.

"We've come up with nothing. Though there have been some violent extremists that claim affiliation with EFC."

"Of course, I know, Henry, but we neither advocate nor tolerate such actions. They have nothing to do with EFC, and are in no way authorized by us. We've repeatedly made that clear to the media."

"The media doesn't care. They think it makes for good news."

"Well, we have to find some way to protect our name. I don't want us to become radicalized by the media like PETA or Greenpeace. We're a mainstream organization fighting for a mainstream idea. To win this battle against obesity and poor nutrition, we need to have everyday Americans believing in us and donating to our cause. The more we get wrapped up with wild ideas or actions, the easier it is for the food industry and its lobbyists to dismiss us as radicals."

"Gina, we agree. Listen, we've come up with an interesting idea.

It involves shifting some resources around, but I wanted Ken to run the idea by you."

"I'm listening," replied Gina.

"Well, as you know, we've assembled some of the most talented operative teams across the globe. Right now we have these teams researching issues like deceptive labeling, improper food handling and contamination issues, and new product registrations and approvals. What if we shift a team to investigate the stories against EFC? If somehow we can root out where the misinformation is coming from, perhaps we can put an end to it."

"Hmmm...I like it," said Gina, and her broad smile lit up the room. She got up from her chair, and started to think aloud. "I don't like the idea of taking resources away from our key projects, but if we can somehow get a better handle on where this misinformation is coming from, maybe we can do a better job of stopping it. Any team in particular you're thinking about, Ken?"

"Tony Gibbs would be perfect for this. He's one of our most experienced team leaders."

"You read my mind," Gina replied.

"Fantastic, let's make the change happen immediately. I'll let you know as soon as we have any new information," said Ken.

"Oh, I did have one more thing before you leave. Do you have a second?" asked Gina.

"Sure."

"Do we have any news on the Redu approval? I haven't heard anything in days."

"Nothing new. We still have no proof of any stacking of the Food Advisory Committee, and we've torn apart the research trials studies, but all we've hit are dead ends. One of our sources did report that Chloe Stiles has an appointment with the FDA Director, Jackie Epps, early next week."

"Damn, I've always had the feeling that Epps is being bought. If only I could prove it."

"We're watching, Gina. Lia Merriman just finished interviewing the last of the researchers involved in the Redu trials. She's coming back to DC today to follow-up on some potential leads," Ken replied.

"Anything promising?"

Ken shook his head. "Nothing yet."

"Okay, I appreciate the information. You both know how important it is that we defeat the Redu approval. IFM must be stopped on this one."

"We know, Gina. I can't speak for Ken, but I'm just not that optimistic," Henry replied, shaking his head. "I think we'll need some kind of miracle."

"I know," Gina replied, "but we can't give up."

"Agreed. I'll get Tony started on investigating where all this misinformation is coming from. Expect daily updates from here on out," said Henry.

FIVE

Plymouth, Minnesota
Thursday, June 3
1:00 P.M.

ANDREW'S DAY was a blur. After a hectic morning of back-to-back meetings, he left work at one o'clock. Nothing would keep him from Ethan's graduation, and he was determined to arrive early and score some good seats.

As the elementary school gym filled to capacity, the laughter and chatter grew. It was a festive occasion for all, and Andrew enjoyed catching up with friends and teachers he had met over the past six years.

Five minutes before two, everyone started to find their seats. Andrew hadn't seen Lydia, so he scanned the crowd once more. Just then she dashed in and looked desperately for an open seat. Andrew stood up and waved to catch her attention then motioned to the seat next to his that he had saved just in case. At first she appeared a bit surprised, but given her late arrival, she was thankful and graciously took him up on his offer.

When the procession of the graduates started, 161 fifth graders dressed in their black and red D.A.R.E. T-shirts circled the gym. As Andrew watched Ethan make his way to his seat, he couldn't help getting choked up and think that his little boy was growing up. He was so proud of Ethan, but in the moment, he also was proud of himself. The past six years had been hard, but he had survived. Ethan was thriving, and Andrew was a vital part of his son's life. Although things were far from perfect with Lydia, they were civil with each other. But they still had a ways to go. Before long they would be co-parenting a teenager, and to be successful they would have to learn to trust each other again.

After fifty minutes of speakers and songs, the graduates crossed the stage to receive their diplomas, circled the gym, and then left for the reception. Parents, grandparents, brothers, and sisters crowded into the cafeteria, which was decorated with streamers and balloons. Andrew quickly found Ethan and his pack of friends huddled around a table of lemonade and cookies. After giving Ethan a big hug, he watched the boys goof around for a bit then visited with other parents and teachers.

It didn't take long for the reception to wind down, and by four o'clock Andrew was home, and then right back out the door for a long run on the Luce Line Trail. By the time he returned and showered, he was starving, so he stir-fried some veggies and a piece of chicken with noodles, garlic, and ginger.

As he sat down for dinner, he set up his laptop on the kitchen island to catch up on work. While eating, Andrew plowed through his e-mails. Over forty had piled up since he had left work, but most were either complete junk or simply pointless.

After taking a break to clean up his dishes, Andrew logged onto IFM's Knowledge Portal to access Becky's files and work on his presentation. Created four years ago, the portal was an innovation to move information seamlessly within and across teams throughout IFM. Too often IFM found itself wasting time and money duplicating research by trying to answer questions that other teams had dealt with years ago. So by typing in just a few keywords, Andrew could quickly access all documents pertaining to Redu's approval process, including Becky's summaries and any original studies or reports.

Redu's development traced back to the mid 1990s when a company out of Australia started to make news with a patented Hi-maize resistant starch made from a non-GMO corn hybrid. This variety was high in amylose, a type of starch featuring long, harder to digest chains of glucose. Resistant starches, otherwise known as RS, occurred naturally in legumes, whole grains, under-ripe bananas, and some other starchy foods. But as developed countries ate more processed foods, resistant starch consumption faced extinction in the average diet. Hi-maize resistant starch presented an avenue to mine a naturally-occurring source that could be incorporated into a variety of foods to improve their nutritional profile.

IFM's interest in the area piqued as consumer interest in health-ier foods began growing. Touting benefits like weight-loss, better digestive health, increased dietary fiber intake, and improved glycemic management, IFM thought RS would be a perfect fit in its new product development pipeline. But after several failed attempts to buy an exclusive right to license Hi-Maize RS, IFM's interest waned as cost and availability issues plagued the project.

Chloe Stiles, who at the time was just an up-and-coming R&D Innovation Director, also disliked the product development limita-tions of Hi-Maize RS. So she had worked to identify a track with higher potential—one that wasn't dependent on nature. Chloe's idea was to chemically alter genetically modified versions of a variety of grains to produce synthetic Ultra-Hi RS (UHRS). This solution not only bumped up UHRS levels of resistant starch 50–100 percent above their naturally occurring counterparts, but also UHRS could now be made from a multitude of grains, thus providing a much broader product development palette. Despite making great progress during the first couple years, Chloe's project was back-burnered in the late 1990s as resources shifted to the fat free fad.

Then, in the spring of 2001 there was a call for "Big Ideas" throughout IFM. Aidan Toole had taken the helm, and he was determined to usher in a new age of growth that would crown IFM as the world's largest food company. Chomping at the bit for recognition and the top ITQ job, Chloe allied with Dan Murdock and made a pitch for synthetic UHRS. Their idea garnered Aidan's leadership team's attention and was chosen as one of three projects to fast track.

After a year of grueling work, Chloe wowed IFM's board with a proprietary process that acylated starch with short chain fatty acids to create CX-4, a line of synthetic UHRS available in four different varieties: wheat, rice, corn, and barley. CX-4 promised net calorie reductions of up to 50 percent without the slightest compromise in taste. Astonished at the potential to be used as an ingredient in cereals, breads, snacks, desserts, and countless other items, the board unanimously agreed. CX-4 was the future growth engine for IFM. Chloe's stock quickly rose with the news, and she was promoted to President of IFM's ITQ function.

Patents were filed for CX-4, and a new consumer-friendly moniker, Redu, was trademarked. The technological creation was heralded in the world of food processing as the Holy Grail—now people could eat more delicious food without getting fat. Finally, technology had prevailed over Mother Nature. But one more giant hurdle lay ahead: getting the FDA's approval for GRAS certification. With a GRAS designation, CX-4, now known as Redu, would be "generally recognized as safe," and could be legally added to all types of consumer foods.

IFM knew the approval process would be challenging. Over the past several decades, FDA approvals had been notoriously long and arduous, with Procter & Gamble's Olestra being one of the most memorable in recent history. Over the course of twenty-five years of development and at a cost of over $200 million, P&G underwent over one hundred animal studies and twenty-five clinical human trials. Finally, after years of debate and narrowing its application to focus on just savory snacks, P&G received FDA approval, albeit with a nasty health-warning label that disclosed Olestra may cause abdominal cramping and loose stools—a pyrrhic victory at best. Olestra's warning was great fodder for late night comedy and helped make the multimillion-dollar launch of Olestra fizzle and fade away.

Determined not to fall victim to such a lengthy and expensive failure, IFM quickly lobbied and gained agreement with the FDA for a more efficient, streamlined approval process that would last no longer than six years. The first, core element of the process was the creation of a Food Advisory Committee, or FAC. This twenty-member committee was formed by recruiting leading food sciences experts with particular emphasis on specialists in the fields of nutrition, diet, and microbiology. The FAC stewarded the approval process and ultimately would make a recommendation to a Regulatory Decision Team (RDT). The RDT was composed of six senior FDA officials, and their recommendation would go straight to the FDA Commissioner for his final blessing.

The approval timeline was broken into three major phases. The first two years were dedicated to product safety testing. After the results of these initial trials were reviewed, any potential issues could trigger a second round of trials. These additional trials would be focused on answering any outstanding questions. After their completion, the FAC would be charged with publishing the data, holding a hearing for public debate, and then making their recommendation to the RDT. Finally, the RDT and the FDA Commissioner would be required to act on the FAC's recommendation within sixty days.

In the first round of safety trials, both the test and control groups of laboratory animals were fed similar diets. However, while the control group received normal food, the test group's kibble had a third of the carbohydrates replaced with Redu. After eighteen months of testing, the benefits of Redu were confirmed. Not only had the control group gained weight, but it was also reporting higher obesity rates. In contrast, the test group was not obese. In fact, its body mass was slightly underweight.

But there were side effects. The most frequently reported was larger, looser stools. There were also reports of violent diarrhea and epithelial cell damage in the intestines and colon. Also, post study evaluation showed modest irritation of the digestive tract, especially among guinea pigs, where there was also a very small increased incidence of cancerous or precancerous lesions.

IFM minimized the side effects and hailed the results as miraculous. But many consumer watchdog groups were not so easily convinced. EFC demanded more testing and argued that moving forward with Redu would be nothing short of a large scale, human experiment. Some critics agreed that resistant starch had potential but feared the unknown, long-term consequences of genetically modified foods, while other skeptics wanted a better understanding of the gastrointestinal irritation and underweight trends. Another flash point ignited around the fact that as these higher levels of resistant starch passed through the digestive tract, mineral absorption was reduced, a side effect whose lifelong impact nobody could predict with any certainty. And, of course, even the most minor increases of cancer garnered unwanted attention.

After debating the issues for three months, IFM notified the FAC it would conduct a second round of testing that included not only additional animal trials, but also significantly more human trials.

A little over two years later, results from the final trials were submitted to the FAC. Statistically, all the studies looked clean. While irritation was still an issue for some, no increased incidence of cancer in test versus control was observed. The test sample continued to be slightly underweight, but it wasn't at a concerning level. Redu impacted mineral absorption, but supplements added to the Redu seemed to be addressing the issue effectively. Some human subjects in the trials did report larger, uncomfortable bowel movements, increased flatulence, and diarrhea, but this was viewed as manageable and to be expected.

After the FAC published the results, hearings and public debate began. While IFM positioned the research as clear support for approval, EFC and other food watchdogs continued to battle. The EFC was particularly alarmed and spent considerable time dissecting the trials. In the process, they identified several suspicious items, and went as far as to claim tampering. They said the research had been altered and falsified by parties unknown. However, the FAC disagreed, and in mid-April, they recommended Redu be approved.

The RDT and FDA Commissioner had until June 15 to act on the FAC's recommendation. While many expected the debate to die down, EFC was unwilling to give up and cried foul, claiming the FAC was biased and stacked. Although most industry watchers agreed IFM would prevail, it looked like it was going down to the final hour.

After poring over the files and taking notes for over two hours, Andrew needed a break. He decided to get up, grab a bowl of ice cream and then check his voice mail at work in case anything had come up while he was out of the office in the afternoon. As he dialed in, he got the dreaded "voice mail is full" recording and braced himself for some disaster. Thankfully, it was just an indicator that he had too many undeleted messages, so he decided to take a couple minutes to clean out his voice mail's inbox. As he was listening and deleting old messages, he heard Becky Clausen's voice. In all the craziness of the past two days, he had forgotten about her message from yesterday morning.

> *Hey Andrew, this is Becky. I'm heading out of town for an urgent meeting. Keep this to yourself, but we've hit a real snag. Some old research just surfaced that may cause a big delay for Redu and your B-Lean Snacks lineup. I'm taking the corporate jet to DC for a strategy meeting with our legal team. I'll let you know more when I can. Please, keep this quiet.*

Puzzled, Andrew sat back down at his laptop, and listened to Becky's message again. He returned to the Knowledge Portal and looked again at Becky's most recent posts, but he saw nothing from the week before she died. He then tried typing in a variety of keyword combinations, but as he read the synopses for each report listed, he realized he had struck out. Thinking back to Becky's message, Andrew focused on her mention of "old research," so he tried searches for "Redu," "CX-4," and "trials" and asked for files five years or older. Still no luck.

Frustrated and about to give up, Andrew remembered that only in the past six years had CX-4 and Redu become synonymous with the project. Prior to the public announcement of Redu, the initiative had operated under at least three or four project code names. Wracking his brain, he could remember only one of the code names mentioned in some old files in his office — Galileo.

Like all IFM code names, it was totally unrelated to the project, and this was by design. The idea was that if someone overheard the code name, they would have no inkling what the project was about. The story Andrew had been told that linked Galileo to CX-4 followed a convoluted, three step chain: (1) the goal of CX-4 was to make overweight people lean, (2) the most famous lean was the Leaning Tower of Pisa, and (3) one of the most famous residents of Pisa was Galileo.

So Andrew typed in "Galileo" and "trials," and after a few seconds of the spinning beach ball, a list of three files popped up. Excited to finally get some hits, he clicked the filenames and opened the documents. As he started to read the first file, the phone rang. He glanced over to check the caller ID. It was Lydia. *It's late for her to call*, he thought. *What could she want?*

"Hello," said Andrew, trying his best to answer with a positive tone. In the background he could hear sirens and lots of voices.

"Andrew, this is Lydia. Ethan was goofing around and fell off the top bunk in his bedroom."

"Is he okay?"

"I think so. He's in a lot of pain. I think he may have broken his ankle. His pediatrician's office was closed, so we're at the emergency room."

"What? Why didn't you call me earlier? Where are you?"

"Maple Grove Hospital," Lydia replied.

"Have you seen a doctor yet?"

"No, we just got here. We're in the waiting room."

"May I speak with Ethan?"

"Sure. Here he is." Andrew could hear the phone crackle as Lydia passed it over.

Ethan cleared his throat, and a muffled "Hi, Dad," came out between sniffling.

"How are you, buddy? You okay?"

"Yeah. I'm just a little scared. Do you think they are going to give me a shot?"

"Well, that all depends. I'm sure the doctors and nurses will take good care of you. Is it still hurting a lot?"

"Yeah, but not as bad as it did."

"Well, I'm going to leave right now, so I'll be there soon."

"Okay," Ethan said, clearing his throat again.

"Hang in there, buddy. I love you. Oh, can you hand the phone back to your mom?"

"Love you, too," he replied, and the phone crackled some more.

"Yes?" asked Lydia.

"I'll be right there."

"You don't need to come."

"Yes, I do. Please call me if you get moved into a room."

"Okay."

Gaithersburg, Maryland
Thursday, June 3
9:30 P.M.

LIA MERRIMAN sat in a dimly lit corner of the Gaithersburg Hilton's lounge, waiting just as Danielle Haley's cryptic e-mail from a mysterious address had instructed. She scanned the bar and tables again and again trying to recognize a face, but all she saw were business people drinking glasses of relaxation on the rocks after a long day's work.

After battling two flight cancellations and rush hour traffic, Lia had made a quick stop at her condo to shower, get dressed, and then drive out to the Maryland suburbs. Her light brown ponytail still felt damp as she nervously twisted it around her index finger. Compulsively, Lia checked her Blackberry over and over to make sure she hadn't missed an e-mail update or phone call.

Finally, thirty minutes after their meeting time had passed, Lia gave up. Enough was enough.

Standing up, Lia dropped some bills on the table for her sparkling water, and as she turned to leave she heard, "Ms. Merriman?"

"Yes," Lia replied. "Danielle? It's nice to see you again and thanks for coming."

"Yes, I'm so sorry I'm late," Danielle replied nervously. "I've been circling outside in my car for almost an hour. I just don't know what to do. I'm so scared."

"It's going to be okay. Let's sit down," Lia said calmly. "Can I get you something to drink?"

"Sure."

After Danielle ordered a glass of wine, Lia chatted with her casually in hopes of getting her to relax and feel comfortable. Finally, when the waiter returned with the wine, Lia asked, "What has you so frightened?"

Danielle paused and brushed wisps of curly brown hair from her face and pulled them behind her ears. She wore a thick pair of glasses, but even they couldn't hide the deep circles beneath her eyes.

"I'm just not sure if I should say anything. I don't want to get anyone in trouble, and Jackie has been very good to me. But something just isn't right," she said, shaking her head.

"Well, start at the beginning," Lia replied, reaching her hand out to hold Danielle's. "You can trust me. I promise I won't repeat a word of what you tell me without your permission. Let me be your sounding board for now."

Danielle looked into Lia's eyes. They hardly looked menacing. Maybe tired and puffy, but certainly not dangerous.

"Okay," Danielle said, squeezing Lia's hand. "One of my jobs as Jackie Epps's secretary is to archive files. Once a year I go through her office, and I pull out any files that are more than two years old. Since Jackie is an FDA Director, there are certain document retention and archiving policies we have to follow. So I sort through the old files, paging through their contents to decide if they should be shredded or archived. If I have any questions on how to handle the file, I'll ask Jackie what she thinks I should do."

Lia nodded. "That's sounds fairly typical for a government office."

"Yes, it is. But you see, last week when I started this process, I transferred a couple bankers boxes' worth of files out of Jackie's office, and I've been gradually working my way through them. But yesterday I realized I must have grabbed some of her personal files by accident. When I started reading through this one file," Danielle reached down into her oversized bag and handed a file over to Lia, "I was shocked. I've marked a couple pages with sticky notes," Danielle continued as Lia opened the manila file folder. "My first instinct was to just put this file right back into Jackie's office. But then I remembered your visit a couple months ago and I found the business card you gave me. So what do you think? Is this information important?"

By this point Lia barely heard Danielle's words. Already immersed in the file, Lia quickly scanned the marked pages. Danielle was right. This wasn't just some random FDA document. It was Ms. Epps's personal notes on the selection of members for Redu's Food Advisory Committee. But instead of a bunch of inter-agency memos and e-mails, it contained a series of outside recommendations to guide Ms. Epps. Not only did it provide detailed support for some candidates, it also assembled ammunition to derail other prospective members.

Lia flipped through the pages to see who authored the work, but with no luck. Then as she re-read the first couple marked pages, she noticed several candidates had asterisks by their names and a handwritten note in the margin that read: "Laura Long's must haves."

Lia's heart pounded as she asked, "Do you recognize the handwriting here?" pointing to the notes in the margin.

"That's Jackie's," Danielle responded. "Do you think this file is important?"

"Yes, it's huge. You see this name here?" Lia said, indicating Jackie's handwritten notes. "Laura Long is the head of a powerful food lobbyist group. I think these documents prove that the FAC assembled for Redu's approval was influenced, and it looks like your boss was involved. Does anyone else know you have these documents?"

"No."

"Have you shared them with anyone else?"

"No, but…I'm just not sure."

Lia reached out and held Danielle's hand again. "I'm sorry. I'm getting ahead of myself. I promised you, Danielle. I'm not going to do anything with this information unless you are okay with it. You understand?"

Danielle nodded.

"I won't lie to you, though. What you found could mean the difference in safeguarding our food supply from a dangerous new food additive. Working in Ms. Epps's office, I'm sure you've heard and read about the Redu debate. This file could stop the Redu approval in its tracks."

"Really? And what about Jackie?"

"I'm afraid your boss could go to jail. That said, so could you if this information comes out later and you've acted as an accessory in hiding it."

"Are you threatening me?" Danielle's tone changed and she pulled her hand away from Lia. "I haven't done anything wrong."

Damn it, Lia thought to herself. "No, I'm not threatening you. And certainly I can't provide you any legal advice. I just wanted you to be aware that it's not as simple as just putting this file back in a drawer anymore."

"Well, I need to think about this some more. Maybe I should go see an attorney first. I think this was all a big mistake. Can I have the file back?"

"Please, I'm sorry if I came across too strong. I'm tired, and this is the first tangible proof we've found to shut down Redu's approval. My excitement got the better part of me."

"I know, but I've got to think about this first."

"Can I at least take a picture of a couple of these pages?" Lia asked.

"No, not yet."

Lia continued to grip the file firmly, not wanting to let it go.

"Please," Danielle said, reaching out her arm, "you promised me."

Reluctantly, Lia handed over the file and asked, "Can we at least agree to meet in a couple days? I can't tell you how important it is that we find a way to share the contents of the file."

Danielle stood up after stashing the file back in her bag. Her eyes flashed across the room, looking for any suspicious onlookers.

"I'll think about it. I have your number. Wait for my call."

LIA COULDN'T BELIEVE IT. After searching for months, she might have blown her first real chance to stop Redu's approval. She had the proof in her hands. How could she have let it go?

Lia walked outside under the hotel's porte cochère and pulled out her cell phone to call Ken. It was well past ten o'clock, but this news couldn't wait. As she glanced down to dial, a car sped through the far end of the parking lot, its tires squealing. *Must be Danielle, leaving as fast as she can, thanks to me,* she thought ruefully.

When the car turned in her direction, Lia raced through the crosswalk to avoid its approach and listened for Ken to answer. On the third ring, the call flipped to his voice mail, but as his greeting started, a man walked up beside her.

"Are you okay?" he asked.

Lia was speechless at first, but then she closed her cell phone and replied, "Yes, I'm fine, thanks."

"I just saw that car speeding through the lot. I thought it was going to hit you. Probably some stupid kids playing a game."

The man paused for a second. "Are you sure you're okay? Can I walk you to your car?"

"That's really not necessary," Lia replied, "but thank you."

"Oh, it's no trouble. I'm glad I can help out. Where are you parked?" he asked, looking around the parking lot.

"Down here," Lia said, motioning one aisle over. "It's not very far."

"I'm in no rush," he replied. "I'm just heading home after a dinner meeting."

"Same here," Lia replied as she approached her car with the man following behind. "Well, this is it—"

Before Lia could turn around to say thank you, the man removed a gloved left hand from his pocket and covered her mouth. Simultaneously with his right hand, he reached around Lia's waist and thrust a nine-inch Stiletto blade up under her rib cage, piercing her lung. In one last movement, he removed the knife from her abdomen and slit her throat. Lia fell to the ground, lifeless in a pool of her blood.

The stranger looked around, reached down for the woman's bag, and then walked away.

DANIELLE HALEY LIVED less than ten minutes from the hotel in a modest two-bedroom ranch on Shady Spring Drive. Her front patio light cast a dim, golden glow on her driveway as she pulled into her carport. Still shaken from her meeting with Lia, Danielle unlocked the side door and slipped into her home, clutching her bag close. All she wanted was to get some sleep. She felt that somehow this was all going to look better in the morning, so she walked back to her room and got ready for bed. After brushing her teeth, she popped a couple of Tylenol PMs and gulped them down with some water from the faucet.

Danielle pulled back the sheets, lay down, and turned off her bedside lamp. As she turned on her side, she saw light streaming down the hallway from the kitchen.

"Damn it," she mumbled, getting up from under the covers, "I thought I turned off all the lights."

It only took a couple seconds for her to make her way to the kitchen and flip off the overhead light. But when she turned around to go back to bed, an arm reached out from the darkness and a hand pressed hard against her face. Danielle struggled briefly, but after drawing in several breaths through the moist cloth clamped against her mouth, a sweet smell filled her lungs and she collapsed.

Her attacker worked quickly, carefully sitting Danielle in a chair with her body slumped over on the kitchen table. It didn't take him long to find her purse by the bed. The manila file folder was there, and after verifying its contents matched the conversation he had overheard earlier, he returned to the kitchen. Walking over to the stove, he turned on the gas burner beneath a teapot to high, making sure the flame did not ignite. Then, setting a specially designed kitchen timer on the counter, he disappeared through the carport door.

The intruder sat parked in his car a couple houses down, observing the house for activity. After waiting fifteen minutes, he was convinced enough time had passed, so he slowly drove down the block and reached over for the remote sitting on the car's console. When he pressed the button, the brilliance of his handiwork exploded, and flames glowed eerily in his rearview mirror as he continued down the street.

Maple Grove, Minnesota
Thursday, June 3
10:15 P.M.

THE DRIVE TO THE HOSPITAL took fifteen minutes, thanks to a heavy foot and no traffic. Andrew was worried about Ethan, but he had sounded okay on the phone. As hard as he tried, he couldn't stop stewing about Lydia. *She should have called me earlier,* he thought. *She would be furious if I treated her like this. She gets upset if I don't call when Ethan has a runny nose.*

As Andrew parked the car, he tried to push aside the petty, negative feelings. Ethan's health was the only priority.

The hospital's emergency room was clean and well staffed. It had opened only a few months earlier, so it had an odd smell of new furnishings and antiseptic.

Andrew scanned the waiting room and didn't see Ethan or Lydia, so he went up to the registration desk. "Excuse me. My son Ethan Hastings was just brought in for a possible broken ankle. Can you direct me to him?"

The receptionist tilted her head to look through her bifocals. "What is his name again?"

"Ethan Hastings."

"Do you have ID?"

Andrew pulled out his driver's license. "Yes, here you go."

"Sir, I have no record of you on the registration forms."

"What? I'm his father."

"I'm sorry, I can't let you back right now."

"Can you call back there?" replied Andrew.

"Do you have any legal custody rights?"

"Yes, I share joint physical and legal custody with his mother," Andrew said with an edge in his tone. He resented the question, and he doubted a mother would receive such treatment.

"Do you have any proof of that?"

"Well, I do at home. I don't carry my divorce decree around with me. Please, can you go back there?" Andrew's face pleaded.

The receptionist looked skeptically at him. He was sure she'd seen everything, and it wasn't the first time that Andrew had been made to feel like a second-class parent. After all, people assumed most divorced dads were just deadbeats.

"Please, my son is hurt. I want to be there for him," Andrew appealed once more.

The receptionist paused and seemed to soften. "Stay right here. I'll go back and check."

Andrew waited by the front desk, pacing. A nearby couple looked at him suspiciously.

Several minutes later, the receptionist returned. "I'm sorry for the delay," she said. "Follow me. I'll take you back."

"Thank you. Thank you so much."

After making a couple turns, the receptionist stopped and knocked on the door. A muffled "come in" sounded from behind it, and they entered the examining room. Ethan was sitting on the examination table with what looked like a doctor on one side and Lydia on the other.

"Hey, buddy. You okay?" Andrew came up and kissed Ethan on his forehead.

"I'm okay, Dad. It just hurts."

The doctor interrupted, "I was just telling your wife—"

"That's ex-wife," said Lydia.

"Oh, excuse me. I was just telling your ex-wife that based on your son's range of motion and reported pain, I think we are dealing with just a sprain. But I'd like to get an X-ray to make sure."

"That sounds great. Thank you, Doctor…" Andrew hesitated, looking at the ID tag clipped on the white coat. "Yes, thank you, Dr. Weiller."

The doctor turned to the nurse in the room. "Can you take Ethan up to X-ray?"

"Am I going to have to get a shot?" asked Ethan.

"No, not if it's just a sprain," replied the doctor.

The nurse pulled up the wheelchair, and Ethan hopped down from the table, Andrew holding his arm to steady him.

"Can I go with him?" asked Lydia.

"No, we have him, ma'am. He's fine, don't worry."

"Don't worry, Mom. I'll be okay," Ethan said with renewed hope now that he believed he wasn't going to get stuck by any needles.

After Ethan had climbed into the wheelchair, Andrew gave him another kiss. "You'll be just fine, buddy."

The doctor left as the nurse wheeled Ethan out. Lydia was

seated in the only chair in the examining room, so Andrew leaned against the wall and stared at the floor.

Finally breaking the uncomfortable silence, Lydia said, "You didn't need to come."

"Yes, I did," Andrew said firmly. "I was worried about Ethan."

"Ethan's fine. I'm here," Lydia said. "At times like these, a boy needs his mother."

"Right. Agreed. And his father, too," Andrew replied.

"Well, we may as well make use of this time while Ethan's away. I've wanted to talk to you about your trip to Hawaii. I'm still not happy."

Andrew rolled his eyes. "We've already worked this out with the mediator."

"I know, but...Well, I just don't like it. I don't want Ethan away from me for two weeks. He needs me."

Andrew took a deep breath. "I know you'll miss Ethan. I'll miss him too when you take your two-week vacation with him. Unfortunately, it's just one of those painful realities divorced families have to live with."

"It's just different for us, Andrew."

"How's that?" Andrew replied. He immediately regretted taking Lydia's bait.

"It's simple. Ethan just doesn't miss you when we're away."

Andrew grimaced. "Oh, here we go again. Just like the drum you beat during our divorce. Is it so hard for you to accept that Ethan loves me? His loving me doesn't mean he loves you less."

Lydia's face tensed and reddened. "Oh, I'm so glad we're not married anymore."

"Lydia, if we're serious about raising a happy and healthy son, we've got to do better than this. We can't let vacations and doctor's visits throw us into a tailspin. Ethan's practically a teenager."

"But—"

"This conversation is over." Andrew turned and left the examining room and stood outside the door, praying Lydia wouldn't follow. He felt his heart pounding through his chest. *Why does she still have such power over me?*

Minutes later, Dr. Weiller returned and said Ethan was fine. It was just a sprain. Ethan was released with an ACE bandage wrap, a pair of crutches, and orders to use children's ibuprofen for the pain. Andrew walked with Ethan to Lydia's car. He was sure Ethan could feel the tension. Divorced children have special instincts for it. But Lydia and Andrew both remained calm for Ethan, and with a hug and a kiss good-bye, Ethan was on his way.

Exhausted, Andrew got home at a little after midnight. In no mood to work, he took a quick look at his computer, printed out the documents he was working on, and shut it down. Marketing plans would have to wait for the morning.

SIX

Wayzata, Minnesota
Friday, June 4
5:18 A.M.

AIDAN'S WIFE, Peggy, had left yesterday for a New York City shopping trip with her college roommate. She had become accustomed to biannual treks to the fashion capital to indulge in the latest styles. For most people, Minneapolis's shopping was great. After all, it was home to the Mall of America. But for Peggy, the Twin Cities simply didn't have enough high fashion to satisfy her hearty appetite.

Aidan was sleeping alone in their massive king-sized canopy bed when his cell phone rang. He was in a deep sleep, and the call seemed like a disjointed piece of some dream. His mind roused from the blissful emptiness and clicked into awareness. As he reached for his phone, he glanced at the ceiling, where his latest high tech device projected the time, temperature and weather. 5:18 a.m. *This can't be good,* he thought. Without his readers on, he couldn't see the caller ID, but he decided to answer the phone anyway.

"Yes, this is Aidan."

"Aidan, this is Laura. Sorry to bother you so early. We have a problem."

The truth was that several problems had cropped up since she had last spoken to Aidan. But with last night's successful elimination of Jackie Epps's secretary, Danielle Haley, and that nosy EFC girl, Lia Merriman, Laura now wanted to focus Aidan's attention on more pressing matters.

Clearing his throat, Aidan tried to shake off his sleep and appear poised and in control despite the hour. "Yes," clearing his throat again, trying to bring his voice to its normal timbre, "tell me."

"We've been scanning your servers for any controversial information relating to Redu. Although we aren't finished yet, we came across an issue early this morning. An Andrew Hastings accessed an old document that referenced some early testing on Project Galileo. The file in and of itself didn't contain any damaging information, but when we vetted this guy a little more, something else came up."

"What?"

"In Hastings's voice mail messages, there was a call from Becky Clausen the morning of the plane crash. She basically told him that the approval of Redu was at risk due to some old research. I'm afraid that with these two pieces of information, he may become a liability."

Still not fully awake, Aidan sat on the edge of his bed, desperately trying to process what he had just heard. What normally would take a split second seemed now to hang in his mind like taffy being forcefully kneaded and pulled into place. Finally, as a synapse or two fired, Aidan asked, "Have you seen any questionable outgoing communication from Hastings?"

"No, we haven't."

"Okay, let's not overreact here. I appreciate you bringing this to my attention. Why don't we start watching this guy? I'll call Dan when we hang up, and let's plan on talking later."

"Agreed. Call me anytime you want."

"Thanks, Laura." Aidan sat back in his bed and rolled over, looking at the empty spot next to him. He missed his wife. Peggy knew the corporate world was tough, and she was always there by his side. He was tired of lying to her about Redu. She knew something was coming between them, but how could he tell her what he'd done? Would she still love him if he told her the whole, ugly truth?

No, I can't tell Peggy, he thought. *I can't risk losing her.*

EFC Headquarters
Friday, June 4
8:10 A.M.

GAITHERSBURG AUTHORITIES contacted Ken Luger early Friday morning to identify Lia's body. She had no identification on her, but after they'd checked car registrations for vehicles near the crime scene, Lia Merriman's name came up. Her face was a match with the DMV's records, but a final ID was needed.

Ken called Gina after leaving the morgue. She was distraught, and rightly so. This was a calamity. Never before had an EFC team member been murdered.

EFC's offices were somber as the news of Lia's death spread. As soon as Gina arrived, she called Henry Usher and Ken into her office.

"What was Lia doing out in Gaithersburg so late? Was it work related?" Gina asked while reaching for a tissue to blow her nose.

"I'm not sure, but I think so," Ken replied. "She came back yesterday to follow up on some local leads. I hadn't talked to her since the day before when she was in Madison. But last night she tried to call me just minutes before she was attacked. I must have been asleep, so her call went to voice mail."

"What did her message say?"

"Nothing. It was strange, just a couple seconds of noise."

"Do you believe the police report?" Henry asked.

"Honestly, no," Ken replied. "Sure, people get robbed all the time. But Lia's injuries were excessive, and the scene was too clean."

"Well, if you're right, that could mean Lia was getting close to something big. Very big," Henry concluded. "Our opponents have been ruthless before, but murder?"

"I know. I've assigned a couple people to start going through her files to see if we can pick up any leads."

"Good. Let's just make sure our teams are on alert, especially everyone on this Redu case. There are a lot of people who want to stop our work, and Lia just paid the ultimate price..." Gina said tearfully, grabbing for another tissue. "I want everyone taking the appropriate measures to keep safe. Got it?"

"Yes."

"How about her family? Have you talked to them?"

"I reached her father this morning. Obviously he was in shock. I offered our help in making any arrangements. I think it would help if you call him as well."

"Of course," Gina replied. "Oh, I meant to ask you earlier. What about the gas leak explosion not far from where Lia was murdered? The news said an FDA employee was killed. I'm wondering if there's a connection."

"I'm already on it."

"Good. I want whoever did this, Ken. We owe that to Lia and her family."

"Agreed," Henry added. "We'll get to the bottom of this."

IFM Headquarters
Friday, June 4
7:30 A.M.

"YOU'RE IN AWFULLY EARLY AGAIN," said Lourdes, poking her head into Andrew's cube.

Andrew jumped and turned around in his chair, startled by Lourdes greeting.

"I'm sorry, I hate it when people come up from behind me and surprise me. We need to get you one of those rearview mirrors on your monitor so you can see when people come into your office."

"Yeah, either that or we all need to wear bells," Andrew said, laughing it off.

"How are you this morning? How was Ethan's graduation?"

"It was great. I'm so proud of him. But we did have a bit of a scare later."

"What happened?"

"Oh, Ethan fell off his top bunk at his mom's. So we all made a late night trip to the ER."

"Really. Is everything okay?"

"Yes, Ethan's fine. He just has a sprained ankle."

"That's good. And the plans deck?"

"Almost done. Just putting on some final touches."

"Well, let me know you've saved your final changes, and I'll print out copies for our meeting."

"Sounds good."

ON HIS WAY into the office, Dan called his secretary and left a message for her to cancel his first couple meetings. Dan's mind was racing after he read Aidan's early morning text: "Urgent. Another issue. Let's talk soon." Although Dan had long ago mastered the look of external calm, the crises of the past several weeks were taking their toll.

After parking his car in the executive garage beneath the main building, Dan made his way up to Aidan's office. Dressed in a dark sport coat, gray glen plaid slacks, and a tailored white shirt that fit precisely across his broad chest and back, Dan was the epitome of IFM style — conservative, athletic, and well-groomed. His sandy brown hair was cut right above the ears and parted on the left. It wasn't gelled or slicked back, but somehow, not a hair was out of place. Weekly visits to his executive stylist kept his hair precise, eyebrows neat, and hands manicured.

Dan's home life looked equally polished. His wife, Shelly, was a former model, and together they had five beautiful kids, a golden retriever, and regularly attended their neighborhood church. Everything about Dan appeared picture perfect. But beneath this whitewashed facade lay hidden years of physical and emotional abuse. Trying desperately to disprove his alcoholic father's toxic words, Dan was determined to win at all costs and demanded absolute perfection from everyone around him.

As Dan exited the elevator, he confidently walked toward his boss's door.

"Is our fearless leader in?" he asked Judy, Aidan's assistant.

"Yes, he's waiting for you. Go on in."

"Thanks."

Walking into the office, he turned briefly and closed the door behind him. "Good morning, Aidan. Sounds like we've got something boiling over."

Aidan stood up and greeted Dan, and they moved over to a conference table. "Laura called me early this morning. They've been scanning our servers. Her team isn't finished yet, but they've identified an issue."

Appearing calm, Dan internally cursed Laura. He was tired of her going directly to Aidan. It made him look like a fool.

"Well, I'm sorry Laura bothered you so early. I had asked her to report back to me with any issues."

"Don't worry, Dan. I've told Laura to call me anytime. Anyway, apparently this guy, Andrew Hastings, accessed an old Galileo file last night. Some file we missed taking care of. It only referenced one of the original studies and had no real information in it, but still. You know him?"

"He's reporting to me while Angie Green is on maternity leave."

"What do you think of him? Is he trouble?"

"He's a nice enough guy. Hardworking, sharp, he sticks to his business and makes sure things get done. He's not our typical marketer, though. He just doesn't seem to have that political savvy and presence that I look for."

Aidan took off his glasses and set them down on the conference table. "Well, there's more. Laura also found that Becky Clausen left Andrew a message the morning she died. She made reference to some big problems that had just come up in the approval process."

"Damn it," Dan said, shaking his head.

"So that's why you're here. I wanted us to check in with Laura and figure out where to go from here."

"What about Chloe?"

"I don't know if Chloe can handle any more of this. Anyway, I want her focused on next week's meetings in DC."

"Agreed. Shall we get Laura on the phone?"

"Yes."

Within moments, Laura was on the speakerphone. "Laura, this is Dan, and I've got Aidan here. I understand we've had some issues develop. Aidan brought me up to speed. Anything new come up since you two spoke this morning?"

"No, nothing new here. As a precaution, I've mobilized a team to start tracking Hastings."

"Really? Aidan and I didn't get that far in our conversation. That's great. I was just telling Aidan that Andrew is temporarily reporting to me. He's one of the managers working on the Redu launch. I know him pretty well. Are we watching him yet?"

"No."

Dan looked intensely out the windows and started tapping his middle finger. "Laura, what if I invite Andrew to go golfing with me tomorrow? It wouldn't seem odd at all since I take out high performers all the time. I can give old Andrew an ego boost and let him know how much we appreciate his hard work. I can even try to get a sense for where his head's at."

"Perfect," Laura replied. "We're putting him under full surveillance, so while he's out with you, we can go through his house, car, and phone. Call me to confirm you've got this set, and we can make it happen."

"By the way, when do you think the remainder of the scan will be finished?" asked Aidan.

"Noon tomorrow. Hopefully this is the last of our issues."

"Amen to that," Dan blurted out.

LOURDES'S REVIEW of B-Lean's marketing plans with the cross-functional team went exceptionally well. She had great command of the room, and she had obviously spent a great deal of time getting the team's input and buy-in.

After returning to his office, Andrew settled in for work. He was tempted to take advantage of IFM's summer hours and enjoy a Friday afternoon outside. But his marketing plans presentation to Dan and the Uncle Chuck's leadership team was in less than a week.

Andrew flipped through his to-do folder. During the week it always became more of a slush pile of papers and notes that he didn't want to lose. So on Fridays he would examine each page and either throw it away, file it, or add it to his to-do list. Near the top of the folder he came across the Project Galileo files he had printed out the previous night. He quickly scanned them, one by one.

All three documents appeared to be project updates from the "BLIT," R&D's top-secret Big Leap Innovations Team. While the first two documents included brief mentions of Project Galileo, the reference to trials was clearly about two other projects in the works—Phoebe and Rachel. But it was the third report that was interesting. Although there were no results in the report, the status update was very clear: "Project Galileo—trials complete."

There was no reference to their success or failure, just that they were complete. *Perhaps these were the trials Becky was talking about in her message,* he thought.

His curiosity piqued, Andrew turned his chair around, logged into the Knowledge Portal, and then entered the keyword query "Project Galileo" and "trials." Nothing popped up. Trying to remember exactly what he had entered last night, he recalled his search training class's advice: the fewer words the better, and avoid multiple words as keywords. So he entered "Galileo" and "trials." Bingo, results. But after reviewing the entries, only two of the three reports came up. The third report referencing the completed trials was missing.

Andrew adjusted his keywords a couple more times, trying various combinations of singular versus plural, caps and no caps, although he distinctly remembered being told capitalizations didn't impact search. He even tried a common typo that slipped through spell check, "trail," with no luck. Puzzled, he decided he didn't have time to get hung up on this right now. Instead, he could ask Chloe for details when they met Monday. So he slipped the printouts back into his folder, added an entry on his to-do list, and forged ahead with his work.

Within thirty minutes, all his papers were organized and his to-do list was up to date, so he decided to grab a bite to eat before the cafeteria closed at one. As Andrew bent over to make sure he had his company ID and wallet, he heard a knock on his cube wall.

"Hey, man. How's it going?" asked Dan. "Getting ready to get out of here and take advantage of summer hours?"

"Oh, hi, Dan. No, not yet. I need to catch up on some work this afternoon."

"Whatcha working on?"

Andrew was puzzled by Dan's visit. Not only was it very unusual, but he was also acting too casual and chummy.

"My team just presented preliminary plans this morning. It's looking great. I wanted to follow up on some issues that need to be locked down by next week's meeting with you and the division's leadership team."

"Sounds good. I appreciate all the hard work. By the way, I meant to compliment you on your meeting with Sales earlier this week. That was good stuff. I think we have them eating out of our hands now. Just like it should be."

"Oh, thanks," said Andrew, a bit in shock with Dan's compliments.

"Do you and your son have big plans for the weekend?"

"No, he's at his mom's this weekend. We're heading out to Hawaii next Friday for two weeks, so he's been at his mom's a lot lately."

"Oh, that sounds like a fun trip. You know, Shelly and I took the kids out there for spring break a couple years ago. We should get together before your trip and I can download some ideas for you."

"That would be great," Andrew replied, thinking this was most likely an empty offer.

"Hey, I've got an idea. How about we hit the links tomorrow? You'd be my guest, of course."

Andrew hesitated, desperately trying to think of a plausible excuse. Spending time with Dan Murdock was not exactly his idea of fun.

Dan saw the panic in Andrew's eyes and moved in to seal the deal.

"Come on, I won't take no as an answer. Golf, a massage at the spa, lunch afterwards. I need an excuse to get away from the wife and kids. You'll be helping me out."

Still taken aback, Andrew saw no way out. With all the enthusiasm he could muster, he said, "Sure, that would be great…"

"Wonderful. I'm a member over at Interlachen. I already have a tee time at nine. Let's meet at quarter till by the starter. Be all ready to go."

"Fantastic," Andrew said, faking a wide grin.

As Dan left, all Andrew could think was *What did I just get myself into?* He hadn't picked up a golf club since last fall, and he had heard Dan was a scratch golfer. At moments like this, Andrew knew he wasn't cut out for corporate life. For most, this would be a golden opportunity to schmooze and self-promote. For Andrew, it was painful and nerve-wracking. Would he say the wrong thing? Would his golf game be good enough? Would he dress and act right at the club? *Damn!* What was planned as a relaxing weekend and catching up on work had all just changed.

Andrew sat back down and picked up his phone to call Josh but only got his voice mail. "It's me. Just wondering if you have plans this afternoon? I need to hit the driving range and would love some help. Long story short, I'm golfing with Dan Murdock tomorrow morning. Yeah, so I'm in desperate need of a quick golf tune-up. I'm going to work a little longer here, but call me back and let me know."

Andrew reached into his drawer and grabbed a granola bar. He had no time for the cafeteria now.

SEVEN

Interlachen Golf Club
Edina, Minnesota
Saturday, June 5
8:25 A.M.

ANDREW MADE sure to arrive early for golf. Showing up late to any meeting with Dan was a clear path to failure. Although still nervous, Andrew felt a little more confident. Thankfully, Josh had been able to meet him yesterday for his second bucket of balls. Josh had a club in his hands since age three, so golfing came second nature for him. After some minor corrections and a little coaching on not trying to kill the ball, Andrew felt ready.

Having some time to burn, Andrew spent a few minutes on the putting green, trying to get some of the kinks out. Fifteen minutes before the tee time, he made his way over to the starter.

"Good morning, I'm Andrew Hastings. I have a nine o'clock tee time with Dan Murdock."

"Good morning, Mr. Hastings. Glad you can join us here at

Interlachen. Mr. Murdock hasn't checked in yet, but let's get you all set up with a cart. Where are your clubs?"

"Right over here," gestured Andrew.

"Fine. So where do you usually play?"

"Oh, just some public courses here and there. Mostly out at Hollydale."

"Very good. Well, don't let Mr. Murdock chew you up out there. He's a fine golfer, and he likes nothing more than to run over his opponents."

"No worries. I just want to play respectably. Anyway, I hear it's never good to beat your boss in golf, and Dan is more like my boss's boss."

Dan walked up in a flurry.

"Good morning, Andrew. How are you?"

"Good here. Beautiful morning out."

Distracted, Dan replied, "Yes, yes, it certainly is. Was a crazy morning at the house with the kids. One of the boys is sick, and it was hard to get out of there." Looking around, Dan turned his head and yelled to the starter. "Can you call your bag boys now? Are we just paying them to do nothing? Get their butts moving. I need my bag now!"

"Yes, Mr. Murdock."

Uncomfortable with his boss's anger, Andrew tried to move on to a more pleasant topic. "So who else is in our foursome this morning, Dan?"

"Oh, well, Rick Dunlop and Ted Harrington were going to play, but I made some excuses and cancelled their invites yesterday afternoon."

"So who did you invite instead?"

"Nobody. It's just you and me. These guys will let me get away with it," nodding over to the starter booth. "I thought it would be easier for us to chat, just the two of us."

"Oh, well, yes, certainly," Andrew stuttered.

For the next four hours, they made their way through the front and back nine. Dan's swing was strong, smooth, and precise. More often than not, his drives were straight and long. Even more impressive than his physicality was his mental focus. A true competitor, he slipped into a steely countenance that was unshakable as he stepped onto the tee, fairway, or green to address the ball. By the eighteenth green, Andrew was a good twenty shots north of Dan's score, but he was quite happy since he hadn't led the twosome on too many wild goose chases to find his ball.

All things considered, the golf outing went well. At times the conversation was a little slow, but Andrew was able to fill in the gaps. If ever at a loss, he would tap into Dan's favorite topic — Dan. By the end of the round, Andrew had heard countless stories of Dan's greatness and achievements. But Andrew still didn't understand why Dan had invited him to play. Certainly he had arranged golf outings with managers before, but they were usually foursomes. A one-on-one session was unheard of.

As the bag boy drove the cart away and took their clubs to be cleaned, Dan asked, "Are you ready for a great massage? I've booked us for an hour with two of the sexiest massage therapists here. Afterwards, we can get a bite to eat."

Despite hearing stories of Dan's many conquests, Andrew was still not ready for the sexy massage therapists comment, and all he could eke out was, "Sure." *How smooth and eloquent*, he thought to himself.

They walked back to the club's Spa and Fitness Center behind the Golf Shop, where they were greeted graciously by the receptionist.

"Good afternoon, gentlemen. How can I help you?"

"Dan Murdock here. I made us a couple massage appointments yesterday."

"Yes, Mr. Murdock. I have you down right here. You're in room three with Paul, and Mr. Hastings, I have you in room five with Vicki."

"There must be some sort of mistake here. I specifically requested Shawna." Dan's face was turning red.

"Yes, I do see that here, but Shawna called in sick this morning. We were able to get Paul Swensen in today to take over her appointments. I don't know if Paul has ever helped you before, but he's excellent and has over twelve years of experience."

"I don't give a crap about Paul's experience. I don't want some dude touching my body." Dan tried to laugh it off, but the scene was no less uncomfortable.

Trying to recover gracefully, the receptionist said, "Well, I'm sorry, Mr. Murdock. All of our other female therapists are booked." Dan's face shook and was getting redder.

Andrew didn't know what to make of this display, but he was getting more uncomfortable by the second. So in an attempt to resolve the tension without further embarrassment, Andrew suggested, "Dan, why don't you take my therapist. Vicki, is that right?" looking to the receptionist, who was nodding enthusiastically. "I don't mind."

"Oh, that would be perfect," added the young girl. "I'll let Paul and Vicki know about the swap we're making, and I'll be right back to show you to your rooms."

———

AS ANDREW AND DAN received their deep tissue massages, a white van with Anderson Electric decals on its side pulled up to Andrew's house. After an all-clear signal, three professionals dressed in khaki overalls exited the van to make a free house call on the Hastings residence. It took them less than a minute to break into the house without leaving a trace of forced entry. Thirty minutes later, they had finished their job. The Hastings home was wired for sound from top to bottom.

———

BACK IN THE PARKING LOT at Interlachen Country Club, a tow truck pulled up next to Andrew's car. After popping the hood and connecting the battery for a charge, the mechanic grabbed his toolbox and opened the driver's side door. Working as fast and precisely as a surgeon, the mechanic made a small, invisible slit in the car's roof liner. Then, after pulling a pair of high-tech tweezers from his overalls, he inserted a pearl-sized transmitter with a tiny filament, no bigger than a hair, that stuck ever so slightly from the ceiling. After locking up, unhooking the battery charger, and closing the hood, the mechanic waited for his partner, who had gone into the locker room and installed a software update on Andrew's phone.

AFTER HIS MASSAGE, Andrew quickly showered and got dressed. When exiting the locker room, he saw Dan, and they agreed to meet by the patio restaurant. But as he wandered outside, his stomach growled impatiently. Remembering a bowl of apples back in the spa, he turned back around and grabbed one. The Granny Smith apple tasted deliciously tart, and Andrew decided to sit down and enjoy it. The entrance to the men's locker room was only a few feet away. He could just as easily wait here for Dan.

As Andrew relaxed and closed his eyes for a moment, his peace was broken by Dan's bellowing voice coming from inside the locker room. He was just one of those people the whole room could hear even when he was whispering. *How annoying*, Andrew thought. He had heard enough of Dan, so he decided to get up and wait for Dan upstairs by the patio after all.

After Andrew paused to repack some clothes falling out of his workout bag, Dan's voice boomed again. But this time Andrew was sure he heard Dan mention Angie Green's name. His interest piqued, he hesitated by the entrance to the locker room to listen. The bits and pieces of the conversation he gleaned didn't make any sense, so Andrew inched into the locker room's entryway further. Finally, he stopped just before reaching the first bay of lockers. He could hear Dan's voice loud and clear now.

"Thanks, Laura. Let's follow that bastard's every little move to see if he is up to anything. Keep me posted."

Andrew was startled by the sound of a locker door slamming closed. Fearing it was Dan's, Andrew took several quiet steps backward, turned around, and quickly walked toward the patio. As he sat on a bench near the dining area, Andrew gathered himself and took a few deep breaths. Dan's words echoed in his head, and he wondered what was going on. *Why is Dan following someone's every move? Who could it be, and how is Angie Green connected?*

Within moments, Dan was right in front of him, grinning ear to ear. "So how was that massage? Release all your tensions and worries?"

"Yes, it was wonderful. I feel so relaxed, it makes me want to just take a nap."

"Me too. I hate to do this, but I have to cancel lunch. The wife just called, and she desperately needs relief from the kids."

"No, that's totally cool, Dan. Thanks for the round of golf and the massage. It was great spending some time with you and getting to know you better." Andrew forced a smile and reached out to shake Dan's hand.

"My pleasure, Andrew. Keep up the good work on the launch. Oh, I was going to suggest this over lunch, but let me go ahead and give you a little advice right now."

"Really, what's that?" Andrew replied innocently.

"You need to be stronger, Andrew. I don't like it when my people look weak or vulnerable. Your wounded, nice guy image isn't going to get you anywhere at IFM. Don't worry, though. Listen to me. I can help coach you."

Andrew wanted to turn away, but just as he was about to release his hand, Dan gripped it even tighter. "Oh, one more thing. Don't get distracted by the Redu approval process. I know it has you worried, but I have it all under control."

Andrew nodded and said good-bye, and then he tried his best to walk nonchalantly back to his car. But he couldn't stop wondering what had just happened. *Why did Dan invite me to golf with him? Just to tell me to be tough and strong like him? And where did this concern over Redu's approval process come from? We hadn't even spoken about it.*

EIGHT

Washington, D.C.
Sunday, June 6
10:00 A.M.

LAURA'S DRIVER, Luis, was off on Sundays. So, for this one day, Laura was left to fend for herself on the streets of DC. Although she made Luis feel guilty for this "privilege," Laura secretly enjoyed having a day on her own. For on Sundays, the rest of the world was put on hold, and Laura made her pilgrimage to see the only surviving member of her family.

The morning drive to Annapolis was usually quite peaceful with little to no traffic. Although Laura would never admit it, when she got behind the wheel of her black Cadillac for her weekly trip, something happened to her. By the time she crossed the beltway, her shoulders began to relax and her lips parted slightly. And without fail, her mind would wander, flashing back to a different time and place.

Born in communist, war-torn Vietnam in 1963, Laura's given name was Long Chung. Raised in poverty, Long's early life was marked with sadness and despair. After losing her father in the war when she was only a toddler, Long faced further tragedy when her mother and sister drowned after their ship capsized during their escape from Vietnam.

Orphaned, Long and her brother Quang found themselves in a refuge camp on the island of Pulau Bidong, Malaysia. Life in the camp was bleak, with little food to go around. Long was shrewd and Quang was fast, so together they outwitted many fellow refugees and, over time, became quite accomplished thieves. But one evening they were caught and savagely beaten. Long's wounds were traumatic, but they healed with time, at least on the outside. Quang, however, was brain damaged as a result, with continuing, unpredictable seizures. He would never be the same.

Over the years, they passed through a series of under-staffed, minimally resourced orphanages, until Long ultimately gave up her hopes of having a family. Who would want to adopt her and Quang? They weren't cute little kids any longer, and Quang's severe mental disability would surely scare off most. But Long was unwilling to leave her brother. Then a miracle happened when a childless couple in Milwaukee decided to adopt them both.

At first life was good in Wisconsin. Long was quick to learn English, and within a year, she was catching up with girls her age in school. Ready to shed her past and become an American, she dropped her given name and started going by Laura Chung, and then Laura Henderson when their adoption was final. Laura's new mother was patient and kind, and together they helped Quang through life, reveling in that occasional smile that would gleam from his otherwise expressionless face.

Happiness, however, was short-lived. Two years after their adoption, their new mother was diagnosed with breast cancer, and within six months she died. Left in the grief-stricken hands of their adoptive father, Laura's and Quang's lives once again crumbled as their dad proved incapable of the responsibility.

Within three months, Quang was turned over to foster care. Laura was devastated and couldn't bear seeing her brother only once a month. But things worsened even more when he was transferred to an institution in Green Bay. Torn from her only real family, Laura begged to go with Quang, but her father refused. Instead, he forced Laura to stay in Milwaukee and become his personal slave—keeping house, cleaning clothes, and making meals.

Laura's freedom from her adoptive father couldn't come soon enough, and the day after graduating from high school as valedictorian, she moved out of the Henderson house. Shortly after, she changed her name to Laura Long, reminiscent of her roots, but still a new beginning. Unable to assume financial responsibility for Quang yet, Laura arranged for him to move to an orphanage in Boston while she attended Harvard on a full scholarship. It was then that her weekly visits became a tradition, a ritual that continued after Quang was transferred to an institution closer to DC.

After almost fifty minutes on the road, Laura pulled into a parking lot behind the Annapolis Adult Home. The historic, three-story, colonial mansion had been converted ten years ago into a private center for adults suffering from ABIs, acquired brain injuries. With a staffing ratio of 2:1, the home's seven residents were in quite capable hands, and for that Laura was very thankful. Although most of the residents' families rarely came to visit, Laura was dedicated to seeing her brother. In fact, since placing him, Laura had only missed one Sunday when she suffered from a bout of the stomach flu.

"Good morning, Miss Long. How are you doing?" Rita asked as Laura walked through the entry hall. The hardwood floors and enameled woodwork shined as light glistened through the panes of the transom window.

"How's Quang?"

"He's had a good week. Only a couple seizures, which is much better than normal. He should be down in a couple minutes. Would you like some coffee while you wait?"

"No, I'm fine, thanks," Laura said as she sat down in the window seat of the home's living room. The well-appointed room was bright and clean, and there was always someone nearby offering help, which made Laura feel more at ease. *After all*, Laura thought, now that she could afford it, *Quang deserves the best*.

NINE

IFM Headquarters
Monday, June 7
7:04 A.M.

ANDREW REALIZED Chloe was being thoughtful to even agree to a meeting, given her busy schedule. But as he hustled through the employee entrance a few minutes after seven, he wished it could have been a little later.

The Caribou Coffee at IFM's Commons was open, and as he approached, he could see Chloe waiting. How could he miss her? She was dressed in an eye-popping floral miniskirt, an open-necked white blouse that showed off her new breasts, and tan heels that must have given her at least three more inches of height and who knew how much pain.

"Andrew," Chloe burst out as he walked up. She gave him a huge hug. "How are you, dear? Don't you look so handsome in your suit."

"Well, with Becky's funeral later today, I thought it best—"

Andrew stopped mid-sentence as he looked at Chloe's outrageous outfit again.

"What are you thinking?" Chloe paused and saw him stare at her skirt, then she laughed out loud. "No, even I'm not crazy enough to wear this to a funeral. For goodness sakes, I'm planning on arriving early so I can sit up front with Becky's sweet family. I brought a change of clothes. It's in my office. I just didn't want to be dressed so drab and serious all day."

After getting their coffee and sitting down, Chloe asked, "Have you spoken to Bill since the accident?"

"I saw him at church yesterday morning. He seems to be holding up well, although I know it's all adrenaline at this point. I gave him a schedule of meals our team is bringing over to his place for the next couple weeks. He was really appreciative."

"You are such a sweetie. Always helping out those in need. But tell me, how can I help you? Your e-mail was a bit cryptic."

"Well, as I mentioned in my message, I've been trying to get up to speed on the approval process. I have my marketing plans meeting with the division and Dan on Thursday, and you know the drill. No matter what anybody says to the contrary, you have to prove you're the expert on everything. And with Becky gone, it's even more important since she won't be in the room to help out in case the conversation goes that way."

"Got it. So what do you need to know?" asked Chloe.

"Well, I've done my homework, and I'm pretty on top of things. Sounds like final approval is due in a little over a week. In fact, the rumor mill has you going out this week for some final, big meetings. Anything you can share about those?"

"Boy, you'd think people would have better things to talk about than my travels," Chloe chuckled. "Yes, I am heading out to DC tomorrow. Nothing to really share about the meetings, just making a big announcement and doing some PR in advance of the approval decision."

"What do you think our chances are? I've heard some rumblings that we aren't going to get approved."

"Where did you hear that?"

Andrew hesitated. He didn't want to create problems, but he also didn't want to be blindsided in his meeting. He needed to be prepared for the consequences. Even though the approvals for B-Lean's raw material inventory pre-builds went far up the line, he knew that when things went south, people at the low end of the totem pole got blamed.

"Well, I haven't told anyone, but the morning of the plane crash, Becky left a voice mail for me. She said a major delay was ahead."

Chloe's face fell like louver blinds being shut. In one moment she shifted from sunny and open to dark and closed. Her smile turned expressionless, and despite her plastic surgeon's best efforts, worry lines rippled across her forehead.

Pausing briefly, Chloe quickly gained her composure.

"That's crazy, Andrew. You know Becky was quite the worry-wart. I'm sure she was just in one of those down moods of hers."

"Well, I saved her message. You can listen to it if you'd like."

Not sure what to say, Chloe finally nodded. "Okay."

Andrew took out his cell phone, dialed into his voice mail, and started fumbling through his messages. "Just one second. I know it's here." After another minute, he put down his phone and said, "That's strange. I know I saved it, but it's not there."

"Don't worry," Chloe said. "I'm sure it was nothing."

"Well, wait a second. I also have some research I pulled off the Knowledge Portal that referred to some early trials being completed. I had never heard of these trials before, and there's no record of them in the FDA approval submission."

Chloe eyes widened as her forehead wrinkles were joined by frown lines. "What? Can I see?" she said. "There must be some mistake."

Andrew pulled out his to-do folder and flipped through its contents three times. *Where is it?* he thought. He had just seen it Friday when he was going through his papers and making his to-do list. Visibly frustrated, he finally said, "I'm sorry, Chloe, I must have left it at my desk or somehow at home. But I'm sure of what I read. There were some trials that happened during the early days of Galileo."

After taking a few moments to digest the conversation, Chloe tried to remain calm.

"Listen, Andrew, I don't know what you saw or what you think Becky told you, but there were no old Galileo trials. I will personally send you every research trial and the results summary if you have any questions. We are just yards away from winning this race with the FDA. Please, please trust me. Everything is okay." Chloe reached out to hold his hand. "I promise. Now just forget all this. If you're worried about your plans meeting, I'll attend and answer any questions that come up. Please, spend your time on great marketing ideas and making the launch a huge success, not on nonsense like this."

Andrew was embarrassed, and his face was red. He knew he wasn't crazy. What was going on? But rather than make a bigger fool of himself, he decided to move on.

"I'm sorry, Chloe. I didn't mean to waste your time here. And thank you. I appreciate your offer to attend my plans meeting. You really don't need to, but I'll forward the meeting notice your way. If it works out that you can make it, that's great."

"Perfect. Now that's enough business. How's that little darling, Ethan?"

"Not so little anymore. He just graduated from elementary school last week. I'm the proud parent of a middle-schooler."

Chloe laughed, tossing back her long, straight mane of black hair. "How wonderful! You know the real fun is just beginning."

AS ANDREW WALKED to his office, Chloe picked up her bag and moved to an alcove behind the coffee house. Grabbing her cell phone, hardly able to contain herself, she dialed Dan. The phone rang and rang and eventually flipped to his voice mail.

"Dan, we have a real emergency here. I was just having coffee with Andrew Hastings. He had some questions about the approval process, and he mentioned the Galileo trials. He also says he got a message from Becky before the crash that said the approval was going to be delayed. I'm going up to Aidan's office right now to warn him. If you're around, join me."

BY THE TIME Andrew got up to his office, he was distraught. *How could I make such a fool of myself? What happened?* he thought.

He put down his backpack, literally dumping out its contents, desperately searching for the Galileo trials document. *Damn, where is it?* Unrelenting in his search, he thought about the files he had out on his desk Friday and pulled them out. Madly searching for that printed page, he thumbed through each file, one by one, with no luck.

From her desk, Steph could hear the racket going on in Andrew's cube. "What's going on in here?" she asked as she walked in, only to see him sitting hunched over, madly searching through his file cabinet.

At first surprised, Andrew looked up and then leaned back in his chair. "Oh, I just made a fool of myself. I was talking to Chloe Stiles about a document I printed out last week, and now I can't find it. I feel like an idiot."

"Andrew, you know that's not true. I'm sure it's here somewhere. Can I help?"

"Steph, I have been through my backpack and my files three times now. Maybe I accidentally left it at home. That's the only place I think it could be."

"Well, just relax. Everyone here knows how intelligent you are, Andrew. One little misplaced paper isn't going to make a difference. Anyway, you are the kindest guy around. That makes a difference."

Still looking around on his desk, Andrew replied "Nice will get you nowhere here. In fact, I sometimes think it is my biggest road-block to getting promoted. Dan Murdock has told me as much."

"Don't talk that way. I've seen too many managers come and

go over the years. You're different. You're special. Don't ever lose that quality."

Andrew raised his head and smiled. "Thanks, Steph. Thanks for reminding me. It's just easy to get down on myself here. Maybe if I get out for a run over lunch it will clear my head."

"After your advertising meeting, you're free from noon on, and Becky's funeral is at three."

"Okay, then a run it is. Maybe I can even get Josh to join me," Andrew replied. "Thanks, Steph. You're always there for me."

OFF THE MAIN CORRIDOR of the executive offices was the executive kitchen, where a breakfast buffet of bagels, fruit, and juices was set up. As Chloe made her way to Aidan's office, she did a quick double take as she passed him in the kitchen helping himself to some breakfast.

"What, your secretary can't get you a plate?" asked Chloe.

"Well, I'm not an invalid…"

While he was serving up some fruit into his bowl, Chloe came up closely to Aidan. "We need to talk. Another leak has sprung."

"Damn, what now?"

"Let's go to your office."

As they turned the corner toward Aidan's office, Chloe heard loud footsteps thumping behind her, and then Dan's voice thundered, "Good morning, Aidan. How are you, Chloe?"

"Thanks for coming up so quickly, Dan. We need to talk," Chloe replied.

Chloe and Dan nodded to Aidan's secretary as they walked by.

"I'm going to be a few minutes, Judy. Can you move or delay my next appointment?"

"Yes, Aidan. Do you need anything else?"

"No, thank you," he said and closed the doors to his office.

"So what's today's panic, Chloe?"

"Sorry to interrupt, Aidan, but before Chloe gets going, I think we've already covered this one." Turning to Chloe, he went on. "You see, Aidan and I learned about the problem with Andrew last week. Laura alerted us Friday morning. It's already been taken care of."

Looking a bit baffled, Chloe questioned, "Really? Then why is he still talking about it?"

"Okay," Dan said, trying to talk slowly and calm Chloe down. "What exactly did Andrew say?"

"Wait a second here. Let's back up. I seem to be the only one who doesn't know what's going on. How did you take care of Andrew?"

"Well, shortly after we found out, I invited Andrew out for a morning of golf, massage, and shooting the breeze. During our little outing, Laura arranged to put Andrew under surveillance. His house, phone, and car are all wired. Andrew can't sneeze without us knowing about it."

"Have we seen anything additional to worry about?" Aidan asked.

"Nope. Pretty boring stuff. He was at home after we golfed and did stuff around the house. Sunday morning he went to church and then worked."

"Well, he certainly was curious this morning. He mentioned a file he found on the Knowledge Portal and then a voice mail he received from Becky."

"Laura has taken care of it. The file has been removed from the portal, and the voice mail has been deleted. Laura's team was also able to find Andrew's printed copy of the Galileo document and removed it."

"Good work," said Aidan. "Sounds like we may have nipped this one in the bud."

"I'm not sure," Chloe said. "You didn't see his face. He was visibly shaken when he couldn't find the Galileo trial info. If he hasn't already, you can bet he's going to go back out there and search for it."

"Well, he won't find it," laughed Dan.

"Dan, you may think Andrew is an idiot, but he isn't. Things just don't disappear for this guy. He's very organized."

"Well, what do you propose we do?"

"I don't know," she said, shaking her head. "I tried my best to get his attention focused elsewhere. He's concerned about getting caught with his shorts down on the approval process at his marketing plans meeting. I told him to focus on great marketing ideas and that I'd be there at the meeting to handle any questions on the approval process."

"That's a great idea, Chloe," said Aidan. "Dan, why don't you just get this guy focused and working on plans? If his energy is there, he won't have time to get distracted."

"Oh, I can make him work. Don't worry. And we'll watch him every second of the day to make sure his nose is to the grindstone and not snooping around where it shouldn't be."

"Sounds good. Anything else?" asked Aidan.

"Wait one second, guys," Chloe said, holding Aidan and Dan by their shirtsleeves. "Why wasn't I in the loop on this?"

"Chloe, we just didn't want to worry you. We knew how upset you were about Becky and your team. We just didn't think you could handle any more," Dan said in his most condescending voice.

Chloe paused and quickly decided not to make a scene in front of Aidan. "Okay, but I don't want it to happen again. Hear me?" Chloe made eye contact with both Aidan and Dan.

"Yes, Chloe. We hear you," added Aidan. "Don't blame Dan for this. I'm sorry. Okay?" The last thing he needed was more feuding.

Chloe nodded, and within moments Aidan had excused both of them. As they walked out of his office, Chloe stopped and grabbed hold of Dan's shoulder. Her fingers were bony thin, but her grip was strong, and her nails were like daggers.

"Listen, Dan, I don't care what Aidan says. I know you're behind this. Hear me and don't forget it. I haven't come this far to be left on the outside. I'm not going to be one of the casualties that you leave behind."

"Is that a threat, Chloe?"

"You can take it however you'd like, Dan. We're on the same team, and I know we can win. But if I have the slightest sense that you're selling me out, you will regret it."

"Duly noted," Dan smirked, and he turned to walk away.

AS THEY EXITED the locker room, Josh and Andrew took the back stairs that dumped them out by the employee entrance. Within a minute, they were running east along Wayzata Bay for a five-mile run.

"So what's bugging you, Andrew? You're awfully quiet."

Andrew was focused on running hard. He was trying to burn the stress of the morning away. He felt like crap, and was in no mood to go to a funeral. "The usual. Work sucks," he replied.

"You care to elaborate?"

"Well, let's see. It's barely past noon, and I've made a complete and total fool of myself in front of Chloe Stiles. Then, I spent almost two hours with Bingham & Morris, and they served up another round of horrible advertising."

"Oh, there has to be a funny story in there somewhere. Come on. What was the worst board you saw the agency present? Which one made you want to just laugh out loud?" Josh knew just how to get Andrew to let his guard down and start talking.

Andrew thought for a second and quickly started to smile. "That's easy. Okay, you know B-Lean Snacks is a new line of calorie-conscious chips, pretzels, and corn puffs with all the taste and none of the sacrifice."

"Yeah. Got it."

"Well, one of the agency's boards was about an organ grinder and his monkey. So this organ grinder guy and his monkey take a break from their street show. The guy sits down on the sidewalk and pours out a bowl of Uncle Chuck's B-Lean Snacks."

"Huh, where did this guy have the bowl?"

"Oh, it was stuffed in his knapsack. Yeah, I know. Kinda crazy. Anyway, the guy starts to eat the B-Lean tortilla chips and decides to toss his monkey a chip. The monkey grabs it and devours it. All of a sudden, the monkey goes rabid, foaming at the mouth, attacking its owner and scarfing down the rest of the bowl. The end shot shows the organ grinder on the ground with this monkey jumping on top of him with a voice-over that says, "Uncle Chuck's B-Lean Snacks. Tastes so good it makes your monkey go wild.""

Josh started laughing so hard that Andrew finally had to chuckle as well.

"I know," Andrew said. "Then they went on about the monkey representing the inner beast in mankind. It was so ridiculous it was funny. What's crazier is that was the board the agency recommended."

"No way. You've got to be kidding!"

"Nope. Seriously, this would be funny if we weren't already six weeks behind on our timeline. This was their third round of crappy boards. It's driving me crazy."

"So what are you going to do?"

"Well, I've requested another round. They won't be ready for another two weeks, so I offered to call into a meeting from my vacation to keep the process moving."

"Great. You pay the price for their incompetence."

"I know. That seems to be how it works every time."

"Hey, did you get my e-mail with the suggestions for your trip?" Josh asked.

"Yes, thanks. It really helped. I made some reservations for surfing and scuba diving in Maui and then that helicopter ride and Nā Pali Coast kayaking trip in Kaua`i. We'll play the rest by ear, but it'll be great to have some things already planned."

"So what else has you so nerved out?"

"Well, my final marketing plan meeting with Dan and the division leadership team is this Thursday."

"Ah yes. You feeling ready?"

"Yeah, although Dan just left a message for me with all these requests for backups in the plan. It will keep me busy 'round the clock for the next couple days."

"Hey, how did your golf session go with Dan the Man? Did you play okay?"

"Yeah, thanks to you. The pointers on Friday definitely helped warm up my game."

"Was Dan cool? Any promotion news?"

Andrew grunted, "Hardly. Oh, he said I was doing a great job, but then at the end he said something about not acting so wounded and offered to help coach me. Not only that, he told me not to worry about the Redu approval from the FDA. He was taking care of that, he said, as if I had asked him..."

"That's odd."

"I know. The whole thing was just weird. I mean, the invite came out of nowhere. Then he was acting like we were best buddies. He made a big deal about getting a great lunch after our massages. Then, all of a sudden, he says I'm weak, and he has to go."

"Hmmm..."

"Yeah. Well, it gets even weirder. After I changed in the locker room, I went to get an apple at the spa's front desk. When I came back, I heard Dan talking. You know how loud he can be."

Josh nodded his head.

"Well, he was talking about how they're now following someone's every move. I don't know. It was like he was having someone tailed."

"Maybe he thinks his wife is having an affair?"

"No, I don't think so. In fact, I'm pretty sure I heard Angie Green's name mentioned."

"Your boss who's on leave?"

"Yeah, that's crazy, isn't it?"

"It is. But maybe she's planning on leaving the company? Or maybe you just misheard. I'm sure at Dan's level he's part of any number of corporate espionage cases or security breaches."

"Really, you think so?"

"Oh yeah. I know in IT we have at least a couple cases a month where there's some employee that is suspected of something. You'd be amazed," replied Josh.

"Hmmm...I would've never guessed."

"So, did you take my advice and give Heidi a call?"

"No, I haven't. I don't know what to say, and I'm so busy with plans and getting ready for vacation."

"Those sound like excuses to me, but I'll let them slide for now. Hey, what do you say we kick it up a notch and make this a real workout?" asked Josh.

"Is that a challenge, Mr. Sargent?"

"You bet."

TEN

Wayzata, Minnesota
Monday, June 7
3:00 P.M.

ANDREW WAS glad he decided to arrive a half hour early. The Wayzata Community Church's eight-hundred-seat sanctuary was overflowing. Becky Clausen's friends, family, and coworkers easily surpassed the capacity. Thankfully, IFM's funeral planner had set up two auxiliary seating areas in the church's fellowship hall and the chapel where monitors and audio of the service were piped in.

The church was impressive. Andrew stared up at the immense white ceiling. Its arcs and curves were simple yet beautiful. Although it wasn't ornate by most standards, the massive organ pipes served as a backdrop to the altar, and they were housed in perfectly enameled white woodwork that also adorned the choir, pulpit, and pews.

Although almost six years had passed, this would still be the first funeral since his parents', and the feelings of sadness and longing rose close to the surface. As the service started, the choir sang

"Amazing Grace," and Andrew immediately choked up. One of his mother's favorite songs, Andrew remembered it playing at his parents' funeral.

Becky's service lasted an hour. After a brief homily from the pastor, Becky's sister, Hope, delivered the eulogy, followed by stories shared by Becky's father and her husband, Bill. The stories celebrated her life and were full of laughs, but they left everyone wanting more — more time with Becky. More time for her precious girls to know the mother who was stolen away from them.

Several men from Becky's family carried out the mahogany casket. Bill followed closely behind, carrying Lizzie in his arms and holding Maureen's hand as she walked slowly by his side. After the family exited for a private internment, the pews slowly emptied. Andrew saw Chloe several rows up but turned his head to avoid making eye contact. He was in no mood to be chatty with her. His wounds were still fresh from his embarrassing, morning meeting.

As he turned to exit through the fellowship hall, he felt someone tap his shoulder and then heard a familiar voice say, "Andrew." At first he thought it was another IFM employee, but then he realized the voice wasn't from IFM. He had loved this voice, and just as he turned, he remembered. It was Heidi's.

Heidi reached out and gave him a big hug. She just held him tight but didn't say a word. No words were needed. She had seen him walk in. She had watched him stare above and wipe his eyes. She knew what he was thinking and was only sorry she wasn't by his side to help.

As their hug started to slow down traffic, Andrew and Heidi stepped back by the coat racks.

"What are you doing here?"

"I'm covering the story for WMSP. I have been since the crash last week."

Andrew stared into Heidi's face. She was so beautiful. Her blue eyes were alive with energy, and they sparkled in the light that streamed in from above.

"Hey, can you wait for me? I need to film just a bit more for my story, but it shouldn't take me long. How about we meet in the chapel in ten minutes?"

"Sure. Sounds good."

Andrew walked over to the restrooms. There was a line out the door, but he was in no rush. After a few minutes, he made his way through. As he was washing up, he soaped up his hands and stared at his face. His eyes were red, and he looked washed out and pale in his dark suit and white shirt. But as he splashed some water on his face, he thought, *Why do I still care?* Unwilling to answer the question right then, he dried off his face, straightened his tie, and then walked to the chapel.

EFC Headquarters
Monday, June 7
5:00 P.M.

"THEY CAN'T get away with this," Gina exclaimed. "We have an eyewitness that saw Lia and Danielle Haley at the Hilton having drinks together. And the police aren't even curious?"

"I didn't say that," Henry said, trying to calm Gina down. "The police acknowledge the coincidence. But after reviewing surveillance tapes from the parking lot, evidence from Ms. Haley's home, and interviews at the FDA, they can't back up their suspicions with any facts."

"How about Ken's team? Have they dug up anything?"

"Nothing. All he's got are a bunch of dead ends. These people are professionals, Gina. You know that, right?"

"Yes, but even pros make mistakes."

Wayzata, Minnesota
Monday, June 7
4:05 P.M.

THE CHAPEL was empty. Only a janitor remained, picking up some programs that were left behind from the service. Andrew stood by the windows and watched the cars line up. The church's parking lot was always a mess. Andrew was amazed at how quickly a group could turn from godly to cutthroat just for a slightly quicker exit. As the parking finally started to empty, he heard footsteps approaching.

"Sorry to keep you waiting. I had to finish up the story in time for tonight's news."

"I understand. I saw your piece last week after the crash. I was over at Josh's. We were both impressed. You always do such wonderful work."

"Thanks, Andrew. I just try to keep it honest and real. But you know that. You've heard me go on and on about what's wrong with journalism today."

"Yes, I've heard that sermon once or twice." Andrew smiled. "Why don't we sit down? Catch your breath?"

"That's sounds nice. I don't have too much time, but it will take the crew a while to pack up." Heidi smiled, and they sat down in the front row of the chapel. "So what have you been up to? It's been way too long."

"Nothing much. Just the same old stuff here. Work, having fun with Ethan, and getting outside. It's pretty simple, but all good. How about you?"

"Too much work. Things are tough at WMSP, so I always feel like I am fighting to keep my job."

"Oh, I hear you there. We've all become disposable. At IFM the motto is "You're up or out," and my clock is ticking louder and louder. If I don't move up soon, there's only one way for me to go."

"Well, they'd be crazy to lose you, Andrew. You're so hardworking, smart, and always looking for creative solutions."

"True, but I stink at the politics. I keep my head down and work, and that just doesn't cut it anymore."

"Are you still working on that big, new product launch?"

"Yes, the B-Lean Snacks line is my baby. We start shipping it in about five months. In fact, that's why I'm here. Becky Clausen was our primary, internal regulatory contact for the FDA approval process. I still can't believe she's gone. Those poor little girls, never getting a chance to know their mom. And Bill. You know I'm not a fan of Lydia's, but I can't imagine raising Ethan without his mom."

"I know. When I was interviewing Bill, he understandably wanted to keep the girls off camera. But he did mention that they kept asking for their mom. They just didn't understand that she was gone."

Andrew shook his head. "This accident just seems so random. I mean, how could it happen?" As Andrew spoke, Heidi turned and shifted her gaze out the window. Andrew may have been apart from Heidi for a while, but he still knew her signals. "Wait a second. What's going on? Do you know something?"

"No, I don't," she paused. "I mean, the investigation is underway, but they still haven't determined the final cause of the crash."

"Heidi, you know something. What's going on? Don't make me wait to hear it on the news."

Heidi looked back at Andrew. His eyes looked so very tired. "Well, there's some talk from the NTSB investigators that the crash was no accident. The wreckage had some residue in the fuel lines that indicates contamination—something that may have caused the engines to fail."

"Oh my God. I can't believe this. I heard the reports that EFC might be involved, but I didn't believe them. It just seemed too far-fetched."

"Well, I agree with you there. I don't think EFC was behind it."

"Then who?" asked Andrew.

"I don't know. But please, don't tell anyone. I'm hoping to break the fuel contamination story on tonight's late news. It would be great if we could have the exclusive on it."

"Heidi, you have my word."

"Thanks. I appreciate it. Hey, it's getting late, and I need to get back to the station."

Suddenly Andrew was determined their conversation wouldn't stop here. "I know you have to go, but do you think we could get together again and talk?"

"I'd love that."

"Well, here's the crazy part. I have my final marketing plans meeting Thursday, and then Ethan and I leave for a two-week vacation to Hawaii Friday night. So the next couple days are insane. Maybe we could get coffee on Friday morning? I'm taking the day off to pack and run last-minute errands."

"Sounds perfect, Andrew." Heidi looked down at her watch.

"I know that look. Get out of here, you. I'll call you later, and we can set a time and place."

They got up from the pew, and Andrew gave Heidi a big hug. As they let each other go, Andrew said, "Thanks for saying hi. I've missed you."

"I've missed you too, Andrew."

As Heidi ran out of the church, Andrew smiled. His body was more than tingling. It was so much more. He felt alive. Andrew walked outside and reached into his pocket to turn on his phone to text Josh. His message was simple. *I saw Heidi. I'm so crazy. How could I have ever let her go?*

ELEVEN

**Plymouth, Minnesota
Tuesday, June 8
7:00 A.M.**

ANDREW WOKE UP a little before seven o'clock. The bright morning sun was shining through the shutters. As he rolled out of bed and walked toward the bathroom, he could hear the noise of electronics downstairs. Ethan had come home with him after their soccer game the night before and was now up early playing video games.

As Andrew came downstairs, Ethan shouted, "Good morning, Dad."

"Hey there, buddy. What has you up?"

"I don't know. Just felt like it."

Andrew shook his head. How come during the school year rousing Ethan was like waking the dead, but on summer mornings, he was up so early?

"Hey, Katie will be over in about thirty minutes. I'd like to make you some breakfast before she gets here."

"I'm down with that, Daddy-O. How about some waffles?"

Andrew glanced at the clock on the microwave and said, "Okay, but you'll need to help. You nuke the syrup and a couple pieces of bacon."

"Just a second. I have to kill one more alien."

"Yeah, yeah." Andrew quickly pulled some mix from the pantry, added some water, and the batter was ready. With a couple more able movements, he retrieved the waffle iron and got it warming up. Then he grabbed some strawberries from the fridge, washed, hulled, and sliced them, and poured two glasses of juice.

Taking a five-minute break to run upstairs and shower, Andrew came back down in khakis and an undershirt.

"Hey, bud, let's get the show on the road here. Come do your part."

The batter sizzled as Andrew poured it into the iron. Steam curled from all sides as the lid closed. Ethan finally made his way into the kitchen as Andrew was setting the kitchen table.

Andrew turned and gave Ethan a big hug and kiss. "Good Morning. Did you sleep well?"

"Yep."

"Hey, is your ankle giving you any trouble? You looked pretty good out on the field last night."

"It feels fine. You don't need to worry."

"Okay, okay. Now, get that stuff warmed up," he said, pointing to the syrup and bacon. "The first waffle will be ready in just a minute."

Although waffles were usually reserved for weekends, the first day of summer break with Dad had to count for something. So Belgian waffles with berries, syrup, and whipped cream made the day a little more special.

Ethan and Andrew joked around over breakfast. During Andrew's time with Ethan, the problems outside of their little family seemed to melt away. As they were finishing up the last bites of waffles, the doorbell rang.

"I'll get it. I bet it's Katie!" declared Ethan. He jumped up from the table and within moments he was shouting, "Good morning, Katie!"

Katie Burke was a sixty-two-year-old native of Mankato, Minnesota, who lived next door to Andrew with her husband, Roy, a retired policeman. With auburn hair, a beaming smile, and radiant green eyes, Katie was always a welcome sight for the Hastings. She adored children, and she had three grown, married sons and four grandchildren of her own. All her boys had joined the military, however, and were posted across the world, so she missed her sons and grandkids dearly. But to help fill the gap, Katie was very involved in nannying for the Hastings, assisting at her church's nursery, and volunteering at a downtown shelter for homeless families.

"Good morning, Katie. How's it going today?" Andrew walked over and gave her a big hug.

"What did I miss here? Waffles? Where's mine?"

"We'll make you some next time if you'd like," said Ethan.

Andrew joined in. " I was just doing something special to celebrate the start of summer vacation at our house."

"Sounds like fun." Katie smiled and tousled Ethan's blond hair.

"Now you probably know Ethan's schedule better than I, but I left all the details on the magnet board. He's got soccer camp over by the Plymouth Creek Center at ten o'clock. I've packed him a lunch. All you need to do is drop him off and pick him up at two."

"Can Mack come over after camp?" asked Ethan.

"That's up to you, Katie, Mack, and his parents. Okay?"

"Katie, please? Please?"

"Sure, we'll give Mack a call."

"Guys, I need to get running. Ethan, you need to pick up the rest of the dishes and finish cleaning up when you're done. No sticking Katie with it." There was a silence. "Ethan?"

"Okay, Okay."

Washington, D.C.
Tuesday, June 8
9:00 A.M.

THE CORPORATE JET landed at Hyde Field in Clinton, Maryland, promptly at nine o'clock. As the wheels touched down, Chloe couldn't help thinking of her team that had attempted to make a similar trek the week before. How unsuspecting they were. Little did they know how quickly they'd become disposable liabilities to IFM.

Chloe sometimes wondered when her corporate shelf life would hit its expiration date. Several years ago she realized her career had reached its summit. Nevertheless, she kept on trying to prove herself. Her therapist attributed this drive to her lifelong desire to gain her parents' approval, to her never feeling like she got the attention or accolades of her brothers. Maybe if she was CEO she could finally earn her father's respect? But as time rolled by, she realized that dream was a delusion. Yes, she could make a move to another company, but what was the point? So as she looked forward in time and pondered the sunset of her career, she pictured a grand retirement. Perhaps IFM would name a new research building after her? How great that would be.

But she'd never let herself be taken out as easily as those corporate lambs who were slaughtered. She was a survivor—a female pioneer in a corporate world where board rooms were still dominated by men. Of course, a few closely guarded secrets would also provide her the consummate insurance policy.

Chloe had a full day planned, thanks in part to Laura Long's scheduling. First up this morning was a meeting with FDA Director Jacqueline Epps. Although booked as a friendly coffee rendezvous between industry colleagues, the veil of secrecy surrounding their get together spoke volumes.

Chloe's public reason for being in town was to meet with the First Lady, Rhoda Fleming. The president's wife had just launched her "Get It Moving" campaign, and over lunch Chloe was excited that she would be announcing a $10 million donation, as well as IFM's pledge to reduce delivered calories to America by 30 percent. Of course, most of that promise depended on the successful introduction of B-Lean across IFM's fast food, snacks, cereals, bakery, desserts, and foodservice businesses.

Chloe's busy day would then close over dinner with Congressman Larry Nesbit (D-NJ) and drinks with Senator John Gilly (R-FL). Of course, these meetings would be in private and off the record as well. Except for the "Get It Moving" pledge, no money would be exchanged today. Laura would handle those details later. Laura's checkbook and an occasional twist of the arm enabled her to have a great ability to transform promises into real commitments, all without the appearance of any ties to IFM.

WMSP-TV Headquarters
Tuesday, June 8
1:30 P.M.

HEIDI HATED the corporate crap, but she knew when to tolerate it. Now was just such an occasion. WMSP's Station Manager, Doug Wietz, had called her in for a meeting. Warren Levin, TriMedia's Network News President, was in town, and Heidi guessed Doug needed her help. As one of WMSP's top reporters, she would play a crucial role in any potential recovery plan for the station. Heidi liked working for Doug and wanted to help him get the station back on its feet.

Doug was a fifty-something guy with salt and pepper hair. Originally from New Jersey, Doug left the network news fast track twenty years ago to join WMSP. At the time, Sven Anderson, Sr. owned the station, but Doug ran it and made all the decision. After Sven's passing eight years ago, his five children had remained relatively uninvolved in all aspects of the company except for one—money. Led by Sven Jr., the Anderson children drained the station financially, forcing several missteps along the way. Aided by the fact that they had no true knowledge of the industry, their desperate attempts to squeeze out every last dime hastened the station's decline.

WMSP's financial troubles were no secret. Layoffs and cutbacks seemed to be quarterly events. The latest rumor was a proposed buyout by the network. Although it had been an affiliate for over five decades, becoming an "O&O" station, one owned-and-operated by the network, was viewed as the latest plan for saving WMSP. Heidi suspected that was the real reason for Warren's visit.

After walking into Doug's office Heidi quickly got down to business and asked, "So why does Warren want to meet with me?"

"He just admires your work," Doug winked. "I want him to appreciate what a great potential we have here, especially if we had his resources."

"I've got it," Heidi smiled. Doug didn't need to say any more. "So where is he?"

"He's meeting with Sven Jr. over lunch. Let's just hope Sven doesn't blow it."

There was a knock on Doug Wietz's office door. Erika Braker was there with Warren. Instructed to greet Warren upon his arrival after lunch with Sven Jr., Erika was out of her league even more than usual. When Warren entered and took a seat, Erika just stood in the doorway, unsure of whether to stay or go. Her awkwardness added to the comedy of the moment for Heidi. Trying to put Erika out of her misery, Heidi finally suggested, "Come on in, Erika. Pull up a chair."

A bit disappointed that the news neophyte was joining them, Warren got down to business.

"Heidi, thanks for meeting with me."

"It's always a pleasure, Warren."

"Well, you're a delight, and I just wanted to make sure Doug and WMSP are treating you right."

"Oh yes, they are."

"By the way, exceptional work covering the IFM plane crash

and then breaking the news of the fuel's contamination. Possible corporate sabotage is always good for ratings. I think the network has picked up your story three or four times already. Are there any new developments you can share?"

"No, not really. The final lab reports aren't due back until this Friday."

"Who would want to do such a thing? Messing with the fuel? Sounds like the work of some teenage pranksters or vandals."

"That's hard to say, Warren. But I don't think we're talking your average vandals."

"Why?"

"To be honest, I don't think we fully understand the crash. The pieces just aren't adding up. All the markings on the wreckage point to a catastrophic explosion. What's in question is whether the explosion was caused by the fouled fuel, or if it had some help."

"What do you mean, help?" asked Warren.

"Well, sugar can certainly ruin a jet engine and cause it to fail, but it's doubtful it would cause a plane to explode."

"So what do you think caused the explosion?" Doug asked.

"I don't know," replied Heidi. "The investigators are a long way from figuring that out."

"What do your instincts tell you?" asked Warren.

Heidi paused. She didn't want her personal theories about the crash floating around, but she knew Doug wanted her to show off for Warren. If it could help the station crawl out from underneath the Anderson family's control, it was worth it. "I think the fuel contamination was used to throw investigators off track."

"But that doesn't make sense," said Warren. "If sugar would take down the plane, why add some other device to make it explode?"

"To make sure the plane went down during that flight."

"Huh?"

Desperate to contribute to the conversation, Erika jumped in. "What Heidi means is that if you use sugar to bring down a plane, you couldn't be sure when the plane would crash."

"Interesting. Then the sugar is just a ruse?" asked Doug.

"That's my latest theory, though I have no way of proving it right now. But if true, it's brilliant since it clouds the real cause of the crash by giving a more obvious reason while also opening up the list of suspects to kids and petty vandals."

"Fascinating," said Warren. "This would be a great piece for an in-depth segment for one of our prime-time network news programs."

"That would be great!" Heidi replied, getting excited as she thought about the possibilities. Being a regular contributor to a news magazine was a network role she would enjoy—all the benefits of a larger stage without the downside of having to move from Minneapolis.

"It's a deal then," said Warren. "Keep me posted and let's see where this goes."

Plymouth, Minnesota
Tuesday, June 8
7:00 P.M.

ANDREW CALLED Katie in the afternoon and asked if she could stay late. He needed to put some finishing touches on his marketing plans pitch. Although he and Lourdes were pretty much done with Dan's last-minute requests, Andrew had set aside Wednesday to mark up his copy with some key facts and then do a couple dry runs to work out the bugs. Finally, at seven o'clock, Andrew walked through the door of his house.

"Hello?" There was no answer. "Come on, where are you guys?"

Andrew set his backpack down and went up to Ethan's room. Nothing. As he returned downstairs, he saw some shadows outside and walked to the back door.

"Ah, there you are." Katie and Ethan were sitting on the back deck, painting. "Wow, that's beautiful, buddy."

"Thanks, Dad. I think it's pretty cool."

In addition to her other talents, Katie was an accomplished

artist. Before any kid could tell Ethan what was cool, he was drawing and painting. After six years, he was quite the artist, and his work was featured often in school art shows.

"Katie, I'm sorry to be running late. If you have to go, please do."

"I told you, it's not a problem. I've got nowhere to go this evening. Roy's off at some Minneapolis Retired Police Officers Association meeting, so we're going to eat late when he gets home. I just need to make a quick trip to the grocery store. "

"Well, I'm glad it worked out, but I certainly don't want to keep you. Ethan, get up and tell Katie thank you and give her a hug good-bye."

After Katie left, Andrew and Ethan headed back out to the deck.

"You getting hungry yet, buddy?"

"Yes, I'm starving."

"Good. I'm going to run upstairs and change so I can get dinner started. When you find a good stopping point, pick up your paints and come inside and help me. I'm making a double batch of chicken rice."

"Yum. But why a double batch?"

"Well, you know I went to Mrs. Clausen's funeral yesterday?"

"Yes."

"I offered to bring her family dinner to help them out. The last thing Mr. Clausen needs to be worrying about right now is putting together meals. So it would be great if you could help out. My plan is to come home around five tomorrow night, and then we can take dinner over to their house. You remember Lizzie and Maureen?"

"Yeah, they're just babies, though."

"I know they're little, but it would be nice if you could play with them for a couple minutes. It shouldn't take long. Just enough time for me to say hi to their dad and deliver dinner. Anyway, I want you to get some of the credit for the dinner. You're going to help me, right?"

"Dad, I don't want to go over there," Ethan said, obviously upset.

"What's up, buddy? What's got you going about this?"

Ethan stood silently as he started to pack up his art supplies. Frustrated, he said, "I just don't want to go, Dad. Isn't that enough?"

"Okay. I'm just trying to understand," Andrew replied. "Here, let me help you with your stuff."

The two stood around the patio table, picking up the paints and cleaning the brushes that were scattered in front of them. Andrew finally broke the silence. "Remember when Grandma and Grandpa died in the car crash?"

"Yes," Ethan replied.

"If it wasn't for the help of some really great friends, I don't know how I could have made it. When somebody close to you dies, it's really hard."

"I know."

"So help me understand, buddy. Why don't you want to help our friends? What's going on inside? Is there something you're feeling that you're trying to avoid?"

Ethan thought for a couple seconds. "It just scares me. Death. It's just sad and scary."

Andrew emptied several bowls of muddied water from Ethan's watercolors over the side of the deck. "I know it is, but we can't just run away from it. In fact, it's our friends and families who help us get through such hard times. So it's our turn to help out some friends."

"I guess," Ethan said reluctantly. "It's just so hard. I feel awkward. I don't even know what to say."

"It's okay, Ethan. You know, we all feel that same way. We all get nervous and uncomfortable. All you can do is be yourself. Just being there for people helps out. I promise."

"Okay."

"So can I count on your help?" Andrew smiled and opened his arms.

"Sure," Ethan replied, wrapping his arms around his dad.

TWELVE

Plymouth, Minnesota
Wednesday, June 9
5:20 P.M.

ANDREW FELT as prepared as he was going to get. Steph had printed out twenty copies of the presentation, and they were sitting on his desk for his eleven o'clock meeting the following morning. Thanks to Dan's requests, the deck was pushing sixty pages, a far cry from the thirty pages Andrew had originally planned. It was done, though, and Andrew was leaving the office early, nothing short of miraculous.

Within twenty minutes, Andrew was home to pick up Ethan. The dinner he and Ethan assembled fit in a couple grocery bags. After a fifteen-minute drive over to the Clausen's, they walked up to the door and knocked.

Andrew asked, "You ready, buddy?"

"Uh huh," Ethan replied hesitantly.

"Just play with Lizzie and Maureen. It should be fine."

Andrew heard a commotion on the other side of the door. As

Bill opened it, Lizzie chased Maureen through the foyer. They both were laughing.

"Come on in, guys. How are you?" asked Bill.

"We're good. We just wanted to drop this stuff off for you. Nothing fancy. Just some healthy food to keep you and the girls going."

"Thank you. I've gotten better at cooking since I became a stay-at-home dad, but I've never really been as good as Becky," Bill said, trying to laugh. As Bill was talking, the girls had made their way over and were now climbing on his legs.

Andrew tapped his son on the shoulder and said, "Ethan, why don't you go play with the girls a little bit. Okay?"

"Wouldn't you like that, ladies?" Bill asked as he started leading Ethan and the girls to the front room off the main hallway. It was filled with pink and purple toys. Bill picked up a few of the girls' favorites and said, "I bet you've never played fairy princess before."

Ethan blushed. "No, I haven't."

"Well, the girls love it. Just let me know if it gets to be too much for you."

Ethan laughed. "I'll be okay. Just don't take any pictures." As Andrew and Bill turned to take the food to the kitchen, Ethan said, "Oh, Mr. Clausen, I just wanted to let you know how sorry my dad and I are about Mrs. Clausen. She was a really nice lady."

"Well, thank you, Ethan. You and your dad are good people."

Andrew cleared his throat and wiped a tear from the corner of his eye.

"Well, let's get this stuff in the kitchen. Do you want it in the fridge, or are you guys ready for dinner?"

"The girls usually eat at six o'clock, so I'll probably serve it right up."

"Sounds good. Let me help you. I have to drop Ethan off at his mom's at six, but I have a few minutes."

Andrew set the bags on the kitchen table and started to unpack them. "So how are you really doing?"

Bill paused to think about the question. "It depends on the moment. The girls keep me really busy, so I don't have much time to mope around. Evenings are rough, though. I put the girls to bed at eight, and it's just so lonely. I was used to Becky traveling, but even when she was gone, she would check in. And you know what a talker she was. Now it's all so different."

"I know you have tons of family around, but if Ethan and I can ever help out, just let me know." Bill handed Andrew some plates, and Andrew filled them with the chicken rice. One by one, the plates were put into the microwave.

"You make single parenting look pretty easy. Becky always said you were one of her favorites, and for Becky, that meant a lot. She never wanted to disappoint you or let you down."

"Yeah, Becky was always great to me. You know, she left me a voice mail the morning of the crash. She was worried about some hiccup in the approval process and didn't want me to be caught off guard."

"Hiccup? Well, I don't know any of the details, but whatever it was, it had Becky wound tight. It seemed like something very bad was going on."

"Really?" Andrew replied with a puzzled look.

"What are you thinking? Is something up?"

"No, it just doesn't make sense. Anyway, I didn't come here to talk about work."

"Oh, don't do that to me, Andrew. My wife just died. I've watched the news. I've heard speculation about EFC being behind the crash and the battle over Redu. Do you know something?"

"No, Bill, I don't know anything. I promise. It just all seems odd."

"What? Come on, Andrew. Shoot straight with me."

"It's probably nothing. It's just that Becky's message that morning was pretty specific. She thought Redu's approval was going to be delayed. She seemed convinced of it. But there hasn't been one single mention of a delay since her death. I even talked to Chloe about it, and she said Becky was a worrywart. Did Becky mention any delay to you?"

"No, she didn't. Just some old product testing results that had some problem."

"Really?"

"What? Do you think Becky did something wrong?"

"No, not at all. There's just something that doesn't add up about what Becky was working on. I've done some digging into all the project team files online, and I can't figure it out."

"Isn't that the nature of these new product launches? Aren't they supposed to be top secret?"

"Yes, but Becky and I have all the same security clearances, and we've been working closely on this approval. All my launch timelines depend on it. It's like she knew something that the rest of the team didn't, and as hard as I try, I can't find out what it was."

"Well, I want to help. If Becky knew something and it got her killed, we need to get to the bottom of it. What can I do?"

"Killed? That's a big jump. I don't know, Bill," Andrew replied, shaking his head. Bill's statement had caught him off guard, but he quickly got back on track. "Did Becky keep any files at home?"

"Yes, but her office was already cleaned out."

"What? You already cleaned out her office?"

"No, not at all. Some heavies from IFM came by the day after the crash to pick up her work stuff."

"Really? That was pretty quick. And insensitive."

"Yeah, I thought so, too, but they said it was just standard procedure."

"Really? Standard procedure?"

"You're welcome to take a look. If you think there's any chance it might help, we should go down there. There are a couple things on her desk, but I'm pretty sure they're just some personal files they sifted out."

Andrew followed Bill as they made their way down into the basement. It was dark, damp, and had a low ceiling. As Bill flipped on the light in the main rec room, another treasure trove of children's toys was revealed.

"It's right back here," Bill said as he opened the door to Becky's office. Other than a computer, a monitor, and a couple folders, the desk was clean. A printer, a couple knickknacks, and some framed photos of the girls adorned the credenza. Bill opened the drawers in the desk and file cabinet.

"See, not much left. Just some files here," Bill said, motioning at the corner of the desk. "But please, feel free to take a look around."

Andrew sat down in the desk chair and thumbed through the stack of folders on the desk. Nothing.

"Is this Becky's laptop?"

"No, that one is ours. Becky had her work laptop with her."

As Andrew looked over at the printer, he saw one of IFM's notorious asset tags. They were plastered all over headquarters. "What about this printer?"

"That's IFM's. Becky got the printer and the monitor when she became a director. Apparently it's standard issue for directors to have home office equipment. Becky was so proud."

"Pretty nice equipment—a 27-inch monitor and that multifunction printer looks like it can do everything. Anything to keep the IFM employees working harder, I guess. Why didn't IFM pick this stuff up when they were here?"

"I don't know. I was in such a daze I didn't even think about it. I guess I should pack it up and give them a call."

Andrew continued to glance through the files in the credenza with no luck. Bill decided to get the computer equipment ready and unplugged the monitor and tightly wrapped up the power and display cords. As he moved over to the printer, Bill stopped short, like he'd just remembered something.

"Wait! Last week, before the crash, Becky asked me to scan something for her. She forgot some papers and needed a copy of them ASAP."

"Where are they?"

"Well, the originals were in a folder on top of her desk. IFM must have packed them up. But I scanned them right after Becky called. I didn't want to forget, so I did it right after the girls finished breakfast."

"Do you have a copy?"

"I should. They should be in my sent mail." Bill sat down and turned on the laptop. As Andrew anxiously watched, Bill slowly made his way through the files. "I can't seem to find the file, but I know it was attached to the e-mail I sent Becky...Oh wait, here it is..."

"Can you print out a copy?"

"Sure."

Within moments, the printer clicked then hummed as the jets deposited their droplets of ink across the page. Andrew picked up the three sheets as they were printed and started to read furiously.

"Becky was right," Andrew muttered to himself. "There was an early set of trials for Galileo, and the results weren't good."

"What?" Bill asked.

"It's a long story, Bill, but I think I may have found something here. I want to check with Chloe about it, but this could be the missing piece of information."

"Chloe? Really? Will this get Becky in any trouble? I know it shouldn't matter, but work was Becky's life."

"No, it won't. Don't worry."

"Do you think it's somehow related to the crash?"

"I don't know. But I promise, I'll keep Becky's name out of it."

Andrew folded the papers and stuffed them in his back pocket. "Let's finish getting dinner on the table."

After heating up the last plate, Andrew placed some berries and salad on the side.

"You sure you guys can't join us?" Bill asked.

"No, Lydia and I try to be punctual with each other." Andrew glanced down at his watch. "Shoot, we're already going to be late." He started patting himself down. "Oh, I must have left my phone in the car. I'll call her when we leave, but we've really gotta get going."

"Okay, but promise you'll come over for dinner again soon and stay next time."

"That would be great," Andrew replied.

Bill and Andrew walked back to the front room. Ethan was wearing a silver crown and a purple feather boa, and he was holding a clear wand filled with glitter and sparkles.

"Looking good there, buddy," Andrew said, smiling at Ethan.

"Thanks, Dad."

"We need to get going. Say good-bye to Lizzie and Maureen."

The girls started holding onto Ethan and wouldn't let him go.

"Girls, come on. We don't want Ethan to be late." Bill picked up Lizzie and held Maureen's hand while Ethan quickly stood up, brushed himself off, and morphed back into himself. "Thanks again for coming over, Ethan. You've been a real sport."

"Oh, it was fun. I miss not having any brothers or sisters."

"Bill, sorry we have to get going so quickly here. Know we are here to help out whenever we can. Okay?"

"Thanks, Andrew. You've been a great help and a real friend."

Ethan and Andrew waved good-bye as they made a quick exit and jumped into the car.

THIRTEEN

IFM Headquarters
Thursday, June 10
4:00 P.M.

T HE MARKETING PLANS presentation to the division leadership team went well. Andrew was disappointed that Dan and Chloe couldn't attend, but he understood how an urgent meeting called by Aidan Toole could easily trump his meeting.

Chloe's failure to even respond to his calls was odd, but once Andrew got in the zone for his meeting, there was no stopping him. The deck was tight and had great flow. Andrew was articulate, sold his ideas well, and anticipated every question. Andrew wished Dan had been there to see it happen. During the meeting, he was no wounded warrior. He commanded the room's attention. He was convincing and powerful. It was a promotion-worthy presentation.

As the Snack's Division leadership team thanked Andrew for his hard work, the weight of the world lifted off of him. It was Andrew's last meeting before vacation, and all that stood between him and Hawaii were some errands and coffee with Heidi. Tomorrow evening, he and Ethan would be on their way to two weeks of fun.

To celebrate the successful end of the marketing plan season, the team headed out to Lord Fletcher's Old Lake Lodge for an impromptu happy hour. Only ten minutes from headquarters, Fletcher's was a Lake Minnetonka classic. Nestled along the north shore, the marina, bar, restaurant paradise was popular among young and old alike. Over thirty team members joined in on the celebration, a tribute to Andrew's popularity with the team, but free drinks and appetizers on the lake sure didn't hurt. What could be better on a sunny, Minnesota afternoon?

Lord Fletcher's staff loved IFM happy hours since there was always lots of food, drink, and big tips. IFM employees were also responsible customers for the most part, although there was a nasty rumor that one of the senior VPs who regularly drank too much at Fletcher's was kindly asked to never come back after he almost ran over a parking attendant and then clipped a stop sign when driving off one night.

The party was still going strong at six, and Andrew was having a great time. Karaoke was getting started, and although he wasn't typically one to get up and sing, Lourdes cajoled him into a group performance of the B-52's classic "Love Shack," something he was going to regret for sure, especially since some team members had their phones out filming the whole thing.

By nine, however, their party had dwindled down to only a handful. Andrew, Lourdes, and Rachel were ready to go. While Andrew had paced himself, having only two beers over the past six hours, Drake Phillips, the B-Lean Snacks Product Sales Manager, had been hitting it pretty hard. As they walked out to the parking lot, Andrew was convinced that Drake shouldn't be driving.

"Hey, Drake, why don't you let us drive you home?" asked Andrew. "I brought Lourdes and Rachel, so I can just drop you off after we stop by headquarters."

"No, no, I'm fine," Drake muttered.

Andrew, Lourdes, and Rachel exchanged glances. They all agreed. He was in no shape to drive.

"Seriously, Drake, you shouldn't be driving. Let us take you home."

"Hey, man, I can't. I need my car. I'm heading out to Milwaukee in the morning for a wedding. I have to be there by noon for golf with the groomsmen."

Andrew rolled his eyes and ran his hands through his hair. He really didn't want to deal with this, but he knew it wasn't right to let a drunken team member drive. So he tried again.

"Okay, Drake, what if I drive your car home? Lourdes, you can just drive my car back to IFM, and I'll cab it over from Drake's place."

"That's crazy, Andrew," Lourdes replied. "What if we just follow you over to Drake's, then you can drive us all back to IFM? Drake, you live over by the Carlson Towers, right?"

"Yep, not too far away," he slurred.

"Okay," Andrew replied, giving Lourdes his keys. "Just follow me. Hopefully Drake here won't get us lost."

Drake and Andrew made their way over to Drake's car. Andrew started it up, pulled out of the parking spot, and hesitated at the exit, looking over his shoulder to where he had parked his car. He saw the taillights of his car glow red and then white as Lourdes put the car into reverse. Suddenly, in a flash of light, the hood blew into the air with an explosive boom, and the car was engulfed in flames. Fiery debris lit the sky and streamed down, flaming briefly, then smoldering on the ground.

Andrew jumped out of Drake's car and ran toward the wreckage.

"Lourdes...oh my God...Rachel!"

As he got closer, the heat became so intense that he was forced to stop. Andrew stood there helplessly, shaking, holding his head in his hands.

Fletcher's emptied as customers flooded into the parking lot to gawk at the blazing, bright yellow fire. Within minutes, sirens blared and lights flashed as the police and Navarre Fire Department arrived. Firefighters quickly attacked the flames, and police cordoned off the area, moving Andrew back forcefully to a safe distance.

FORTY MINUTES LATER, Andrew sat in the back of an ambulance. Although unharmed, he was having trouble calming down enough to fill the police in on the events leading up to the explosion.

As much as he tried, he couldn't figure it out. Why did this happen? Were there any survivors? How could there have been? Lourdes and Rachel might as well have been holding a bomb in their laps from the size of the explosion.

The paramedic handed Andrew a bottle of water, and he took a couple of sips. Andrew continued staring out into the night as another officer sat down next to him.

"Andrew Hastings?" asked the officer.

"Yes, sir."

"My name is Officer Laetner. I understand that it was your car?"

"Yes, it was. Do you have any idea why it exploded?"

"I'm sorry, I don't. It will probably take a while for us to figure it out."

"Okay."

"We're trying to get hold of the victims' families. Do you have any contact information?"

"I'm sorry, I don't," Andrew replied flatly. *The victims*, he thought. *More victims*. "They were both coworkers of mine. I'm sure IFM has some family contact information on file."

"Thanks. Can you wait here one moment?" the officer asked.

"Sure."

The policeman and paramedic walked over to the officer's car, talked briefly, and returned.

"We have a couple options here, Mr. Hastings. Do you have any family nearby?"

"Yes, my son. He's at his mom's house tonight."

"Your wife?"

"No, I'm divorced."

"Okay, well, we could also take you over to Methodist Hospital and have them check you out."

"Why? I'm not hurt."

"I know, but you're obviously in shock. It'd just be good to have someone who can keep an eye on you."

Andrew nodded. "How about a friend's house?"

"Sure," replied the officer. "I'd like to call ahead and make sure they're home."

"Her name is Katie Burke. She's my next door neighbor."

Andrew reached into his pocket for his phone and gave the officer Katie's number. Along with his phone, Andrew had pulled out several folded sheets of paper. It was the Galileo trials information. As he unfolded the papers, he shook his head and stuffed them back into his pocket with his phone.

The officer stepped away for a couple minutes, and then returned. "I'm going to take you over to Ms. Burke's home. She's waiting for you."

———————————

THE BACK OF THE POLICE car was clean. Andrew stared out the windows.

"Can you open a window for some fresh air?" Andrew asked.

"Here ya go," the officer replied.

The wind felt good on his face, and with each breath, his mind came back into focus. Soon it was racing. Reaching into his pocket he pulled out the Galileo trial information again. *Why's all this happening?* he thought. *All these deaths can't be an accident.* Then in a flash it finally hit him. *That bomb was intended for me.*

As the officer turned into his neighborhood, Andrew put the papers back into his pocket and pulled out his phone. He wasn't sure if someone was following his every move, but if they were, their job was about to get a whole lot harder. He slipped the phone between the seat cushions of the cop's car.

Katie and her husband came out to the car as the police officer drove into the Burkes' driveway.

"We're here," said the officer.

"Thanks."

As Andrew and the officer got out of the car, Katie came up to Andrew and gave him a big hug.

"Are you okay?"

"I'm fine."

"Mr. Hastings, an officer will call you tomorrow with an update and a complete accident report for your insurance."

"Thanks."

Andrew followed the Burkes into their home, and when the door closed, he said, "I need to take a shower. Can I use yours?"

A bit taken aback, Katie replied, "Of course. Let's get you set up in our guest bathroom."

As they walked upstairs, Andrew asked, "Do you have a robe and maybe some old clothes of Roy's I could borrow?"

"Oh, yes. I'm not sure how well they will fit you, but we can find something." Katie left Andrew by the bedroom door. "I'll be right back."

Andrew's mind was still racing. *How am I going to do this?* he thought. Before Katie returned, he carefully removed the Galileo trials report from his pocket, stripped down to his boxers, and then threw his clothes into a pile on the other side of the room. He didn't want to take any chances. Surveillance technology was getting smaller all the time. Who knew what kind of devices might be planted on or around him. He went into the bathroom and turned on the shower, hoping the rushing sounds of water might further muffle any listening device.

"Okay, here we go," Katie said as she turned into the guest room and glanced into the bathroom. "Oh my, I'm sorry. I didn't realize you'd already undressed."

Andrew pulled Katie into the bathroom, grabbed the robe from her hands, and closed the door. "Katie, listen to me very carefully. I need your help. I know you're going to think I'm crazy, but someone tried to kill me tonight. That's why my coworkers are dead. I don't have much time. Go get Roy, and come back here."

"What?"

"Please, go get Roy."

Frightened, but still calm, Katie opened the bathroom door and quickly ran downstairs. After returning with Roy, they all three crowded into the steamy bathroom, and Andrew closed the door.

"What's going on?" Roy asked. "Why are we all standing in my guest bathroom with the shower running and you dressed in my robe?"

"I need your help, Roy. I'm in trouble." Andrew held up the folded pages from his pocket. "I don't know why, but everyone who has known about this information has been killed in the past week or so. Maybe I'm just being paranoid, but I don't want anybody listening to our conversation, and this is the best way I could make that happen on such short notice."

"Andrew, you don't really think somebody is spying on you and trying to kill you, do you?"

"Katie, ask yourself, how often do you see your car just blow up? Then add to that, how often does your coworker's plane explode in mid-air? It's just too coincidental, especially when you add in this information I have in my hand."

"What's in the papers?" Roy asked.

"I don't want to tell you. I don't want you or Katie any more involved than you have to be."

"I've still got some friends in the Minneapolis Police Department. Do you want me to call them?" asked Roy.

Andrew thought for a second. The Galileo trial results proved nothing. It might derail the Redu approval, but he had no proof of wrongdoing and no solid evidence that someone was trying to murder him. "I don't think they can help me. Right now all I have are some coincidences and these papers. I can't prove they're linked."

"Well, the police can take your statement, and depending on what you've got, they may start an investigation," Roy replied.

Andrew shook his head. "And in the meantime? I'm sure someone wants to hurt me." Then in a sudden flash of panic, Andrew looked up. "Oh my God. If they've done any homework at all, they know Ethan is my world. He's in danger, too."

Roy and Katie looked at each other. Katie's eyes darted back and forth. Before Roy could say anything, Katie asked, "So what can we do?"

"I need you to help us disappear."

FOURTEEN

**Plymouth, Minnesota
Thursday, June 10
11:00 P.M.**

THE BURKES WALKED next door with Andrew to his house. Roy flipped on the lights, Katie turned on some music, and Andrew went to work.

Five minutes later, there was a knock on the door. It was the Goldwaters, neighbors and mutual friends of Katie, Roy, and Andrew. Katie gave them a hug and welcomed them in. She repeated the same excuse she had made over the phone. Andrew wanted some company, and she explained what happened at Lord Fletcher's. Over the next twenty minutes, six couples Katie had called from the neighborhood dropped in. It wasn't the usual Minnesota get together, but tonight was not just any ordinary night.

Andrew worked silently in the basement. He had already gathered a tent, sleeping bag, the suitcases and backpacks that were packed for Hawaii, and the bike and its pump from the garage. He started rummaging through his storage area. He knew it was in there, but he grew anxious as every second ticked by, hoping the entertainment upstairs would buy him more time.

Finally he found it—the Burley bike trailer. Ethan hadn't ridden in it since he was five, but Andrew wasn't thinking of using it for that. He wanted it to hold some gear. With a little air, it should work. Quickly, Andrew attached the trailer to his bike and pumped up the tires. After loading the gear and strapping on his backpack, Andrew clipped on his helmet and was ready to go.

Then, as the voices and shuffle of feet from the party sounded above him, he lined up the bike and trailer so it was a straight shot out the basement door. With a deep breath, he opened the door, jumped on his bike, and peddled with all his might.

The darkness was unnerving, not only for fear of what might be out there watching and waiting for him, but also for concern over accidentally riding into a ditch or getting in a wreck. But Andrew had made a well-worn path to the Luce Line over the years, and within a moment he could see the trail ahead. The weight of the Burley made the bike unruly, and as he climbed the hill up to the trail bed, he realized he didn't have enough speed. Scared and frustrated, Andrew hopped off the bike, and with all his might, he dragged it and the trailer up the incline and onto the crushed limestone trail.

Once on level ground, he got back on his bike. Andrew's heart pounded, and he breathed hard as he peddled like he never had before, unsure if he'd been seen. He continued at an aggressive pace until finally he cut north and headed toward Baker Park. Andrew knew the park well. He and Ethan had camped there many times. His goal this visit was very different.

Once Andrew made it to the park, he gathered some dry branches and twigs to make a small fire. By the dim, flickering light, he set up his tent, and then dug though his backpack in search of a notepad and pen. His escape into the night appeared to have worked, but his mind couldn't rest—at least not until he knew Ethan was safe.

He started making lists, jotting down notes, and trying to think of everything he had to do in the next twenty-four hours.

For now all he wanted was to escape with Ethan to some place safe. He could figure out a more detailed plan later.

Finally, at three o'clock, Andrew set his travel alarm clock, inched down into his sleeping bag, and tried to close his eyes. Images of the explosion tortured him. How could Lourdes and Rachel be gone? It wasn't fair. More devastated families mourning their loss. In that moment Andrew realized he couldn't attend any funerals or truly mourn the loss of his friends. For now, striking back was the name of the game. Whoever did this had to be stopped.

FIFTEEN

T HE FIRST GLIMPSES OF SUNLIGHT inched over the horizon shortly before five. After getting up, Andrew packed up his stuff and grabbed a granola bar from his backpack.

Determined to avoid his neighborhood and paths near IFM, Andrew headed east on Highway 6 and picked up the Luce Line a couple miles east of his house. From there, Andrew biked over to Theo Wirth Park, where he followed trails south to Lake Calhoun. A couple blocks west of the lake, Andrew found some dense bushes to hide his bike and trailer. Then, he walked down to the jogging paths and waited.

With so many IFM employees living nearby, Andrew did his best to remain inconspicuous. He wore a cap on his head with the bill set low to cover his eyes. Also, rather than just stand out by the path, he picked a nearby tree and stretched his hamstrings and quads tirelessly.

It was definitely a gamble whether Josh would be out running this morning, but Andrew was willing to take the odds. The weather report had called for rain from noon into the evening, so if Josh were going to get in his run today, it would have to be now.

Shortly before seven, as Andrew leaned into the tree for the hundredth time, he saw a jogger who looked like Josh. The gait, the shoes, the hair, the pace — it all matched. As the figure got closer, Andrew started to jog, taking it slow at first to make sure the man would pass him.

Just as the runner caught up to him, Andrew looked quickly to his left, confirmed it was Josh, and said, "Hey man, it's Andrew. Keep running. Don't stop or say anything. Just keep going. I need your help."

"Andrew…What the heck…You okay?"

"Don't talk yet. Lourdes and Rachel were blown up in my car. We may both be in big danger."

Josh listened in disbelief as Andrew told him the details of the past twenty-four hours. As they neared the southwest edge of the lake, Andrew took them off the lake path, and they ran along some side streets in a residential neighborhood. There were less people on this route, and it would be easier to tell if they were being tailed.

"Do you think we're being followed?" asked Josh.

"Maybe," Andrew replied. "I hope not. If they were following me, I hope I lost them last night, but we can't take any chances."

"I'd do anything for you, Andrew. How can I help?"

Andrew pulled a cord from around his neck. Attached to it was a travel documents holder. "Here. I made a list of what I need. I know this is asking a lot. The stuff on here isn't cheap. I need it today, but I promise I'll pay you back."

"I'm not worried about that," Josh said as he started to scan the list. "Wow, I'm gonna be busy."

"Yeah, about that. You've got to go into work. Everyone knows we're best friends, so they may be watching you, too. You need to act like everything is normal, so you can't be doing this from work. But maybe you go into work a little late and then finish the rest this afternoon. I don't know."

"Don't worry. I'll find a way to get this done."

"Did you see the notes about the car?"

"Yeah. You need the car parked by Minnehaha Falls by two o'clock and keys dropped off in an envelope at the Egg & I by one. I'll need to start on that item first."

"Thanks."

"Do you have a plan, Andrew?"

"I'm working on it. My first step is to get Ethan out of town safely."

"That's great, but you know, you can't do this alone, especially with Ethan. Let me help."

Andrew thought for a moment. "What if you join Ethan and me this weekend? You can help me come up with a plan?"

"Perfect. I know just the place, too. Remember my uncle's hunting lodge up north?"

"Yeah, we went up there a couple years ago with Heidi," replied Andrew.

"Maybe we could go up there? It's private and isolated."

"Josh, that would be great."

"Done. Let me make a couple calls to make sure it's free. If it's not, I'll come up with a Plan B and leave a message with the car keys. Either way, I'll give you directions to where we're going."

"Josh, thank you, but…remember. Whoever is doing this, is watching. We have to assume they'll be trying to follow you, too. Use another car, not your regular one. Don't bring your cell phone, they're so easy to track, and then make some stops along the way, to make sure you aren't being tailed."

"I'll be careful. Now get going, and be safe. I'll see you later tonight. Deal?"

"It's a deal."

Plymouth, Minnesota
Friday, June 11
8:00 A.M.

KATIE ARRIVED at Lydia's house promptly at eight o'clock. Although she tried to act normal, it was hard after the previous night. Katie gave Ethan a big squeeze as Lydia walked up.

"If I didn't know better, I'd think you two hadn't seen each other in months."

Laughing it off, Katie said, "Well, sometimes a night without this guy seems like an eternity."

"You're telling me. I don't know how I'm going to survive without him for the next two weeks. Going to Hawaii without me!"

"Mom..." Ethan said sternly.

"I know. I told you. I'm happy you and your dad are going," Lydia said, trying her best to be supportive.

"Well, I don't know who is going to miss you more, your mom or me," Katie interjected. "But I'm sure you'll have a great time with your dad."

"I've got to get to the bank, honey," Lydia said, grabbing her purse and another oversized bag. "I'll be home by five o'clock so we can check in before your dad picks you up."

"Okay, Mom. Have a great day." Ethan kissed his mom good-bye.

"I love you, sweetie."

"Love you too, Mom."

As Lydia pulled her car out of the driveway, Ethan returned to the television.

"Where do you think you're going, buster?"

"I thought we could just relax this morning."

"Sorry. I've got a surprise for you this morning."

"Really? Am I going to like it?"

"I know you will. Let's get all your stuff together."

Within five minutes, Katie and Ethan were on their way. As they pulled out of the driveway, Katie turned off her cell phone. At Andrew's request, she was driving Roy's car, and she was to use only cash. She carefully watched out her rearview mirror to see if they were being followed. Even if they were, Katie was ready. Between the history museum, the science museum, and all the twists and turns she planned in downtown St. Paul, she was determined nobody could follow her today.

Minneapolis, Minnesota
Friday, June 11
10:00 A.M.

ANDREW SPENT the morning in a dive motel near Uptown. He didn't expect much from the room, and it delivered. It fit his only requirements — the front desk accepted cash and didn't ask for ID. All he really needed was a place to stay out of sight, store his stuff, and make an important phone call.

Sitting down on the edge of the bed, Andrew picked up the hotel phone and dialed a number scribbled on the back of an envelope.

After several rings, a voiced answered, "Hello, Donny Dahl speaking."

"Yes, Donny, my name is Andrew Hastings. My neighbor, Roy Burke, gave me your name. He said you two used to work together in the Minneapolis Police Department."

"Of course. How's Roy doing?"

"He's well," Andrew replied, but he was in no mood to chit chat. "Roy said you might be able to help me out with something."

"Sure. What's going on? Wife cheating on you?"

"No, no. Nothing like that. I just want to find out if my house is bugged."

"That should be easy enough. Who do you think is listening?"

"That's a long story, and I don't have a lot of time right now. Whoever it is will probably have some pretty advanced technology. My address is 16250 9th Avenue North in Plymouth. How soon can you get out there?"

"Well, it's Friday. How about early next week?"

"No, it has to be sooner, like right now."

"Tomorrow morning first thing is the best I can do, and that'll cost extra."

"That's fine. I assume you can let yourself in without a key. I'll follow up with you in the morning."

THE RAIN STARTED shortly before noon. Andrew thought about calling a cab. He had the cash, but he finally decided it was better to bike around the city. The less contact he had with other people, the better. So, at quarter till one, he pulled out a rain jacket from his luggage and biked over to the Egg & I. Mike Brayley, the owner, had become friends with Josh and Andrew over the years. Brunch at the Egg & I was a tradition after a hard Sunday morning run. So when Andrew walked in, Mike greeted him with a handshake and a warm cup of coffee.

"Wet day to be biking there?"

"I know. Anything to get in some extra exercise, I guess."

"Really? I saw you on the news this morning. They had a whole story about your accident over at Fletcher's. Are you okay?"

Andrew's face turned pale. "Yeah. I'm okay."

"They said two women died in the explosion. Is that right?"

"Yes…" Andrew hesitated.

"Oh man, that's horrible."

"I know, Mike. It is. I thought some exercise would help take my mind off of it. Anyway, Josh arranged for an envelope to be dropped off here for me. I hope you don't mind."

"No, of course not. I've got it right here," Mike said, handing over a large white envelope. "Sorry for the questions. Just wanted to make sure you're okay since you look like hell."

"Thanks, Mike. I'm going to be fine. I just need to get away for a while. My son and I are going to Hawaii, so that should do the trick."

"Fun. That should take your mind off your troubles."

"I hope. I can't wait. I gotta run here, but thanks for the envelope. See you when I get back."

"Yeah. Sure. Take care, man."

As Andrew left the diner, he zipped the envelope into his rain jacket and put on his helmet, and then he biked on to the park.

MINNEHAHA PARK was empty. The rain had kept almost everyone away. A barbecue was going on by one of the pavilions, but as Andrew glanced over, he saw dozens of people gloomily huddled under a shelter and guessed it was some forced-fun company event.

The light crowd made finding the car Josh arranged much easier. Andrew took the envelope from his jacket, ripped it open, and as he tilted it slightly, a key slid out. After pressing the unlock button on the remote, he shook his head and laughed. He should have expected as much from Josh. The lights blinked on a black Acura MDX.

Without wasting any time, Andrew loaded up his bike, stripped off his jacket, got into the front seat, and turned on the car. Cold and wet, he turned on the heat, and then he looked in the white envelope.

Inside he found a map with directions and a note that said, "Lodge is available. Garage code is 5197. Key is in a clay flowerpot on the garage shelf. See you tonight. Be safe."

SIXTEEN

St. Paul, Minnesota
Friday, June 11
3:55 P.M.

IT WAS TOUGH for Andrew to be out of contact with Katie all day. He knew it was for the best, but all he wanted to do was make sure they were okay. After stopping back by the motel to pick up his gear, he shopped for supplies at Walgreens, and then drove to St. Paul. There he waited in a parking deck at a downtown hotel. Finally, a few minutes before four, Andrew pulled into the Science Museum's parking lot. As he turned the corner and saw the glass enclosure by the elevators, Andrew's prayers were answered. Katie and Ethan were standing there, waiting.

Quickly pulling up in the car, he jumped out and gave Ethan a big hug. "Hi, buddy. How's it going?"

"Good. Katie and I had a fun day. We were all over St. Paul."

"I know. I can't wait to hear all about it. Go ahead and get inside."

As Ethan climbed in, Katie put a bag of stuff in the backseat and closed the door.

"Katie, I don't know how I'll ever be able to thank you."

"Just come back soon. If we can do anything, let me know. Okay?"

"Thanks. Now here's a note for Lydia. Can you give it to her?"

"Sure. I can also try to explain," replied Katie.

"No, please don't. The note will do. You've already stuck your neck out far enough for me."

"Okay, I understand. You have me worried, Andrew."

"I'm sorry, Katie. I just want to be careful."

"I know you do. I promise, not a word to Lydia. I'll try to do my best to calm her down."

"Thanks, Katie. Hope to talk with you soon." Andrew hugged Katie good-bye.

He jumped back into the car, and before he could even fasten his seat belt, Ethan asked, "What's going on, Dad?"

"Can you hold that question for just a little bit? Why don't you find some music on the radio?"

"Whose car is this?"

"Ethan, I need your help. I'll tell you more, but for right now, we need to get out of here, and I need to concentrate on driving."

Ethan was good at reading his father. He could feel the intensity, and he knew his dad wasn't joking around. Andrew exited the parking ramp and maneuvered through downtown traffic. Determined to free himself from the gridlock, he changed lanes and strategies every few seconds. Finally, out of frustration, he decided to try the GPS. He was reluctant to use it at first, but surely there was no way it could be traced to him. After plugging in their destination and choosing off-roads, he felt he had done all he could to avoid the worst part of the bottlenecks. Finally, after thirty more minutes, they turned onto Highway 10. It was busy, too, but getting up north on a rainy, Friday night in the summer was slow no matter which way you went.

As they started to leave the metro area, Andrew knew it was time to come clean with Ethan. He didn't want to scare him, but he had to tell him some basics.

"How about dinner, buddy?" Andrew asked. "This GPS system says there's a drive-in restaurant right around the corner."

Ethan smiled tentatively. "Sure, I'm hungry."

Andrew turned into the parking lot and then pulled up alongside one of the speakers. After placing their orders, Andrew rolled the window back up and apologized.

"Sorry I've been so cranky, Ethan."

"Are you okay, Dad?"

"Yes, but I need to be honest. We're in danger. Something horrible has happened, and I'm not sure who's behind it, but we're going to be okay."

For the next thirty minutes, Andrew told Ethan what had happened, and Ethan peppered his dad with questions. Andrew tried to keep the explanations simple, but there were so many unknowns. Some of it made sense, but Andrew just didn't know who was behind the plane crash or the car bombing that killed Lourdes and Rachel. They were going to come up with a plan, though, and Josh was going to help them figure it out.

"What about Mom? Does she know? Is she going to be safe?" Ethan asked.

Andrew knew the question was coming. "I gave Katie a note to give to your mom. I told her someone tried to kill me last night. I couldn't tell her much more, or she might be in danger, too."

Ethan looked more worried. "Do you think she'll be okay?"

"I think so. As long as she listens to what I wrote."

"Since when has Mom listened to you, Dad?"

"I know." Andrew paused. "Hey, as soon as we have a plan and I know we're safe, we'll call her. I promise."

"Okay. What about Hawaii?"

"Hawaii will have to wait. We have our whole lives to make that trip. Today we just need to make sure we're safe."

Andrew reached over the console and squeezed Ethan's hand.

"It's all going to be okay. I promise."

Andrew wished he felt as confident as he sounded, but he had to reassure Ethan. Hope was all they had at the moment, and Andrew clung to it with all his might.

Leech Lake, Minnesota
Friday, June 11
10:00 P.M.

BETWEEN THE TRAFFIC and a dinner stop, the drive up north had taken longer than expected. Andrew and Ethan drove onto the peninsula around ten o'clock, after crossing a small, concrete bridge that provided reliable, year-round access from the mainland. Except for a sliver of moonlight, it was pitch black, and Andrew drove very slowly. When he spotted two buildings up ahead, he parked the car right where he was and grabbed the flashlight from his bag.

"Come on, let's go find the key."

When they opened the car doors, the sounds of all sorts of bugs surrounded them. Andrew flipped on his flashlight and pointed it toward a building on the left.

"I think the garage is over here," Andrew declared.

After fumbling around for a while, they opened the garage, found the key to the house, and unlocked the front door. Andrew felt inside the door and finally flipped a set of switches. Spotlights lit up all around the house, illuminating the main foyer. Inside, a magnificent slate hallway greeted them with a dozen wooden cubbies lining one wall and several locked gun racks and cabinets on the other.

"Wow, they must do some serious hunting here," Ethan said.

"Yes, they do," Andrew replied as he led Ethan through the main hall of lockers and past the guns. In front of them was another door that led outside. Through the sidelights they could see a screened-in back porch and beyond it, lots of green grass lit by the outdoor spotlights.

"If I remember correctly, the living room and kitchen are over here to the left." As they turned, Andrew flipped the switches by the doorway, and a magnificent two-story, vaulted living room, kitchen, and eating area came to life. The walls were paneled in knotty pine and adorned with prized heads of moose, elk, and deer. The focal point of the living room was a huge stone fireplace that climbed up to the ceiling. Leather chairs and sofas provided plentiful seating in front of the fireplace, and a huge weathered, wool rug stretched across the floor and added subtle charm and rustic sophistication to the room. Playing cards, poker chips, and other board games sat nearby, and the room evoked images of relaxing, laughter-filled evenings spent by the fire.

Beyond the living room were the kitchen and main eating area. The kitchen was equipped like a small restaurant and boasted a huge island, granite counter tops with rough hewn edges, over-sized appliances, and distressed cherry cabinetry. To the right of the kitchen was a long, rectangular table with two benches on either side. Capable of seating twenty people, it created a sense of grand simplicity.

"Dad, this place is awesome. What's up there?" Ethan pointed up a massive staircase made of pine timbers that led up to a cat-walk with railing that extended across the entire room.

"Those are the bedrooms."

"Can we check them out?"

"Why don't we bring in our bags, and you can choose a room for us."

"You sure Josh won't mind?"

"I'm sure."

After getting settled, Andrew and Ethan explored the lodge a little more before getting ready for bed. They prayed as they did every night, but Ethan added a special request to keep them all safe, including his mom.

———————

ANDREW PACED BY THE FRONT DOOR, peering out the windows every minute or two, looking for Josh. It was well past one o'clock, and he had expected him by midnight at the latest. Getting more nervous by the moment, Andrew glanced over to the gun cabinets, wondering where the keys were. He hadn't shot a gun since he took riflery in camp when he was a kid, but with the right motivation, he was sure he could do just about anything.

Andrew went back into the living room and turned on the television, attempting to distract himself by flipping through the channels. As he halfheartedly stared at a Shamwow infomercial, the sound of footsteps on the wooden deck outside attracted his attention.

As the front door squeaked open, he heard, "Hello. Andrew?" Heidi came from around the corner and saw Andrew standing in shock. "Surprised?"

"Yeah, to say the least."

"Well, I couldn't just let you stand me up for our coffee date."

"Heidi, I'm so sorry. I just didn't want—"

Heidi interrupted. "No need to explain. I chased down Josh. He filled me in. Now let me give you a hug."

Heidi set down her bags and gave Andrew a big hug. As she held him close, she reached up to his shoulders and then stroked the back of his head and neck.

"Thanks for coming," Andrew whispered.

As they slowly let go, Heidi looked up into Andrew's blue eyes. "So, how's Ethan?"

"He's okay. He fell asleep upstairs a while ago."

"Poor guy. A lot to take in for sure."

"Yeah, it is. And I know he's worried about his mom. To be honest, I am, too," Andrew laughed nervously. "Bet you never thought you'd hear me say that."

"Oh, I know you don't want anything bad to happen to Lydia. She's Ethan's mom, after all."

"So where's Josh?"

"He should be here soon. We drove separately. I think my interfering slowed him down. He insisted on playing a game of secret agent to make sure nobody was watching or listening to us."

"Really?"

"Yeah, really. Two different bars, passing notes, no cell phones, the whole deal."

"Good for him," Andrew replied.

"You know, last night when I heard about your car exploding, I tried to call you, but you didn't answer."

"Yeah, I ditched my phone before I got home."

"Then, when you didn't show for coffee, I gave Josh a call at work."

Just then, the front door opened again. "Hello," Josh exclaimed. "You'd think someone would lock these doors with all the crime out here."

"Well speak of the devil," said Heidi.

"Can somebody help me out here? I've got my hands full."

"Yeah, yeah, here we come, Josh," replied Andrew as he and Heidi headed for the front door.

"Boy, you're right, you do have your hands full," said Heidi.

Andrew grabbed several bags from Josh's arms, and Heidi gave Josh a hug.

"How was your trip up?" Heidi asked.

"Uneventful, thank goodness."

"Well, that's good. Listen, I'm going to grab a room upstairs and wash up. I'm sure you guys have some catching up to do."

Heidi ran upstairs, and after setting down the bags, Josh came over to Andrew and reached his arm around him.

"Hey there. Good to see you. How's Ethan?"

"Safe, asleep, but anxious for sure."

"Well, that's normal. I'd think he was crazy if all this didn't have him a bit wound up."

"Yeah, you're right. Thanks for the surprise by the way."

"Huh?"

"Ah, Heidi?"

"Oh yeah. Well, there was no way to call you and ask. Anyway, she was determined to come up here."

"Kind of like old times?" said Andrew.

"Sorta..."

"So you sure you weren't followed?"

"It would have taken a miracle, Andrew. Per your instructions, all cell phones were left at home, and I borrowed some cars for Heidi and me from my dad. I watched my rearview mirror like a hawk, and I know Heidi said she would do the same. How did your trip go?"

"Good. I didn't see anyone following us either. We stopped for dinner, and I was watching the road, too. Oh yeah, thanks for the car. Pretty nice ride."

"Oh, that. I know the guys at that dealership. It was my best bet to get you a car fast with no real names on the license tag or registration."

"Well, thanks."

Josh walked over to the dining room table and started to unpack the bags he had accumulated.

"Looks like you have been busy shopping."

"Well, you gave me quite the list. I was lucky, though. After our half-day Friday at work, I stopped by my dad's house to set up the logistics for the cars. Anyway, his assistant was there, and she offered to do all this legwork for me."

"Did you tell her anything?"

"No, I just said it was all graduation and wedding gifts for friends. Pretty good cover, huh?"

"Wow, you're a pretty great gift giver," replied Andrew as they emptied the bags. Once again, Josh had purchased top of the line stuff. What must have been over $10,000 in gear lay on the table.

"So why did you buy four laptops and iPhones? I only asked for two."

"Well, by the time I went over to Dad's, I already knew Heidi was on my trail. Then I thought, well I can't leave Ethan out, so I bought a couple extras just in case. You know, Heidi could be a real asset for us. She's a reporter, for God's sake. This detective work is her job."

"I know, I know. I just hate to get her involved."

"Andrew, you know she isn't going to walk away. Anyway, you could be sitting on the story of a lifetime. You think she's going to miss out on that?"

"Yeah, you're right," Andrew said, still not quite sold on the idea. "So what's in this bag over here?"

"About $30,000."

"Really?" Andrew opened up the paper bag and poured it out on the table. "Wow, I don't think I've ever seen this much cash anywhere."

"Well, I stopped at two banks, and my dad's assistant went to one. We only withdrew $9,000 in cash from each bank to avoid that cash transaction reporting thing. Dad's assistant also got ten VISA check cards with $500 each on them."

"We should be set for money."

"Yep. One less thing to worry about."

As Heidi came downstairs, she saw the stacks of twenty-dollar bills on the table.

"What's going on here, a drug deal?"

"Just some cash for Andrew to help keep him invisible for a while."

"Boy, you guys have been thinking ahead. You ready to get to work on a plan? It's still early, not even two o'clock yet."

Andrew yawned and replied, "I think we should start fresh in the morning. I could barely sleep at all last night, so I've been up for over forty hours."

Heidi considered giving Andrew a hard time, but as she looked at him, she could see he was fading fast. "Yeah, I think you're right. We could all use some sleep."

SEVENTEEN

IFM Headquarters
Saturday, June 12
7:15 A.M.

"WHAT THE HELL is going on?" asked Chloe. "I practically handed the guy over to you. Instead you kill two of his coworkers. What kind of operation are you running?"

Laura Long shook her head at her desk in Washington, DC. She hated taking the blame for others' incompetent mistakes. But the quicker this conference call went, the better, so she gave no excuses.

"We blew it. You're right," replied Laura.

"So do we have any leads?" Aidan asked, tapping his fingers on his desk.

"None. After the accident, we tracked down his cell phone. We found it in the police car that took him home. But then he disappeared. He must know we're after him."

"How about his son?" asked Dan Murdock. "Are you tracking him?"

"We tried. Yesterday morning his sitter took him to the Minnesota History Museum. Somewhere in all the exhibits, we lost them. All we know right now is the woman came back to Hastings's ex-wife's house without him at about five. Last night Hastings and his son were supposed to travel to Hawaii for vacation, but they didn't check in for their flights."

"Have you talked to his ex-wife? She despises Andrew. Maybe she knows something," Chloe said.

"No, we haven't talked to her yet. We're waiting for the right opportunity."

"Damn it, Laura," said Dan. "This is all spinning out of control. Do we even know what evidence Andrew has?"

"Just what Chloe told us."

"You heard the message, Laura," added Chloe. "All he said was that he found a document about the Galileo trials and wanted to talk to me ASAP."

"What about his friends? Has he made any contact?" asked Aidan.

"We're working on that. Cell phone service shows his best friend, Josh Sargent, slept at home last night, and his car is parked at his condo."

"He's an employee of ours as well. You going through his stuff?" asked Chloe.

"Already done. It's all clean," replied Laura.

"So what do we do, Laura?"

"Aidan, I think this guy is just running scared. He's got to show up sometime. How long can he hide out with his son? He can't have that much cash on him. We're watching his bank account and credit cards. Just be patient. We'll find him."

"Laura, we haven't gotten to where we are by being patient," replied Aidan. "Get us answers now!"

Leech Lake, Minnesota
Saturday, June 12
8:10 A.M.

THE SUN SHONE brightly through the window above Andrew's bed. As he slowly gained consciousness and rubbed his eyes, he could tell it was well past daybreak. But only after checking the clock by his bed did he realize it was already after eight, and Ethan was gone.

Andrew jumped out of bed, raced downstairs, and quickly surveyed the main floor. Nothing. Panicking, he cried out, "Ethan? Where are you?"

"Out here on the deck," Ethan replied.

The sliding glass door to the deck was open with only a screen in its place. Andrew flung open the flimsy screen door frantically.

"Good morning. What's wrong?" Heidi asked.

"Hey, Dad, you didn't tell me Heidi was coming."

"Yeah. Well, she surprised me, too." Andrew came up to Ethan and gave him a big hug. "What are you eating there?"

"Just some handfuls of stale cereal," Heidi replied. "How did you sleep?"

"I think pretty well."

Ethan laughed. "When I woke up, you were totally out. You even had a little stream of drool coming from the corner of your mouth."

Feeling foolish and shaking his head, Andrew pretended to punch Ethan in the head. "Thanks, bud. Selling me out right here in front of Heidi. So where's Josh?" Andrew asked.

Heidi nodded over her shoulder. "He took the boat out earlier to pick up some food for the weekend. He got back a couple minutes ago."

"Wanna see if he needs some help with the groceries?"

Ethan and Heidi ran ahead as Andrew paused to look out across the lake. The hunting lodge sat on a seven-acre peninsula in the southeast corner of Leech Lake. Although the lake surrounded them, outcroppings of trees gave it a private feel without stealing from the beautiful vistas of the lake. Off the deck was a grassy field that stretched west to the water's edge, where a couple docks and garages held boats, fishing poles, tackle, and every other conceivable piece of recreational gear for a lake.

Josh was kneeling on the dock, tying down a sleek arrow-shaped speedboat. He was dressed in tattered khaki shorts and some flip-flops, and his tanned back flexed as his arm reached to tie down the final line. Behind him, the lake opened up. The water was glassy blue with lily pads and lake grass sprinkled near the shore. As Josh stood to appreciate his handiwork, Andrew could hear Heidi and Ethan ahead.

"Looking good there, Joshua," proclaimed Heidi.

"Ethan, is your dad up?"

"Yeah, he's coming over right now," replied Ethan, pointing over his shoulder. "We're here to help with the groceries."

Josh waited a couple seconds for Andrew to get a little closer, then yelled, "Good morning, Andrew. Why are you moving so slowly?"

"Just looking around. I forgot how beautiful this spot is."

"Yeah, it's pretty special. It's been in our family for over a hundred years. Dad tells stories of coming out here with his great-grandpa. Generations of Sargents have fished and hunted duck in these waters. I guess that's why there's so much wildlife around," Josh laughed. "We were never very good hunters. More of an excuse to get outside."

Andrew had finally caught up with Heidi and Ethan, who each grabbed a bag from Josh.

Andrew looked over to Ethan and said, "Hey, buddy, take these inside. I'll be there in a minute. We'll get you fed and then set up for some fishing. Sound good?"

"Yeah!" Ethan tore off across the grass toward the main house.

Andrew grabbed a plastic grocery bag then asked, "Hey, can we get those phones you bought set up? I need to make a call."

"Already done. I set them up this morning. I programmed in

our numbers. Heidi's already got hers. Your phone and Ethan's are on the kitchen island. I thought you'd like to give it to him."

"They're pretty sweet," exclaimed Heidi. "They've got an HD camera, full Internet, and texting. You can even video chat with them."

"Josh, you think of everything. Thanks." Turning to Heidi, Andrew asked, "Can I borrow yours for a second?"

"Sure. You calling Lydia?" Heidi said, handing him her phone.

"No, not yet. I'll call her as soon as we have a plan," Andrew said, walking away from the shore, looking for a spot protected from the breeze. He dialed Donny Dahl.

"Hey, Donny, Andrew Hastings here. Just wondering if you had a chance to go by my house this morning."

"Yeah," Donny replied, hesitating while munching on some sort of snack. "I was there first thing this morning." More chewing and gulping. "You were right. The place was covered. Some real high tech stuff, too. Somebody spared no expense."

Andrew stood by the trees in silence. On the one hand, he expected this answer. But hearing it made the nightmare seem so much more real.

"You there? Andrew?"

"Yes, I'm here. Just thinking. You didn't touch anything, did you?"

"Nope. I was in and out in thirty minutes."

"Do you think anyone saw you?"

"There was a car parked up the street with some guy in it. He may have seen me. I got his plates. I can run them if you want. My guess is it's a rental, though."

"Could they see you inside with any cameras?"

"No, they were only running audio. They probably just heard me rustling around with my equipment."

Andrew thought for a second, "Yeah, go ahead and run the plates."

"You have any idea who's doing this?"

"Yes and no, Donny."

"You need some more help?"

"Yes, I'm sure of that. I just need to come up with a plan first."

"That's cool. Give me a call whenever."

"Hey, one more question, Donny. You know anyone who can do forgery work?"

"Depends. What kind?"

"Passports."

"That's serious stuff." Donny hesitated. "I don't know of anyone right now, but I'll ask around."

"Thanks. I'll call you in a day or two," Andrew replied, walking back toward the docks.

"So, Mr. Mystery Man, what was that all about?" asked Heidi.

"No mystery," Andrew replied, looking down at the phone. "I called a PI yesterday to check out my house. He just searched it and says it's crawling with bugs."

"Well, at least it proves you're not crazy," added Josh.

Heidi came up to Andrew and put her arm around his waist.

"Let's get Ethan fed so we can set him up fishing. Then we'll have a chance to talk."

Plymouth, Minnesota
Saturday, June 12
9:00 A.M.

"KATIE, YOU have to know something. Please," Lydia pleaded.

"Come on in and sit down," Katie replied. "Can I get you some coffee or juice?"

"A cup of coffee please. Skim milk and some sweetener."

"Okay, just one second. Oh, which do you prefer—pink, blue, or yellow sweetener?"

"Yellow."

Katie had never kept anything from Lydia before. She didn't have to. Of course, Lydia had tried to pry and learn about things at

Ethan's dad's house. But early on, Katie declared she was Switzer-land—neutral and impartial.

This time was different, though. Lydia didn't know where Ethan was, and Katie knew at least some details about Andrew's escape. But if her true allegiance was to Ethan, then his safety was para-mount, so she believed keeping silent was the best course.

As she came back with a mug of coffee and sat down, she pat-ted Lydia on the knee.

"I know you must be terribly worried. But I really don't know anything more than I've already told you," Katie said. "Andrew just told me he needed to pick up Ethan a little early. He said he tried to reach you but couldn't, so he gave me that note. I'm so sorry." She left it at that. Yes, there were some little lies in there, but not much.

"You never told me what the note said. Can I see it?"

Frustrated and angry, Lydia tossed the note over to Katie.

Dear Lydia:

I'm so sorry to do this. Something terrible has happened. Someone tried to kill me last night, and I fear for Ethan's life. The killers will try to find me by getting Ethan, so I'm taking him somewhere safe. Please, don't try to find us since they may be watching you, too. We will try to contact you when we can. Given the situation, you should disappear as well.

I promise I have done nothing wrong, and our son's safety is my only concern. Lydia, I know I'm asking a lot, but please trust me.

Andrew

After reading the note, Katie closed her eyes and took a deep breath. "You saw the news reports, Lydia. Andrew's car exploded at Lord Fletcher's. Two of his coworkers were killed. I think you should trust him."

"I'm worried that he's kidnapped Ethan and I'll never see him again. That's every divorced mother's nightmare."

"Blame it on me, Lydia. I did it. I let Andrew take Ethan early. The point is, I'm worried about them. I honestly believe Andrew is in trouble."

Lydia looked up and saw the concern in Katie's eyes.

"Have you called the airlines or their hotel in Hawaii? How about Andrew's cell phone?" Katie asked.

"He's not answering his cell phone, but that's not the first time that's happened."

"And the hotel? Have they checked in?"

"No, they haven't."

"Lydia, don't you see? He's on the run. Maybe you should follow his advice and disappear for a couple days, too. What do you have to lose?"

"Well, by that time he could be halfway across the world with Ethan in some country that doesn't extradite kidnapping parents."

"You don't really think Andrew has kidnapped Ethan, do you?"

"I'm not sure of anything anymore. All I know is that Ethan's my life." Lydia started sobbing uncontrollably. Her pain was real. Katie could see it in her eyes and in the trembling of her hands.

"I'm so sorry." Katie reached out to hug Lydia. "Andrew said he'd contact you as soon as he can. Please, be patient. It'll be okay."

ANDREW, JOSH, AND HEIDI sat around a table on the back porch, eating breakfast and drinking coffee while they watched Ethan fish off a nearby dock. The conversation started with Andrew sharing everything he knew from the beginning. He recounted Becky's voice mail, the documents he found on IFM's Knowledge Portal, and their mysterious disappearance. Then he went on about his conversations with Dan and Chloe. He couldn't be sure, but they had to be involved. Finally, he passed around the report he got from Bill Clausen. It seemed simple enough. It was only three pages long, but the secret, animal research trial showed a definite causal relationship between IFM's synthetic resistant starch formulation and intractable gas, bloating, abdominal discomfort, and diarrhea. The link to intestinal cancer was also suspected but as yet unproven. Andrew was convinced that this research was connected to the plane crash and his car's explosion. The papers reeked of death.

Heidi told Josh and Andrew what she had learned about the plane crash. Although it would be hard to prove, she was certain the crash wasn't caused by sugar fouling the engine. If that had been the case, it would have been impossible to time the crash so strategically. There had to have been some other reason, and there was evidence on some of the recovered pieces of debris that the plane had been burned by an intense external heat from an explosion that wouldn't have occurred if only the internal fuel line had failed.

"So let's take a step back from all this information. Who are the suspects?" asked Josh.

"Well, EFC keeps getting bantered about with the crash, but I just don't think they did it," said Heidi. "If we believe the same entity was responsible for the crash, Andrew's car explosion, and the bugging of his house, it becomes even more far fetched to think EFC is connected in any way."

"I agree," said Josh. "If this document is true, there might be some damaging information out there that could derail Redu's FDA approval. If anything, EFC or IFM's competitors would love to get their hands on this information, not get rid of it."

"I know. IFM is trying to bury something," Andrew said, staring out over the lake then looking up. "After all, millions are riding on this launch. Aidan Toole has bet the bank on this one."

"You're right," said Josh. "I was reading an article online in Monday's *Journal*. It said that when IFM applied for FDA approval, Wall Street speculation drove IFM's stock price up from $40 per share to over $67. If the FDA approves Redu, analysts predict IFM's stock will break the $80 barrier since no real competition exists in this ultra-low calorie, great-tasting food space. However, if the FDA rejects it, Wall Street estimates have the stock price falling to $30 or lower."

"Sounds like feast or famine," added Heidi. "I bet if you take a look at the options riding on this deal, Aidan, Chloe, and Dan each has $250 million or more at risk."

"I'd guess Aidan has at least twice that riding on it," said Andrew. "Not to mention the blow to his ego if his prized launch went up in flames and our stock crashed."

"Our stock?" Heidi asked. "That's awfully friendly talk about the company you believe just tried to kill you."

"Yeah, I guess you're right. It's just hard to change your allegiance so quickly," replied Andrew.

"So we have a motive. How can we prove it?" asked Heidi.

"I think my first step is to visit Wally Babin at Iowa Agriculture and Technology University. It's his report here," Andrew said, holding the papers in his hand. "He at least might know about issues during the Galileo trials. Maybe it can lead us to more?"

"Okay, that's a start," said Heidi. "But how are we going to link this to IFM?"

"Who do you think is doing the dirty work? I'm sure Aidan is keeping his hands clean."

"Good question, Josh," Andrew said, rubbing his fingers against his temples, trying to relax. "There has to be some communication trail from Aidan. My guess is that Chloe and Dan are also involved, but I'm not sure how much deeper into the board or leadership team this goes."

"Andrew's right," said Heidi. "If this is playing out like we think, Aidan has had some serious help. I'm not sure from where, but I'd bet it's from some incredibly smart and dangerous allies outside IFM. Josh, could you do some sleuthing when we get back? Check e-mail and voice mail systems for any traces?" asked Heidi.

Andrew jumped in. "Josh, I don't want you getting in trouble."

"Don't worry. I'll be careful. I don't mean to brag, but I can run circles around our IT group."

Andrew stared back toward the dock and watched Ethan cast his fishing rod.

"How am I going to keep Ethan safe? I can't just bring him along as we try to figure this out."

"Do you think Lydia is going to listen to the note you wrote? Maybe Ethan could go away with her?" Heidi asked, already knowing Andrew's answer as he shook his head in disapproval.

"I don't know. Sometimes her emotions cloud her decision-making when it comes to anything regarding me. Do I think Lydia would knowingly hurt Ethan? No. She adores her son. But can I count on Lydia to listen to me and hide Ethan? No."

"You're right," Heidi replied. "Could he stay with Katie? Or a distant relative?"

"I've already asked Katie to do too much. I've put her in a tough spot where she can't tell Lydia everything she knows. Anyway, I'm sure whoever is behind this is looking closely at anyone I know. And you guys know my family tree. Ethan and I are it. I've got no one."

"What about my family?" Josh asked. "I've got tons of cousins. I'm sure one of them would be more than happy to help out."

Andrew paused to think.

"Do you think Ethan will go along with it?" Heidi asked.

"He might have to," Andrew replied. "We don't have a choice."

EIGHTEEN

Washington, D.C.
Sunday, June 13
8:00 A.M.

"WHAT? You don't have a single lead for me?" Laura yelled into her phone.

Skylar Brin knew the verbal beatings would continue until he had something. He was even tempted to make something up, but if she ever found out, he'd be found dead in a ditch the next day. He knew Laura was not to be fooled with.

"Some guy entered the Hastings house, and your man didn't even get a license plate?"

"That's right."

Sweat was starting to form on Skylar's brow. It was getting harder to hide it these days. His hairline was betraying him. Just some tufts of brown hair were left. The hair at his temples had already receded deeply into the crown of his head. He wasn't a big man. Five feet six inches, maybe 130 pounds—hardly what you'd expect from a tough guy. But time and again over the years

Skylar had proven himself to Laura. Big brutish guys were a dime a dozen. Laura knew that to have someone of Skylar's intelligence in the field was invaluable.

She tried to regain her composure. Monday was right around the corner, and Laura couldn't afford for another day to go by without some morsel of progress to dangle in front of Aidan's eyes.

"I know it's a long shot, but how about the fingerprints? When can I expect results?"

"Ann is tapping into the FBI database. End of day at best," replied Skylar. "But remember, we lifted seven partial prints off the doorknob of Hastings's front entry. Who knows if we even got this guy's print."

"I need something, Skylar," Laura replied. "I'm going out for the next six hours. Work some magic now."

Leech Lake, Minnesota
Sunday, June 13
9:30 A.M.

THE BLUE AUDI S5 CONVERTIBLE carved through the turns as the wind rustled through Andrew's hair. His gaze was lost in the huge clouds that billowed above the lake like whipped cream piled atop a banana split. Only the cherry on top was missing. He couldn't believe Josh had convinced him that they had to make this trek together. When had his life gone so off track that he needed to learn how to shoot a gun?

Josh turned onto a gravel road with a large sign posted for the Cass County Sporting Club. This wasn't some fancy golf or tennis club. It was a gun club. Set in the country, a couple miles off the lake, it consisted of one main wooden building and a smaller maintenance shed out back. In the distance, there were several cabin-like structures, each focusing on a different kind of target practice.

They parked in the gravel lot next to the main building, and before Josh had put the car in park, he asked, "You ready?"

"You really think I need to do this?"

"I don't want you to get killed. I want you to have some way to protect yourself and Ethan, so I brought a couple shotguns, rifles, and handguns from the lodge. I also have some ammo."

Andrew sat there shaking his head. Being able to defend himself and Ethan took on new meaning now, and he couldn't just ignore the possibility of danger. When they left the safety of Leech Lake, there would be real danger waiting. No, it wouldn't be just waiting. It would be looking for them.

"Come on. Heidi's taking care of Ethan. Let's do this."

After paying the attendant, Josh led Andrew out to the range, where they met Hal, the club's instructor. Dressed in generously sized khaki shorts, a white T-shirt, and a vest with all sorts of pockets, Hal's first job was to take Andrew through an hour-long course on gun safety. He spoke carefully and methodically, occasionally tugging at the tip of his near-white beard as he tried to emphasize the deadly implications of not heeding his instruction.

The first stop was target practice with rifles. Josh had brought a Winchester M70 and a Remington M700. Hal taught Andrew the basics while Josh watched and occasionally tossed out some advice.

After Andrew got situated at his station, he quickly learned his first painful lesson. Despite being warned a couple times to hold the butt of his rifle right in the crease between his shoulder and chest as he squeezed the trigger, Andrew suffered the pain of recoil. But after fifteen minutes, Andrew was getting the hang of it, and more often than not, he was at least hitting the target. So as Hal continued to give Andrew tips, Josh stepped into his own station, raised his rifle, and in a split second, was ripping the bull's-eye to shreds.

Handgun practice was next, and it wasn't any easier. On television it looked so simple. Just point and shoot. But learning how to hold a gun very still, developing perfect sight alignment, and pressing the trigger without moving your hand or other fingers were difficult tasks to master. As Andrew grew frustrated, he lowered his gun and looked over to Josh, hoping he could learn by example. Shot after shot, Josh hit the bull's-eye. When the range instructor gave the all-clear signal, Andrew walked over to Josh and said, "How did you do that?"

"Well, I've been around guns my whole life, and I've always seemed to have a knack for it."

"Hmmm . . . Maybe it's just your gun. Look how fancy yours is. What's that thing by the trigger?"

"It's a laser sight. I bought it with the gun. I hope I never have to use it."

Annapolis, Maryland
Sunday, June 13
10:55 A.M.

LAURA DROVE to Annapolis. She had wanted to go into the office, but it was Sunday, and Quang needed her. She could always go in later if necessary.

After waiting in the home's living room, Laura jumped up as she saw Quang come downstairs, greeting him quickly in Vietnamese.

"Quang, how are you? Are you feeling well today?"

There was no response, but Laura nodded as if she understood her brother.

The nurse's aid then asked, "Are you ready to go out with your sister? I bet you will have fun."

No response.

"What do you have planned today, Laura?"

"The usual. We'll walk around the college then stop for lunch. Quang loves the butterscotch malts they make at that diner near the State House. Sometimes he'll even start to smile for me. And you know how much sis likes to see you smile," Laura said, reaching over to caress Quang's empty visage.

"Sounds like fun. You have a great time. See you in a couple hours?"

"Yes, we should be back by three. Come on, honey. Let's get going," Laura said, reaching over to hold Quang's arm.

———————————

Leech Lake, Minnesota
Sunday, June 13
9:45 P.M.

THE SECOND DAY of thoughtful planning was winding down as the sun faded across the lake. Although an occasional, forced joke broke the tension as they sat around the bonfire and roasted s'mores, the mood was still tense. But as the sparks were swept away into the darkness, Andrew's thoughts drifted to tomorrow. A deadly game was afoot, and this sanctuary in the woods couldn't protect them any longer.

NINETEEN

IFM Headquarters
Monday, June 14
7:15 A.M.

CHLOE SAT in Aidan's office with Dan across the table and played nervously with her breakfast of blueberries and a bottle of pomegranate juice. Rarely did she eat an IFM manufactured breakfast. She needed something healthier and full of her morning antioxidants.

"What's taking her so long?"

Dan cast a sideways glance at Chloe. He knew she didn't have the stamina for this work.

"Calm down," Aidan replied. I'm sure Laura has made some progress. She's never let me down."

"But what are we going to do?"

"We're going to stop this guy and plug this leak for good."

Chloe seemed to take solace in Aidan's confident voice, only to be jolted as his office phone rang.

After glancing at the caller ID, Aidan answered.

"Good morning, Laura."

"Yes, Aidan, how are you?

"Okay here. Dan and Chloe are right here with me. So tell me, any news?"

"Yes, we have a break."

Chloe's eyes lifted, and Aidan inhaled deeply. Dan's face stared motionless down at the cosmic-shaped speakerphone.

"I just got a call from my team in Minneapolis. It appears that Hastings has involved a private investigator named Donald Dahl. We observed him entering the Hastings house on Saturday morning, and were able to confirm his identity with fingerprints we pulled."

"Any idea why he hired this Dahl guy to go into his house?" Dan asked.

"Well, our bugs picked up Dahl's entry. He didn't make much noise, but it sounded like he was using some equipment to detect our devices."

"So Andrew is definitely on to us?" Chloe asked.

"Yes, it would appear so. But we're watching Dahl closely, and I think he'll lead us to Andrew."

"Good work, Laura," Aidan added as he started to rub his hands and discretely crack his knuckles.

"I'm certain Andrew can't stay in hiding long. We're watching his bank accounts, credit cards, and passport. He and his son can't just vanish."

"Well, keep us posted. We can't let them just disappear. We all agree. Andrew knows too much."

"And if we find him, what about his son?"

"We'll cross that bridge later," Aidan replied, massaging his right temple. "I don't know what choice we really have..." His voice trailed off.

"What's the word from Jackie Epps at the FDA?" Dan bellowed. "The fifteenth is tomorrow. We should be hearing something any time now."

"I haven't heard anything, but no news is good news. We—"

Dan jumped in. "Laura, you can't drop the ball on this. I don't care how busy you've been tracking down Hastings. We must have this approval now! I have sales teams chomping at the bit, and I've promised them we're ready."

"Calm down, Dan. As soon as I know something, I'll call Aidan. And if you'd like, let's plan on talking at eight tomorrow morning. We can update on both of these matters."

"But—" Dan was all ready to start a tirade, but Aidan gestured to cut if off and interrupted.

"Sounds good, Laura. Can everyone here make it?"

"This is my top priority, Aidan. I'll be here," replied Chloe.

Dan nodded as his thumbs went to work adding the meeting to his schedule.

WMSP Headquarters
Monday, June 14
9:15 A.M.

HEIDI TOOK one more gulp of coffee before knocking on Doug Wietz's door. It had been a very early morning, and she needed some caffeine. She and Josh had left the lodge at four o'clock to get back in the cities before eight. After some deft maneuvers to avoid being observed, they were back at their respective jobs, but this time they each had very important, personal agendas.

Doug Wietz had just set down last week's ratings reports when Heidi entered.

"Am I interrupting?" she asked.

"No, just looking at our latest numbers. Looks like we are up some, thanks in large part to your coverage of the IFM crash."

"That's good news. It's been a while since our audience numbers were up."

"I know. It's cause for celebration!" Doug exclaimed, throwing his hands up in the air. "Between this news and our great weather this weekend, I'm the happiest guy around. So how was your weekend? Did you get a chance to get out and enjoy the sun?" Doug asked.

"A little, although the weekend wasn't at all what I expected," Heidi replied.

"What do you mean?"

"Well, that's why I'm here, Doug. I need to go out on a special assignment. I received another lead on the IFM plane crash, and I want to explore it."

"Tell me more."

"Doug, I can't right now, and I'm hoping you can just trust me on this one."

Doug hesitated. Normally he would press, especially in this sea of newbie reporters and staff he was stuck with. But with Heidi, it was different.

"You're one of the best reporters out there, Heidi. I trust you implicitly. What support can we provide?"

"None right now." She paused. "I'll try to call in every few days. Just know that it may be a bit difficult. And if you can, I prefer if we keep this very quiet—just between you and me."

Doug looked over at Heidi. She was always very serious about her work, but he could sense a whole new level of commitment. "Okay. Okay. Just promise me you'll call if you're getting in over your head."

"I promise." Heidi nodded.

Plymouth, Minnesota
Monday, June 14
12:15 P.M.

LYDIA STOOD LOOKING into her refrigerator, trying to muster up some appetite to maintain her strength. Although she had called in sick to work, after half a day at home she felt no closer to being able to handle the real world. Ethan was on her

mind. She was more than worried. She was distraught. Tired of feeling helpless, she picked up the phone, contrary to Katie's advice.

"Hello, is this the police? My name is Lydia Sands. I'd like to report a kidnapping."

Dubuque, Iowa
Monday, June 14
7:00 P.M.

THE DRIVE down to Dubuque was picturesque but long. Andrew wanted to be extra cautious, so he avoided all the main roads and for most of the trip travelled down the Great River Road, hugging the banks of the Mississippi River. By the time they checked into their hotel, they were both tired. Ethan relaxed on the bed watching TV while Andrew worried about Lydia. How were they going to keep her safe? There certainly didn't seem to be any easy answers.

Just then Andrew's phone lit up with an incoming call. Finally, something that could make him smile.

"How are you guys doing?" asked Heidi.

"Good here," Andrew replied. "One second, though." Andrew turned to Ethan. "Can you turn that TV down? I can barely hear Heidi."

Ethan shot his father a disgusted look and said, "There. Satisfied?"

Andrew decided to let Ethan's attitude slide for now. They were both tired and on edge, so he replied, "Thank you."

"Sorry, Heidi. You still there?"

"Yeah. Sounds like you've got a grumpy guy there?"

Andrew turned and walked toward the bathroom and asked, "How about you? Where are you?"

"I'm good. I got out of Minneapolis a little after two. I'm at a convenience store about fifteen minutes outside of Dubuque. Had to get some gas."

"You're paying cash, right?"

"Yes, Andrew. Don't worry, I'm not leaving a trail."

"So did you have any trouble?"

"Nope. I spoke to my boss this morning. I'm on a special assignment. He didn't ask for details."

"Fantastic! And no problems getting out of town?"

"Andrew, you'd have to be magician to have trailed me."

"Great!"

"Have you heard from Josh? Can his cousin take care of Ethan?" Heidi asked.

"Josh just texted me. It's all set up."

"And Ethan? Does he know?"

Andrew shook his head. "No, I thought I'd break it to him when I knew for sure."

"How do you think he will take it?"

"He won't like it. He's going to feel like I'm just dumping him. But it's the safest option, right?"

"Yes," Heidi replied. "I think it's your only option, other than taking Ethan with us."

"I know…" Andrew's voice trailed off.

"So where am I heading?" Heidi asked.

"Oh, I'm sorry. We're checked in at the Holiday Inn downtown under the name Richard Moore. I have an adjoining room for you—room 521. Do you need the address?"

"No, I can pull it up on my phone. I'll come straight up. Maybe we can get dinner together?"

"Perfect. I'm starved."

"Cool. Can't wait to see you."

"Me too."

Five miles behind Heidi, a white Toyota Highlander had pulled over on the side of the road. As Heidi turned back onto the highway, a dot on a screen inside the stopped vehicle started to blink. A voice from inside the SUV cut through the silence. "Let's get going, Tony. She's moving."

Minneapolis, Minnesota
Monday, June 14
7:15 P.M.

FRESHLY SHOWERED after his workout, Josh threw on some sweats, turned on the television in the living room, and drew his blinds. Doing his best to act normal, he walked out his front door and checked to see if anyone was watching. When he was convinced the coast was clear, he grabbed his backpack and slipped downstairs to the second floor. Just one door down from the stairwell there was a room with a plaque outside that said "Guest Suite." As head of his condo association, Josh had the only key, and he had decided to rent out the suite for the next several weeks.

After setting down his bag, Josh went right to work making sure his new office was safe. Surely by now IFM was listening to all his actions upstairs. He was just betting they didn't have video, and he hoped his escapes downstairs would go unnoticed. But he thought he'd soon find out as he set a trap, gluing a thin, clear filament between the closet door and its white, wooden frame. As long as the door remained closed, the thread would stay in place. But if someone came snooping, it would break and fall.

Pleased with his handiwork, Josh walked over and knelt down by the TV stand, pulling out a special network router from his backpack. An early morning call to the cable company on the way home had upgraded the line for Internet service. If everything went as planned, he'd be ready to set up his operation the following night when he was sure it was safe. Some special programming he had worked on was already infiltrating IFM, and he was anxious to review its results.

TWENTY

IFM Headquarters
Tuesday, June 15
8:00 A.M.

CHLOE AND DAN assembled in Aidan's office. Judy knocked then cracked open his door. "I've got Ms. Long on the phone for you. She said she's been trying to reach you on your cell phone but had no answer."

"Oh, I must have the damned ringer off. Just transfer her to my desk phone. I'll put her on speaker."

A few moments passed as Judy walked back to her desk and transferred the call. The anticipation in the room was palpable. Dan and Chloe stared anxiously as Aidan answered his phone.

"Good morning, Laura. I hope you haven't been trying to reach me long."

"Good morning, Aidan. No, not long at all. Do I have just you on the line? I wanted to speak with you first."

Aidan exhaled. This didn't sound good. Trying to maintain

some semblance of a poker face he grinned and said, "You can speak freely. Chloe and Dan are here, but we're all in this together."

Laura paused for what seemed like minutes. "Well, I'm sorry to report, I don't have good news."

"Oh my God," Chloe declared.

"Please, please," Laura interrupted. "It's not horrible news. It's just not the news we wanted. The FDA has decided to delay their decision."

Aidan sat tapping his finger on his desk.

Dan jumped in. "Damn it, Laura. Do you have any details why?"

"I spoke with Jackie Epps last night. Despite all her attempts to force a decision, Candy Presho has been very successful in getting the ear of FDA Principal Deputy Commissioner Tillman."

"Everyone knows she has connections to EFC," Chloe added. "I'm sure Gina Sills is behind this."

"I can't be sure," Laura replied, "but I wouldn't be surprised."

"So what do we need to do?"

"Well, we can let this run its course, or we can make one last push."

"I don't want to leave this to fate," Dan said.

"Neither do I," Aidan added.

"I thought you'd say that," Laura replied. "So here's what we're going to do. Aidan, I'd like you and Chloe to come to Washington this Friday. I'll set up a series of meetings that will close this deal once and for all. Tillman has apparently set the final announcement date for July 1 with the decision meeting scheduled for June 28. If we go in this week, we can hit them hard and go back again before the decision meeting if needed."

"Agreed. I'll let Judy know to clear my calendar."

"Aidan," Dan said. "I totally agree, but I'd like to be part of this visit. Chloe's been unsuccessful in closing the deal, and I think I can be helpful in these meetings."

Chloe leaned forward and stared down Dan, slowly shaking her head. She was ready to spit fire, but she was also confident Aidan would defend her efforts.

"What do you think, Laura?" Aidan inquired.

Chloe was shocked.

Laura took a thoughtful pause and said, "No, I disagree. Chloe's been very effective. I think bringing in Dan will seem like we're trying to gang up on people. It's logical that you come, Aidan. You're Chloe's boss. You're the reinforcements. Dan's presence isn't needed."

Relieved, Chloe finally uttered, "Thank you, Laura. I appreciate at least your vote of confidence."

"Okay, it was just a suggestion," Dan added, satisfied with the deadly jab he had inflicted on Chloe. "I trust your judgment, Laura."

"So do we have any news on Hastings? What's that detective up to?" asked Aidan.

"We're following Dahl, hoping he leads us to Hastings. Nothing to report yet. We did hear something interesting from Hastings's ex. Apparently, she called the police department and reported her son as kidnapped."

"Really? She must be pissed that Andrew has disappeared with him," Dan added.

"Oh, she is. But when the officer questioned her on the phone, she revealed that Andrew was supposed to have Ethan for vacation for the next two weeks."

"Yeah, so how did the officer leave it with her?" Chloe asked.

"She said they hadn't checked into their hotel and then mentioned some note that Andrew left her that said she was in danger. She went in last night to file a missing persons report, but we haven't seen it show up yet in any databases."

"Do you think there is any way we can use her?" Dan asked.

"I don't think we should rule it out," Laura replied.

"Keep on top of this one, Laura. Now's not the time to get shy."

"Agreed, Aidan. Ms. Sands is under our watch. We will pull her in if needed. Also, since Hastings doesn't have any family, I've instructed my people to start researching all of his friends and their families. If Hastings is on the run, he may be looking for a place to hide with his son."

"Makes sense," Dan said. "We need to root that bastard out."

"I think that's it," Aidan interjected. "I've gotta run. I've got some board members coming in town this morning, and they're going to be very concerned about Redu. Please, Laura, keep us posted on any news. Oh, also I'd like some details on our meetings in DC so Chloe and I can be fully prepared."

"Will do, Aidan. Expect them by end of day tomorrow."

"Thank you, Laura," Aidan replied and then hung up.

"Well, looks like we need to hold off the celebrating." He glanced over at Chloe and said, "Now's not the time to get down, just even more focused. Got it?"

"Totally," said Dan as he started to leave.

"We'll bring home the win, Aidan. You and me in DC," Chloe added then quickly turned to catch up with Dan.

As Aidan's door closed behind her, Chloe shouted ahead, "What the hell was that?"

Dan turned. "What do you mean?"

"Hmmm...What the hell do you think I mean? Let me see if I can remember your exact words. 'Chloe's been unsuccessful in closing the deal...'"

"Oh, don't take my words out of context."

"What?" Chloe said, raising her voice in the otherwise silent executive suite.

"Stop making a scene."

Realizing she was attracting attention, Chloe dug her nails into Dan's arm and whispered, "Follow me or you'll find out what a real scene looks like."

Her face was red and flush with anger. Dan could dismiss her, but he didn't want to create an even bigger scene. The secretaries loved to talk, and all they needed right now was a rumor of dissent in the executive ranks. So Dan relented and followed Chloe to a nearby conference room.

As she closed the door, Dan said, "So what do you want from me?"

"I want respect, Dan. I'm not going to be another victim of yours. I've told you that before, but apparently you didn't take me very seriously."

"So are you threatening me, Chloe? Now that's funny," Dan said, inching closer into her space.

Chloe couldn't believe her ears. She had seen Dan disembowel plenty of people over the years, but she honestly believed it would never be her. It made sense, though. The closer Redu's approval came to hitting the rocks, the more Dan would want to deflect blame, and she was the only person left standing next to him.

"Get your cocky ass away from me, Dan. I'm ready for you. I've got dirt on you that could take you down. Not just here at work, but everywhere. Your whole life will crumble into pieces."

"Really? Come on, Chloe. Tell me. Hit me with your best shot! I dare you."

Chloe wanted to so badly. She wanted to knock him to his knees. But she knew she still needed him, so his secret was safe for now.

As Chloe slowly gained control of her anger, she finally took a deep breath and said, "Test my patience one more time, and you will regret it. I promise, Dan. You have no idea what I know about you. Consider this your final warning."

Dubuque, Iowa
Tuesday, June 15
10:00 A.M.

IOWA AGRICULTURE & TECHNOLOGY University, known as IAT by the locals, was located a mile west of downtown Dubuque. Brick buildings, a green canopy of trees, and a quadrangle gave it the feel of a classic college campus. Although its survival was questionable at one point, recent wins in its Agriculture, Biochemistry, and Food Science programs had brought renewed life to the campus. Fundraising campaigns over the past five years had brought in unprecedented donations, and four new buildings had just been completed with two more on the way. As with many things in life, success begot success, and enrollment was up and upgrades in its faculty were finally taking hold. IAT was not only back on its feet; it was viewed as a new model for prosperity in the world of private colleges and universities.

The normally bustling campus was quiet this morning. Students had left for summer break in late May, and a light load of summer school classes left a skeleton crew of faculty and students. Administrative and research-oriented buildings were still busy, but nothing could replace the flurry of student life during the fall and spring semesters.

Agnes Legare walked across campus for her nine o'clock appointment at the new, four-story McNaulty Food Sciences Center. The latest jewel in IAT's crown of achievement, the center was state of the art, thanks to its namesake, Todd McNaulty, PhD. Dr. McNaulty, head of the Agricultural and Food Sciences programs at IAT, was a keystone to the turnaround. Championed as one of the brightest research minds around, he was also a charismatic fundraiser. Todd was a busy man, though, and when asked yesterday for a press interview, he had handed it over to Agnes. Usually more than happy to crow his successes to the media, Todd said the reporter's request for a meeting seemed more information-oriented. So as IAT's public relations representative, the task fell in Agnes's lap. She was instructed to call Todd only if she thought the story merited his attention.

Outside the McNaulty Food Sciences Center, Andrew pulled his car up to the curb on Campus Drive. Heidi checked herself in the vanity mirror one last time while Ethan sulked in the back seat. He was still upset by his dad's plan to drop him off with Josh's relatives.

"Good luck, Heidi," Andrew said.

"What do you mean?" Heidi smiled. "I'm Roxanne Dixon." She flashed a WMSP press ID she had forged yesterday morning. She had made several, including ones for Andrew and Josh, using some of her fellow reporters' names, just in case.

"Knock 'em dead, Roxanne," Andrew said, leaning over to give her a hug. "Be careful."

"Don't worry. This is just another day in the life of a reporter."

"THANKS SO MUCH for agreeing to meet with me on such short notice, Ms. Legare."

"Oh, please, Roxanne, call me Agnes. We like to have an informal atmosphere here at IAT. Most professors and students are on a first name basis."

"Really? That's certainly different than when I was in school."

"Yes, we believe it's one of the things that has helped the rebirth of our school. Rather than adhering to the old hierarchal model, we believe using first names helps create an atmosphere of collaboration."

"Very interesting. Sounds like the makings of a whole new story. Today, though, I'm trying to get some information about some research trials that were conducted here."

"Oh, we're very proud of our research work. We've built quite a reputation over the past several years. Of course, I can't keep track of all of our accomplishments, but I'm familiar with many of them. Which study were you looking for information on?"

"Well, it involves the Redu trials. The ingredient is up for approval, and the FDA is supposed to be making a decision today. I was hoping to get some background from the research team in advance of the FDA announcement."

"Oh, great. It's always wonderful when we can be in the press for such prestigious work."

"Well, as you probably know, there has been a lot of debate over Redu's approval."

"Oh yes, yes, but that's all garbage. You know, those food watchdog groups. If they had their way, they wouldn't approve the use of table salt."

"So I was hoping to meet Dr. McNaulty and speak to one of

his research assistants, Wally Babin. He coauthored some of the early research for the Redu trials."

"I don't recognize that name, but of course, I don't know everyone here. We're just too big for that."

Roxanne nodded in agreement but said nothing, waiting for Agnes to fill in the uncomfortable silence.

"I guess I could call him up to see if I could set up a meeting for the three of us."

"That would be great," Roxanne replied.

"Just wait one second, and let me make a couple phone calls."

Agnes stepped out smiling, phone in hand, only to return a changed woman.

Lips pinched tightly, she stood by the door after shutting it. "Oh, I'm sorry that took so long."

"That's okay. I really appreciate your help."

"Well, to be honest, I don't think I'm going to be able to help you much. Mr. Babin no longer works here."

"Do you know where I can reach him?" Roxanne asked. Heidi could already tell Agnes's response as she shook her head.

"I'm sorry. It's against university policy to provide contact information for former employees."

"Well, is there someone else I can talk to about the trials?"

"You know, I called around, and there really isn't. Again, sorry I couldn't have been of any assistance." Agnes was still standing, and she opened the door to the conference room. Their interview was over.

Roxanne shook Agnes's hand and headed for the building's entrance. After she had left, Agnes stayed behind in the conference room, just as she had been instructed.

———

ANDREW GRABBED for his phone, anxious to hear about Heidi's meeting. "Any luck?" he asked.

"Nothing," Heidi replied. "At first Agnes was all helpful and excited. Then she left for over ten minutes to make some calls. When she came back in, she was as cold as she could be. I think someone higher up, probably McNaulty, told her to clam up. Maybe somebody got to him."

"Right. Looks like we move on to Plan B."

"Yep."

"We'll pick you up in a minute."

———————

WITHIN A MINUTE after Heidi's departure, none other than Dr. Todd McNaulty showed up and greeted Agnes in the conference room.

"Was that her? Blond shoulder-length hair, blue eyes, gray slacks, white blouse?"

"Yes, she just left."

"Did she ask any more questions?"

"No, I did just what you asked. I was firm."

"Great."

"I'm sorry. I didn't realize we were silent on Redu press coverage."

"It's okay. We had a spate of this happen a couple years ago. Looks like the final Redu decision has dredged up some new coverage."

"I guess," Agnes said, shrugging her shoulders, still a bit confused by the whole situation.

"Well, please let me know if there are any additional press or information requests on the Redu approval. If there are, please vet the request, and get rid of them. Under no circumstances is anyone to be given access to my staff, my labs, or me. Okay?"

"Yes, sir."

———————

AFTER STRIKING OUT AT IAT, Andrew and Ethan picked up Heidi and dropped her off at Wally's last known address, the McNab apartment building. Heidi knocked on several neighbors' doors. When none of them answered, she wandered into the building's first floor laundry room, where she found a young Asian woman moving her wash into a dryer.

"Excuse me, could you help me one second?" Heidi asked.

"Yes, what do you want?" the young women replied with a heavy accent.

"I was wondering if you know a friend of mine. His name is Wally Babin. He used to live here."

"Ah, yes. I know Wally. He's a very funny guy. He lived a couple doors down from me."

"Well, this is kind of a strange circumstance, but Wally and I used to date many years ago. After we broke up, I found out I was pregnant. I didn't want him to feel obligated to take care of us, so I just never told him.

"I don't want anything from Wally now, but our son just turned ten. He wants to meet his father. So, I decided it was finally time to tell Wally. But Wally's trail ends here in Dubuque. I know he worked at IAT and lived here. Do you know where he is now?"

"Wally got into a biochemistry PhD program at Madison. Full ride."

"University of Wisconsin Madison?"

"Yes. He moved there about a year ago."

"Oh, that's great. I can't believe it. Maybe we can finally reconnect. I've looked and looked online, and he's not on Facebook or anywhere. It's like he just disappeared."

"Yes. I haven't heard from him since he left. But if you find him, please tell him Lan Tan says hello."

Long & Company Headquarters
Tuesday, June 15
1:00 P.M.

LAURA COULDN'T REMEMBER a worse string of days.

After hanging up with Aidan, she gathered her team and ripped them to shreds. She was tired of their incompetence.

As she was sitting back down at her desk, trying to gather her thoughts, Joy walked into her office.

"What the hell do you want now?" Laura barked.

"I've got Dr. McNaulty on the phone for you. I tried to take a message, but he insisted I interrupt you."

"What does that stuffed shirt want?"

"He didn't say. I'm sorry."

"He probably got wind of the FDA delay and has some scheme to make money on it, that greedy bastard."

Joy stood there, afraid to ask. But after several seconds passed, she finally squeaked out, "So do you want to take the call?"

"Sure. This day's going to hell anyway."

Joy quickly ran to her desk, and within moments Todd was connected.

"What's so important?" Laura barked.

Todd was used to Laura's brusque responses. "I have some interesting news to report."

"We already know the FDA is delaying their decision."

"What? I hadn't heard that. Why?"

"We're still trying to get to the bottom of it, but claims that the FAC panel was stacked seem to be gaining traction."

"I warned you of making it too obvious."

"So you're calling to gloat?"

"No, I'm not. We had an interesting visitor here today. Some reporter."

"What?"

"Yes, she was asking for Wally."

"Damn it," Laura replied. "What did you tell her?"

"Nothing. I didn't even meet with her. When my PR person notified me that the press was asking about Wally, I told her to get rid of the reporter and to give her nothing."

"Who's this reporter anyway?"

"Hold on one second. I have her name written down here

somewhere. She was a drop dead gorgeous blond. Here it is. Her name is Roxanne Dixon. She's with WMSP."

Laura's wheels were turning. It seemed too much of a coincidence, and she started Googling. Yes, WMSP did have a blond reporter named Roxanne Dixon, but she was hardly a bombshell.

"Todd, do me a favor. Are you near a computer?"

"Yeah. I'm at my desk right now."

"Go to WMSP's website and check out Roxanne's picture."

"Just one second," Todd replied.

Laura could hear the clicking of keys. When they stopped, she asked, "Is that the woman you met?"

"Well, I didn't actually meet her, Laura." Todd paused. "But from the glimpse of her I got as she walked out, she was much prettier."

"Okay, now go back to WMSP's main page and locate Heidi Pearson."

More clicking noises sounded in the background. Suddenly, Todd exclaimed, "That's her. I'm sure of it. That's the woman that was here."

"Hmmm...Did you see anyone with her?"

"No. I was just glad to get rid of her so quickly. Why do you ask?"

"Well, her former boyfriend is a major loose end."

"Oh." No further explanation was needed. Todd was quite familiar with Laura's terminology. "What are you thinking?" he asked.

"Well, it's almost a shame that she doesn't know where Wally is."

"What do you mean? You promised me. Nothing happens to Wally."

"I know. I know. That was probably one of my more stupid deals with you, but Wally is safe for now."

"Laura?"

"I was just thinking we could have set a trap for Heidi with Wally. And who knows. She seems like a smart one. She may figure this one out anyway.

"Todd, I gotta run here. Anything else?"

"Well, no. Just don't forget your promise. Keep Wally safe."

"Yeah, yeah. Later."

Laura immediately dialed Skylar Brin and got his voice mail. "Get a team in Madison now. Watch Wally Babin. Hastings and his ex-girlfriend are trying to find him."

Minneapolis, Minnesota
Tuesday, June 15
8:10 P.M.

JOSH TRIED his best to keep his routine. Things had to appear normal. So after going for an evening run, he showered and turned on some music. The station really didn't matter. He just needed some noise. Then, he closed the blinds and made a quick exit downstairs with a couple pieces of fruit in his hands and his backpack slung over his shoulder.

His spyware had been at work for over thirty-six hours now, and he was anxious to see what he'd caught. Cautiously, he exited the stairwell, making sure nobody was watching. Then, he ducked into the guest suite and checked out his primitive trap by the closet door. It looked undisturbed. He was good to go.

As Josh powered up his laptop and waited for it to launch, he called Andrew.

"Hi, Josh," said Heidi.

"Huh? What are you doing answering Andrew's phone?"

"Oh, he's in the bathroom with Ethan. He threw his phone in my purse. I'm back to being his pack mule."

"Where are you?"

"Well, we're in Madison now having dinner at some Italian place on State Street."

"Madison?"

"Yeah, we found out that Wally Babin left Dr. McNaulty's lab a year ago to get his PhD in biochemistry. They acted very odd at IAT when I mentioned his name. They went from helpful to get the hell out of here in two minutes."

"You talk to him yet?"

"Yes. We found him listed in the online student directory. Andrew called him from a phone in the library. They're meeting for lunch tomorrow at the Memorial Union Terrace."

"Great, but be careful. If this guy is important in the puzzle and you just went poking around, they may be watching him now."

"I think we have it covered. Andrew made it clear to Wally to be careful and even mentioned that someone might be watching. What was odd was that Wally didn't even question that idea, which makes me think even more that he knows something."

"Hmmm...Sounds promising."

"So how's your work going? Do you have anything so far?"

"Not yet. I've combed through all the files on IFM's servers, looking for details relating to the trials. Nothing has shown up there. I was able to tap into Aidan, Chloe, and Dan's computers, so I'm searching them as well. Oh, and I was able to hack their webcams, so we should have recordings of any conversations they have near their laptops."

"Very good. Those should be interesting, especially with the FDA delay."

"Yeah, that news hit headquarters like a rock."

"Wall Street didn't like it either. IFM's shares tumbled $16. You can believe that left quite a dent in some pockets," Heidi added.

"I know. I hold a fair number of IFM shares and options myself."

"A mere speck in your portfolio, I'm sure, Mr. Sargent."

"Yeah, yeah. Anyway, what I was going to tell you is Aidan issued a statement via the intranet, trying to spin the news. He said something like this was just a modest setback. He painted a smiley face all over it."

"I bet."

"Well, I need to get going," Josh replied. "Any sign of Andrew?"

"No, not yet. Want me to have him call you?"

"No, just tell him I say hi, and I'll post anything interesting in the secured, digital cloud I've set up. It's going to take me a while, though. I have twenty hours of video and over three hundred e-mails to review. I'll send you guys a link so you can check it out in the morning."

"Mr. Hi-Tech. We're lucky to have a geek like you on our team."

"Thanks, Pearson. Coming from a nerd like you, I'll take that as a compliment."

TWENTY-ONE

Madison, Wisconsin
Wednesday, June 16
5:00 A.M.

T HE DAHLMANN CAMPUS INN was a perfect location for their stay. Right in the heart of Madison, it was only a couple minutes walk from the Memorial Union and offered easy access to both the University and State Streets. Since there were no standard, adjoining rooms available, Andrew sprung for the Presidential Suite. He just didn't like the idea of Heidi being out of earshot, so the extra expense was well worth the peace of mind.

Anxious to comb through the files Josh had uploaded, Andrew was up before daybreak. The catch in Josh's net was already rich and teeming with damning information. Yesterday morning's update with Aidan, Chloe, Dan, and this lobbyist, Laura Long, was particularly revealing. This despicable team had all but admitted to killing his friends. And as Andrew learned more from Josh's detailed research on Laura Long and the multitude of lobbyist groups she led, he grew increasingly scared of the monster that was chasing them.

There was no underestimating this group. One slip was all it took. They had already found Donny Dahl, rendering one of Andrew's few allies useless. Who knew what else IFM could do with so little? His friends' families were already under investigation, so there would be no tucking Ethan away in a safe corner of the universe. Although the thought of going head to head with this group was frightening, he was ready to go to DC if that was what it took to reclaim his family's safety.

Heidi woke up a few minutes later and began reading over his shoulder. She devoured the information as well, every so often whispering "Did you see this?" disgusted by their enemy's achievements. They had to be stopped. She agreed with Andrew—there was no choice but to bring Ethan along. And then there was Lydia, dancing on the edge of a cliff, ignoring Andrew's note. Somehow they had to help keep her safe, but how, without endangering themselves? As Heidi and Andrew traded ideas on Lydia's safety, a groggy Ethan entered the room.

"I hear you talking about me and Mom. What's going on?"

Andrew looked over at Heidi, and she nodded. "Well, it looks like our plan to drop you off with Josh's cousin in Chicago isn't going to work out. So for now, you're coming along with us."

Ethan smiled and hugged his dad. "But why? What happened?"

"Josh found out that there are some evil people at IFM that are behind all of this. They're prepared to do anything to hurt me. They're looking for us, they're already checking out friends and—"

Ethan interrupted. "What about Mom? Is she okay?"

"Heidi and I were just figuring out how to help her and keep her safe," Andrew replied.

"Is she okay?" Ethan asked again.

Andrew didn't want to go into all the details, but he also couldn't lie. So he tried to keep his answer short and simple.

"Yes, she's okay. We just need to get her a message that we're safe and convince her to hide until we fix this."

Relieved, Ethan sat down next to his dad. "How 'bout we make a video of me? I know she'd like to see me. I can tell her what we're doing and ask her to go hide out. I'm sure Josh can put it up in that data sky you guys have been talking about."

"You mean the data cloud?"

"Yeah, that. Maybe Josh can send her some anonymous e-mail, or I can call her at work and give her the link and some password."

"I think you've got a pretty smart kid here," Heidi said, nodding with approval.

"No big deal. Any other problems for me to solve this morning?" Ethan asked.

Andrew reached out and scrubbed Ethan's bed head with his fingers. "Maybe you can work on a way to get clean? I don't think your mom wants to see a messy boy. Hit the showers."

"Okay," Ethan said, running to get ready.

"Oh, what do you want for breakfast?" Andrew called. "I'm going to order up room service."

Andrew heard a muffled "waffles" as Ethan jumped in the shower.

ANDREW ARRIVED FIVE MINUTES before noon — just enough time to get the lay of the land and scan for any trouble. As he looked around, he couldn't help being impressed by UW's Union. It was situated on the shore of Lake Mendota, and Andrew could only imagine what it was like when school was in full session — bands playing, boats out on the lake, ice surfing and skating in the winter, and lots of beer — a recipe for some great collegiate fun for sure, especially if early on you learned the skill of moderation.

Lost in thought, Andrew jumped when a voice whispered, "Mr. Hastings?"

Andrew turned and was surprised to see a young man in a wheelchair.

"Wally?"

"Yes," Wally replied, reaching out his hand to shake Andrew's.

"Sorry, I just wasn't expecting…"

"I know. I guess I should have told you to just look for the handicapped guy, but I try not to define myself by my disabilities."

Andrew recovered quickly and shook Wally's hand.

"Okay then. You said this was urgent. Let's get talking."

After finding a table away from most of the crowd, Wally and Andrew ordered lunch, and Andrew asked some innocent questions about Wally's background. By the time their food arrived, however, Andrew was ready to drop the bomb.

"So you were Dr. McNaulty's lead graduate student on the Redu trials?"

"Yes, I coordinated the activities of multiple locations, coauthored some research, and managed several study coordinators and a couple of statisticians."

"That's interesting," Andrew replied as Wally used the break in conversation to take a big bite from his cheeseburger. Then Andrew continued, "Now, was it your job to rig the trial results?"

Wally gulped, almost gagging on his burger, his eyes bulging. After struggling for a couple seconds, he managed to gasp out, "What?"

"Oh, you heard me. You rigged the trials."

"Where are you getting your information?"

"You were the only person other than Dr. McNaulty who had broad enough access to pull something like this off."

"Just wait one second here. First off, where do you get off assuming the trials were rigged?"

"I already know that. You see, what I didn't tell you, Wally, is I used to work at IFM. In fact, I was a marketing manager getting ready to launch B-Lean Snacks. It's a new product that IFM is coming out with, and it's chock full of Redu. Would you like a couple bags? Oh, that's right, you know how bad that stuff can be for your gut."

Wally put down his burger, wiped his mouth, released his chair's brake, and started to back up from the table. "I think our conversation is over."

"Oh no, Wally. If you know what's good for you, you'll want to see this." He pulled three crumpled sheets of paper out of his pocket.

Wally's curiosity was piqued, and the more he thought about it, he figured the more he knew the better. After all, this was the first time somebody actually knew his real role on the Redu trials, other than Todd.

"You see, very few people who have seen this report have lived to tell about it. Seven people died on IFM's corporate jet when it crashed in a field just southeast of Minneapolis. Then, two team members of mine were blown to bits in my car. Yeah, it was supposed to be me," Andrew said, his voice raised.

"Calm down," Wally whispered. "You're attracting attention."

Andrew looked around and saw several nearby tables were checking him out. Wally was right. He needed to calm down, but he had to make his point.

"Okay, I'm sorry. I'm not crazy, Wally. I'm just scared. I'm on the run with my son because I know Redu isn't as safe as it has been billed. I haven't seen the real data. I just know early trials happened and they showed a definite connection with gas, bloating, abdominal discomfort, diarrhea, and maybe cancer. This was your research, Wally. So my guess is you know a hell of a lot more. And as IFM looks to close the lid on each leak, there's only one place for you to go, Wally. Six feet under."

Wally's face reddened. He wasn't stupid. He'd had the same thoughts. Todd had promised to protect him, but he knew forces bigger than Todd were in control.

"Join me, Wally. Help me save my son, please. I know it's scary. But you must already be scared by your own shadow. Is that any way to live?"

Wally cleared his throat. "You certainly have some very passionate beliefs, but your assumptions are all wrong. Get me a couple bags of B-Lean chips. I'll eat them. I'll eat a whole case of them. They're perfectly safe. The results proved it."

Swirling in dismay, Andrew looked up into the sky for some answer. Perhaps Wally was the wrong guy? Or maybe Wally just felt safer in the grip of IFM and Laura Long. Andrew took a couple deep breaths, trying to regroup his thoughts.

"Okay, do me one last favor, Wally. Google these names." Andrew grabbed a clean napkin and wrote three names: Becky Clausen, Lourdes Perez, and Rachel Sears. "These people are dead now because of what you're covering up," he said as he handed Wally the list. "Oh, and one more thing." Andrew reached into his pocket, pulling out his wallet. "Here's a picture of my son, Ethan. He's eleven. If you don't help me, I don't think he will see his twelfth birthday." Andrew turned Ethan's fifth-grade picture over on the table and starting writing. "Here's a special e-mail address just for you, Wally. If you change your mind, and you want to stop living a lie, just shoot me a note. Be careful, though. They could be watching you." Andrew paused and looked around. "I just hope for both of our sakes they aren't out there right now."

Andrew paid the bill, shook Wally's hand, and walked back to the hotel. He had failed.

———————————

A SCRUFFY-LOOKING man dressed as a student watched the two men shake hands, and then pulled a cell phone from his pocket.

"Skylar."

"Yes."

"We just made a positive ID on Andrew Hastings. Wally Babin led us to him just like you promised."

"Perfect. Now you know your instructions. Take care of the problem as soon as you have a clean shot. Got it?"

"Don't worry. My boys will get the job done."

TWENTY-TWO

Madison, Wisconsin
Wednesday, June 16
1:00 P.M.

AFTER GETTING BACK to their room, Andrew broke
the bad news to Heidi while Ethan played video games.
For twenty minutes, Andrew recounted the details of his lunch
with Wally, beating himself up for not being more convincing.

"I'm sure it didn't go that badly, Andrew," Heidi said. "You
didn't expect Wally to confess to rigging research results on the
spot, did you?"

Andrew sat dejected in a chair, staring out at the capitol. "Heidi,
I failed. We're no closer to getting out of this mess."

Despite being immersed in his game, Ethan overheard the
conversation, and he decided to help Heidi. "Dad, it's going to
be okay."

Although Andrew didn't know how, he realized having a pity
party in front of Ethan wasn't the answer.

"You're right, buddy. We can do this. Are you ready to make that video for your mom?"

"Yes," Ethan replied enthusiastically. "I worked on what to say while you were gone, and Heidi helped me edit it. Here, check it out." Ethan handed his father a piece of paper that had a script of sorts scribbled out on it.

Andrew read through it, nodding as he went along. "Looks good. I think it gets the point across to your mom without revealing too much information that could get us in trouble."

"Yeah," Ethan replied. "Heidi really helped me out with that."

"Well, I've got my phone right here," Andrew said, pulling his phone from his pocket. "Are you ready to film?"

"Sure."

Andrew tapped on his phone and set the camera to video.

"Where should I stand?" Ethan asked.

"How about over here," Heidi suggested. "The wall will provide a good neutral background, and if I move a couple of these lights, your mom should be able to see you clearly." Heidi started moving things around, getting the scene set.

"Lucky we have a pro in our midst, aren't we, Ethan?"

Heidi paused and made some final adjustments with the lights. "Now, how's that looking?" she asked.

"Perfect," Andrew replied. "You ready?"

"Yep."

"Okay, when I say 'action,' you start. Got it?"

"Sure," Ethan replied.

"Okay, here we go in five, four, three, two, one, action."

Ethan looked straight into the phone and started to talk.

Hey, Mom. I just wanted to let you know that I'm safe and I'm doing fine. Dad was right, though. Some very bad people are looking for us, and they will do anything to stop Dad from uncovering the truth. Please, listen to me. You could be in danger, too. Find a way to sneak out of town for a while, but be careful. Just use cash, leave your cell phone at

*home, and don't log onto any computers. Dad's sure
they're watching you, so make sure they don't follow
you. I love you, Mom, and I want you to be safe.
Please, do this for me. Okay?*

*At the end of this video, you will see some instruc-
tions on how we can keep in touch via e-mail. When
you're safe, and sure nobody is watching you, follow
those instructions so we can make sure you're okay.*

*I love you, Mom, and I can't wait to hug you when
this is all over. Talk to you soon. Bye.*

Ethan waved to the camera then paused. "How did I do?"

"That was perfect," Andrew replied.

"You sure you don't want to be a TV reporter, kiddo?" Heidi added. "You nailed it in one take."

Ethan smiled. "So when will Mom get this?"

"I'm not sure, but I'm going to upload it to Josh right now. I imagine he will send it on to your mom after work this evening or early tomorrow morning."

"Cool. Hopefully Mom will be somewhere safe by tomorrow night. Maybe we can even talk online?"

"Maybe," Andrew replied, "but we've got to follow Josh's lead on this. He's doing everything he can to keep both you and your mom safe. Okay?"

"I know," Ethan replied with a hint of disappointment and impatience in his voice. "So what's next? Where do we go from here?"

"Well, we don't have any more leads here," Heidi replied.

"That's true. I think it's time for us to head to DC. If Wally Babin isn't going to share his secrets, maybe we need to learn more about Laura Long and how she's helping IFM."

Heidi nodded with approval. "I don't have any better ideas. In fact, I think it's our only option."

Cleveland, Ohio
Thursday, June 17
1:00 A.M.

A SIXTEEN-HOUR road trip to Washington, DC, was hardly appealing, but the idea of getting on board an airplane and using their IDs was far worse.

Heidi tried her best to keep things fun and light, spicing up the drive with her best repertoire of games and songs for the car, but they all were tired. After stopping for a quick dinner outside of South Bend, they called Josh and updated him on their day. He agreed with moving on to Washington and said he would concentrate on infiltrating Long & Company's servers. Josh passed on the latest news on his end. He had received Ethan's video for Lydia, and it was already scheduled for delivery tomorrow morning via her work e-mail. No, they didn't have to worry. It would be impossible to track the source. It was bouncing all over the world before it arrived, and all traces would disappear an hour after it was opened.

By eleven o'clock, both Heidi and Andrew were exhausted. There was no way they could make it all the way to DC, so they decided to stop in Cleveland. The airport exit had multiple hotel options, so Andrew pulled off the road, and they found a room at the Castleberry Inn & Suites. Clean and comfortable, the hotel featured a pool and fitness room. Some exercise in the morning would help start their day right.

Their room was a suite on the first floor, overlooking the swimming pool. Ethan had seemed comfortable with Heidi staying in the same room in Madison, and Andrew didn't like the idea of being separated, even with an adjoining door, so Heidi took the bedroom overlooking the pool, and Andrew and Ethan bunked up front on a pullout sofa.

Heidi and Ethan fell asleep quickly, but Andrew couldn't relax. The sagging sleeper sofa certainly didn't help, but even more troubling was the fact that he couldn't turn off his mind.

He kept replaying his meeting with Wally, wondering what he could have done differently. Then his worries drifted to what they were going to do in DC. Was this just a fool's journey? How could they possibly succeed? Finally, by one o'clock, he had tortured himself long enough, and in desperation he started to meditate, forcing the negative thoughts out with prayer. As he concentrated on taking slow, measured breaths, his eyes grew heavy and his heartbeat slowed.

Lost in meditation, worlds blurred, and his awareness slipped from the room. The whispers in his ears seemed otherworldly, but then the unmistakable click of a card key and a crack at the door brought Andrew back to the room. Still in a fog, he tilted his head, his heavy eyelids opening briefly, then all of a sudden, opening wide in terror.

"Do it quickly," the whisper said. "They're going to wake up as soon as you start."

Some tool reached through the gap in the door, ready to cut the safety latch. Andrew rolled over, pretending to be asleep, and reached underneath Ethan. Then, as quietly as he could, he pulled his son in close to pick him up, stood from the bed, and tiptoed into the back bedroom.

"Heidi," he whispered. "Get up. Someone's breaking in. I've got Ethan. Get the gun."

Dazed, Heidi sat up straight as Andrew crouched down behind the bed, setting Ethan on the floor beside him. Heidi quickly realized what was happening and rolled off the bed, fumbling by the nightstand and grabbing her backpack.

"Got it," she said.

By now, Ethan was awake, and they all huddled behind the bed.

"Do you think we can get out of here?" Andrew said, looking at the patio door to the pool.

"Give it a try," Heidi said as she pointed the gun to the hallway that led to the front room.

Andrew pulled back the curtains in front of the sliding glass doors then quickly closed them. "Oh my God, there are men out there, too."

"Damn it," Heidi whispered. "Reach in my bag. Get the other gun."

Suddenly, gun shots sounded out by the pool.

"Dad, they've got the door open. Someone's coming! I hear them coming!"

Then, what sounded like voices from the door to their room shouted, "Stop or we'll shoot." After a brief pause, more guns fired in rapid succession, this time from the front room.

"What's going on?" Heidi asked.

Then the crackle and beep of a walkie-talkie was followed by another voice saying, "All clear."

The voice inside the room responded, "Clear here."

"They're coming back," Andrew whispered. "Ethan, stay low. Heidi, you ready?"

"Ready," she replied, her gun shaking in her hand as she aimed toward the front room.

"Mr. Hastings. Are you there? Ms. Pearson? Are you okay?" the man's voice called out as lights turned on in the room. "I know you must be frightened. My name is Tony Gibbs. I'm here to help you. Is your son okay?"

Heidi and Andrew looked puzzled. Tony Gibbs? They weren't going to fall for any tricks, so they kept their aim locked ahead.

The man continued, "We don't have much time. We need to get out of here now. Can I come back?"

"No. I'll shoot," said Andrew.

"Please, trust me," the voice replied.

"Who are you?" Andrew asked, holding his aim steady.

"I'm working undercover for the Ethical Food Coalition. We've been watching Ms. Pearson for almost two weeks now to find out what her investigation of the plane crash uncovered. You just met Wally Babin for lunch. They were watching you. They followed you here."

"Who? Who are they?" Andrew asked.

"Their organization's name is CALF, and it's run by Laura Long. It stands for Council for American Liberties and Freedom, and they've been working with IFM on the Redu launch. I'm guessing you know something that might endanger the FDA approval, so they want you dead."

Heidi turned to Andrew.

"We don't have much time. More may be coming, and then the police. Please, I'm coming back. I've put down my gun. My hands are raised."

TWENTY-THREE

Washington, D.C.
Thursday, June 17
2:00 A.M.

LAURA LONG STOOD BY her living room window, watching the lights twinkle over DC. She was tired of waiting, so she picked up her phone. They should have checked in by now.

"Larry, what have you heard?"

"Nothing. That's the problem," he replied. "We lost contact with our team around one thirty, right after they went in."

"What? How do you lose contact with four henchmen tailing some guy off the street, his ex-girlfriend, and an eleven-year-old kid?"

"I don't have any details. Police are on the scene at the hotel. Gunshots were heard, and fatalities have been reported."

"Damn it, Larry, this was our shot! They didn't see us coming."

"I know."

"I'm tired of the screw-ups. Get me the facts. I'll be in at seven. I want answers, Larry. Answers!"

Akron, Ohio
Thursday, June 17
3:00 A.M.

THEIR EXIT had been quick. Tony had led them out of the back bedroom and around the three dead bodies in the front room, warning them not to touch anything. Heidi had tried to shield Ethan from seeing the bloody corpses with their terrible gaping wounds, but there was no way he hadn't gotten at least a glimpse.

After grabbing their bags, Tony and his team had loaded them into a white Toyota Highlander while another group drove off in Andrew's MDX with instructions to "hide it." Within an hour, they were in the connecting suites of a hotel in Akron, Ohio.

Finally, around three o'clock, after Tony suggested they lie down, Ethan collapsed, Andrew holding him, gently stroking his forehead.

"I think he's asleep," Andrew whispered.

Heidi nodded. "Are you okay?"

"Still pretty wired. Where's Tony?"

"He's waiting for you in the other room."

They didn't know much about their new friend, Tony Gibbs. He explained how he worked for Gina Sills and the Ethical Food Coalition. They claimed to be the good guys, but based on the dead bodies they had left back at their last hotel room, it was hard to tell. Dressed in black from head to toe, Tony had dark, salt-and-pepper hair and wrinkles that whiskered about his brown eyes. Although he looked like he could be in his fifties, something about him seemed much younger.

"Can you stay with Ethan? I don't want him waking up without one of us here."

"Of course," Heidi said, reaching out her arm to help Andrew up.

"Thanks," Andrew said, pulling Heidi in close. "I'm sorry I've gotten you in such a mess. I almost got us killed tonight."

"We're okay, and that's all that matters," Heidi replied, putting her hands on Andrew's shoulders.

As Andrew held Heidi even closer, something deep within him took over, and without thinking, he kissed her. Not just any kiss. What started with sweetness and innocence quickly turned into something deeper. Then Andrew slowly pulled away while gently caressing her face and said, "I love you."

Heidi smiled, staring into Andrew's steel blue eyes. Tears welled up and spilled onto her cheeks. "I love you, too. More than I ever thought possible."

Andrew held her tightly, gently kissing her cheek and along her neck.

"Oh, how I've missed that," she whispered in his ear. "I wish we could do this all night, but...Tony."

"I know." And reluctantly, with one last kiss, Andrew let go of Heidi and walked into the adjoining room.

Tony got up immediately. "Is everything okay?"

"Yes, it is. Thank you for saving our lives." Andrew hesitated then asked, "Are you sure we're safe here?"

"For now, yes. We should get moving soon, though. I'm getting some new transportation for us. We have some connections nearby, so we should have it in a couple hours. Would you like to sit down?"

"Yes, that would be great," Andrew said as they moved over to a round table near the window.

Tony nodded. "I'm sure you have tons of questions."

"I do."

"Where do you want to start?"

"How about the EFC? I've heard of it, but why should I feel safe? I mean, you guys have a reputation for violence, like tonight, and blowing things up like that Nutrisense infant formula plant a couple years ago."

"Well, as you'll learn, reputations can sometimes be earned, and other times manipulated and foisted upon you. IFM and CALF like nothing more than to paint us as extremist, violent terrorists, undeserving of public support. All I can do is promise you that tonight's violence was a last resort. When we picked up this group following you, and then intercepted some of their communications, I knew I had to act quickly to save your lives. I gave them one chance to stop their attack. When they didn't, I stopped them."

"Who are you? How did you end up here? And why do you care?"

Tony paused. "Well, never in a million years did I think I would be living this life. A little over ten years ago I was living my dream. My wife and I lived in Southern California. I worked on San Diego's SWAT team, and I loved it. But then it all just came apart."

Andrew waited for an explanation, but none came. "So what happened?"

"My world unraveled."

Again, Tony just stopped. So Andrew continued to press. "How?"

Tony took a deep breath. "My daughter died."

Andrew's face creased in pain. A pain no parent ever wants to know, but can only imagine.

Then Tony continued, "No, she didn't die. She was killed."

Tony leaned forward and pulled out his wallet. "Here are a couple of pictures of her. Her name is Bella." Consciously choosing the present tense. "The one picture is of Bella, her mom, and me when she was just a couple months old. The other picture was taken when she had just turned five. She was killed about two months later."

"She's beautiful," Andrew said, looking into the sweet, innocent eyes of this precious girl. They were Tony's eyes—big and wide, and a rich, chocolate brown.

"I'm so very sorry."

"Thank you." Tony paused, taking one more look at his photos before carefully returning them to his wallet. "You know, they say when you lose a child, you're never the same again. It's so true. But I think when your child is killed, so carelessly murdered, you either wither and die, or you fight with all your might to make a difference. You fight a battle for change to make sure it never has to happen again. That's how I ended up here, Andrew."

"I don't understand. How did your daughter die?"

"Bella was killed by a kid's meal at Emma's. The cheeseburger was contaminated with E. coli 0157:H7."

The pieces started to fall in place. Andrew remembered that Emma's, IFM's fast-food burger chain, had a devastating E. coli outbreak years ago. Twelve children and one adult died, with hundreds more hospitalized. It was a dark period in IFM's history, and although IFM leadership did its best to bury it, people continued to talk about it whenever another food poisoning scare popped up in the news.

"I didn't work at IFM at the time, but I've heard some details of the incident."

"Incident? Really? Such an innocent-sounding word," Tony replied. "I hate that word. I've heard it so many times. Hell, I used to say it as a police officer. But it comes nowhere near describing what really happened. IFM, the meat packers, and the corporate farmers that raise our nation's cattle on horrific, inhumane feedlots killed my daughter. My daughter was killed because of the complete and total failure of our food system."

"I'm sorry, Tony. Now that you say it, I can see how that word minimizes what really happened."

"No, I'm sorry. I shouldn't react that way, especially with you. Words like 'incident' are just part of our vocabulary now. Unfortunately, we just don't realize how words are used to manipulate us and sanitize real tragedies. They give companies like IFM a way to win the PR war by saying, 'Oh, that's too bad' and expressing sympathy without acknowledging the deeper problem. So we shed a tear and move on, only for the same tragedy to be repeated again and again because the underlying problem hasn't been addressed."

"I guess I've just come to accept that, in general, our food is safe."

"Well, that's where EFC comes in," Tony replied. "Unlike some of the other crazier left wing groups out there, EFC is really trying to promote a more centrist agenda. After Bella died, I changed in so many ways. I asked more questions. Finally, I decided that to make sense of her death, I had to do something. So I resigned my position on the SWAT team at the SDPD and started working for EFC."

"Wow, that's a big change. What did your wife think?"

Another scar was sliced open. Tony looked down again and unconsciously started twisting his wedding band around his ring finger with his thumb.

"My wife is dead, Andrew." He finally lifted up his hand and removed the band. "Tanya committed suicide six months after Bella died. She felt like she had failed as a mother to protect her child, and it destroyed her."

TWENTY-FOUR

Long & Company Headquarters
Thursday, June 17
8:30 A.M.

LARRY RUEHL and Ann Verbena were sitting at the conference room table with three other associates and Skylar Brin on the speakerphone. Larry had never seen Laura so furious and out of control. Although no one was able to provide any details, four men were dead, and Andrew Hastings was still free.

After shredding Skylar for his field ops team's complete and utter failure, Laura moved on to Larry and Ann.

"Now where the hell are those surveillance tapes from the hotel?"

Before Larry could jump in, Ann replied, "I'm working on it, but it's not as simple as hitting copy, paste, and send. I'm hacking into police servers trying to get them."

"Is that attitude I hear? Stop making excuses for your inadequacy and get it done. Damn it all. Why the hell is it so hard to find people that don't make excuses?"

Finally, after chewing out her team and peppering them with demands, Laura realized she was getting nowhere. Even she understood you could beat your people for only so long.

She got up from the conference table and went over to a white board. She was rarely one to stray from her electronic gadgets, and the room fell silent as she picked up a marker and started drawing circles and thought bubbles across the board. In one circle there was "Hastings × 2 + Pearson" with four thought bubbles coming off it: "getting help?"; "from whom?"; "where are they?"; and "going where?" Then, across the board another circle read: "Known Leverage Points: (1) Wally Babin, (2) WMSP/ TriMedia, (3) Lydia Sands, (4) Dahl?"

Laura put down her marker, and the room stared, waiting for their orders.

"This is how I see it," Laura started. "The only thing we really know is that Andrew, his son, and Heidi Pearson are together. We don't know if they're getting help, but it's a mystery to any of us how they could be so successful eluding us on their own. We also don't have a clue where they are or where they are going. Does anyone disagree?"

No one had the courage to speak up.

Laura continued, "Okay, I'll take that as complete agreement. So I figure we can continue and just wait for some good fortune to drop in our laps, or we can start shaking some trees. Larry, take notes. I don't want to repeat this."

Larry, the new secretary designate, turned to a clean sheet in his notepad.

Laura went on, "First, let's get a new team back in Madison watching Wally 24/7. I don't want him scratching his ass without us knowing it. Got it?"

The room nodded in unison, and Larry scribbled away.

"Second, between all the companies we do business with, I'm guessing there is several billion dollars' worth of media that I can influence." Thinking out loud, Laura wondered, "What would happen if I threatened to pull spending at TriMedia if they didn't help us shut up Heidi Pearson? What do you think?"

"Brilliant," Larry said without lifting his head, determined to capture her every word.

"Third, let's get Lydia Sands. She's leverage with the Hastings boy. I'm not sure if her ex will risk himself or his child for her, but it's worth a try." On a roll, Laura barely paused for a breath. "And fourth, what the hell's going on with that Dahl guy? We know he had some early contact with Hastings, but it's dried up. Now that's pretty unusual. Damn it, find out why."

Minneapolis, Minnesota
Thursday, June 17
10:30 A.M.

LYDIA HAD already missed three days of work, and people were starting to ask questions. So Thursday morning she was back at the bank, unfortunately just in time for a lending compliance meeting. The provisions of the latest Consumer Financial Protections Act had resulted in so many changes, and compliance-consulting firms were now making a fortune educating lenders across the country. Although Lydia was far above the minutia of everyday lending, her presence at this meeting was more symbolic and intended to demonstrate how seriously Great Sioux National Bank regarded following the new regulations.

Right after the morning break, the discussion had moved into amendments to Truth In Lending disclosures. Bored out of her mind, Lydia flipped open her phone to check her messages, first in her personal e-mail account, and then for work. As she scanned her work inbox, one e-mail caught her immediate attention. The sender's name was odd, but the subject line couldn't have been clearer: "Hi Mom."

Within moments she had clicked open the e-mail to read the message:

Hi Mom:

I'm safe here. Attached is a video I made for you. Please, listen to me and follow the directions at the end of the video. You're not safe.

Love, Ethan

P.S. This message will disappear from your inbox one hour after you open it for safety reasons.

Unable to view the video on her phone, Lydia reached down, grabbed her purse, and ran up to her office. All she could think was *Ethan is safe. My baby is safe!*

———————

I-76 East
Thursday, June 17
11:30 A.M.

DESPITE ONLY A FEW HOURS of sleep, Tony had the group up and moving by eight o'clock. The local news had reported the shootings at the Castleberry Inn & Suites with only vague descriptions of Andrew, Heidi, and Ethan and no mention of Tony or his team. But Tony didn't want to press his luck, and during his conversation with Andrew in the wee hours of the morning, they had agreed: Washington was their only option.

Going toe to toe with Laura Long didn't scare Tony, but he had to run it by his bosses at EFC. Gina Sills had worked very hard to keep her organization clean, so breaking into Long & Company's office might cross the line.

Tony had arranged for two new cars to transport the Hastings group and his team to Washington. Tony drove Andrew, Heidi, and Ethan, while three other members of his team followed behind, looking for anything suspicious. As lunchtime approached, Ethan started lobbying for some fast food. At first, Andrew just said, "No, we need to keep moving," hoping to hear Tony's suggestions of where to eat, but Tony didn't bite. Finally, when Ethan saw a sign for Betty's Farmhouse, he begged to stop.

"Betty's is my favorite, Dad. Please, can we stop? I mean, it's not just a burger joint. We can get something healthy there. It's like a farm."

Tony smiled, and Andrew couldn't help feeling like a parental failure. He braced for a lecture from the food cop. Then Tony surprised Andrew.

"I've got a deal for you, Ethan. We can go to Betty's if you promise we can talk more about where all this food comes from."

"Sure," Ethan said confidently, "I hear my dad lecture me all the time about this. Betty's is good stuff."

TWENTY-FIVE

Minneapolis, Minnesota
Thursday, June 17
2:05 P.M.

LAURA REACHED Aidan on his way back to the office. He was busy that morning polishing IFM's public image at a groundbreaking for a local, IFM-supported food shelf. Laura wanted to keep the call brief. She thought Aidan deserved an update, but she didn't want Chloe and Dan's bickering to get in the way. So she purposely chose a moment that was sure to avoid them.

After a brief prelude, Laura came clean on the foiled attempt to capture Hastings in Cleveland. Without missing a beat, she quickly moved on to a new plan she was formulating, and she promised to share more details during his visit.

Plymouth, Minnesota
Thursday, June 17
3:15 P.M.

ETHAN'S PLEA had worked. After seeing his video, Lydia decided to get out of town for a while. She wasn't sure all the precautions were necessary, but she played along and withdrew five thousand dollars from her bank account and announced a leave of absence until her son was found.

Shortly after three o'clock, Lydia was packed and ready. Her cab would arrive in fifteen minutes, and although she hadn't been to a bus station since college, she figured it was a good place to get lost. With four different bus tickets in hand, she would be able to at least blur her trail for a while.

As she stood by her bed ready to zip up her bag, Lydia went through her mental checklist one final time, making sure she had everything she needed. Then, when the doorbell rang, she ran downstairs in a panic, thinking the cab was early.

"Ms. Sands?"

"Yes."

"I'm Officer Sundy, and this is my partner Officer Jennings," the man said. Both flashed their badges in unison. "We're following up on your missing person report from earlier this week."

"Yes, do you have information?"

"We think something may have happened with your son. We believe he was involved in a shooting in Cleveland and may have been kidnapped. Can you identify him in this photo?"

"Is he okay?" Lydia asked, anxiously waiting as the officer pulled the photo from a file.

"Is that your child?"

Lydia grabbed the photo from the officer's hands. It was blurry and black and white, but it was unmistakably Ethan.

"Yes, this is Ethan. What happened? When?" Lydia could feel her world crashing around her. "Is my baby all right?"

"Yes, but we can't share the details with you here. We need you to come with us downtown."

Washington, D.C.
Thursday, June 17
4:35 P.M.

ANDREW, HEIDI, ETHAN, AND TONY were driving into DC during afternoon rush hour. Traffic was slow, but since they were going against the flow, it was still moving along.

"I'm sorry we don't have time to stop off at a hotel first. Gina has a dinner meeting this evening, and I think it's crucial we get in front of her sooner than later. If our plan is going to work, we don't have much time at all," Tony said.

"I agree," Andrew replied. "Anyway, I don't like having Ethan out of my sight. Given all I have seen the past week, it worries me."

"That reminds me. You guys still interested in that quick course in self-defense?" Tony asked.

"Yeah," Ethan replied.

"Hold on one second," Andrew said. Then looking over to Tony, he continued. "I know Heidi and I'd like to learn some more about self-defense. Let me think more about Ethan coming along."

"Come on, Dad," Ethan said between making sounds and arm motions that were supposed to resemble some form of martial arts.

St. Louis Park, Minnesota
Thursday, June 17
3:45 P.M.

THE DRIVE into the police station downtown was quiet with the officers sitting up front in the white, four-door, unmarked car. Twenty minutes into the trip, when Lydia finally looked out the windows and paid attention to her surroundings, she asked, "What route is this?"

Officers Sundy and Jennings didn't reply.

"Where are you taking me? This isn't the way downtown."

Something was wrong, and as the car slowed for a stoplight, Lydia decided to make a run for it. Without making any quick movements, she slowly reached for the handle of the rear right door. *Damn it*, she thought. It wouldn't open. Starting to panic, Lydia tried to lower the window, but it was locked as well.

Then, from the front of the car, Officer Sundy bellowed, "Just relax and stay put." As he turned around, the barrel of his FN 57 semiautomatic pistol was pointed at her head. "Cooperate, and I won't have to use this. Get the picture?"

EFC Headquarters
Thursday, June 17
5:15 P.M.

GINA SILLS'S updates with her top aides, Henry Usher and Ken Luger, had kept her close to Tony's progress. The latest report of shootings in Cleveland was very disturbing, but Tony assured Ken it had been a last recourse, and his surveillance tapes would prove there had been no other options.

It was a clean job. Tony was her best operative, and Gina trusted him implicitly, but she was still worried. EFC could not fulfill its mission if it acted amorally, and even a tiny swirl of doubt could paralyze its efforts. But what had started out as chasing down misinformation surrounding the IFM plane crash was turning into a potential gold mine. Nevertheless, she was running out of time to stop Redu's approval.

As Gina walked into the room with Ken and Henry by her side, Tony immediately got up to say hello.

"How are you, my dear?" Gina asked, running over to hug Tony.

"I'm good." Tony held Gina tight. "How long has it been?"

"More than a year," Gina replied, staring into Tony's dark eyes. He was a little more weathered than she remembered, but his rugged good looks hadn't faded. His frame was modest, but it was lean and muscled.

"Too long."

Gina's heart raced as she felt the power of Tony's arms around her and she flashed back to a time when they were a couple. But the pain of Tony's loss had been too much weight for them to carry, and what had been a summer filled with passion soon fizzled despite many heartbreaking, late-night conversations. Gina understood, but of all the men she had dated, Tony felt like the one she should have never let get away.

Before Gina became too lost in his hold, she gently pulled away and asked, "So who do we have here?"

"Oh, excuse my poor manners," Tony declared. "Gina, I'd like you to meet Ethan Hastings, his dad, Andrew, and their friend, Heidi Pearson. Oh, and these are two of Gina's associates." The two men stepped up. "Ken Luger, my boss, and Henry Usher, Gina's right hand man and Chief of Operations."

Gina, Henry, and Ken made their way around the room, shaking everyone's hands.

"It sounds like you've been on quite the journey the past week," Gina said as she gave Ethan a handshake and gentle hug.

"It's been crazy and frightening," Ethan replied.

"To say the least," Andrew joined in. "Our world has been flipped completely upside down. And if it weren't for the help of your team and Tony here, I don't think we'd still be in the game."

"Well, I'm glad we could help," Ken said. "It's great when you find yourself in the right place at the right time."

"I just hope you don't see us as some vigilante group," Gina added. "That's not who we are."

"No, not at all," said Heidi. "As we sat huddled down in our hotel room, shots being fired all around us, I wasn't sure we'd make it. Then Tony walked in like the cavalry."

"He's our best guy in the field." Gina smiled at Tony. "Now, I understand y'all must be worn out," she said, her southern accent slipping out. "After last night and then your long drive today, I'm sorry to ask you to come in here so late in the day. But I'm meeting Candy Presho for drinks later, so I don't have a whole lot of time."

"Candy Presho? Where have I heard that name?" Andrew asked.

"She's the Deputy Director of the FDA's Office of Applied Research and Safety Assessment. We've been good friends since med school. To be honest, if it wasn't for Candy, I think Redu would have been approved by now. She's been a thorn in the side of the Regulatory Decision Team, and to date she has at least won some traction with Joseph Tillman, the Principal Deputy Commissioner of the FDA."

Impressed, Heidi said, "Well, sounds like you have some influence in this town."

Gina laughed, her smile warming up the room. "After almost twenty years leading EFC, I'd hope I have some. But up against a lobby powerhouse like CALF, I feel like a ripple in the ocean.

"Big Food companies like IFM want to get us to eat more so they can make more money. That's why the EFC exists. We're desperately trying to get the message out and increase awareness of what people are putting in their bodies. But our voice is just so small, especially compared to these huge food manufacturers and agribusinesses and their lobbyists."

Andrew was nodding his head. "Well, we hope to even the game out a bit. As you know, we have a report by Wally Babin proving the link between early Redu formulations and chronic gas, bloating, abdominal discomfort, and diarrhea. We also have proof that IFM has been working with CALF. That alone would be a PR disaster for Aidan Toole."

"True, but there's nothing illegal about having a lobbyist like Laura Long working for you," Henry Usher added, somewhat stiffly. "Can I see that report you're talking about?"

Andrew pulled it out of his pocket and handed it to Henry.

"What do you think?" Gina asked.

After scanning the report's contents, he replied, "At best it may reopen some questions about Redu's safety. We'd need proof that the formulation of synthetic resistant starch tested here was the one submitted to the FDA for approval, or at least a precursor. In fact, this report doesn't even mention Redu by name. Without that, this is just another failed ingredient trial."

Andrew replied, "I know, but we also have conversations recorded where Laura and Aidan all but admit to killing people to get Redu approved. Since the time I learned of these early, secret Redu trials, I've been watched, and when I refused to give up searching for the truth, they tried to kill me. I'm convinced the survival of my family is dependent on exposing the truth and taking down IFM, and we'd like your help."

"Do you have them actually admitting to killing anyone or doing anything illegal?" Ken asked.

"No, but that's why we need your help. I know IFM is guilty. I just need more proof."

Tony had coached Andrew and Heidi before the meeting. He wanted in on the plan, but the idea had to come from Andrew. Gina, Henry, and Ken would reject it without consideration if the idea came from Tony and it was labeled an EFC-generated plan.

"We want to break in to Long & Company's offices. We'd pose as a special night crew of carpet cleaners. Tony helped us do some of the groundwork, and we think it's feasible. I've got one of the best IT guys around on my team. He assures me that if we can just get access to Laura Long's network via some computer or portable device, he should be able to snag any documents we need to prove our case."

"Like what? What types of documents are you hoping to find?"

"E-mails, voice mails, or files that prove IFM sabotaged their own corporate jet and blew up my car. Evidence that proves IFM stacked the FAC panel or altered Redu's product safety testing results. We want access to all of Laura Long's files. I'm sure we can find evidence there that proves IFM has acted illegally."

"And what type of support are you asking for?" Ken asked.

Tony jumped in. "Basic logistics and some security support. I'd really like to assist Andrew and Heidi. I think it will be too challenging for them to execute this alone."

"Let's say we go along with you on this, and you find something. It's unlikely any of this evidence could be used in court," Henry replied.

"That's a question for the courts to decide," Andrew interjected. "Right now, we want to live to see tomorrow, and if we don't do anything, I think it's only a matter of time until IFM catches up to us."

Heidi continued, "As you know, there are two courts out there—the legal courts and the courts of public opinion. We don't have to dot our i's and cross our t's to win in the court of public opinion. Hopefully, the information we obtain can help us gain enough leverage to bring more people to our side, like Wally Babin. If we can sway a couple folks like him who may have legally obtained information, we can sink the Redu approval, IFM, and Laura Long."

"Yes, Mr. Babin," Ken said, imagining the possibilities. "We've suspected that he and his boss, Todd McNaulty, have been tampering with these trials all along."

"Oh, I agree. When I spoke to Wally, he was visibly shaken, and that alone makes me believe he was involved," Andrew replied.

"Interesting, but what about the ethical question? I mean, breaking in? That's not legal, and I definitely don't want EFC's good name being attached to it."

"I pride myself on being a very ethical reporter, Ms. Sills—"

"Please, call me Gina."

"Okay." Heidi smiled. "Gina, I don't casually disregard the

legality of what we are trying to do. That said, I do believe we have run out of options."

Gina stared up at the ceiling, trying to navigate some solution. She wanted to nail IFM and Laura Long more than anyone. She still couldn't help believing they murdered Lia. Turning to Tony, Gina asked, "What exactly do you need in terms of support?"

"Six to eight people."

"EFC people?"

"Not necessarily."

"Total cost?"

"Twenty thousand," Tony replied.

"Let us think about it overnight," Gina said. "I can't promise anything, but I feel like we at least understand the situation. Any other questions? Ken? Henry?"

St. Louis Park, Minnesota
Thursday, June 17
4:30 P.M.

IN AN ABANDONED WAREHOUSE near the Cedar Trail and the BNSF railway in St. Louis Park, Lydia strained to hear her captors in the room next door. She was tied to a metal chair in a storeroom, and the space was dark except for a dim, overhead light. Despite being empty and swept clean, a damp, mildew smell permeated the room and made Lydia's eyes itch and body crawl as if the invisible contamination were seeping into her skin.

"Yes, we have her, Larry," said Skylar Brin.

"Did you have any trouble?" Larry asked over the speakerphone in the makeshift office.

"No, she cooperated for the most part," replied Rufus Pilot. "She bought our story until she realized we weren't heading downtown."

"Good. Well, make sure she doesn't escape. If you make another mistake, I don't think Ms. Long will keep you around."

"Don't worry," Rufus added. "I'm keeping my eyes on her. She's a hot little number. Before this is over, I want me some of that."

"Rufus," Larry replied, "her days may be numbered, but if Laura finds out you touched her, I wouldn't want to be you. So shut the hell up, and keep your hands off her. Got it?"

Rufus was ready to tell Larry where to go when Skylar interrupted. "Yes, we understand Larry. I'll get out a cattle prod if I need to keep this ass under control."

TWENTY-SIX

Washington, D.C.
Thursday, June 17
7:03 P.M.

CANDY PRESHO sat at a corner table of the Library Bar at The Melrose Hotel. Usually, coming into the district after work for a drink was out of the question, but tonight was special. She needed to meet with Gina in person. Things were heating up, and Candy needed help.

Gina arrived a few minutes after seven, naturally radiant despite the frenetic pace of her life. The mere sight of her made Candy envious. Gina had always made life look easy, and despite being the same age, Candy looked at least ten years older, with lines and wrinkles deepening with every night's sleep. Gina's caramel skin was as smooth and flawless as most thirty-year-olds'. *Damn her*, Candy thought as she gave her graduate school girlfriend a hug.

"Thanks for coming into town to meet with me," Gina said, giving Candy a peck on her cheek.

The two sat down in the richly appointed room with gold

medallion upholstered chairs and rich mahogany bookcases adorning the walls. Candy surveyed the room again. There was nothing illegal about her meeting with Gina, but during such a high profile approval like Redu, the Commissioner probably wouldn't be happy.

"I didn't see anyone coming in," Gina said. "I think we're good."

"Sorry to be so paranoid. Normally I'd like to make an evening of this and catch up, but everyone is feeling the pressure in the office these days."

"What's going on?"

"I'm telling you, Gina, I've seen a lot over my years, but nothing like this. Politics and the federal agency biz can be a rough game, but this has been taken to a new level."

"So what's different?"

"Some people are freaking out. When Joe Tillman announced the decision delay, it's like someone lit a fire beneath us. Yes, I have my supporters, but several people have come up to me and said point blank, 'Stop holding up the decision or you don't have a future here.' I know Jackie Epps is behind it. We're supposed to be equals, but she's got another one of the directors, Sam Gallatin, under her thumb, and they are teaming up and trying to steamroll right over me."

"Watch out, Candy. I'm almost certain Jackie's dirty. Did you hear about the death of her secretary?"

"Yes, I did. Horrible gas explosion at her home."

"I know. I can't prove it, but I think her death is somehow related to the murder of one of our agents, Lia Merriman."

"Really?"

"Yes, so above all, be safe."

"When did being an advocate for safe food become a dangerous job?"

"I know. We're living in scary times," Gina replied. "How about Tillman? What's he saying about Redu?"

"He's a big supporter of mine, but yesterday he said he was at the end of his rope. He can't delay the decision any longer. He's set the final meeting date for June 28. Unless I have real proof of wrong-doing or about the dangers of Redu, he'll recommend approval."

"Damn it," Gina replied. "We both know Redu is dangerous. It's just one more concocted ingredient in our industrialized food chain."

"I agree, but my hands are tied. I can't do any more."

"I know, Candy. You've gone to bat on this one, and I appreciate it." She reached out and held her dear friend's hands on the table.

Then, from across the room, a flash of light jolted the tranquil room, followed by a "Smile!"

Candy looked up, and Gina turned her head. "Damn it," Candy whispered. "I can't believe she's here."

Jackie Epps, with smartphone in hand, was standing across the room taking a few more pictures. In between shots, she said, "Isn't it funny to run into the two of you here? This certainly is a small town. Do you mind if I sit down?"

"Oh, that would be great." Candy grinned, trying to think quickly. "Gina and I were just talking about our grad school days. One of our classmates is getting married, and we're in charge of the bachelorette party. Isn't that crazy at our age?"

"That sure is," Jackie replied. "And to think, I would have guessed you were talking about work. But I know you're smarter than that, right Candy?"

THE INTERSECTION of colonial charm and DC style came to life on Georgetown's Wisconsin Avenue. With some of the best shopping and restaurants in DC, this street was a favorite of locals and travelers alike.

Tony arranged for three rooms in the Georgetown Inn. Heidi and the Hastings were in a two-bedroom suite, flanked by rooms occupied by Tony and his team. Although most travelers would choose to dine out at one of the many neighboring cafes, Heidi, Andrew, and Ethan stayed in. This was no vacation. They knew

Laura Long's people were looking for them. They hoped she hadn't realized how close they really were.

After ordering room service, Tony joined them and together they updated Josh over their secure cell phone connection about the past twenty-four hours. It was hard to believe that just a day ago they had been driving innocently to Cleveland, only to be attacked in the middle of the night by CALF's operative team. Josh was silent as Andrew narrated the scene. Somehow this dark, surreal world had taken on a familiar form, but when they were faced with real, heart-stopping death, the terror of their situation took on a completely new dimension.

"Well, compared to you all, things are pretty quiet on this end," Josh replied.

"Anything to report?" Heidi asked.

"The good news is, it looks like Lydia listened to your message."

"What did you hear?" Ethan asked.

"Her message at work says she's on a leave of absence. I don't know where she went, though, and that worries me."

"What do you mean?" Andrew asked.

"Well, I don't know all the details, but Aidan talked to Chloe and Dan late in the day. He referenced a call from Laura and some four-pronged plan."

"And?"

"No details, but the plan is supposed to put pressure on every known link to you and Ethan."

"Lydia definitely would figure in there."

"Dad? What are we going to do?"

"Your mom is very smart, buddy. She got your message, and she's left town. Josh will keep us posted if he hears anything from her."

"I promise I will," Josh replied. "I'll keep listening in at IFM for more details. Okay, Ethan?"

"Thanks, Josh."

"So where do you guys stand on breaking into Laura Long's offices?" Josh asked.

"We pitched the idea to Gina Sills, and now we're waiting to hear if she'll back us up. I don't know how we can pull this off without her team's help."

"Do you need me to come down to DC this weekend?"

"No, Josh, we need you there in Minneapolis. You're our best eyes and ears, and the more movements you make, the more suspicion you'll arouse."

"You feel like you're safe?" Tony asked. "You sure they aren't watching you?"

"Oh, I bet they're watching. But I've just arranged a nice hidden retreat here. After getting home, I turn on the television or some music, take a shower, and then disappear downstairs. I've set up shop in the guest suite in my condo building."

"Don't get complacent. You sure they don't know you're there?"

Josh shared the details on his filament trap. Not satisfied, Tony went on. "I can have a team there by morning. You sure you're okay?"

"I'm fine. I agree with Andrew. The more activity around me, the more likely we are to raise a red flag."

"Okay. Just don't get over-confident. Make sure you have an emergency plan to get away quickly."

"Understood. Let's talk details on the break-in."

"What do you have?" Andrew asked.

"I've uploaded onto our data cloud the script you need to infiltrate CALF. There are instructions linked to it on how to download it to your laptop and transfer it to a USB flash drive."

"Are you sure this will work?" Tony asked.

"I've tested it here. You never know what security we'll find, but I think it's pretty clever. It can beat all of the security systems that have been peddled by vendors at IFM."

"Josh is a tech wizard. If he says it will work, you can bet on it," Andrew added. "So how do we get it on their network?"

"That's the tricky part. You'll have to upload it on a computer that's logged into the network."

"How are we going to be able to do that?" Heidi asked. "I'm sure every workstation there is password protected."

"You're right, but here's where we bet on human nature," Andrew explained. "I'm guessing that there's at least one employee in that office who writes their password down and keeps it close by under a keyboard or mouse pad or in a desk drawer. It's one of the biggest security risks out there, and I'm gambling Long & Company hasn't been able to break that bad habit."

"I know people do that at the station all the time," Heidi replied.

"Do you know how you're going to get into the building in the first place?" Josh asked.

"As carpet cleaners," Andrew said. He, Heidi, and Tony had worked this out earlier on the drive to DC.

"Carpet cleaners?" Josh sounded incredulous.

"That's right, Josh," Tony interjected. "We've got the uniforms and cleaning equipment all ready."

"Hmmm...Okay, you're the expert, Tony."

"Our plan is to strike tomorrow evening, after everyone has left. It's a Friday night, so hopefully the offices will be empty."

"How are you going to get in?"

"We need to forge some paperwork to get through building security. I'm thinking an e-mail from the office manager? Any chance you can help us on that, Josh?"

"I'm on it."

"Hopefully we'll arrive after the cleaning crew has left. We need to make sure we can have as much access to the offices and computers as possible."

"Makes sense," Josh replied. "Just remember, if you're having trouble we can always try to hack into Long & Company's network using a smartphone — though our chance of getting the right employee's phone might prove even more difficult."

"I agree," Tony replied. "One more thing. I think it's a real possibility that Gina will reject our plan, and I'm concerned about paying an outside team."

"Money's not an issue," Josh said without hesitating.

"Really?" Andrew asked.

"Really."

Tony was bewildered by the banter.

Heidi finally let Tony in. "Yeah, it just so happens our best friend here is a billionaire."

"You don't seem like the normal stuck-up, rich guy."

"Oh, he is." Heidi grinned. "He just does a great job hiding it."

"Thanks, Pearson. I appreciate the kind word."

"Anything else to cover?" Andrew asked.

"Not that I can think of," Josh replied.

"Good. Tony's taking us through a basic, self-defense class later just in case. After our scare in Cleveland, we're thinking the more we know, the better."

"Ethan, too?"

"I haven't decided yet. I'm sure Tony's men would keep him safe while Heidi and I take the class, but we will see."

"Oh, let him go, Andrew. There's no harm in it. Is there?"

Tony jumped in. "And it'll be a great way for him to get to know the entire team."

"Okay, okay," Andrew replied. "He can go."

"Yes," Ethan said, pumping his fist in the air.

TWENTY-SEVEN

Washington, D.C.
Friday, June 18
8:10 A.M.

"DO YOU THINK you were set up?" Henry asked.

"I'm sure of it," Gina replied. "I mean, what are the chances?"

"What do you think Jackie is going to do with the photos?" Ken asked.

"That kept me up all night. I'm guessing she is going to share them with Tillman, flaunting them as proof that I'm unduly influencing Candy."

"Do you think she'll leak them to the press?"

Gina shook her head, "I don't think so, Henry. If she leaks them, she's making her boss and his boss look bad. She can inflict the most damage by discrediting Candy privately."

"You didn't mention our suspicions about Lia and Jackie's secretary, did you?"

"No, but I wanted to. It would have been pointless, though. Jackie would have denied any connection."

"So what are you going to do?" asked Ken.

"Well, it has me mulling over this Hastings operation more. Before I met with Candy, I had pretty well made up my mind to pass. But now?"

"I agree, Gina, but once we cross the line, don't we become as guilty as IFM? And the press uses a different yardstick with us. Big companies are assumed to be very self-motivated, so the public doesn't blink an eye if there is some corporate mischief going on. Hell, they expect it. On the other hand, a non-profit like us that is trying to help? The press loves nothing better than to turn our image around as some evil-monger promoting its self-serving agenda."

"You're right. But beyond the politics there are some very basic human elements here. The Hastings are in desperate trouble. Is there any way we can help them while remaining ethically intact? And then there's Lia. I'm sure she was murdered, but we have no proof. If we had access to Laura Long's files, maybe we could connect the dots."

"I've got an idea," Ken interjected. "What if we fire Tony?"

Gina looked shocked. "What?"

"Hold on one second," Ken appealed. "Just listen. If Tony is no longer an EFC employee, he's acting on his own accord. He can hire his own team and work with Hastings directly."

Gina thought for a couple seconds. Then with complete conviction she said, "You know, I apologize. I think I've lost my way on this one. Ken, I'm sorry I put you in the position of coming up with this option. Just hearing it made my skin crawl—no offense. This isn't the way a real leader should act, hiding behind lies and letting others assume all the risk. I'm starting to act just like all the politicians around here, and it's not right.

"The only thing worse than breaking the rules is abandoning your friends when they're willing to go to bat for you. Tony has been with us for a long time, and he's been faithful to a fault. He

believes we need to do this, and I trust him. Saving the Hastings'
family and friends is reason enough. If we kill Redu, prove Lia
was murdered, and take down IFM along the way, then so be it.
And if there's hell to pay, I'm ready to take the blame.'"

———————————

WHEN LAURA LONG'S call came through, Warren Levin
leaned back in his chair. It seemed like he had just made his tax-
deductible contribution for Freedom of Speech Now, Ms. Long's
media-focused lobbying group. But it didn't take Warren long to
realize he was on the other side of the table this time.

"So what do you want me to do?" Warren asked.

"I need you to rat out one of your reporters."

"You're kidding me, Laura. We're a media company."

"A media company that benefits from over $5 billion in advertis-
ing from the companies I work with. Come on, Warren, do the
math. Restaurants, food companies, pharmaceuticals, they're all
customers of mine. I make a couple calls, tell them how dangerous
your operation is, and your ad revenues will dry up."

"You wouldn't."

"I don't think you want to test me on this one. I appreciate your
business, but Freedom of Speech Now is a very small operation
in comparison to what I'm working on here. Besides, you know
what I've done for you and your company. You don't want me
working against you, do you?"

"Laura?"

"Sorry, Warren. Get in line, or I flip the switch. Just realize,
you're in for a long fall. I'm feeling generous today, though, so
I'll give you twenty-four hours to think about my proposal. But
I warn you, Warren. Don't come back with the wrong answer."

———————————

IFM Headquarters
Friday, June 18
10:00 A.M.

ART JACOBSON wasn't shy with Aidan Toole when it came to supporting his sales team. He went straight to the CEO's office, walked in, and sat down without an appointment.

"Aidan, my teams are starting to jump ship. What are you going to do?"

"Art, I need you to stand with me. We're going to get this done."

"You know how it is. My guys hate to lose face. Hell, presentations have been set up across the country, and we aren't going to have product samples to taste. Shoot straight with me. Is this approval going to happen?"

Art turned as there was a knock at Aidan's door and Dan walked in.

"Sorry I'm late, Aidan," Dan said, walking across the room. "Art, how are you? We need to get out of here and enjoy some golf one of these days. You free this weekend, man?"

"Good morning," Art said, shaking Dan's hand. "No time for golf. The regions are calling. They're trying to hold things together, but they're really nervous."

"Did Aidan share the latest?" Dan asked.

"No, we just started," Aidan replied.

"So tell me," Art said. "Did the approval come in?"

"No, but I'm going out to Washington with Chloe for a final push with some key players. Art, I'm telling you. We're almost there. I don't want you or your team worried."

"Aidan, we're beyond worried. My guys are panicking. The Klout top-to-top is next Tuesday. Dan, you promised my team you'd be ready."

"Aidan and I will both be at the meeting. If we need to, we can reschedule some meetings. We're in this with you guys," Dan said, slapping Art on the shoulder.

"Dan, if we reschedule meetings, we're sunk," Art replied. "We may as well just roll up the launch for this year. Is there any chance we can have product samples available for these meetings?"

"Sorry, the FDA prohibits it," Dan said, shaking his head. "I don't think we have a way to get around that. What we're hearing, though, is that the FDA is meeting in late June for a final announced decision. I'll have our sales warehouse ship on July 1 with my call. Also, we can scramble and get some samples put together into gift boxes. We can promise customers we meet with before the July 1 deadline that they will receive a special gift box of samples overnighted to them directly."

Art thought for a few seconds. It wasn't ideal, but they were dealing with the federal government here. Besides pushing for a delay, he was stuck. His bonus payout and options were dependent on a successful launch, which meant $25 million worth of reasons to continue to push hard.

"Okay, I'll rally my team. But July 1 is as far as we can push it. If we fail to get approval by then, we're going to have to punt. Got it?"

"Yes, we do," Aidan replied.

"Oh, and not only do I expect to see both of you at the top-to-top, but I want Chloe there, too. Klout makes us jump through hoops even in the best of circumstances, and their CEO, Randy Mueller, is a real health nut. Ever since he had a heart attack five years ago, he's been making a huge nutrition and wellness push in their stores. Chloe's key to answering any of his concerns. Heck, maybe she can even flirt with Randy to get him off our backs."

"I'm not sure Chloe is our best bait for that one, but I bet you have some hot salesgirl in your fold who is," Dan laughed.

"Just make sure Chloe is there. I trust her, Dan," Art replied, walking to Aidan's door.

"Don't worry, Art. She'll be there," Aidan replied, shaking his hand as he left.

As Art walked down the hall to his office, Aidan closed the door.

"Dan, thanks for your help. It feels like the walls are closing in on us."

"Don't worry, boss. We'll get it done."

"I know."

"So when do you and Chloe head out to DC?"

"We leave in an hour. Meetings start up at two o'clock."

"Who are you meeting with?" Dan asked as they sat down by Aidan's desk.

"Laura has us meeting a string of congressmen and senators, mostly from the House Committee for Energy and Commerce or the Senate Committee on Health, Education, Labor, and Pensions. I've gone through the list, and I've met with all but two of them before. It should be pretty straightforward. They're pro-food, pro-business. I just need to rattle their cages, beat the drum, and remind them how we've helped them in the past. Chloe will reassure and answer any technical questions they have and make them feel like our government has done a disservice to our citizenry by further delaying Redu. I think it should play pretty well."

"Any FDA meetings?"

"We'll be meeting Jackie Epps, but she's already in our pocket," Aidan replied. "Laura would rather have congressmen or senators pressuring the FDA to move. Jackie will update us in person. Believe me, if I sense any doubt, we'll be doing more."

"Good. Any updates from Laura on our Hastings problem?"

"She's working on that plan I mentioned last night. She wants to make more progress on it before revealing it, but she did mention a piece of it."

"What?"

"Her team has Hastings's ex-wife. She's in some warehouse until we're ready to play that card."

"Great. It feels like we're getting the upper hand again. I like it," Dan replied. "When do you get back?"

"Late Saturday afternoon. Maybe earlier if we can pull it off. Just depends on how the meetings go."

"Keep me posted. I'm here, ready to do anything you need."

"I'm glad I can count on you, Dan."

Washington, D.C.
Friday, June 18
12:00 P.M.

GINA GAVE Tony carte blanche to assemble the finest team he could on short notice. Always a step ahead, Tony had already been making calls. By noon his crew was ready to meet Andrew, Heidi, and Ethan. Tony had reserved an aerobics fitness room on the second floor of the Potomac Health Club for their initial gathering. Learning some basic self-defense moves would be a great way for everyone to get to know each other.

On the top of his team's list was Esperanza Valdivia. In her early thirties, Essie, as she liked to be called by her friends, was a spitfire. Packed in a ninety-eight-pound package with a bob of dark brown hair, Essie quickly dispelled any lingering myths that size was an unbeatable advantage in the game of personal warfare. The rest of Tony's team consisted of Ed Schaumburg, Ricardo Rasner, Rudy Muschett, and Liz Swisher.

After some quick introductions, the group moved into their lessons. With Ed acting as the first assailant, Essie showed the team the power of the foot, both as a weapon and as a target for injury. Ed's job was to assault Essie from behind, and as his attack pulled Essie in close, she lifted her knee up high, then using her heel, she pretended to slam down on his toes with all her might.

"Most of the bones in your foot are tiny," she said, "but your heel is one of the strongest bones in your body. It doesn't matter what your attacker's size is. You nail their toes or instep, and not only will they double over in pain, but they won't be able to chase you worth crap. Let's practice it."

After going a couple rounds with Tony's team, Essie demonstrated the next move with Ricardo. Tanned, with dark receding hair, Ricardo was barrel-chested, and his biceps bulged from his tight black shirt.

"Now there's another option to slamming the vulnerable part of the foot. Let me demonstrate," Essie said, and then looked over at Ricardo. "Come on, big guy, give me your best."

Ricardo rushed toward Essie from behind, faking an attack. In an instant, Essie raised her knee and then pretended to slam her foot back at Ricardo's knee.

"Did you see that?" Essie asked. "The knee is a very vulnerable joint. Nail them here, and you can immobilize them."

Ethan looked on intently. No more being afraid of the bullies he might face in middle school.

Essie continued, "The key here is, after you hit the knee, keep sliding that heel down the shin. Even if you miss the knee and get the shin, you'll still inflict some damage. Got it? Let's line up again and practice it."

After a series of practice drills covering several additional techniques, Essie's workshop came to a close.

"Awesome! You guys have been great! I just want to teach you one more thing. Okay?" She paused to make sure she had everyone's attention.

"The goal of all this training has been to break free from your attacker. In the vast majority of cases, you're much better off to struggle to get free than to go with your attacker. When your attacker has you alone on their turf, that's when your chances go down significantly. So do whatever you have to do to prevent being caught."

"Like what?" Ethan asked.

"Scream for help, scream fire, scream rape. Do whatever you can do to get people's attention," Essie replied.

"What if nobody is around?" Heidi asked.

"Do anything you can to delay your assailant or to get them in a situation where you can get free easier.

"So, Ethan, let's say you've been unable to get free. What could you do to delay your assailant?"

Ethan's eyes looked up to the ceiling as he thought. "I could puke on them."

"Good idea. I'm not sure if most of us can get sick on command, but if you can, that might work. What's important is that you come up with a plan that works for you. Come up with a couple different ideas, think them through, and practice them if it makes sense. The point is, always have a plan, act quickly, and never let your attacker get the upper hand."

TWENTY-EIGHT

Washington, D.C.
Friday, June 18
4:00 P.M.

FOR THE LONG afternoon and evening of meetings, Laura had reserved a quiet section of The Oval Room, one of DC's power restaurants. Just across the street from Lafayette Park, and a short walk to The White House, The Oval Room was prestigious and well appointed. Although its sophisticated, contemporary decor and top-notch food were enough of an attraction for most, Laura chose it for other reasons.

Tucked away in a corner of the restaurant was a spacious, private meeting room. It was behind these walls and doors that the political game of Washington was played. There were rules to this game. Politicians had pontificated about them for decades. But like many games, there were ways to win that either involved getting around the rules, or bending them ever so slightly that it just didn't matter—at least not in the eyes of the politicians or their benefactors. And that's why the walls of this place were so important.

The fourth meeting of the day was with Senator John Gilly, chairman of the Committee on Health, Education, Labor, and Pensions. Chloe had visited with the honorable Senator Gilly less than two weeks ago. A sixty-two-year-old, four-term senator from Florida, Senator Gilly was facing a challenging Independent in the fall elections. For some reason, Gilly's constituencies were growing frustrated with over a quarter century of promises with little action. The hope of a new voice, one not in the pocket of big business, was enticing to some. But so many voters had given up on the notion that any representative could actually be clean, especially after the muckraking campaigns that Senator Gilly was accustomed to running.

"Good afternoon, Senator," Aidan said, shaking John's hand. "I believe you know Chloe Stiles, IFM's President of Innovation, Technology, and Quality."

"It's so good to see you again, John," Chloe reached out to shake his hand.

"And of course, our hostess, Ms. Long," Aidan continued.

Senator Gilly nodded to Laura. They knew each other well, but he decided to keep his distance.

As the group got seated comfortably around the table, a waiter rolled in a fresh set of hors d'oeuvres on a draped service cart and placed it next to the senator. Several minutes of chit chat filled the room, but once the drink orders were served, the doors to the room were closed, with instructions to keep them shut unless buzzed.

The senator took a mighty gulp from his Maker's Mark scotch and decided to jump-start the conversation. He had learned over the years that Midwesterners seemed to go around and around before getting to the issue, and as a brash East Coast guy, he just didn't have the patience for such tactics.

"So what's on your mind, Aidan? I'm sure this meeting is more than a social call?"

"And I'm sure you have a pretty good guess," Aidan replied coyly. "I do."

"So why don't you tell me. Why are you having such a hard

time making things happen?" Aidan asked, quickly turning the tables on his ally.

John Gilly rollicked with a deep belly laugh as his turkey neck swayed disgustingly beneath his chin. "Well, good man, I thought you knew more about how this world worked."

Aidan was in no mood to mince words with the senator. "If we're talking about broken promises, then I know very well how it works. Because last time I checked, you've been the beneficiary of generous contributions that I happen to control. And I must admit, I haven't seen much of a return on my investment lately. Perhaps I need to find a new senator who can actually make things happen?"

The senator laughed again. This time, the laugh was different. Gone was its dismissive tone. The senator was now in search of a friendlier conversation.

"Aidan, let's not throw around any threats. We've had a great relationship over the years. I'd hate to see us part ways," he said, sporting a wide grin. Then, the grin disappeared, and his eyes narrowed as he continued. "There's a lot of fine work we can do for Americans. As you know, right now, some crucial food safety legislation is in committee. I'm sure you realize how important it is that we strike a proper balance in this legislative work. After all, people are mad about all the food recalls that are going on. There are going to have to be some changes."

Aidan interrupted. "I'm sure you will do right by us with this legislation, John. That is, if you have a chance. You see, I'm not here to discuss the latest churn on the food safety bill, and you know that. So let's cut the crap. What the hell is going on with the FDA's approval of Redu? I'm tired of playing the piñata in this governmental game. We were promised an approval by June 15, and according to my calendar, you're now well past that deadline. Maybe the government can operate on such a sliding schedule, but the world of business cannot."

"But—"

"I don't want buts, Mr. Senator. I want action."

"But—" he tried one more time.

"No. No buts, John," Aidan said. He was in control of this meeting, and he was not going to let some slippery senator begin a pointless filibuster. "Now, I believe Chloe answered all of the safety questions that you had. Is that correct?"

"Yes, but—" the senator started.

Shaking his head, Aidan raised his voice. "Have we answered all your questions about the product's safety?"

"Yes," the senator replied.

"Then the only conclusion I can come up with is that this issue must not be high on your priority list."

"No. No, Aidan, that's not true," Senator Gilly replied.

"Then how in the hell can you explain what has happened, John?"

John thought for a moment. Simple, direct answers did not come naturally. "Aidan, I've applied pressure. I assure you, Redu's approval is on the top of my list. It's these damn bureaucrats' fault. Unlike your corporation, our government doesn't have one, final decision-maker. Hell, I was surprised by the delay, and I'm sorry. I promise you, as long as your detractors have nothing up their sleeves, you'll be fine."

Aidan interrupted. "John, that's not good enough anymore. If you're on my team, you need to make it your business to know what's up everyone's sleeves. You and I have had the last of our surprises. Now get to work if you still want to work in this town. Got it?"

WHILE TONY AND ANDREW SAT at a crowded table in the suite, Ethan lay down on a nearby sofa and played a game on his iPhone. Floor plans and checklists covered the table as the team reviewed every detail for the break-in.

After some debate, Andrew convinced Tony he wouldn't be satisfied with a support role. He was entering Long & Company's offices. His family's life was on the line. After some final wrangling, the teams were decided. Andrew, Tony, Essie, Ed, and Ricardo would crew the internal mission with Rudy and Liz providing back-up support in a van. Heidi wanted to join as well, but Andrew needed her with Ethan, so she agreed to stay behind with some additional security reinforcements Tony had retained to protect their suite.

Liz then helped each team member dress for the mission. After handing out dark gray jumpsuits emblazoned with a KarpetMaster logo, she equipped each member with communications gear. Finally, Liz selected some "accessories" to morph each team member's look. Andrew's disguise was easy—a little temporary hair-dye, glasses, ball cap, neck tattoo, and mustache made him a new man.

The final step involved a run-through of the operation. After conferencing in Josh, Tony led the group through the plans, step by step.

"Let's start with building access. We've got the forged paper-work taken care of. Josh, thanks again for your last-minute help. What was the name of the office manager?"

"Her name is Elizabeth Fitzsimmons. I've written an e-mail that will appear to come from her Long & Company address confirming access for KarpetMaster. The timestamp will be around four, but I've set it for a delayed delivery. Hopefully this will avoid any problems with security attempting to contact her for verification."

"Perfect. How about surveillance?"

"I've hacked into the building's management company's files. They show live surveillance in the entry, lobby, and elevator banks. It looks like Long & Company's offices have cameras, but noth-ing live."

"Hear that, team?" Tony said, trying to get everyone's atten-tion. "Everything we do will show up on the surveillance tapes, but up in the offices, no one will be scanning them until the next morning, right?"

"Correct," replied Josh. "However, as soon as I get access to Long's servers, I will delete those video files. So if all goes well, there should be no trace."

"Good. But let's not get careless. Keep your heads down. Don't glance up for any reason. If something goes wrong, I don't want our faces plastered on some FBI wall."

Tony tried to make it seem like he was talking to the whole team, but Andrew knew the detailed instructions were meant for him.

"Got it," Andrew confirmed.

"Now let's walk through the process of uploading the spyware. We've copied Josh's script onto three flash drives, and each has been tested per his instructions. Josh, I know you've written this all down, but I'd like us to review it together one more time," Tony requested. "So exactly how long will it take for this script to load?"

"Once you plug in the USB drive, it will take the computer about ten seconds to recognize the program. It's all auto-executed, so there's nothing to do except wait. It will take maybe a minute to upload the file, and then several minutes to run the script. As soon as the script has run, the computer will reboot, and we should be in."

"And what exactly will this script do?" Tony asked.

"Basically, it installs spyware that will watch and record an admin login's username and password. Once I've obtained that information, I'll use it to log in and then create a new, secret admin account that will enable us to access any information whenever we want."

"So once we are logged onto a computer, we should only need about five minutes to complete the job?" Andrew asked.

"Yes, that's right."

"Sounds simple enough," replied Tony. "Next, let's nail down exactly how we are going to do this. After we enter Long & Company, we will divide into two teams. I'll be a floater and provide any necessary support or cover. On each team one person will operate the carpet cleaning machine while the other moves stuff off the floor and looks for hidden login IDs and passwords. Ricardo and Ed, you are working the machines. Essie and Andrew, you're moving stuff around and looking for IDs and passwords. Now when we find one, the machine operator is to keep working, hopefully in an area that will screen Andrew or Essie as they access the computer. While the spyware is being installed, we'll stay busy in the office by moving stuff around or pretending to work on a stain."

"You make it sound easy, Tony," said Heidi.

"Well, if we're alone in the offices like we're planning, it should be a piece of cake."

"That's what I like to hear," Andrew said.

JACKIE EPPS was Laura's final guest at The Oval Room's private dining room. Jackie made sure to leave enough time before this meeting for a quick stop at a nearby drugstore to pick up the eight by ten photos from her encounter with Gina the night before.

"These are priceless," Laura quipped. Jackie had outdone herself, although she still owed Laura big-time for "cleaning up" the fiasco with her secretary, Danielle Haley.

"Well, your tip was what made it possible, Laura," Jackie replied.

"Laura, these are perfect," Chloe joined in. "If this doesn't prove to Tillman that Ms. Presho is in EFC's pocket, then what will."

In a rare moment, Laura grinned, pleased at the progress of the past twenty-four hours. "I agree. And Aidan, I must say, you were quite impressive today. You know, I work with many leaders in your position, but I've seen few tackle these political giants so handily."

"Well, thank you, Laura."

"Between your performance and Jackie's win here, I'm confident that we are going to be successful." Then Laura's tone changed ever so slightly that Jackie almost missed it. "Now, if we can just tie up some remaining loose ends."

Jackie looked puzzled briefly, but she knew better than to ask. She had already seen firsthand what loose ends meant.

"Aidan, can you and Chloe still meet first thing in the morning to discuss the rest of our plan?"

Aidan glanced at his watch. He really wanted to get home to spend most of the weekend with his wife. He missed her.

"Chloe and I agreed on the flight out here that we'd like to head back first thing tomorrow morning. Is there any chance we can discuss whatever you had planned for the morning after we get home?"

Laura looked at Aidan and Chloe, then she turned toward Jackie and stared.

"Oh, I'm sorry. I can go. I've overstayed my welcome."

"Not at all, and thank you, Jackie. It was great seeing you, and we certainly appreciate all your help. You've got quite a future in front of you, Ms. Senator," Aidan joked. "You can expect our full financial support when you decide to announce your candidacy."

Then Chloe echoed Aidan's comments, and Jackie gathered her photos and left.

"Sorry, Aidan, I just didn't want to discuss these details with her."

"No, I understand."

"Here's the deal. I don't want to wait to go through the rest of our plan. Several pieces are already underway, and I want to make sure you're on board."

"Is it too late to meet now?" Aidan suggested, glancing down at his watch. "How long do you think it will take?"

"About an hour," Laura replied. "A couple team members were going to join us since they are more involved in the details." Laura paused momentarily then picked up her phone. "Hold on. Let me make a couple calls."

THE KARPETMASTER CREW waited patiently in the lobby while their van circled outside to avoid questioning by some prying policeman. After waiting for over ten minutes at the security desk, Andrew started to doubt their plan. But when the security guard finally found the e-mail from Long & Company's office manager, questions over the forged paperwork evaporated and the carpet cleaning team was immediately escorted up to the penthouse offices. To their surprise, however, the offices weren't empty as expected. A man dressed in matching green pants and shirt with 'Vance Cleaning' and 'Esteban' embroidered on his chest promptly greeted the crew.

Esteban quickly came up and shook the security officer's hand. They apparently knew each other quite well, and they used the opportunity to catch up on each other's family. Tony nodded reassuringly to his team. He knew things were already falling off plan, but they could handle this. After waiting several minutes, Tony politely interrupted their conversation and asked, "I'm sorry, but we'd like to get started. If you can point us in the right direction."

"Who are these guys?" Esteban asked.

"Carpet cleaners. Ms. Long's orders."

Esteban seemed concerned. "I hate when this happens." Turning to Tony, he said, "You guys better be good. I don't want to get blamed for any messes you leave."

Tony stepped up. "Don't worry. We've heard Ms. Long can be tough to please."

Esteban laughed. "That's an understatement if I've ever heard one."

Wanting to get to work, Tony said, "Why don't we get my team started over here, and then you can quickly show me around and point out any areas of concern."

Esteban took Tony up on his offer, and said good-bye to the security officer. While the two teams got to work, Esteban gave Tony the tour. The decor was simple, clean, and contemporary. Glass offices lined the perimeter, with cubes forming a maze in between two corridors. Ms. Long's office was on the far end.

"Be very careful not to disturb anything in there," he cautioned. "Only I'm allowed to clean Ms. Long's office. I don't want to get fired for your mistakes."

Tony nodded. "If you're going to be here for a couple hours, you're welcome to check our work."

"Ms. Long's is my last office for the night," Esteban replied.

"After I double-check my team's work, I'm leaving. I'm guessing I'll only be here another thirty minutes."

Good to know, Tony thought to himself. *We can make this work.*

HEIDI AND ETHAN stayed up playing cards while waiting for news from Andrew. Originally, Andrew had wanted Ethan in bed and asleep, but he finally relented after Heidi intervened. After all, how did Andrew expect either of them to get any rest while he was out on this dangerous mission?

"Gin," Ethan said flatly, laying down his cards. Normally, Ethan would be jumping up and down, but the evening had cast a long shadow over their card game.

"That's the fourth hand in a row you've won. Are you cheating?" Heidi said, trying to lighten the mood.

"No," Ethan replied. "Just working the odds like Dad taught me."

"Ah, great. Another little stats genius here, huh?"

Ethan tried to smile. "I guess."

As Ethan started to deal the next hand, Heidi's phone vibrated on the table, and she picked it up. "Hey, Josh, what's up?" she asked, holding the phone in the crook of her neck as she gathered up her cards and started organizing her hand.

"Andrew's gone?" Josh asked.

"Yeah, they left an hour ago. Why?"

"I was just reviewing video cam files from Aidan's office. Something's wrong."

"What?"

"Lydia's been kidnapped."

"Oh my God," Heidi said, dropping her cards to hold her phone closer. "Do we know if she's okay?"

"Who?" Ethan asked. "What's wrong? Is Mom okay?"

LARRY RUEHL arrived at the office at ten thirty. On his way

in he saw Esteban, just heading in to clean Ms. Long's office. Plenty of late nights had put Larry on a first name basis with Esteban and most of Vance Cleaning's crew.

"What's all the noise, Esteban?" Larry asked as he entered the offices.

"Carpets being cleaned. Ms. Long's request."

Larry nodded. It didn't take any more explanation. What Laura wanted, Laura got. What else would explain his showing up to work late on a Friday night? Already annoyed at having to cut a promising date short, he asked, "Is there any way they can keep it down? We're going to have a meeting in Laura's conference room in about five minutes."

Esteban nodded. "I will have them close doors in offices as they go, then do the hallways after you leave. Will you be here long?"

"I'd guess about an hour or so."

"Okay," Esteban said, quickly running over to talk to the KarpetMaster crew's foreman.

"Thanks," Larry replied. As he walked down the hallway to Laura's conference room, he looked through the glass-walled offices and saw two crews dutifully at work.

AFTER ESTEBAN FINISHED giving Tony instructions, Tony walked over to one of the offices and closed the door.

"What's going on? Is something wrong?" Andrew asked, quite aware of the activity outside.

"Nothing. Just somebody who came in late to work. Esteban asked me to make sure we keep the noise down. He told us to do offices first and to keep the doors closed. That shouldn't be a problem." Tony smiled. "You guys find anything yet?"

"No such luck."

"Well, let's keep looking. I'm going to tell Essie what's up."

"Okay," Andrew replied as Tony walked out and closed the door behind them.

Ed motioned over to the wastebasket, and Andrew turned

around, picked it up and placed it on the credenza. Then, from the corner of his eye, he saw three figures walking past him down the hall toward Laura's office. The glass of the office wall had a three-foot opaque strip running horizontally a foot off the floor to provide privacy. But as Andrew caught a sideways glimpse of the people walking by, what he saw was unmistakable. Chloe Stiles and Aidan Toole had just arrived.

"CALM DOWN. It's going to be okay," Heidi said.

One of the security men posted in the room next door entered and asked, "Is everything okay in here?"

As Ethan buried his face in Heidi's shoulder, she nodded to the man, and he stepped back into the other room.

"Where is she?" Ethan asked as he pulled away from Heidi.

"We don't know. All we know is that she's been kidnapped."

"But why? Why did they kidnap her?"

Heidi shook her head. "None of this makes sense. It never makes sense when people do mean stuff like this. But don't worry. We're going to win this. Your mom is going to be okay."

"WE'VE GOT to get out of here."

"What?" Ed said, not hearing Andrew over the noise of the steam-cleaner.

Andrew motioned to him to turn off the machine.

"What?" Ed asked again.

"We've got to get out of here."

"Why?"

"I just saw two top IFM executives walking down the hall with someone. Something's not right."

Ed stood there thinking for a second. "Okay, you work the machine. I'll go find Tony."

Andrew kept his head down, rubbing the same patch of carpet back and forth for what seemed like hours until Ed returned with Tony.

After Andrew flipped the machine off, Tony asked, "What's wrong?"

"Tony, they're here. We've got to get out of here. I just saw Aidan Toole and Chloe Stiles walk by this office with someone. Something's happening here right now."

"Maybe I should go check them out?"

"No, I've got a bad feeling about this."

"Calm down, Andrew. It's going to be okay. Let's hold on for a few more minutes. Essie just signaled me. She's found something."

———————

LAURA PARADED Aidan and Chloe down the halls of her kingdom. Although it didn't compare with the grand scale of IFM's headquarters, power emanated from its sleek glass and brushed steel decor. As they sat to gather around the conference table, Larry greeted the guests.

"We should be able to get started in one minute. We're waiting on our data and network expert, Ann Verbena. She just arrived. She'll be in any second," Larry said.

Laura rolled her eyes in disdain.

"We appreciate you meeting with us on such short notice," Chloe added. "I'm sure it's not too often that you get called in so late on a Friday night."

"You'd be surprised," Larry replied with a glancing glare at Laura.

"Ugh, what's all this noise going on here?" Laura asked. "Can't they keep it down?"

"They're cleaning the carpets, like you requested," Larry replied.

"What? I did no such thing. I hate that perfumed smell. It'll give me headaches for weeks."

"But Esteban said they let in a special crew just for you."

"Well, he's wrong."

Puzzled, Larry looked over at Laura and said, "Really? Hold on one second. Let me find Esteban. Stay right here."

TEN MINUTES HAD passed, and what had looked like a promising list turned out to be a bust. The IDs and passwords on it must have been used for something, but not for network access.

"We need to get out of here, Tony," Andrew said. "Our plan was for nobody to be here, but this place is crawling with people."

Reluctantly, Tony agreed, and he signaled Essie's team that they needed to move out.

While rolling their equipment down the hall to the elevator lobby, they donned their communications gear. Then, just as they turned to exit through the glass doors, Esteban rounded the corner and shouted, "Stop, they're getting away!"

Suddenly, three more men appeared from behind Esteban, guns drawn, and from the other end of the hallway, another man, dressed in khakis and a blue shirt, ran toward them, gun in hand.

Andrew froze, panicked and in disbelief as Tony grabbed him, pulled him through the glass doors, and said, "Run! Quick! Down these stairs!"

Essie, Ed, and Ricardo were down two flights when a voice sounded through their earpieces, "The van is waiting on the north side of the building!"

Andrew's adrenaline kicked in as he bounded down the steps. Despite his newfound speed, Tony was right on his heels, pressing him on.

"Hurry, they're in the stairwell," Tony's voice whispered through their gear.

Bullets started to ricochet down as the men fired.

"Don't stop," Tony said. "Keep running."

Ricardo was leading the way down when Liz's voice called out from the van. "Warning, two men outside. Warning, two men outside."

"Damn it," Tony muttered. "Take them out, Liz. Take them out. Ricardo, Ed, clear security."

Tony and Andrew caught up to Essie, who stood momentarily by the fire exit's door.

"Cleared," Ricardo's voice sounded.

"Go," Tony called. "Now!" He shuttled Andrew behind Essie into the lobby.

"Liz? Status? We're on the move."

"We're clear," Liz called over the earpiece. "Driving up to the east curb now."

Running through the lobby, Andrew saw two men sprawled on the ground. They appeared alive, but they were no longer a threat. Bursting through the lobby doors onto the sidewalk, he saw two more disabled bodies on the ground and the van just twenty feet away. As its doors slid open, Liz quickly motioned and then disappeared as the first team members lunged into the van.

Shots peppered the night air. The goons weren't far behind.

Following Essie, Andrew dove for the van, turning his body before hitting the interior wall. As Andrew rolled back upright, Tony jumped through the door, shouting, "Move!" Then as he reached to slide the van door close, his body fell limp.

As the van raced away from the building, Essie cried out, "I've got him! Liz, help. Close the door, damn it! Close the door!"

TWENTY-NINE

Washington, D.C.
Friday, June 18
11:15 P.M.

"WHAT THE HELL is going on?" Aidan asked.

"I'm sorry," Laura replied. "It appears as if some group was posing as carpet cleaners to get into our offices. From what we can tell, they were trying to access our network."

"Did they get anything?" Chloe asked.

"No," Ann Verbena replied. "But I'll be doing some extra security checks to make sure."

"This is crazy, Laura. Does this happen often?"

"Never, Aidan. Never."

"Do you think it could be related to our project?"

Laura tried to play it cool with Aidan. She had to remain in control of this operation.

"It could," she replied, "but to be honest, I have a lot of enemies out there. We'll check the security tapes and follow up with authorities."

"Was anybody hurt?" Chloe asked.

"Four men were tasered downstairs. They'll be okay," Larry replied. "We're pretty sure we hit someone as they were escaping. We'll check nearby emergency rooms for any leads."

"Anyway, I apologize. I'm guessing after all that commotion, you may just want to reschedule for the morning?" Laura asked, ready to change topics.

Aidan looked at Chloe, who said, "It's up to you."

"No, let's do it now," Aidan replied. "I want to get home."

"WHERE'S THE EMERGENCY KIT? Get bandages," Essie yelled.

Andrew saw the orange box by his foot, grabbed it, and quickly found some bandages. "Got them," he said, kneeling next to Essie.

Tony's body lay slumped on its side.

"Press the bandages firmly against his wound."

The left side of Tony's scalp was covered in blood. Andrew had never seen a gunshot wound, and certainly not one to the head.

"Like this?" he asked.

Essie nodded and quickly checked Tony's vital signs.

"Is he going to be okay?" Andrew asked.

"I'm not sure. We need to get to the closest hospital, and fast. Ed, call Ken. We're going to need his help."

GINA DECIDED to sit up in bed and watch some television to distract her anxious mind. Henry had promised to call once the team checked in, so old reruns of *Password* on the Game Show Network kept her company as she waited nervously. But after she answered the phone, it didn't take Gina long to learn the mission had gone terribly wrong.

Tony was in surgery. Henry went on about Ken handling things, but Gina didn't care. She was going to the hospital no matter what. Tony needed her.

———————

AS THE TEAM walked through the door, Ethan ran into his father's arms. Heidi and Ethan had already learned the news of Tony's gunshot wound from their guards. Heidi walked up to Andrew and joined in the hug.

"I'm so sorry," she said. "I don't know how to tell you this, but we have more bad news."

Ethan stepped back to look up into his father's eyes. "Mom's been kidnapped."

THIRTY

Washington, D.C.
Saturday, June 19
7:00 A.M.

L ARRY DIDN'T WANT TO TAKE any chances, so he ordered twenty-four-hour guards until the crisis was over. After Laura left, he requested an immediate shakedown of their network. Ann was to check every nook and crevice of their systems. Information was their currency, and if anything leaked, it was all over.

When Larry left, Ann diligently tested their systems throughout the night for any possible attack. But even when she was satisfied that their operation was clean, she didn't stop. It was too much of a coincidence that their offices had been broken into just as this IFM matter was boiling over. If Long & Company was a target, IFM had to be as well. So she used her IFM network privileges and poked and prodded until she struck a vein of gold.

"You found what?" Larry asked, nearly dropping his phone from the crook of his neck.

"There's a leak. I'm sure of it."

"What? They got in?"

"No, not here, Larry. Someone's hacked into IFM."

"What the hell! Are you sure?"

"Yes. I'm just not sure who yet."

"Can you lead us to them?"

"I think so. It will just take some time."

"Do it, Ann. Do it. I'll call Laura. We'll both be in within the hour."

THE SMELL OF COFFEE wafted under the door of the adjoining suite, waking Heidi. Knocking softly, she quietly peered in and saw Andrew and Essie sitting by the window, holding cups.

"Any word on Tony?" Heidi asked.

"His surgery went well," Andrew replied. "He's still in a coma, but his vitals are strong."

"Good," Heidi said. "And long term?"

"It's too early to tell," Essie joined in. "Although his skull was fractured, he only suffered an epidural hematoma. Apparently it could have been a lot worse."

"That at least sounds hopeful, right?"

"Yes," Essie replied. "And Gina's there with him. She said she'd call us as soon as she has any updates."

Walking up next to Andrew, Heidi held him tight and asked, "Did you get any sleep?"

"Not much, but I've got a new plan," Andrew said with renewed confidence. "Laura Long and IFM aren't going to be so lucky this time. They're all going down."

"GREAT WORK, ANN," Laura complimented. "I knew you'd be a great asset to our team."

Larry looked askance at Laura, surprised at her uncharacteristic praise. But he decided to enjoy Laura's newfound admiration of Ann rather than fight it.

"How long will it take? Can we bring in some others to help speed it up?"

"Twelve to twenty-four hours." Lost in admiration for the perpetrator's handiwork, Ann said, "Whoever's behind this really knows what they're doing."

"We'll get you some help," Laura said. "Larry, bring in some support. She can't continue like this all night." Then looking down at her phone, she said, "Excuse me, I need to get this," and she stepped outside Ann's office.

"Great job, Ann," Larry said, grinning. "I knew you could win her over."

Ann couldn't take her gaze from her screen. "Well, don't congratulate me yet. But a juicy bonus when this is all over would be nice."

"Ann, if you can pull this off, I think there will be a lot more than a bonus in store," Larry replied as Laura walked back in.

"Great news. Warren Levin is on board. Hopefully we'll have a lead on Pearson by tomorrow."

THIRTY-ONE

Washington, D.C.
Sunday, June 20
7:05 A.M.

"HAPPY FATHER'S DAY," Ethan crowed.

Andrew sat up, his eyes gritty from another night of tossing, turning, and precious little sleep. As his vision finally focused, he saw Ethan and Heidi proudly serving him breakfast in bed, with Essie, Ed, and Ricardo in the wings.

"What's this all about?"

"He insisted," Heidi replied as Ethan set the tray on his father's lap and gave him a big hug.

"All of your favorites!" Ethan declared. "Raspberries, pecan waffles, and hash browns."

"Oh, buddy, how special. Thank you!" He pulled Ethan in for another hug and kiss.

As Essie, Ed, and Ricardo came in around the bed, Andrew continued, "I'd invite you all to join me, but I don't think there's anything you can eat here. Maybe some berries, but I don't think they're organic."

"What do you mean?" Essie replied. "The food police, as you like to call us, have ordered some pancakes and fruit in honor of the occasion. They'll be up any minute."

"Ah, the allure of junk food."

"On occasion, as a treat," Essie replied. "Anyway, I need you ready for today."

Andrew glanced at his watch. "We need to leave in about an hour and a half."

"Yes. After we're done with breakfast, we've got to get into our disguises and then over to the condo."

"That's why we started so early, Dad. And I wanted to surprise you."

"Well, you got me, buddy. I'd almost forgotten it was Father's Day."

"Here, open my gift," Ethan said, reaching over to the nightstand and grabbing a package. "Heidi helped me wrap it."

Andrew read the card that was tucked under the bow.

Dear Dad,

I'm the luckiest kid around. You've always been there for me. Thanks for being my Dad.

Love, Ethan

"And what do we have here?" Andrew said, ripping through the wrapping paper and opening a box. As he carefully removed the tissue paper, Andrew revealed a watercolor painting. "Oh, Ethan, it's beautiful. It's our house."

"Yeah, I've been working on it all week. See, I don't just play video games."

"Ethan, you're quite the artist," Essie added.

"Yes, my guy is amazing. Thank you, buddy."

"Well, I know you always tell me you like gifts that I make." Ethan started to sniffle, and a tear came down his face.

"Are you okay?" Andrew asked.

"Oh, Dad." Ethan broke down and cried. "I'm afraid. I don't want you to go. I want Mom to be free. I want us all to be home."

"I know, Ethan. I know." Andrew held his son tightly, never wanting to let him go. "But today is going to be our day. Once we get the upper hand, we're all going to be safe again."

St. Louis Park, Minnesota
Sunday, June 20
7:30 A.M.

"WAKE UP," Rufus said, kicking the cot.

"I wasn't asleep," Lydia replied, turning over.

"Whatever, princess. Your breakfast is ready."

Lydia looked at the tray. "What's that?"

"Biscuits and gravy. I got it just for you."

"I don't eat crap like that. Can I just have a piece of fruit?"

"Stop your whining," Rufus said as he sat down to eat Lydia's breakfast. Then between gulps, he looked over at his prisoner and grinned, gravy dripping from the corners of his mouth. "I bet I can think of some ways to make you happy."

Lydia cringed. "Don't even think about it. You disgust me, you pig!"

Rufus laughed, more food spilling from his mouth. "You can call me anything you want, lady, but I'm gonna get me some of that before this is over," he said, looking at her thighs.

Washington, D.C.
Sunday, June 20
10:00 A.M.

ANDREW STARED intently at the ramp leading from The Residences at The Ritz-Carlton's underground parking. Josh had come through for Andrew once more with some key intelligence. Not only had he located Laura Long's Georgetown condo, but after hacking into her building's records, he had also learned that every Sunday around ten o'clock, Laura exited the garage. Josh wasn't sure where she went, but he told Andrew to be ready.

Not knowing how close Andrew would have to get to Laura, Essie went all out on his disguise. His persona today was a nerdy professor. Wearing a wig of disheveled brown hair, a full shabby beard, and a pair of dark, horn-rimmed glasses, he was truly unrecognizable. Hopefully, his look could blend in wherever Laura's day took him.

They had arrived an hour early, just in case Laura broke from her regular schedule, but promptly at ten Laura's black Cadillac turned onto K Street.

As the white Prius pulled into the street behind the big black sedan, Andrew said, "Don't lose her."

"Would you rather drive?"

Andrew shook his head no. "You know DC's roads. Just don't let her spot us in the rearview mirror."

THE TABLE WAS LITTERED with pizza boxes, sandwich wrappers, and greasy French fry containers. Besides a half dozen bathroom breaks, Ann had remained attached to her computers for almost thirty-six hours. Larry had come in early to help out in any way he could. But Ann seemed to work best alone, so he had holed up in a conference room next door.

Then, suddenly, Larry heard a large thud pound the wall, followed by, "I've got it, Larry. I've got it."

Larry jumped from his chair and ran next door to Ann's office. "What do you have?"

"The data stream traces back to Minneapolis. It's coming from some condo on Lake Calhoun."

"Give me the address."

Ann handed a printout to Larry.

"Thanks. Now go home, get a shower, and go to bed. Please."

Annapolis, Maryland
Sunday, June 20
11:30 A.M.

THE TOYOTA PRIUS was parked down the street from the Annapolis Adult Home, waiting for Laura Long. Dressed in light khaki shorts, a polo shirt, and a small backpack, Laura emerged with a short, pudgy Asian man with thick black glasses. He was dressed in denim shorts, a purple and black Raven's T-shirt, tube socks, and some type of walking shoes. As the two slowly made their way down the street, it didn't take long for the Prius's occupants to realize Laura's friend suffered from some kind of disability.

"You sure you want to go alone?"

"I've got this," Andrew said confidently.

"Good luck."

Andrew got out of the car and walked up the opposite side of the street from Laura and her friend. As the couple wandered through the St. John's College campus up to Maryland Avenue, Andrew watched them from a distance, keeping them within view. When Laura and her friend stopped for lunch at a local restaurant, Andrew decided it was time to eat as well.

He took a corner seat at the diner's counter.

"Would you like to see a menu, sir?" the waitress asked.

"No, just some black coffee and toast. Thanks."

Then, grabbing several discarded sections of *The New York Times* off the counter, Andrew pretended to read as he discreetly surveyed the space. The Asian couple was seated in the far corner of the room near the restrooms. He watched their table closely as they ordered, then when Laura handed her phone to her companion to play with, Andrew seized on his window of opportunity.

Andrew casually walked up to the server station as Laura's server punched in the order. "Excuse me, I need some help."

"Yes," the waiter replied, wondering if this guest was in need of a menu, napkins, or silverware. As it turned out, he couldn't have been more wrong. After listening to the man's request, he pocketed the most generous tip of his career.

Ten minutes later, the Asian couple's lunch arrived. But just as the waiter was about to serve them, he lost control of his tray. Two plates of food and a milkshake tumbled onto the table and all over the couple's laps.

Laura quickly jumped to the aid of her companion while cursing the waiter for his clumsiness.

Sitting back at the counter, Andrew thought to himself, *Yes, my plan's working.*

"I'm so sorry, ma'am," the waiter said. "Here, let me help you and your friend get cleaned up." He escorted the couple back to the restrooms, Laura verbally assaulting him the whole way.

Trying his best to remain calm, Andrew slowly walked over to the table. Appearing to help out as he passed by, he picked a plate up off the floor and set it on the table. Subtly, he palmed the cell phone Laura's companion had left on the table and placed it in his pocket, then he promptly retreated to the diner's counter, acting overwhelmed by the entire mess.

By now Andrew's heart was pounding. He had to work quickly. After sitting back down, he pulled the phone from his pocket and touched its screen. Relieved to see it was still unlocked, he quickly maneuvered through the settings menu to get Laura's phone number. Next, he reached into his breast pocket and pulled out an inexpensive, pay-as-you-go phone. With a few taps he entered Laura's phone number and hit send. Within seconds, Laura's phone vibrated, and Andrew opened the message. Josh's script now lay waiting to be synced with Long & Company's network. With a couple more taps, Andrew deleted all traces of his text and put Laura's phone to sleep.

Dropping some cash on the counter to pay his bill, Andrew picked up the wad of newspapers and waited for the busboys to finish cleaning up the mess around Laura's table. As soon as they left, he got up to make his approach. But just as he was about to return the phone, he saw Laura and her friend return with the waiter.

Damn it, he thought. *I told that waiter to take his time helping them clean up.*

Turning sideways to let the group by, Andrew quickly made a detour to the restrooms. As the men's room door closed, his mind started to race. *How am I going to return Laura's phone now?* he thought. *What if she notices it's missing?* In a sudden, decisive move, he realized waiting wasn't an option. He was just going to have to go for it.

Stepping out from the bathroom, he took a deep breath before turning the corner. Then, as he walked past Laura's table, he fumbled and dropped a couple sections from his stack of newspapers. Bending over to pick them up, Andrew then stood up so that he was face to face with Laura and asked, "Excuse me, is this yours? I found it on the floor by your table."

Minneapolis, Minnesota
Sunday, June 20
11:30 A.M.

AFTER RETURNING from his workout, Josh showered and changed, then slipped downstairs with his backpack. He was ready to work. Settling in quickly, he sat down at the desk, fired up his laptop, and squinted over to the framing around the closet door, moving his head back and forth, expecting the overhead light to glisten off the filament. After trying to catch the light several times, he finally got up. Then, as he walked to the doorway for closer inspection, all he could think was, *Shit!*

Annapolis, Maryland
Sunday, June 20
12:45 P.M.

ANDREW SPOTTED Essie, and as he approached her car, he dropped his new, pay-as-you-go phone in the trash. He didn't want to take a chance having it tracked back to him.

Before he could even get seated, Essie asked, "So how did it go?"

"Well, for a couple seconds I thought I was going to get caught. I had to go face to face with her. Thank goodness for your disguise. She didn't recognize me."

"So you did it?"

"Yes." Andrew smiled. "Let's get out of here."

As they cruised back to Georgetown, Essie peppered him with questions. After giving her a quick run-down, Andrew called the hotel. When Heidi answered her phone, he shouted without introduction, "We did it."

In the background he could hear Heidi repeat his news and then a wave of cheers and applause in response.

"That's amazing. I can't wait to hear the whole story." Then Heidi added, "We just got some great news here, too. Tony's out of his coma. His brain function is looking really good."

"Oh, that's wonderful. Thank God."

"One second. Ethan wants to talk to you."

"Dad, are you okay?" he asked.

"I'm great," Andrew replied. "We should be back in less than an hour."

"Can't wait! Can we head home now and get Mom?"

"Soon, Ethan. I promise."

Long & Company Headquarters
Sunday, June 20
12:50 P.M.

"DID YOU GET HIM?" Larry asked.

Shifting his phone to his other ear, Skylar replied, "No. One second he was getting ready to start work, the next he bolted."

"What happened?"

"I don't know what spooked him, but he grabbed his pack and tore off down a bike trail before we could catch him."

"You get to tell Laura this time," Larry replied. "She's going to kill you guys."

Washington, D.C.
Sunday, June 20
2:15 P.M.

AS SOON AS Andrew and Essie returned to the hotel, Andrew shared all the details of his face-to-face encounter with Laura Long. Although it was too soon to celebrate, they were making progress. Once Josh got into Long & Company's servers they were sure to finally have the information they needed to take down IFM and secure Lydia's safety.

After reassuring Ethan that his mom would be safe soon,

Andrew stole a moment alone with Heidi. Slipping away to the bedroom, he held Heidi close.

"It's been quite a day," Heidi said, staring deep into Andrew's eyes.

"I know. You've risked everything for me, and I love you—"

Suddenly Ethan barged into the room with a phone in his hand. Surprised, Andrew stepped back from Heidi. For a second he didn't know what to say, but then the words came effortlessly.

"Ethan, I'm sorry. I've been wanting to tell you about Heidi and me, but I just wanted to make sure—"

Ethan interrupted. "Dad, do you think I'm clueless? Please, I could tell over a year ago that you loved Heidi. I'm just glad you're together. Heidi's the best! Now before you go off on some deep, parental talk about this, Josh is on the phone," he said, handing the phone to his dad.

Andrew smiled. He should have known better than to try to outsmart Ethan. "Thanks, buddy, but you're not getting out of that talk."

Andrew held up the phone to his ear. "Josh, where have you been? I've been trying to reach you. Did you hear the news?"

"Yeah, but I've been kinda busy here."

"Anything wrong?"

"Well, I've got good news and bad news. Which do you want first?"

Andrew drew a deep breath. "Hit me. Bad news."

"They found me. I'm on the run."

"You okay?"

"Now I am."

"Damn! What happened?"

"I didn't have time to ask questions. I just ran."

"Where are you now?"

"A hotel outside of Eau Claire."

"So is that my good news?"

"No, the good news is actually great news."

"What? Are we in the servers already?"

"No, but this is just as good."

"What? Tell me."

"So as soon as I got set up here I wanted to make sure our data cloud was secure."

"And?"

"Everything is fine. But while I was checking things out, I noticed you had mail."

"What?"

"Andrew, Wally Babin e-mailed you. He's ready to help us."

THIRTY-TWO

Madison, Wisconsin
Monday, June 21
11:00 A.M.

THE DANE COUNTY Regional airport was settling down from the Monday morning rush. Wally had made it through security and now sat nervously near his gate. He had followed every last detail of the precise instructions that Andrew had e-mailed him yesterday evening. Using his real name, he had booked a ticket on Delta flight 436 to LaGuardia, departing at 11:46 a.m. But the plan wasn't for Wally to really take that flight, and as he compulsively checked his watch again, he realized it was time to hit the bathroom.

Rolling into the handicapped stall, Wally locked his chair in place and waited. Five minutes later, there was a knock on the door.

"Hello?" Wally said.

"Is there toilet paper on the roll?" a voice replied.

That was the code, so Wally opened the stall door, letting in the stranger, and quickly closed the door behind him.

"So, you need any help?" the stranger whispered, removing his gray T-shirt and Packer's hat.

"No," Wally replied as he took off his Wisconsin Badgers sweatshirt, hat, and dark sunglasses.

The stranger's features were quite similar to Wally's. Both had brown hair and eyes, fair skin, and modest builds. Someone had done great work on such short notice.

"Okay, here's my stuff," Wally whispered, handing the stranger his clothes. In return, Wally got the stranger's clothes, and the two quickly dressed, each feeling uncomfortable being half naked in a men's room stall with another guy. "Here, can you open this up?" Wally asked, handing the stranger a cane that folded open into a seat. "Place it close to the door so I can latch it after you leave."

Wally hoisted himself from his wheelchair using the stall's rails and maneuvered himself onto the small seat. After Wally motioned at their bags, the stranger picked them up and helped Wally switch their contents. Then, after Wally handed the stranger his backpack and boarding ticket, the stall door opened, and the stranger rolled away in Wally's wheelchair. Wally quickly closed and locked the door, waiting nervously for his next visitor.

WMSP-TV Headquarters
Monday, June 21
11:30 A.M.

"GOOD MORNING, Doug," Sven Anderson, Jr. said, knocking at the door.

"Good morning. And for what reason do I have the pleasure of your visit?" Doug replied sarcastically.

"What do you mean?"

"How long have we known each other now? Twenty years? Even when your dad was around, the only time you'd stop by was when you needed something. What is it today? Sports tickets? Press pass?"

"Doug, I'm surprised. You know I have a genuine interest in our station here," Sven replied.

Unwilling to engage in an argument, Doug replied, "Sure. Just kidding around with you, Sven. So seriously, what brings you in today?"

"Well, I was curious about our news coverage. Warren Levin phoned me this morning to tell me Heidi Pearson has been off the air for over a week now. What's going on?"

Doug laughed. "I didn't even think you watched our news. And to think, I pegged you for an ESPN SportsCenter guy."

"Come on, Doug. I watch our news every night, and I've been missing Pearson. Where's she been?"

"She's on a special assignment," Doug replied.

"Really? Sounds interesting. What's the story about?"

"Why do you care?" Doug answered flippantly.

"Come on, Doug, I deserve some respect here," Sven said sternly.

"Okay." It was much simpler to appease Sven than argue.

"So you didn't answer my question. Where is she?" Sven said, continuing to press.

"I don't know. Heidi asked to leave a week ago. She hasn't checked in since. To be honest, I'm getting worried."

"Have you called her?"

"I tried, but she's not answering her cell phone."

Frustrated, Sven finally barked, "Doug, we need to find her now. This is important. I'm not paying her to be on some vacation."

"Where the hell did you get that from? I'm genuinely worried that she's in trouble."

"Just find her, Doug. Find her now, damn it! And let me know as soon as you do." Sven leaned down onto Doug's desk, trying his best to intimidate.

"Sure, Sven," Doug nodded. "I'll get working on that ASAP."

———————

Madison, Wisconsin
Monday, June 21
12:15 P.M.

THIRTY MINUTES after Wally's flight to New York took off, he emerged from the restroom stall with a new wheelchair and Ricardo walking by his side. After they made their way through the security exit, they took the elevator downstairs to pick up a cab to the Wisconsin Aviation terminal, where a private jet was refueling, fresh from its flight from DC. Josh had arranged for some first class transportation to unite Wally with their team and whisk him away without a trace.

As the crew helped Wally board, Andrew came up to him and said, "Welcome. Did our plan go smoothly?"

"A cakewalk." Wally smiled. "I'm guessing somebody's going to be quite surprised when I don't get off that plane in New York."

Andrew laughed. "I'd like you to meet our group here. First, there's my son, Ethan. I gave you his picture a while back."

"So you did, Andrew," Wally said, smiling. "It was very helpful, actually, in convincing me to take action."

"Nice to meet you, Mr. Babin," Ethan said, shaking his hand.

"And this," Andrew went on, "is my girlfriend, Heidi."

"Hi, Wally," Heidi said. "We're so thankful you're joining us."

"Yes, we are," Andrew added. "You already met Ricardo. This is Essie. Watch her, she's a lot tougher than she appears. And then in the back there are Ed, Liz, and Rudy."

"Don't get up," Wally said. "It's very nice to meet you all. Thank you again for helping me."

"Well, we're not safe yet. Did you bring your files?"

"It's all right here," he said, gripping his backpack. "Where are we heading?"

"The Windy City. We're joining up with the rest of our team there. So sit back and relax. Wheels up in ten minutes."

IFM Headquarters
Monday, June 21
3:00 P.M.

ON CUE, trays of packaged and meticulously displayed snacks, cereals, desserts, and baked goods were ushered in. Everyone seated at the table got up to admire IFM's accomplishment.

"And here's our line-up," Aidan declared. As if he were showing off his newborn children in the nursery, his babies were shielded behind a wall of acrylic glass. Waxing poetic, Aidan went on, "With these revolutionary foods, we will transform the way the world eats. No longer will there be that painful choice: to be hungry and thin or to be fat and happy," Aidan quipped. "Now you can eat to your heart's delight without worry."

Art Jacobson tried to add to the cheerleading in a more down-to-earth fashion, but Randall Mueller, Klout's CEO, stared blankly.

"These products are truly amazing, Randy," Art said. "They are going to fly off your shelves. We can't wait for you to see our displayable pallet programs with customizable options. They will be perfect for January's kick-off to weight-loss season."

"So do we get to taste this stuff?" Randy asked, baiting his trap.

Dan stepped in to help Aidan and the sales team out. "Any day now, Randy. We've got a case of all different samples ready to send your way."

"Oh, that's right. I did read about that pesky detail in *The Journal*. Let me see if I get it right?" Randy said, touching his right temple as if to conjure up some memory. "The FDA didn't approve your tasty little concoction."

"No, no," Aidan jumped in. "The decision was just delayed." He nodded his head reassuringly.

"You guys, you just don't get it!" Randy said, raising his voice as the IFM big wigs tilted back their heads ever so slightly to brace for a hit. "I'm so tired of seeing crap like this peddled onto our shelves. Companies like yours force it into our stores. Do we have a choice? I mean, you'll be spending some $80 million trying to convince every household that B-Lean is the best thing since sliced bread. So they'll come pouring into our stores, and what do we say? Do we turn them away and say, 'No, we don't stock this artificial garbage.' No, we can't. I mean, I guess we could take a stand, but that would just get our valued customers mad at us."

Shocked and stunned, Aidan was speechless, so he let Art rally the cause first.

"Sounds like you aren't pleased," Art said in a blinding understatement of the obvious. "What exactly has you concerned?"

"Art, is this stuff safe? Really? Is it safe?" Randy paused. "I've read the debate in the press. Intestinal distress? Scarring to the epithelial lining?"

Chloe, trying to help, replied, "Oh, that's only in a very small number of cases."

As the words tumbled from her mouth, she wanted to pull them right back in, but it was too late. As she glanced over at Aidan, Dan flashed her a look of controlled rage.

"That's freaking wonderful, Ms. Stiles. I don't care how small a percentage it is. When a customer comes back into our stores complaining about your products, where will you be? Counting your fat profits? Cashing in your stock options? And all the way claiming everything is okay?"

Aidan finally regained his footing, trying to retrench. "Randy, you're obviously upset and misinformed. Let's sit down and talk about your concerns logically."

"Aidan, have you looked at the statistics? Less than 20 percent of Americans trust food companies to develop and sell food that is safe and healthy for themselves and their families. Do you know why?"

Aidan started to fire up his pat answer. This was a regular one he had to field out on the road. But Randy didn't want to hear his answer.

"I'll tell you why, Aidan. Do you know how many recalls we managed last year? Well, to be honest, I lost count. Peanut butter, ground beef, spinach, sprouts, chicken, ground turkey, cereal, eggs, popcorn, chips, baby formula, and chocolate. The list goes on. It's spiraling out of control. Don't you get it? You can hardly pull up the news on Yahoo without reading about another recall, each one bigger than the last."

"But—"

"Excuse me, Aidan, I'm on a roll here. People want safer food. They want real food, not some genetically modified concoction. You and your buddies here are missing the boat. There's a revolution going on outside. You and companies like yours can either embrace this change or become modern day buggy whips salesmen as you fall from favor. I, for one, don't want my company to fall victim. I refuse to have a deaf ear. Do you know what is the fastest growing category in our store?"

"Organic—" Aidan started to reply.

"Yes, organic anything, up double, triple digits."

"Yes, and we are now driving that growth in several categories," Dan squeezed in.

"Oh, yes, that's right, Dan. Is that your new organic cola or French fries?" Randy replied sarcastically. "I know your guys are hard at work trying to bastardize organic foods. Isn't that what you've done with all health and nutrition claims? Hell, you've turned the phrase 'all natural' into a couple deceitful, dirty words. Daze, confuse, and legislate loopholes that muddy the waters. After all, a confused consumer just might give up and buy a fruit snack, thinking it's actually good for their kids. Isn't that the game?"

"Randy, stop acting so high and mighty here," Dan finally rebuked, tired of the lashing. "You and your fellow retailers are hardly victims."

"Do we share some blame? Sure. But enough is enough!" Randy replied. "That's why you'll have to put up with me ranting and raving. I've come to meetings like this for four years now, asking for real solutions. I want nutritious answers that will help end obesity. Get with the program. You're on the wrong side of this issue."

Aghast and speechless, Art jumped in before Dan could rally an attack.

"Randy, I really appreciate your honesty here. This stuff really comes from your heart. I can tell. I wonder if there is a way we turn this into a win-win." Art was starting to spin. "We've got a room set up over at Gianni's. What if we wander over there a little early and get a couple drinks, then dinner. I know Aidan, Chloe, Dan, and I would love to figure this one out with you."

"That would be great," Randy replied. "I'd love to partner with you guys on making some real changes."

Chloe and Aidan started to nod along as Dan stared off dismissively.

Art then laughed out loud, and in a half-joking manner he started to retest the waters. "And maybe if we promise you some progress, you'd be able to figure out a way to stock our B-Lean lineup." More laughing. "Let's get going. I'm thirsty!"

Chicago, Illinois
Monday, June 21
3:30 P.M.

JOSH BEAT ANDREW'S CREW to Chicago and had already set up shop. Four lakefront suites were a little rich, even for him, but he was in no mood to cut corners. In fact, he was ready to celebrate. Late yesterday Laura had synchronized her phone, and by morning his new, administrative ID was up and running, searching for documents containing a list of keywords he had compiled with Andrew and Heidi's help at the lake. Documents peeled off Long & Company's servers right and left. Yes, it would take some time to review them, but his friends would be there soon to help.

Wayzata, Minnesota
Monday, June 21
10:00 P.M.

ART'S ATTEMPT to wine and dine Randy had little impact. Despite hours of drinks and grand promises to collaborate on a new path of wholesome food, Randy decided to draw a line in the sand. For now, Klout would not accept IFM's line-up of B-Lean products. As the dinner broke up around ten o'clock, Dan stomped out of the restaurant with Chloe just steps behind, walking down Lake Street.

"Where'd you park?" Chloe asked.

"The ramp was full earlier. Up Walker Street," Dan replied curtly.

"Same here." Chloe paused. "I think that was the worst top-to-top meeting I've ever attended."

"Thanks to you."

"What?"

"You heard me. Did you see the look Aidan gave you when you said, what was it, 'only a small number of cases'? You're done, Chloe, and I'm tired of defending you."

"Defending me? Hell, you've been anything but a staunch supporter lately, Dan."

"Aidan and I are going to have a talk tomorrow. If this house of cards is going to fall, it's going to have a name-to-blame written on it, and it's going to be yours," he laughed.

"What? You're giving up?"

"No, I can't give up. But you've failed, Chloe. You said you could deliver, and here we sit, still waiting for FDA approval, and our second largest customer is bailing on us. Do you know what happens when other retailers get wind of this?"

"It's not good."

"Not good? That's a hell of an understatement. When a retailer like Klout turns down your new products, it's like a tidal wave. Customers will defect right and left, second-guessing because they think Klout knows something they don't." As Chloe stopped at her car, Dan turned back so he could continue his verbal attack. "Yeah, Aidan is not going to like this. Dust off that resume, sweetie, or get ready for the corporate graveyard."

Chloe laughed. "You know, something deep inside told me it would come down to this with you someday, Dan. I've seen you stick it to so many suckers over the years. So it's just my turn, I guess."

"Maybe," Dan replied, smiling slyly from the corner of his mouth.

"Well, I warned you, Dan. I've taken out quite the insurance policy. I'm going to take you down. Just watch."

"Hell, sure, Chloe. Good luck."

"I've got the paperwork all ready, Dan. Hmmm…" she thought. "What will it be? A call to Human Resources? Or maybe I'll leak an anonymous story to some industry rag like *Branded*? Talk about the corporate graveyard. You'll be buried." Chloe's face reddened. She was determined to stand up to this bully once and for all.

"Come on, Stiles. Hit me with your best shot!"

"Oh, I'd hate to threaten your puffed up, egotistical self. But I hear Angie Green is a big fan of yours."

Dan's face emptied, the smile wiped completely from its place. "What?"

Chloe, laughing, said, "You heard me. Angie. You know that direct report of yours who's on maternity leave with your baby? How curious that her same exact job, reporting to you, will be waiting for her when she comes back next week. And so many others wanted that job. What a shame. It does sound like some sort of preferential treatment was going on. At least that's the rumor I'm starting. Boy, this has all the makings of a messy sexual harassment case, doesn't it?"

"Chloe, now you've gone from incompetent to crazy."

"Really? You know, Dan, I'm one of those curious sorts. So I just got this wild idea to hire a detective. I've got some great pictures of you and Angie if you're looking for some photos for your next holiday card. Oh, not to mention the paternity test results."

"What?"

Laughing again, Chloe said. "Yeah, I felt bad yanking a hair from the baby's head when I visited Angie. He started to cry like crazy. But it felt good snatching a hair off your head a month ago."

As the color started to return to Dan's face, an uncontrollable rage built inside him.

"So sorry, Dan. Your time is up."

Chloe turned, laughing out loud while opening her car door. Then from behind her, Dan's meaty arms reached up and grabbed her neck. As she started to cry out, he realized he had gone too far. But he had no options left. In one twist, Chloe's bony vertebrae snapped, and her head fell to the side, silencing her for good.

DAN DROVE WEST in Chloe's car, searching for the perfect spot. It didn't take long for him to get past civilization. He knew he could get rid of the evidence. He didn't have a choice. Dan turned onto a dirt path that appeared to lead nowhere and parked the car miles off the main road in some thick brush. Convinced he just needed to stay calm, Dan searched Chloe's car for ideas. With cigarettes and a lighter from her purse, and a siphon from an emergency kit in the trunk, Dan hatched his plan.

Situating Chloe's limp body in the driver's seat with a cigarette in her hand, he soaked her purse with fuel from the car's gas tank. Then with a flick of the lighter, Dan watched the fire create an eerie glow inside the BMW. Suddenly, the flame found her long, dark tresses, and poof, they were gone. A moment later her entire body was covered with fire.

THIRTY-THREE

Chicago, Illinois
Tuesday, June 22
11:00 A.M.

GINA TOOK the first flight to Chicago Tuesday and arrived at the Ritz by eleven o'clock. She felt horrible leaving Tony's side, but the doctors reassured her that his recovery was going extremely well. And when she talked to Tony about Andrew's success, Tony squeezed her hand. It was then that Gina realized that she should go. Tony wanted to win this battle against IFM more than anyone. IFM had to be stopped and held accountable.

After taking a moment to greet Gina and learn more about Tony's condition, Andrew introduced her to Josh and Wally. Then he gathered the group around a large table in his suite. Set in front of Gina's seat was a three-inch binder with over two dozen tabs in it. Page by page the team took her through the damning evidence that was sure to stop Redu in its tracks and put a whole host of characters behind bars.

Wally took Gina through his documents first. He had secretly kept digital copies of all his Redu files as an insurance policy. Severe gastrointestinal problems had plagued the chemically derived, genetically modified Ultra-Hi Resistant Starch since the very beginning, and despite higher butyrate levels in the colon, legitimate animal testing suggested long-term cancer risks were real. Improvements to the formulations ameliorated some issues, but the bottom line was the same. Redu exceeded the body's capacity to pass through undigested material. Gastrointestinal tracts weren't meant to be a trash chute for "plastic" food.

In order to get the results IFM needed, little manipulations here and there quickly turned into all-out tampering of the results. By the final round of testing, IFM had invested too much time and effort to give up, so they pulled out all the stops. In animal testing, the control group's food was altered to mimic the increased incidence of gastrointestinal issues and cancers in the test group, thereby making any differences in control vs. test group evaporate. However, the most blatant abuse occurred in the human trials when actual responses were altered and reallocated between the test and control samples in order to assure results that would support Redu's approval.

Dr. Todd McNaulty was complicit in all the activities. It all started innocently enough with relatively minor lies that helped fund his labs at IAT. As the lies got bigger and bigger, McNaulty had tried to put his foot down, only to be blackmailed by Laura with disclosures that would destroy him professionally. By that point it was too late. Dr. McNaulty's indiscretions turned into outright fraud. Wally unknowingly fell into a similar trap. What was originally implicit trust in Dr. McNaulty's ethics quickly backfired, and Wally became yet another tool in Laura Long's engine of deceit.

After the last of the Redu studies was complete, Dr. McNaulty arranged for Wally's move to UW–Madison's biochemistry program. McNaulty told Laura that it was better to have Wally move on and fall off the radar. Given the opportunity, Wally did just that. But after a visit from an EFC detective and then Andrew last week, Wally was convinced Dr. McNaulty couldn't protect him any longer. He had to make a choice.

When Wally's review was complete, Josh took the group through highlights from data skimmed off Long & Company's servers. Ms. Long's love of technology had left a rich trail of data. The files corroborated Wally's story. Millions of dollars had flooded into Dr. McNaulty's labs in exchange for his work. Yes, the transgressions were fairly innocent at first, but soon he was in too deep. Laura Long owned him, and he feared for his life. Bribery, blackmail, and murder were Laura's tools of the trade, and she used them ruthlessly.

Digital trails also proved that IFM had used Ms. Long to stack the FDA's FAC panel with a carefully selected group that was sure to rubber stamp Redu's approval and discount any criticisms from organizations like EFC. Additionally, cash payments and political contributions to countless senators, congressmen, and federal employees, including Jackie Epps, were discovered. Finally, Josh also found e-mails and voice mails that implicated Laura and IFM in the crash of Becky's jet, Andrew's car explosion, the murders of Lia Merriman and Danielle Haley, and Lydia's kidnapping.

"All of this is beyond my wildest dreams," Gina said. "Finally the good guys have won a battle against corruption and greed." Hesitating, tears falling down her cheeks, she continued, "Tony will be so proud of you all. I know I am. So let's call the press and watch these empires fall!"

"We've got the press piece covered," Andrew said, nodding over at Heidi, "but before we do anything, we need your help once more." Andrew hesitated. "Ethan's mom has been kidnapped. Before we give this information to anyone, we need to make sure she's safe. I've been working on a plan to free her. Can we count on your support?"

"Of course," Gina replied, "but I have one condition."

"What's that?"

"We need to have some real authorities involved. The police? The FBI? Someone."

"But, Gina, after all of this, I don't trust anyone. Not the police. Not the FBI. IFM's connections run too deep."

"Andrew, I want to help you, believe me. But after what happened last week, we can't do this alone. We need someone who can look at the situation objectively and provide some support. Fair?"

Andrew couldn't argue, and as he thought hard, the name of one person he could trust came to mind.

Long & Company Headquarters
Tuesday, June 22
12:00 P.M.

"I'VE NEVER SEEN such incompetence!" Laura yelled. "Despite having multiple opportunities, you've managed to fail each and every time."

The beating had continued for over an hour. Then there was a knock at the conference room door.

"Yes," Laura screamed.

Ann opened the door, looking serious.

"I'm sorry, Ann. I'm giving this bunch of losers a final piece of my mind. What do you need?"

"Uh, I've got some bad news to report," Ann said hesitantly. "Someone broke through our security. They accessed our servers."

"What?" Laura said, her face trembling and moist with sweat. "How bad?"

"It looks devastating."

"What happened? Who did this?"

"I don't know who, but I've figured out how. The malware was uploaded via a smartphone onto our network."

"Who? Whose phone did this, damn it?" she yelled at the top of her lungs, clenching her short, manicured fingers into her own flesh.

Ann paused before finally saying, "It was your phone, Ms. Long. Your phone."

WMSP Headquarters
Tuesday, June 22
1:30 P.M.

"DOUG WIETZ," he answered, not recognizing the number.

"Doug, it's Heidi."

He got up from his desk, closing his office door. "You okay?"

"Yes, I've got the story."

"Shhh..." he said. "Don't tell me anything, Heidi. Something's up."

"What?"

"I'm telling you, something's not right here. Sven came in here asking about you yesterday. He's all pissed off that you're not around."

"So?"

"Heidi, not to hurt your ego, but I've heard Sven mention your name only a handful of times over the years. I'll take that back. A couple of those times he thought your name was Harriet."

"What does he want to know?"

"He wants to know where you are."

Heidi was speechless.

"Heidi?"

"Yes," she said, finally responding. "Never underestimate the criminal mind, Doug. I never thought corruption and greed could run so deep."

"What do you mean?"

"Never mind," Heidi replied. "Can you help me set a trap? It could mean the downfall of Sven Jr."

"Count me in," Doug said without hesitation.

"We're leaving for the Twin Cities in a few minutes, but we've still got our rooms here in Chicago for the night. Let's just see if anybody shows up."

"Heidi?"

"Don't worry, Doug. They can't track us. I'll have our tech guy set up a camera or something to watch."

"Us? Tech guy?"

"Yeah, we've got quite the operation set up. Anyway, give me three hours lead, then let Sven know I'm checked into The Ritz-Carlton at Water Tower Place. We have four suites on the twenty-ninth floor under the name of Hodges. You need to watch Sven, though. Find out where that little weasel is going with the info. Got it?"

"Yes, but Heidi, what's going on?"

"Doug, everything is just fine. One of us was kidnapped, but we're working on getting her freed."

"Kidnapped? Who? This sounds insane."

"Believe me, it's been a wild ride. It's not over yet, but expect a call in two or three days. Thanks."

Minneapolis, Minnesota
Tuesday, June 22
7:00 P.M.

A MAN DRESSED IN RAGS made his way through the downtown Minneapolis homeless shelter. He didn't pay much attention to the various services that were available. All he wanted was dinner, and when he saw one of the servers ahead, he knew the menu was perfect.

After he got some salad and a roll, a woman in her sixties asked him, "Would you like some veggies with that? I've got carrots, potatoes, or beans."

As the man lifted his head, a familiar voice said, "Katie, it's Andrew."

Katie gasped and was ready to cry out when Andrew whispered, "Just act normal," followed by "carrots, please," in his regular voice.

Katie swallowed her excitement and started to serve the man while whispering, "Are you okay? And Ethan? Lydia hasn't been around for almost a week. Is she with you?"

In a hushed voice, Andrew said, "Ethan and I are fine, but they've kidnapped Lydia. I'm working on a plan, but I need some help. I don't trust anyone. I need Roy's help to recruit some police officers he trusts."

THIRTY-FOUR

Stockholm, Wisconsin
Thursday, June 24
8:30 P.M.

A S THE EVENING STARTED TO FADE, Heidi and Andrew went for a drive. The stated purpose for their trip was to make a couple untraceable phone calls as far away from their new St. Paul headquarters as possible. But Josh also knew the couple needed some time alone. So he stayed behind with Ethan while Heidi and Andrew drove east, taking a moment for themselves.

As they passed River Falls and headed south, they stopped in Stockholm, a small Wisconsin town perched on a wide stretch of the Mississippi called Lake Pepin.

The couple walked down through the campground and spotted the pay phone Josh had chosen for their calls. But before getting down to business, they followed a path out to a man-made point constructed of rock and sand. There, arm in arm, they watched the water glistening blue then orange as the sun melted over the distant trees. Andrew was content to let the time pass in silence. Heidi knew this was his way. Words would only make it harder for him. But Heidi needed the words. She couldn't let him slip away into danger without saying good-bye.

"Are you worried?" she asked, finally breaking the silence.

"Hmmm…" he thought. "It's like the feeling when you've studied really hard for a final exam. You know you're prepared, but you're scared of the random question the teacher might come up with. So yes, I'm worried, but not because we aren't prepared."

"I don't want to lose you. Not again. Not like this."

"Shhh…" He held her tightly and stared into her eyes. "I love you, no matter what. It's that simple. Now, let's stop talking about what can go wrong. We have some calls to make."

Heidi made her call to Doug first. She confirmed their Chicago hotel room had been raided hours after they left, and Doug shared a trail that led from Sven Jr. to Warren Levin. They were part of this conspiracy as well.

Heidi would add the last twists to her news story. At eight o'clock tomorrow night, Doug would receive a link to her completed segment along with a wealth of documentation. All Doug needed to do was to make some final edits, get legal clearance, and have a news crew positioned in downtown Minneapolis.

Andrew was next. As he dialed the phone, he realized he was looking forward to confronting Dan at last. But as the call flipped to voice mail, Andrew shook his head in disgust. Even the sound of Dan's arrogant voice was painful.

"Dan, Andrew Hastings here. So sorry I missed you. I think it's time for us to catch up. Rumor has it you've been looking for me. We've dug up some real interesting information here. Are you ready for a wardrobe change, 'cause the stuff we've found could earn you an orange jumpsuit. If you want all this to go away for you and your friends, bring Lydia and $2 million in cash to the Mall of America transit station tomorrow night. Get on the 6:02 train. I'll call your cell phone with more instructions.

"One more thing. No tricks, Dan. Something tells me orange isn't your color."

THIRTY-FIVE

Minneapolis, Minnesota
Friday, June 25
5:45 P.M.

DAYS OF PAINSTAKING PLANNING were complete. Now was the time for action. They took refuge in the St. Anthony Falls Visitor Center. Andrew had reserved the entire facility for a "private tour," thinking it could provide safe harbor near his designated meeting location. A calm resolve fell upon the group in this final hour, and they quietly listened to the tour guide. By the end of the tour they stared in silence, lost in thought, watching the tumbling whitewater roar over the fall's concrete apron.

The Dakota Sioux recognized the power of these falls centuries ago. For them, this was a sacred place nestled along the shores of what they called Hahawakpa or "river of the falls." The falls had remained relatively untouched until the 1800s, when the United States pushed the Dakota to "sell" their land. Soon after, the US Army started construction of Fort Snelling, and it wasn't long before the profit potential of this special place was exploited.

Tunnels and dams were built to harness the falls' power. Railways were added to bring in grain and timber and transport out flour and lumber. But in 1869, tragedy struck when the falls collapsed, weakened from the abuse of industry. Undeterred, the government built dikes and more dams, and a wooden apron was put in place to cover the falls' breech. "Progress" continued as more mills were built, and by 1880, Minneapolis was crowned the "Flour Milling Capital of the World." But after World War I, that title started to tarnish, and slowly the old mills closed. Industry moved on, and in its exodus the area was left in ruin.

Its rebirth was slow, but when an old railway span named the Stone Arch Bridge was converted into a pedestrian and biking byway, the area began its renaissance. More and more trails opened, the ruins of the mills were attended to, and finally Mills Ruins Park and the Mill City Museum opened. Slowly it all took root, and the people returned. Warehouse lofts, coffee shops, store fronts, artist studios, writers' workshops, and theater all grew and thrived. The riverfront metamorphosed. Although its natural, untouched beauty was no longer, it cast aside the ugly residue of industrial abuse, and was reborn anew.

Andrew looked down at his watch and nodded to Josh, Heidi, and Essie. As he turned to Ethan, he closed his eyes and entered a zone of calm and confidence.

"So, are you ready, buddy?"

Ethan's stare lingered for a couple seconds. Finally, he turned and said, "I'm scared, Dad."

"I know. So am I, but we're so close. Your mom's going to be all right. We've got some great friends watching over us. We just need to stick to the plan."

Ethan nodded.

"Now, you stay with Heidi. Josh, Essie, and I are going to get your mom. You guys are going to be safe here.

"See you in a few minutes." As he stood up, Andrew closed his eyes again and flipped a switch deep within him. Survival is humanity's most basic instinct, and in the journey since Becky's last message, Andrew had learned not only how to survive, but also how to live once again.

"Let's do this." Andrew said, smiling.

"Please be careful," Heidi said, pulling Andrew back in for one last kiss. "We'll be right here waiting for you."

Essie, Josh, and Andrew entered the elevator to leave the building. When Andrew turned, he said one last good-bye. He gave a wink to his family, then the elevator closed and swept him into the chaos outside.

AS THEY EXITED the Visitors Center gates, Andrew shook hands with Ricardo. "Where's Rudy?"

"He's already at his post by the river."

Andrew, Essie, and Josh walked up the road while confirming the final details of their plan. Then, after saying a brief good-bye, Josh and Essie broke off to join Roy. His team of police friends was in place and ready to protect Andrew if something went wrong.

It's showtime, Andrew thought as he reached for his phone.

After what seemed like an interminable number of rings, he finally heard, "This is Dan."

"Well good, you can follow orders, Dan. I thought you only gave them. This must be hard for you."

"Let's just get this over with, Hastings."

"I'm good with that, Dan. Just don't try anything funny. You don't want the whole world to find out what a criminal you are."

"Cut the crap. Where do you want me?" Dan snapped back.

"Exit your train at the Downtown East station. From there I want you to come over to a little courtyard right outside the old Whitney Hotel on the Portland Avenue side. You know the place?"

"Yes, I do. When do you want me there?"

"You should be getting off the train any minute, so let's say ten minutes. Just you, Lydia, and my money."

"What the hell! We can't get there so quickly."

"Yes, you can. Oh, and make sure you don't bring any of your goons with you. If I see even one of them, the deal is off, and your face is all over the headlines."

"I—"

"Just do it, Dan." Andrew hung up, wishing there was a way to slam his phone down to make his point.

———

BUILT IN 1879, the Standard Mill had survived several expansions and conversions over the years. Its most recent incarnation was a six-story luxury condominium named The Whitney Landmark Residences. In its shadows, a tree-lined courtyard was constructed between two neighboring buildings. Large, white and gray stones defined the area, and created an oversized chessboard.

Andrew stood inside the doorway of an adjacent building, checking his watch, waiting for Dan.

Cloudy skies threatened rain as the streets of Minneapolis hummed with activity. Horns honked and traffic backed up on Washington Avenue as a Twins game, two plays at the Guthrie, and a medical device convention flooded the sidewalks of this historic city with throngs of people.

In the distance, Andrew could see them walking up Fifth Avenue South. At first it was just the faint image of two figures rushing along. Then, as they got closer, Dan's tall stature next to Lydia's petite frame created quite the identifiable contrast.

As they approached, Andrew's heart pounded louder and louder. Taking a moment, he closed his eyes and said a brief prayer.

Finally, Lydia and Dan were standing there in the middle of the chessboard, waiting for him to make his move. With one final, deep, cleansing breath, Andrew emerged and confronted his future.

"Lydia, how are you?" Andrew asked.

"I've been better, but I'm okay."

"Good." Andrew turned his head toward Dan. "Let's make this quick and painless. First things first, let her go now."

"But—"

"Dan, let her go."

Reluctantly, Dan released his hand around Lydia's tiny wrist. "There, she's all yours."

Andrew stepped toward her with a note in his hand. "I'm sorry you were pulled into this. I hope I can explain it all to you, but for now I just want you to get out of here. Please, take this and follow the directions, okay?"

Andrew searched for some acknowledgement. Finally, Lydia reached out and held Andrew's hand as she took the note. "Thank you for trusting me. Now please, Lydia, hurry. You must go."

Lydia smiled as she read the note. Suddenly, she turned and disappeared down some stairs in the corner of the courtyard that led to the river.

"So what do you have for me?" Dan asked.

Andrew dropped the backpack off his shoulder and unzipped it, pulling out an accordion file.

"It's all here, Dan—all your dirty secrets. It's such a shame to hand it over. The boys in prison would love a new bunkmate."

"Spare me the lecture. Just give it to me."

Andrew handed it to him, and without hesitation, Dan tore into it, almost like a kid at Christmas. But this time it wasn't presents he was opening. It was the key to preserving his life.

"Don't worry. It's all there, Dan." But that didn't stop him. Dan continued thumbing through the papers, shaking his head back and forth.

"You and your little gang have been quite busy."

"A little luck and lots of perseverance."

"Now, this is the only copy?" Dan asked.

Andrew chuckled. "No, that wasn't part of the deal."

"What?"

"Dan, I never promised that. This stuff is my insurance policy. Believe it or not, I don't trust you."

"Well, then you're not getting this money," he said, motioning to the duffel bag he had dropped on the ground.

"You must be dumber than I thought," Andrew replied. "Keep your damn money. All I wanted was my family safe."

"Oh really. You wanted that bitch back?"

"Stop right there," Andrew interrupted. "We're done here."

Dan laughed. "That's where you're wrong, Andrew."

LYDIA PRESSED the buzzer at the St. Anthony Falls Visitor Center's gate, looking around for Ethan. She was free, but not until she could hold her little man again could she be happy. The gate buzzed back, and a man walked up to greet her.

"We've been waiting for you, Ms. Sands."

"Thank you, but where's my son?" Lydia replied urgently.

"The elevator is over there," Ricardo said, pointing to the main building. "Press 'O'—" but before he could finish, Lydia had run off.

The elevator slowly climbed the two stories. It was an interminable wait, but when the doors finally opened, her pain was gone.

"Mom," Ethan exclaimed, rushing into her arms. "Are you okay?" he asked, not letting her go.

"Mommy's fine. I'm so glad you're safe."

"Oh, it's so good to see you. How was Dad? Is he okay?"

"I left him talking to that man, Dan. His note said he would be here soon."

Still overwhelmed, Lydia finally started to get her bearings and looked around the room. "Oh, Heidi, what are you doing here?"

"Josh and I have been helping Andrew and Ethan out."

Lydia nodded. "He's lucky to have good friends like the two of you."

"Yeah, Mom, you'd be so proud of Dad. From the moment this all started, he's been worried about you."

"Really?" Lydia appeared shocked, shaking her head. "After all that's happened?"

"Yeah. He arranged all of this. He saved you."

As soon as the words were out of his mouth, a voice from the fire stairwell cut short their reunion. "So who do we have here?" The voice was new to Heidi and Ethan, but it was all too familiar to Lydia.

"DAN, I'M TIRED of your games. I'm outta here."

"Stop, Andrew. I think you're going to want to wait."

"For what?"

"This isn't over. I imagine right now, I've got myself several more hostages."

"What?"

Dan laughed. "I told you before, Andrew. You're too weak. Don't ever underestimate me."

"DID YOU MISS ME, sweetie?" Rufus grinned with his FN 57 in hand.

Turning toward the voice, Lydia, Ethan, and Heidi realized their troubles weren't over.

"Do you know him, Mom?"

"This is one of the men that held me hostage, honey," she said, pulling Ethan in closely, guarding him with her body.

"And a bonus?" Rufus's eyes bulged, examining Heidi. "A two-for-one deal—"

"Shut up, you ass," Skylar said, joining his partner from a separate entrance on the observation deck side of the Visitor Center. Then, turning to his hostages, he said, "Let's get this straight. Behave, and you won't get hurt."

Heidi knew how this went. Maybe they would be safe for now, but it wouldn't last. The quicker they could escape, the better, and when she had a chance, she nodded ever so slightly to Ethan.

"What are you going to do with us?" Heidi asked.

"No questions. Keep quiet."

"But I have to go to the bathroom," Ethan said in a panic, starting to cry.

"We don't have time. You've gotta hold it, kid," said Rufus.

"Please, I'm nervous. I have to go now. The bathroom is just down these stairs," Ethan said, crying harder, pointing to the doorway, starting to wiggle and squirm.

Lydia looked strangely at her son and Heidi.

"Come on, Rufus, let the kid go."

"Damn it, Skylar, you're too soft."

"I've gotta go now. Please," Ethan begged.

"You afraid of some kid?" Skylar asked. "Here, I'll take him. I could use a pee myself." Grabbing Ethan by the shoulder, Skylar escorted him into the restroom.

The two had barely left when Rufus pulled Heidi in front of him, holding a gun to her head.

Unfazed, Heidi started up. "You know, you're not going to get away with this."

"Shut up."

"Our guards will catch you."

"Really?" Rufus laughed. "We've already hauled their sorry asses out of here along with the staff. You're all alone."

Heidi was afraid of that, but she wasn't above bluffing.

"What about the police? They're due here any moment."

Suddenly shrieks echoed from downstairs. "Rufus, something's wrong," Skylar shouted. "The kid's on the floor making strange noises. I think he's having a seizure."

"What?" Lydia exclaimed, rushing to the stairs.

"Stop right there." Rufus turned, pointing the gun to halt Lydia's exit.

Skylar kept yelling, "Help! I need some help."

In that split second, Heidi saw her chance. Quickly, she raised her knee and slammed her heel down on Rufus's foot with all her might. Then, to finish the job, she reared her head up into his face, breaking his nose and knocking him and his gun to the ground.

Lydia ran from the doorway and quickly picked up the gun, pointing it straight at Rufus's head.

"Now don't say one word, you sick bastard," Lydia whispered.

Heidi scrambled to her feet and ran downstairs, stopping outside the hallway that led to the restroom. As she listened to the man's screams, she waited for the right moment. Then, just as the cries for help paused, Heidi lunged into the bathroom. Ethan was sprawled out on the floor, writhing as the man hovered over him, gun in hand. Before Skylar realized what was happening, Heidi lifted her leg and kicked him in his temple, sending his body across the room and smashing his head into the toilet. When the gun fell to the floor, Ethan quickly picked it up and pointed it at his former captor. The man lay unconscious, his face bloodied from the crushing blow.

Suddenly a shot fired upstairs. Ethan looked desperately at Heidi and screamed, "Mom," then sprinted up the steps, gun in hand.

Lydia stood there shaking, the gun now by her side. Rufus lay there motionless on the ground, a bullet in his head. When she saw Ethan she turned and held him close, trying to protect him from the violence she had just committed.

"Thank God," Heidi gasped as she came to Lydia's side. "Are you all right?"

"Yes," she said, still shaking. "He wouldn't stay there."

"I know. It's okay. You're alive, and that's all that matters."

"We need to get going, but let me tie up the guy downstairs first. He's in pretty bad shape, but I don't want him chasing us."

Heidi reached into her backpack, pulled out the power cord for her phone, and ran downstairs.

"We're okay. It's going to be okay," Ethan said, holding his mom tight.

———

"I DON'T BELIEVE you for one second, Dan," said Andrew. "This is just another one of your tricks. Maybe a delay tactic for some of your friends to arrive."

"Really? But if you're wrong—"

"Didn't you hear me, Dan? I've got extra copies of all this. If anything happens to any of us, it goes public."

"Well, maybe you'll change your mind. Watching your child suffer can do amazing things for a father."

"I'll kill you first, Dan."

———

LYDIA AND ETHAN ran out of the Visitor Center as Heidi directed the group down into Mill Ruins Park. Crossing under the Stone Arch Bridge, they raced down the path as they followed a stream from the old waterpower tunnels' tailrace.

"Where are we going?" Lydia asked.

"The Guthrie," Ethan replied. "Hurry."

"Why the Guthrie?"

Heidi jumped in, trying to get Lydia to move faster, "It's our back-up safe house. There are two performances going on this evening. It should be easy to get lost in the crowd. In our contingency plan, we identified a spot on the Endless Bridge where we could safely meet and hide. Once we're all there, we can call the police."

"Sounds like someone has been busy, thinking of everything," Lydia said, trying to catch her breath.

"Yeah, Dad's been great."

"So how did you know what was going on back at the Visitor Center?" Heidi asked.

Lydia smiled briefly through the agony of running. "Well, Ethan has always had a steel bladder. He hasn't acted like that since he was four or five. Then, when he started having a seizure, I knew something was up, so I played along."

Before long they were past the ruins and had made their way across two small bridges.

"You okay, Mom?"

"Yeah. I guess I need to get back on the treadmill. I'm not used to all this running."

"We're getting close," Heidi said as she cut off the road and started running up the hill.

Heidi effortlessly bounded up the steep dirt path, slowing down only to wait for Ethan and Lydia.

"Come on, Mom, you can do it."

Heidi glanced ahead to the Guthrie's rear entrance. It was clear. But as they started to cross the street, a car came speeding toward them, blocking their path.

"Damn it, they're here!" Heidi yelled. "Come on. This way, upstairs to the restaurant. Hurry!"

Two men jumped out of the car, while the third stayed behind.

"They're coming. Hurry," Ethan said to his mom.

As they reached the top of the stairs, Heidi thought they could make it. The restaurant's entrance was just ahead. The pre-show dinner crowd was sure to be busy. If they could only make it inside, they could disappear in the crowd. Then, as she turned to check Lydia's progress, an arm reached out and grabbed her.

"Stop right there."

In seconds, another set of arms grabbed Ethan and Lydia.

"I've got a gun right here in my jacket. I want the three of you to follow my associate. I will be walking ten feet behind you. If any one of you makes a move or says a word, junior here dies."

———————————

THE SKIES DARKENED as clouds blew in from the west. The wind swirled in the tree-lined courtyard, sweeping leaves around and around as the two men stood waiting. Finally, after ten minutes, Dan's confidence seemed to waver as he glanced down at his watch yet again.

"I think I've waited long enough," Andrew said, and he started to walk away.

"I wouldn't do that," Dan shouted. "Stop, damn it! Stop!"

Andrew looked over his shoulder and shook his head in disgust. Then, just as Andrew was about to turn the corner, Dan's men marched their three prisoners up the stairs and into the courtyard. Dan grabbed Ethan, twisting his arm behind his back.

"Scream for your father or I'll break it," Dan ordered.

"Dad," Ethan cried out.

Instantly Andrew ran back to the courtyard, briefly looking overhead as he got closer.

"Stop it, Dan. Stop it right now," Andrew said, his face icy with resolve.

"That seemed to get your attention," Dan chuckled. "They always say a parent is specially attuned to their child's cry for help."

"Don't touch him. I swear, I'll kill you."

"I don't think you're in any position to be threatening me," Dan said as he kept a strong grip on Ethan. Then looking over to his three men, he asked, "Where's the van?"

"It should be driving up within the minute, Mr. Murdock," one of the men replied.

"Perfect," Dan said, turning his attention back to his hostages. "You failed, Andrew. Just like you always have. Finally, I've got a team of professionals with me that can handle the job.

"Now I expect everyone's cooperation here. When the van arrives, each of you will get in without a fight, or I'll break this kid's arm. And it will only get worse from there. Got it?"

Andrew nodded, and then looked over to Ethan, darting his eyes above once more. Through his pain, Ethan could still see his father's glance, and he tried to remain calm and hold still.

Before Dan knew what was happening, four bullets sliced through the air from atop a nearby building. Josh, Roy, and two of Roy's police buddies hit three of the four targets. Dan's three henchmen were taken out. However, the fourth shot, intended for Dan, missed and ricocheted off the ground. As Dan turned his head to see what had happened, Andrew's fist smashed against his face, crushing his nose and left eye socket. Ethan seized the moment and snapped Dan's pinky with his free right hand. Finally liberated from the man's grasp, Ethan ran into his mother's arms. Then, as Andrew ran over to make sure Ethan was okay, a white van rounded the corner, screeching its tires as it pulled up beside the courtyard.

"Go! Run!" Andrew screamed. "I'll meet you there."

Heidi grabbed Lydia and Ethan, and rushed them down the steps, back toward the Guthrie's rear entrance.

As Dan struggled back to his feet, Andrew yelled, "No. No, you don't," and landed another blow to his face as the van careened to a stop.

Confident that the men in the van had orders to kill, Andrew bolted in the opposite direction of Heidi's path, hoping to become bait and ensure his family's safety. After sprinting to the end of the block, he turned left onto South Second Street to make his way to the Guthrie's front entrance. Running at full tilt, he could see the theater crowd starting to form ahead. As he reached the mass of people, Andrew weaved through them, at one point jumping into the street, barely missing an oncoming car.

He was a block and a half away from the theater's main doors when the skies finally opened up. Thunder and lightning crackled through the warm, wet air as the light drizzle quickly turned into a torrent of rain. Charging forward, fighting through the crowd, Andrew wiped the water from his face, keeping focused on his path ahead. Then, behind him, he heard wheels squealing up the street. As he turned for a quick look, the white van sped toward him, leaving a wake of pedestrians in its path.

Afraid the van would cut him off before he reached the Guthrie's main entrance, Andrew crossed the street and entered the building through the side doors of a restaurant attached to the theater. Without the slightest pause, he darted among the crowded tables, knocking over several people along his way. As he ran through the bar, he could see the street through the building's inky blue glass. Then suddenly the van crossed two lanes of traffic and burst onto the sidewalk in front of the theater. After the vehicle lurched to a stop, Dan and two other men jumped out.

Knowing his exact path, Andrew made it past the hostess stand and into the theater. Crossing the lobby then turning left, Andrew dashed up the escalator, excusing himself as he stepped on toes and pushed people aside. Halfway up the four-story trip, Andrew turned, only to see Dan clearing a path behind him. *Damn it*, he thought. *How the hell is he still standing?* Andrew flew up the stairway.

The crowd at the top of the escalator platform was thick as theatergoers made their way to the two different stages. Andrew bobbed left then took an immediate right, running full speed up the Endless Bridge lobby. As he raced with all his might to the refuge they had planned, Andrew suddenly realized slipping underneath the draped table was too risky. Dan was too close. Unable to turn around, Andrew decided the outdoor observation deck was his only choice.

———

STILL TRYING TO CATCH THEIR BREATH, Heidi, Ethan, and Lydia huddled beneath the table. Peering through a slight gap in the drape, Ethan carefully watched from one end while Heidi observed from the other. Andrew had spotted their last ditch sanctuary the night before when his team scouted out the building. He insisted they needed one more place to hide, just in case.

It was a simple but elegant solution—a ten-foot long, counter-height table behind the bar, draped in black. It appeared unassuming enough to escape notice, making it the perfect spot to hide until the authorities arrived. When Andrew had asked the bartender if he would mind some visitors under the table the following night, the bartender had hesitated. Indeed, the request was bizarre. But a generous tip helped the young man overcome any concerns.

Heidi, Ethan, and Lydia waited anxiously. The bar's business had slowed down since the three of them had slipped underneath the cloth. Although there were some customers nearby, most stood by the windows of the cantilevered lobby and watched the storm. Heidi glanced at her watch. Their time was running out. In less than ten minutes, the final seating bell would ring, and the theater's lobbies would empty.

Desperate to know what was going on, Heidi dialed her phone.
"Josh, where's Andrew?" she whispered. "Is he okay?"

"I don't know. He ran off after he punched Dan. But then the van picked up Dan to chase him down."

"Damn it!"

Just then a figure shot past Ethan, opening the observation deck's patio door.

"Heidi, that was Dad," Ethan whispered. "I'm sure of it."

"What? Are you positive?" she asked.

Before she knew it, Ethan started to slide out from under the drape.

"Wait, no. Lydia, grab him. Don't let him go."

But it was too late. Ethan slipped out and left through the patio door, Lydia chasing after him.

"Josh, get here quick. The plan's falling apart. Ethan saw his dad run out onto the observation deck. He just left, and then Lydia followed him."

"Damn. I'm inside the building now. I'll be right there."

"Hurry!"

Heidi scrambled to where Ethan had been sitting and peered out from beneath the table as yet another figure ran out onto the deck.

Oh my God, she thought.

NIGHT ARRIVED PREMATURELY as the storm-darkened sky emptied a deluge upon the riverfront. Pausing for a second, quickly trying to come up with a miracle, Andrew remembered an alcove off the lower deck that led to an emergency exit. As he started down the concrete steps he heard a shout, muffled by the pounding rain.

"Dad," Ethan yelled. "Where are you going? We're all right here."

Andrew's heart sank. Then before he knew it, Lydia popped out the door as well.

Running back up the steps, he grabbed Ethan's hand. "Hurry. Come on. Both of you," he yelled.

Ethan and Andrew were already at the base of the stairs when Andrew realized Lydia was missing. As he turned to look back, he felt his world shift. Dan was herding Lydia down the stairs, a gun at her head.

"Ethan," Andrew yelled over the storm. "There's an emergency exit back there. Get out of here, and sound the alarm."

"But, Dad?"

"Do it now," Andrew screamed in desperation.

Within seconds, alarms sounded as Ethan escaped. *Thank God!* Andrew thought. *At least Ethan's safe.*

The sky lit up as slivers of lightning snarled across the heavens. Dan slowly made his way down the steps, being careful not to slip on the slick concrete.

"Where's Ethan?" Lydia cried.

"Shut up," shouted Dan.

"He ran down the fire escape," Andrew shouted out.

"Thank God he's safe," Lydia replied.

"I said shut up. Both of you. Now!"

"What now, Dan?" Andrew replied with a new sense of power. "The police will be here any second from the alarm. There's no escaping."

"You should know me better than that, Hastings. I never give up."

"Well, I think *you* underestimated *me*, Dan. There are some things in this world I won't give up. Now let her go, damn it!" Andrew said, starting to walk slowly in Dan's direction.

"I'm not afraid of you anymore, Dan," Andrew went on. "I once thought you cast an untarnished image. Smart, successful, wealthy, with a picture-perfect family. I felt flawed and defective. I felt like I had to be fixed. And if I was lucky, just maybe, I could be successful like you. But you know, the truth is, I couldn't have been more wrong. You are the flawed one, Dan! You are defective! You use people, and you'll do anything to further yourself. I'm telling you, Dan, that's all going to end right here!"

The sermon had worked, and Dan shifted his gun's aim to

Andrew. Now within five feet, Andrew stopped and looked at Lydia.

"Let Ethan know I'll always love him."

Her eyes narrowed, trying to comprehend his words.

Then, just as Andrew took a final leap toward Dan's gun, a piercing red beam of light cut through the darkness from above. Two shots rang out. Andrew and Dan fell to the ground.

Sirens blared as police cars, fire trucks, and ambulances encircled the Guthrie.

"Help!" Lydia screamed. "Help!"

Josh and Heidi came running down the stairs.

"Oh my God. Is he breathing?"

Josh moved quickly to turn Andrew over and pull him off Dan's body.

"He's been hit in the chest, but there's a pulse. Lydia, go get some help. Hurry."

The gunshots had been heard, and help was on its way. The police cordoned off the area, and paramedics rushed to Andrew and Dan. It was too late for Dan. Josh's aim was precise and deadly. If only he could have taken his shot a moment earlier.

The police found Ethan hiding in a corner on the fire escape. As the officer walked him back up the ramp to the observation deck, he saw his dad lying there, surrounded by paramedics.

THIRTY-SIX

Minneapolis, Minnesota
Friday, June 25
11:00 P.M.

NEVER HAD A NIGHT seemed so long as Ethan waited with Heidi, Josh, and his mom for news about his father.

Then, as the surgeon walked up, they each searched her face for the slightest hint of success. And when she smiled, they realized their prayers were answered. The surgery was successful. Andrew was in ICU. He would be fine.

Still not completely satisfied, Ethan asked, "So when can I see my dad?"

"He should be out of ICU in a couple hours, and in a room by morning. Maybe you should go home and get some sleep," replied the doctor.

"No, you don't understand what we've been through. I'm staying right here." Ethan looked up at his mom, and she nodded.

———————

THEY WERE BREAKING every hospital rule, but after Josh explained to the nurses the events of the past couple weeks, they made some gracious exceptions.

The sunrise cast a golden glow throughout the hospital room. In the rich morning light, Andrew awakened and slowly looked around the room, then smiled.

Ethan was sleeping on the extra bed in the room. Josh and Lydia were balled up uncomfortably in reclining chairs. And by his side, Heidi was asleep, holding his hand. Andrew moved his fingers ever so slightly, and he realized she wasn't asleep as her eyes flashed wide open.

"Welcome back, mister. You gave us quite the scare." Reaching over, Heidi caressed Andrew's cheek.

"I'm sorry. This wasn't exactly in my plan."

"I know."

"I see Ethan over there. Is he okay?"

"Yeah. The trooper tried his best to stay up all night. He finally gave out an hour or so ago when they moved you into this room."

"How about everything else?"

Heidi picked up the morning paper from her lap. "The nurse dropped this off a couple minutes ago. You did it."

Andrew smiled and laughed, wincing from the pain.

"The paramedics couldn't save Dan. The FBI arrested Aidan for multiple charges, including fraud, bribery of government officials, and nine counts of murder. Chloe is still missing, but an officer in Delano found her BMW. It was torched, but inside there were human remains."

"How about Laura?"

"The FBI is still looking for her. It turns out that guy she was visiting in Annapolis was her brother. They've both disappeared."

"And what about Jackie Epps and Dr. McNaulty?"

"In federal jail, awaiting arraignment. Same with a long list of senators, congressmen, and FAC members. Oh, and Sven Anderson Jr. and Warren Levin were arrested as well."

In disbelief, tears streamed down his cheeks.

"That's the man I love. I'll take a man who can express his true feelings any day of the week," Heidi said while lightly cupping her hands around his face.

Andrew sniffled, slowly reached for Heidi's hand, and then cleared his throat. "Just one more thing would make this moment perfect," Andrew said.

"What's that?" Heidi smiled curiously.

"Will you marry me?"

"Hmmm...Let me think about that one," Heidi said, teasing.

"Come on. I'm in no position to beg."

"Okay. Enough thinking. Yes...yes...yes...Andrew, I can't imagine living my life with anyone else but you. Of course I'll marry you."

THIRTY-SEVEN

Kaua`i, Hawaii
Saturday, August 7
6:00 P.M.

AT THE BASE of Mt. Makana on the shores of Ke`e Beach, the couple gathered before their friends and family. Thirty white chairs were arranged neatly in three ocean-side rows. Three chairs were draped in white, with a single white rose on each seat, in honor of the friends they had lost.

Everyone who was invited attended. The list was short, but each guest held a special place in their hearts, especially their friend Tony, who was doing well enough to come and expected to make a full recovery.

Their ceremony was informal. Ethan was Andrew's best man, and Josh agreed to be Heidi's "maid of honor" on one condition—he didn't have to wear a dress. As the wedding party made its final preparations, Lydia straightened Ethan's tie and combed his hair one last time. Then with a kiss, she wished him luck, gave Andrew a hug, and left to join the other guests.

As Heidi walked onto the beach with Josh by her side, she was nothing short of radiant. Her hair was pulled back in a shimmering pearl headband, and she wore a simple, white-linen, ballerina-length dress with soft pleats and spaghetti straps. In her hands she held a small bouquet of pink roses. Josh helped steady her as they walked barefoot toward the bamboo altar wrapped in white silk organza and native orchids.

Andrew beamed brighter and brighter as Heidi approached. Smiling over at Ethan, who stood right by his side, Andrew could hardly believe it was all happening.

Finally, hand in hand, joined before the minister, they smiled, looked deeply into each other's eyes, and exchanged their vows and rings. As they kissed before the altar, the minister proclaimed them man and wife and said, "So they are no longer two, but one. Therefore, what God has joined together, let man not separate."

EPILOGUE

Geneva International Airport
Sunday, August 15
6:35 A.M.

T HE COUPLE disembarked from their plane and proceeded to Swiss Immigration Control. The line to pass through was relatively short, and after waiting for a few minutes, they were waved on to the next officer.

"Your travel documents?" he asked.

The Asian woman handed him two passports and paperwork she had completed on the plane.

"Mr. and Mrs. Chung?"

"Yes, I'm Long Chung," she replied.

"What are you plans in Switzerland?"

"We have a layover here. We'll rest here for two days before taking the final leg of our journey to Ho Chi Minh City. We are going home."

The agent glanced at the Vietnamese passports and travel

documents again. "I see your flight arrived here from Havana. What was the purpose of your travel?"

Ms. Chung knew that telling the truth about Cuba's lax extradition laws and friendly attitudes towards wealthy, international criminals wasn't the right answer, so she politely replied, "We were there on holiday."

"Do you have any items to declare?"

"No."

"How about you, sir?" The officer turned, looking at the gentleman.

"No, he doesn't—"

The man interrupted, "I'd like to hear from your husband, ma'am."

Ms. Chung contained her anger. Her new life didn't afford such luxuries yet. "Sir, this is my brother. He is disabled and can't speak."

The agent looked at the Asian man once more. He was staring down at the floor with a blank gaze.

"Fine," he replied, looking a bit embarrassed. "Proceed."

Long and Quang walked slowly toward baggage claim.

"We're almost home," Long said, holding her brother's arm. "I know this has been such a hard trip for you. Are you tired?"

Quang raised his head slightly as if to acknowledge his sister.

"Today we can rest up. Then tomorrow all we have to do is visit a couple banks." Long paused, as if she were hearing Quang's response.

"Yes, then we fly home. So much has changed since we left. I don't think we'll even recognize it. But I have a good feeling about our move." She paused once more. "There are many opportunities at home for an enterprising capitalist."

Author's Message

A novel such as *Fat Profits* inevitably leads readers to ask questions as they try to bridge the worlds of fiction and reality. Since the topic of food is so important to me, I thought I'd be proactive in answering some of the questions I most frequently receive, and hopefully help readers on their own personal food journey.

First, many people, especially those who know I'm a veteran of the food industry, ask me, "Is *Fat Profits* real?" No, it is not real. *Fat Profits* is a complete work of fiction. The people, the company, the products, and all aspects of the book represent my imagination and not real life. Writing *Fat Profits* has been a four-year long "hobby" of mine, and as such, I chose to depict a divorced father working in the food industry in the Twin Cities only because I am familiar with those settings and character backgrounds. In no way does that mean *Fat Profits* is at all autobiographical. When you're trying to learn how to write fiction, and you're writing as a hobby, it's very helpful to at least be familiar with your subject matter since you don't have the time or money to research every single aspect of an unfamiliar field.

Many readers are also curious to find out if I think something like *Fat Profits* could happen in real life. Unfortunately, my answer is yes. First, let me be very clear. Most of the people I've met and worked with in the food industry are honest, hard-working people just doing their jobs. They aren't actively trying to deceive people or plotting against the so-called "food cops."

In fact, most of them deal with the same struggles we all have in trying to do their best and put a healthy meal on the table. That said, for as much good as I know exists in humanity, there is still a very persistent sliver of evil. Greed and self-consuming egos are realities of our corporate and political worlds. That's what makes novels like *Fat Profits* so timeless. Regardless of the industry, if power is in the hands of a few, dishonest people, unethical behavior will flourish. If you don't believe me, just look through history or check out some recent headlines.

"But what about the food industry itself? Is it really so bad?" That's a tougher question to answer. When I first started working as a food marketer, I didn't think any issues existed. But along the way there were some red flags that I more or less dismissed. For example, when I worked at a candy company in the early 1990s, the confection industry had the rallying cry "25 by 95." What it meant was pure and simple—they wanted Americans to eat more candy. In 1980, annual candy consumption was 16.2 pounds per person. By 1990, consumption was up to 20.1 pounds per person, but that wasn't good enough, so the industry created the 25 pounds by 1995 mantra. Sometimes food companies insist that they aren't trying to get people to eat more. Instead they argue they merely want to increase their share of the pie by stealing from their competition. This confection industry example disproves that story. But times were different in the early 1990s. The issue of obesity was still in its infancy, and the food industry didn't have to hide its true intentions yet.

A second instance when I questioned the food and beverage industry's motives was when I was interviewing at Coca-Cola in the mid 1990s. At the time, Coca-Cola's latest corporate vision was to be "within arm's reach." Such a call for ubiquity may raise some eyebrows, but when Coca-Cola went on to describe their desire to increase the one billion servings of Coca-Cola products that were consumed each day by stealing from the forty-seven billion servings of other beverages consumed daily (most of which is water), the picture starts to get clearer. Although one can quickly understand how this strategy would be good for Coca-Cola's profits, it's alarming that little to no concern was shown for the impact on public health. Again, times were quite different, and this incident was just prior to the obesity epidemic hitting the headlines.

While these examples illustrate real-life corporate behavior, the underlying truism isn't hard to grasp. Corporations are in existence to make money, and to do that, they need to sell more. Wall Street's expectations are relentless, and if a food company fails to deliver, their stock price is punished. So, at the end of the day, food companies are very highly motivated to sell more food. It's this never-ending push to sell more that is at odds with our health. Some companies do an okay job navigating this challenge ethically, while others fail miserably.

Although most food companies are acting within the law, we have to remember, just because it's legal, doesn't make it right. No too long ago, tobacco companies were able to legally use lifestyle advertising to depict their products. Most of it portrayed aspirational or emotional messages filled with vivid imagery: Marlboro with its quintessential cowboy or Vantage with groups of friends having fun "alive with pleasure." Somewhere along the way, we decided it wasn't right to portray unhealthy tobacco products in that way. Unfortunately, since many food companies seem incapable of using judgment that is aligned with our public health interests, I believe government will need to step in and regulate the advertising of unhealthy food products, just as it had to ultimately do with tobacco.

So what do I believe? I think people do have the right to eat whatever they want. However, I think food companies have a moral responsibility to be extraordinarily clear about what is in their products, how they are made, and how they impact animals and our environment. Furthermore, food companies must be truthful about their product benefits and end the use of unsubstantiated, misleading product claims. Food companies would like you to believe that it's impossible for them to live up to these standards, but that's just an excuse.

Until this happens, what should every consumer know about Big Food companies? Andy Bellatti asked me this question in an interview for his blog, *Small Bites*. In my opinion, there are three basic principles that consumers should never forget:

1. **Big Food is profit-driven.** Don't be fooled into thinking a brand or the food company that owns it cares about you or your health.
2. **Think critically.** Most claims and advertising by Big Food companies are meant to manipulate you, not educate you. Read your labels and do your research.
3. **There is no free lunch.** Over the long-term, you always get what you pay for. Cheap food is very expensive once you add up the true costs — like the taxes you pay to subsidize Big Food companies, health consequences like obesity or diabetes, the devastating harm to our environment, and the inhumane treatment of animals raised within the industrialized food system.

Finally, regarding the chemically derived, GMO resistant starch (Redu) mentioned in *Fat Profits*, there is no such thing. Real, naturally-occurring resistant starch in legumes and a variety of other foods is great for you, and we should all try to eat more of it. Processed food manufacturers, however, have started to use resistant starch additives in foods. Although these additives appear to be derived from non-GMO sources, I personally shy away from them because I'm trying to eat foods that have been minimally processed. In my food journey, I've chosen to embrace Mother Nature rather than try to outwit her. Goodness knows I'm not perfect, but I do my best to eat more fresh, organic foods and minimize the amount of processed food in my diet.

So what can you do if you're interested in eating better and improving the health of our food supply? Joining a CSA and shopping at your local farmers market are great first steps. But more than anything else, it's crucial that you become informed. I've included a resource list at the end of the book that contains more information to help get you started on your food journey, but only you can decide what's right for you. We will all have differing opinions, and I don't think there is one right answer.

When you figure out what you believe, make sure your voice is heard. Too often, corporate interests drown out the voices of everyday consumers. So speak up and share your opinions with friends and family. Vote with your wallet, and only buy products that are in sync with your food morals. And finally, make sure to let your elected officials know how you feel by voting and telling them where you stand.

Connect Online

Are you interested in learning more about what's really in your food? Would you like updates on my latest book news? Then connect with me online. You can subscribe to my blog, like me on Facebook, or follow me on Twitter. And if you enjoyed reading *Fat Profits*, please recommend it to your friends and family. Whether it's a tweet, like, share, e-mail, or old-fashioned conversation, you can help make a difference by spreading the news about my debut novel.

Website & Blog: brucebradley.com

Facebook Author Page: facebook.com/brucebradleyauthor

Facebook Book Page: facebook.com/fatprofits

Twitter: twitter.com/authorbruce or twitter.com/Fat_Profits

Resource List

Books:

Appetite for Profit, Michele Simon
Eat, Drink and Be Healthy, Walter C. Willett, M.D.
The End of Overeating, David A. Kessler, M.D.
In Defense of Food: An Eater's Manifesto, Michael Pollan
Fast Food Nation, Eric Schlosser
Fed Up For Lunch, Sarah Wu
Folks, this ain't normal, Joel Salatin
Food Fight, Kelly D. Brownell, Ph.D.
Food Matters, Mark Bittman
Food Politics, Marion Nestle, Ph.D.
Food Rules: An Eater's Manual, Michael Pollan
Good Calories, Bad Calories, Gary Taubes
Good Meat, Deborah Krasner
Mindless Eating, Brian Wansink, Ph.D.
The Omnivore's Dilemma, Michael Pollan
Poisoned, Jeff Benedict
Recipe for America, Jill Richardson
Tomatoland, Barry Estabrook
Twinkie Deconstructed, Steve Ettinger
The Unhealthy Truth, Robyn O'Brien and Rachel Kranz
What to Eat, Marion Nestle, Ph.D.

Websites:

100daysofrealfood.com (Lisa Leake)
appetiteforprofit.com (Michele Simon)
blog.fooducate.com (Hemi Weingarten)
brucebradley.com (Bruce Bradley)
civileats.org (Civil Eats)
cornucopia.org (The Cornucopia Institute)
cspinet.org (Center for Science in the Public Interest)
eatingrules.com (Andrew Wilder)
eatwellguide.org (Eat Well Guide)
eatwild.com (Eat Wild)
ewg.org (Environmental Working Group
foodandwaterwatch.org (Food & Water Watch)
fooddemocracynow.org (Food Democracy Now)
foodpolitics.com (Marion Nestle, Ph.D.)
foodroutes.org (Food Routes)
grist.org (Grist online magazine)
landstewardshipproject.org (Land Stewardship Project)
markbittman.com (Mark Bittman)
michaelpollan.com/resources (Michael Pollan)
organicconsumers.org (Organic Consumers Association)
politicsoftheplate.com (Barry Estabrook)
preventioninstitute.org (Prevention Institute)
rodaleinstitute.org (Rodale Institute)
slowfoodusa.org (Slow Food USA)
smallbites.andybellatti.com (Andy Bellatti)
summertomato.com (Darya Pino, Ph.D)
takepart.com (TakePart)
weightymatters.ca (Yoni Freedhoff, M.D.)

Documentaries:

Fat Sick & Nearly Dead
Food, Inc.
Forks Over Knives
King Corn
Super Size Me